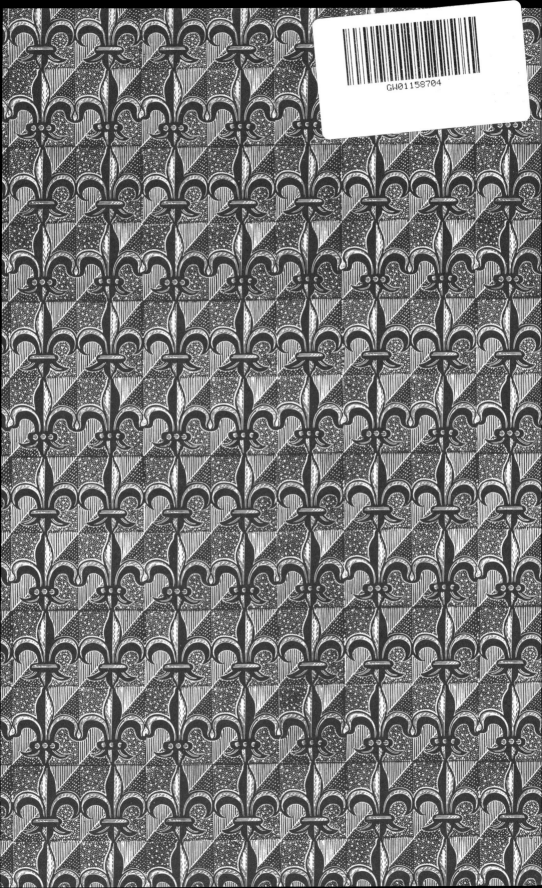

GOOD
GRIEF

GOOD GRIEF

Sally Brampton

SINCLAIR-STEVENSON

First published in Great Britain by
Sinclair-Stevenson Limited
7/8 Kendrick Mews
London SW7 3HG, England

Copyright © 1992 by Sally Brampton

All rights reserved. Without limiting the rights under copyright
reserved, no part of this publication may be reproduced, stored in or
introduced into a retrieval system or transmitted, in any form or by any
means (electronic, mechanical, photocopying, recording or otherwise),
without the prior written permission of both the copyright owner and the
above publisher of this book.

The right of Sally Brampton to be identified as author of
this work has been asserted by her in accordance with the
Copyright, Designs and Patents Act 1988.

British Library Cataloguing in Publication Data
A CIP catalogue record for this book is available from the British Library

ISBN 1-85619-109-5

Photoset by Rowland Phototypesetting Limited
Bury St Edmunds, Suffolk
Printed and bound in England by
Clays Limited, St Ives plc.

For J.P.

CHAPTER ONE

HILDAMAY Smith was a spinster. 'Spinsterhood,' she said to her friends, 'is a state of grace.'
    It was the morning of her thirty-fifth birthday. She stretched happily in the expanse of her big, empty bed, sat up, arranged into a pile the numerous pillows with which it was cluttered, sank back and picked up a magnifying mirror. She looked at herself every morning, as soon as she woke up. She liked to be sure that she was still herself. She was. She smiled.
    Hildamay needed her smile. She had six. Each one brought her something different. She practised each of them every morning. Hildamay was not vain. She thought vanity was for fools; fools who thought too much about themselves and too little about other people. It was other people who brought you what you want. She used her face with the utmost care, arranging it in different ways at different times. She would make its planes and curves settle into sadness or lift into happiness and, when they saw that particular composition, people would try even harder to make her form it again. She was not beautiful. Sometimes she looked downright ugly.

But people felt compelled to watch her. Hildamay was, at least among those people she knew, and even did not know, clever. And on the whole people – both men and women; she saw no distinction on this point – find cleverness uncomfortable.

She knew that and made public her blue eyes, blonde hair and pink mouth. Her mind was her most personal possession. She did not offer it freely to all the world, as others do – both the bad as well as the good parts – but slipped it in, unnoticed. She only set it free for seconds at a time. It flashed out, sharp and shining, and was back under its protective cover before most understood what had snapped, so stingingly, around their heads. Those who had understood looked at her dubiously, until she smiled. She kept a special smile for such occasions. Hildamay had spent many hours perfecting that smile. It was so childlike in its hugeness, so shining with complicity, that those who had seen her stinging cleverness were immediately comforted. The rest of the world simply felt protective towards her.

There was only one person on whom that smile did not work. Liz Valentine, her closest friend, would stare coldly at her until she replaced it with her normal face. If the stare were not enough she would say, 'Hildamay Smith, get off that stage,' and Hildamay would laugh and stop it.

Hildamay gazed at her smile with admiration. The telephone rang. Still smiling, she picked it up.

'It's me,' said Liz. 'I am going to have a child.'

Hildamay stopped smiling. 'You could have an abortion,' she said. 'I hear they're awfully good these days. There's one they do with a vacuum pump. It's rather like having a Hoover attachment shoved up inside you. Two seconds and there you are. All spick and span and clean again.'

'No, you idiot,' said Liz. 'I mean I want to have a child. I've been lying in bed trying to decide with whom I shall have it. And you are going to be its godmother.'

'But I am an atheist,' said Hildamay.

'So?'

'So, I won't know what to teach it. I won't be able to tell it about God. I know nothing about God.'

'You know about the world, don't you?' asked Liz.

'Yes.'

'Well, that's far more useful. Tell it about that. And by the way, you have to look after it if I die.'

'Why should you die?' asked Hildamay.

'Because people do,' said Liz, and rang off.
Hildamay rang her back. 'Are we having lunch?'
'Of course we are,' said Liz. 'It's Wednesday, isn't it?'
'I just thought you might be busy.'
'Busy doing what?'
'Busy having children,' said Hildamay.
'I could hardly do that without discussing it with you, could I? You have to help me choose the man. And anyway, it's your birthday.'
'I know,' said Hildamay, and put down the phone.
'A child!' she exclaimed. 'Why on earth does she want a child?' She knew the answer perfectly well. She knew that what Liz really wanted was a child and a man. But Liz said that men weren't what they used to be.
'Oh, why bother,' she would say. 'They're all married, or gay, or still love Mummy.'
'Well, get thee to a nunnery,' said Hildamay cheerfully, for she was of the opinion that most men were emotional cripples by the time they had reached their middle thirties.
'Helpful,' said Liz drily.
'True,' said Hildamay.

Hildamay sighed and, picking up the magnifying mirror, returned to the more immediate matter of her smiles. She practised all six with intense and elaborate concentration. This exercise complete, she addressed her face, starting with her nose. It was broad in the middle, blunt at the tip, and tilted to show what she considered to be an indecent display of nostril. She wrinkled it with disdain and began mentally to place other noses on her face. She could find none to her satisfaction and so gave up and fretted for some minutes about the lines which cracked around her eyes.
'Smoking,' she murmured and resolved, as she did every morning, to give it up. 'Or maybe just give up make-up,' she said aloud to the empty room and lit a cigarette. She sat in thoughtful silence for some minutes, squinting through the smoke, then picked up the mirror once again, and, raising it to within an inch of her nose, examined her eyes.
She blinked at their bright blueness, wondering if the colour would fade with age, and remembered seeing the first signs of decay, the evening she had stood smiling cheerfully in front of her bathroom mirror; stood smiling until she had noticed the remains of

the day's eyeshadow. 'Revlon's Perfect Brown, it was,' she now murmured out loud, caught in the lines around her eyes, like mud shining dull in the dusty tributaries of a dried-out river. 'Age!' she had whispered, fumbling in shock at her eyes in the cool glass of the mirror. The next day she had gone out and bought a pot of eye cream, 'Guaranteed to reduce visible signs of ageing'; rushing home that night to her bathroom mirror where she had stood gazing at herself in a sort of wonder, like a girl who has just lost her virginity, patting the pale cream into the cracks around her eyes.

That little pot of eye cream had stood alone on the shelf in her bathroom, its gilt and porcelain sophistication forlorn next to the old tortoiseshell comb and ancient pot of Vaseline. Before the eye cream, Hildamay had never so much as picked up a pot of moisturising lotion, and had used the same tube of lipstick for ten years.

Somehow, that had all changed. From those first pale fumblings, from that tiny little jar, had grown an obsession.

'Extraordinary,' murmured Hildamay to her own reflection.

'Extraordinary to be in love,' she added, practising her conciliatory smile in her magnifying mirror, 'with a moisturiser.' Then she shrugged ruefully and, smiling at herself apologetically, put down the mirror and climbed out of bed. Smoothing down the starchy white linen sheets, she flung a faded old American quilt across the rumpled expanse of the bed then walked across the room and leaned against the door of the bathroom. She gazed in at the room, at the walls covered with shelves, each crammed with bottles and jars. When Hildamay felt depressed she went to Harrods' beauty hall and wandered through its cool, marbled rooms, pausing here and there to squeeze a pearl of some perfumed unguent on the inside of her wrist. The salesgirls knew her well and spoke to her as a friend. She paused to chat with them for hours about the merits of collagen or extract of placenta; much as other women discuss men. They were grateful for her interest. Their days were long and their customers hard.

She would hurry home with her small packages in their shiny, gilded cartons, unwrap them, dip her fingers into their pale contents and sigh with delight. Then came the ritual of arranging them, which she did tenderly and with great care on the already crowded shelves.

In the centre of the bathroom stood an old, ceramic claw-footed bath big enough for a person to lie down in fully, and in the corner was a big, square white ceramic tiled area surrounded by a low wall. A tap was set at waist height against the wall, and on the tiles sat a low pale wooden stool, a bucket and a fat bar of creamy coloured soap. A silvered mesh basket held a sponge, a loofah, a body brush and a plastic lozenge-shaped thing with a curved handle to its top and a dimpled, soft rubber pad to its underbelly.

Hildamay would sit on the stool and wash and scrub herself all over then rinse herself with pails full of warm water. Only when she was thoroughly clean would she climb into the bath and lie soaking in the oily, scented water. It was the Japanese manner of bathing; precise, ritualistic and, to Hildamay anyway, infused with an impeccable logic. When she visited Japan, Hildamay had at first been bemused by this novel method of bathing but soon found herself so absolutely in sympathy with it that, when she got back to London, she found it impossible to climb unwashed into the bath and lie in dirty water.

She spent hours bent over the sink in her old bathroom, soaping and rinsing herself with flannels. The carpet under her feet grew damper and damper until gradually the patch became mildewed and rotten. At first she did not notice for it was the ritual more than the method which she had come to find indispensable. She began to understand that it was not so much Japanese cleanliness that she admired but the manner in which they compartmentalised and anaesthetised emotion, rendering it malleable, harmless even. In the secret, ritual manner of bathing they cleansed both body and soul. She spent more and more time in the bathroom and as she cleansed her body, so she wiped the stains of other people and the mess of their emotions from her mind.

Before long the bathroom came to seem to her another world, a world both secret and precious.

She stood one day in her old bathroom and smelled the rank dankness of mildew and looked at the towels which other people used and at the soap with which other people washed their hands and longed suddenly for a quiet, secret place where she would be alone. Completely alone. So she called a builder and a plumber and instructed them to cut her bedroom in half and place in it a bathroom, which she had carefully and painstakingly designed. They thought her mad, and said so often, but she simply smiled her most vulnerable, pleading smile and made them cups of tea and they worked twice as hard, finishing the bathroom in a matter of weeks instead of months. The morning they left she walked into the bathroom carrying a stiff wooden brush and a bar of hard milled geranium rose soap and spent the whole day scrubbing, cleansing off all traces of them. In each corner of the room she placed little heaps of scented incense pebbles which she left burning for twenty-four hours until the walls and carpet were infused with their sharp, clean smell. Then she arranged the room, placing everything in a precise pattern which she never again altered or disturbed.

White towels were piled up on the floor, which was carpeted in thick cream wool. After she had soaked for exactly ten minutes in the hot, scented water, Hildamay would step out of the bath, and wrap herself in a towel, big as a sheet. If there was time, or if she needed to think, she would sit on the floor in the scented, warm air. She had on occasion spent whole days lying wrapped in towels on the cream carpet, musing. The bathroom, which led off her bedroom, was kept locked. Guests went to the old, smaller one down the hall. Not even her close friends knew that the locked door in her bedroom led to a bathroom. They all assumed that it was a cupboard and teased her about the size of her wardrobe. Even Rita, her cleaning lady, whom Hildamay trusted with her most intimate secrets – her underwear, her telephone messages, the lies she sometimes told – did not know it was there. Hildamay would lock the door and feel as if she was in another world. A world that nobody else knew existed.

The telephone rang again and she jumped, momentarily startled. She did not pick it up but waited for the answering machine, which was placed on the floor by her bed, to whir into action.

'Hildamay? Hildamay? Are you there? It's me. I mean, it's Kate. Oh, you're not there. Now I don't know what to do. Will you get this message, do you suppose?' A child screamed in the background. 'Well, you'll have to.' Kate's voice sounded frantic. She seemed to be wrestling with something and was breathing heavily. 'It's Ben. He says he'll be late back from the office and couldn't I drink champagne with you some other time? Oh, happy birthday. I forgot to say it and it was what I rang up to say. Oh, I hate these things,' she added, quite crossly. 'It's silly. Saying happy birthday to a machine. Well, I'll have to ask Mary to stay late. That's it. She's coming to clean anyway and she's always complaining that she never has any money. She can earn some tonight. That's it. So I will be there after all. Oh, darling, stop it. Don't do that. I said *don't do that*!' The telephone went dead.

Hildamay smiled at the silent telephone as if it were at Kate she smiled. She loved Kate; sweet, slow, simple Kate. But she had no idea why. 'Habit, I suppose,' she said thoughtfully. If they met now, they would never become friends. We never would meet now, thought Hildamay, remembering Kate's kind, round face shining out from the gloom of the typing pool. She had lent her her Tipp-Ex, that first morning, and taken her to the canteen for lunch, tucking Hildamay comfortably under her wing as if she, Kate, had been forty, not nineteen. She had talked incessantly about Ben then, just as she did now. 'Ben,' she said, 'is my *raison d'être*.' She said it as if he was a piece of dried fruit.

Kate had never stopped disapproving of Hildamay's life, which made Hildamay feel cheerful, for she disapproved of Kate's.

'It's about time, Hildamay, that you found yourself a decent man and settled down.'

'Now why would I want to do that?' said Hildamay obediently. Kate had been saying the same thing for the past fifteen years.

'Because it will make you happy,' said Kate firmly.

'Fucking makes me happy, settling makes me dull,' said Hildamay, grinning.

'You are not to have casual sex.' Kate looked prim, her face pink. 'It's dangerous.'

'I'm never casual about sex,' drawled Hildamay. 'I take it very seriously.'

'Oh, really, Hildamay,' said Kate, flushing. 'You are the absolute limit.'

Smiling at the memory of Kate's prim, pink face, Hildamay stepped back into the bright square of her bedroom and from there into the long, dark corridor which led to the kitchen. She stumbled, momentarily blinded by the gloom, and felt the polished wood floorboards cold under her bare feet. When she bought the flat, in an old mansion block in Bloomsbury, it seemed to her so like a strange plant with its dark, narrow stem of a corridor out of which sprouted big light rooms, bright as flowers, that she painted the corridor a deep green and all the rooms in pale, brilliant colours. Now she stepped suddenly into the brightest of them all, the kitchen, painted the yellow of daffodils. The room winked cheerfully at her as she opened the fridge and took out a quarter bottle of champagne. 'Happy birthday,' she said, pouring it into a fragile crystal flute and drinking to herself. It was a habit she had maintained since her eighteenth birthday when she had decided that, since she was always going to live alone, she might as well be happy doing it.

She had not been surprised when her mother died and left her completely and, finally, alone. It had always seemed to her inevitable that she should leave. Her presence, even when she was alive, had been but dimly felt by her daughter. Since her father's disappearance, her mother had lived in some shadowed place. Her body remained but the spirit had long since departed. Hildamay understood, even as a very small child, the effort it took her mother to live in the world. Her resolute cheerfulness, her unrelenting optimism were affirmations of life, little pinching reminders to a mind that suspected it might already be dead. 'It will be all right,' she told her small daughter every morning over breakfast. 'What will?' daily wondered the child and, finding no answer, grew cynical and weary. 'Today is a new day,' said her mother, nodding brightly over the soapy water. Hildamay had ever after thought of mornings as shiny and bright. Perhaps that was why she liked them so much. But evenings to her were little deaths.

Neither mother nor daughter was surprised by her death. What surprised Hildamay was her mother's sudden vehemence, her eager grab at life before she died. 'Learn to love, Hilda. It is not good to be so alone.'

'Yes it is, Mother,' she said aloud. 'Yes, it is.'

Hildamay sat at the scarred wooden kitchen table drinking champagne and thinking of her mother. She heard her soft, scolding voice. 'Champagne, Hilda? At breakfast? I don't know who you think you are, my girl. Really I don't.'

A smile twisted at the corners of Hildamay's mouth. Her mother had never known who she thought she was. Even down to her name.

'Hildamay? What kind of fancy label is that? Hilda you were born, my girl. Hilda you will die.'

Hildamay was the name her father had given her. The only thing he ever had given her. Her father. She sighed. She did not like to think about him and so did not, but turned instead to the brightly wrapped parcel which lay on the table. As she started to unwrap it, the phone rang.

'Hello,' she said, but had scarcely rounded off the 'o' when a deep voice said, 'Darling!'

'Hello, Cassie.'

'Hello, darling, darling Hildamay. Happy birthday. Are you having a nice day? Isn't it a gorgeous morning? I've just been out in the garden, barefoot in the frost, and my narcissi are all cream and gold and the sky all pale and pearly. I woke so early and just bounded out of bed feeling full of the joys which is surprising really because I drank such a lot of champagne last night. But it was worth it. To drink so much champagne, I mean. There was this man with the most fabulous mean green eyes and once I'd got a bit of, you know, courage, I went and talked to him and realised that really his eyes weren't mean at all but green like the underside of a new leaf, tender and fine and terribly shy.'

Cassie Montrose – she had always called herself by her full name, Cassandra, until a numerologist told her that with that combination she would never amount to much – was creative director of an advertising agency. She regarded her work as something of a religious experience, 'Bringing colour and illumination to the world. I like,' she also said, for Cassie was fond of words and used them to excess, 'to paint pictures with words.' Cassie's canvases were abstract, florid and very large.

'I'm drinking champagne now,' said Hildamay to interrupt the present creation.

'Darling! How perfectly wicked of you. But of course you are. It's your birthday and a girl should always drink champagne on her birthday. Did you get lots of gorgeous presents?'

'Yes,' said Hildamay, who had just finished unwrapping her parcel.

'Oh, what, what? Do tell.'

'A pair of Chanel earrings.'

'Oh! Who from? Do tell, do tell!'

'Certainly not,' said Hildamay, who had bought them for herself.

'Oh, you're so horrid, darling. They're from one of those millions of men you have tucked away. I'm convinced there are *hordes* of them shut up in that cupboard in your bedroom. Gorgeous men with leonine hair and yellow eyes flecked with gold. The door's always locked. Do you only let them out at night?'

'No,' said Hildamay truthfully, then added, 'I let them out in the morning. I only like sex at dawn.'

Cassie, who was convinced that Hildamay had lovers whom she

refused to introduce to anybody, said, with absolute understanding, 'I see.' Then dubiously, 'Dawn, darling?'

'Dawn,' said Hildamay, bored with the turn the conversation was taking.

'All right, darling,' said Cassie, who, when sober, was extremely sensitive to voices. 'Shall I see you this evening? For your birthday champagne?'

'Of course,' said Hildamay.

'And Delilah?' asked Cassie warily. She was nervous of Delilah who was a psychologist, which made Cassie nervous enough, but Delilah had always seemed to her too cool and clever, particularly after she, Cassie, had had a few drinks.

'Yes,' said Hildamay.

'Liz?'

'Naturally.'

'And Kate?'

'If she can get somebody to look after the brats.'

'Oh, Hildamay,' said Cassie. 'They're perfectly sweet.'

'Sweet they are not,' said Hildamay. 'They're too much like their father to be that.'

'He's not so bad,' said Cassie, who was of a charitable temperament and, moreover, thought that a husband, any husband, was a sacred being.

'I suppose not,' said Hildamay, who was eager to have a bath. 'See you at seven.'

'Can't wait, darling.'

Hildamay sat, naked, on the wooden stool in her bathroom, Chanel earrings clipped to her ears, and soaped herself thoroughly. The telephone rang again. She could hear Delilah's measured tones echoing through the answering machine.

'You probably are there, listening, but as it's your birthday, I forgive you.'

'Generous of you,' said Hildamay loudly.

'I'm going to be a bit late. A patient. Seven-thirty at the latest. Goodbye.'

'Bye bye, Delilah,' sang Hildamay, and then began to sing a song, a particular favourite of hers. 'Last n-i-i-ght I had a bit of masturbation. It was no nice! I did it twice!' she sang, grinning at herself in the mirror, hair plastered to her head, ears twinkling with

Chanel gold. 'Beat it! Heat it! Bang it in the door!' she yodelled, 'smash it, crash it, bash it on the floor! They say that sexual intercourse is really rather gr-a-a-a-and! But I prefer to take it in my clammy little hand. Beat it! Heat it!' she sang to her reflection in the mirror. Her breasts were too big. 'Bash it! Crash it!' she yelled, flattening them with both hands, turning this way and that to see the effect. There were those who admired them. She was not one of them.

There were two things in life which Hildamay did not like. Building sites and Rigby & Peller. She could be walking along a road minding her own business, thinking about quantum physics and wearing a sack, but her breasts would always find the nearest building site and the men perched high on the scaffolding would always find her breasts.

'I'd like to get a load of those, darlin',' they would shout. And she, humiliated, dumbstruck, reduced to vulnerable, quivering flesh, would shuffle past, shoulders tensed to control her treacherous breasts.

'Something to make them look smaller,' she murmured to the woman at Rigby & Peller.

'I don't know why Madam wants that,' said the fitter, briskly cramming them into stiff little strips of elastic and lace. 'Now, if Madam would just bend forward, we could tuck them in properly. There we are. Don't you look lovely?'

And Hildamay would stare at her reflection in the mirror, her breasts encased in their prisons of lace, standing like stiffened, snowy cones on her chest.

'Madam has nice, firm breasts,' sighed the woman with satisfaction. 'Some of the ladies, well. You can see why they might get upset. We have to scoop 'em off the floor sometimes,' she added, her huge breasts jiggling with laughter.

Hildamay stopped singing, looked at herself and frowned. Her arms were strong and muscular, as were her shoulders and back. The whole set of her upper body was firm, capable. It tapered down to her waist, which was smallish. She looked at her waist and felt cheerful. Then she looked at the rest of her body which flared out over big, rounded hips and fleshy, high buttocks, and felt less optimistic. Her thighs were solid and well muscled, her calves well shaped and her ankles fine. Still, Hildamay did not like her body. She thought it altogether too fleshy and longed to be slight and small and interestingly boned.

Hildamay loved food. And food loved her. It seemed to attach itself to her, clustering around her hips and her thighs or clamping itself on to the fleshy expanse of her upper arms.

'The only part of you that's thin,' she said regretfully to her reflection, 'are your hands.' The man in the jeweller's had told her that she had anorectic fingers. She considered them, then pinched a fold of skin from the back of one hand. This was the age test. The quicker it snapped back, the more slowly the skin on the body would age and grow slack. She watched the raised fold with dismay. It did not seem even to move, let alone snap. 'Good grief,' she said to her reflection and walked cheerful and sweet smelling into the bedroom.

CHAPTER TWO

HILDAMAY was a high-heels girl. 'The last of the breed,' she reflected sadly. In her wardrobe was a collection of fifty pairs of shoes. Snub-toed, peep-toed, pointy-toed and each with a slender, high heel that elongated her calves and pushed her bottom up and out to give her hips a helpless, hopeful swivel. Men watched Hildamay as she left a room, their eyes fixed on the promise of that soft, well-rounded posterior. Hildamay Smith could be hard in her demands, but she left her male colleagues with the conceit that they could be harder still, should the need ever arise. That it had not, and probably never would, curiously did not seem to occur to them.

'Hope springs eternal in the young man's penis,' said Hildamay to herself as she sat on the tube. She thought about penises all the way to Baker Street. She thought of them fondly, for Hildamay liked penises. In fact she liked them very much. She liked to hold them, clasping them firmly to feel their velvety resilience against the palm of her hand. She liked to feel them between her legs, push them up and inside her. They never failed to give her pleasure.

What she did not like was the mess they caused. Not the physical mess, for she took pleasure in sleeping on the damp patch. It was the emotional mess that she did not like.

'I love you,' said the mouth attached to the head attached to the last penis she had put between her legs.

'What?!' she had said, with genuine shock.

'I love you,' it repeated, and kept on repeating until Hildamay was forced to admit that she did not love it back. How could she, when she had known it for only a week?

'But love is like that,' said the man concerned.

'No, love is not like that,' said Hildamay. 'At least mine is not.'

He smiled at her fondly.

He's going to say, 'You funny little thing' next, thought Hildamay with dismay.

'You funny little thing,' he said tenderly.

Hildamay screamed so loudly he jumped out of bed.

'Why did you do that?' he asked crossly.

'I thought I felt the earth move,' said Hildamay.

'You funny little thing,' he said, climbing back into bed, and proceeded to lick her breasts.

'Good grief,' said Hildamay.

He was unhappy when she did not respond to his calls or his letters or his bouquets of flowers or, even, his tender, yearning face. 'You are cold, Hildamay,' he said bitterly. 'You are incapable of love,' he added, a note of hope creeping into his voice. Hildamay registered the hope, and knew what it meant. It challenged her to admit that she was afraid, frightened of love. Then he could be her saviour, her rescuer, her knight in shining armour come to thaw the ice queen and take her from this cold place and into the warm, living world. This he, only he, could achieve. Hildamay had looked at him, gently. His hope brightened. 'Yes,' she said. 'I am incapable.' He had left, gone charging off with his optimistic penis to boast to his friends of his adventures and to be consoled with tales of cold women.

Hildamay sighed and got off the tube. She walked up the stairs, turned to the left and walked down the long corridor to the platform where she stood, waiting for the Bakerloo line. The train arrived and she got on, sitting down to face a poster. It was for a dating agency. 'Don't let love and life pass you by', said the advertisement. She wondered what love really had to do with life.

'Are you married?' people would ask her.

'No,' she always replied. 'I am a spinster.' And she could see them looking at her strangely, but whether it was pity or contempt or simply envy which lit their faces, she did not know. Nor did she care.

Liz told everyone that she was divorced. She said it was easier. 'If I say that I am alone,' she complained, 'I am looked at strangely. But if I say I am divorced I am regarded with sympathy; someone thought me worthy enough to marry.' She laughed bitterly. 'It is true that it is better to have loved and lost than never to have loved at all.'

Hildamay wondered if it was really true, and thought about her mother.

Hildamay's mother died much as she lived. Politely. The tumour in her breast and the swollen lymph glands in her armpit had given her trouble. Quite a lot of trouble, really. But she did not like to make a fuss. And so she had not but ignored the tumour until it grew to the size of an orange and began to suppurate. It was the smell that drove her to the doctor. She could not bear the thought of smelling bad. In the latter months of her life she had taken to wearing a fragrance, gardenia, which blended with the unmistakable smell of rotting flesh to form a cloying, sickening odour. Everybody pretended not to notice except one small child on a bus who kept saying, 'Mummy, Mummy, that lady smells bad,' until Mummy, who had a red face and hard eyes, had whisked her to the back of the bus and distracted her with the promise of a McDonald's. After that Hildamay's mother never went out again.

Hildamay had sat in the hospital and watched her mother's face turn grey with pain.

'Shall I call a nurse?' she asked.

'Oh, no, dear, I don't like to bother them,' her mother replied, smiling bravely.

'But that's what they're here for, Mother. To be bothered.'

'No, dear. They have so much to do,' she sighed faintly. 'And they earn so little money. So little money for all that work.'

Elizabeth Margaret Victoria Smith knew about having very little money. She saved the unusable slivers from bars of soap so worn away that even a child's hand could not hold them, and sewed them into little foam pouches which she decorated with embroidered violets. 'Look at how well it foams, dear,' she would say to Hildamay with real pleasure. Everything in her mother's house was patched and darned. Even the titles on the spines of the books in the bookcase were reworked in shiny black Biro. Every scrap of fabric, every piece of thread, every square of wrapping paper was hoarded. Even the cat, Maisie, was a hand-me-down and was bald in patches.

Her royal names had not secured a royal income or even a reliable husband. Margaret – her mother had thought it too presumptuous to call her Elizabeth – had married, not so much beneath herself as completely and utterly outside of herself. She had never met anyone like Johnnie Smith before. 'Not John!' he would protest. 'Never plain John Smith. Plain John's dull, but Johnnie? He's quite another fellow!' In all the years that she had lain in her narrow bed dreaming of the man who would one day bend his face to hers and obscure her present with his future, she had never been able to summon a man like Johnnie Smith to her imagination. Somehow, she summoned him to her life. Why a man as impossibly good-looking, as clever, as funny and as talented would want her she never did understand. She married him, despite her mother's protestations. She became Maggie Smith, although she remained a Margaret in spirit. Johnnie would have none of the Margaret. He wanted a Maggie: 'Wild, spirited, a dreamer,' he teased.

When her daughter was born she chose a name that was as plain as any she could think of. She wanted no hopeless dreams or false ambition to disturb her daughter's equilibrium, none of what she called her husband's 'daft, romantic ideas'. Hilda she was born and Hilda she would live. But Maggie weakened on her way to the registrar and added May as a second name; something sweet, something fragrant, something to soften the blow of Hilda.

She never understood why Johnnie Smith had come into her life so she understood it when he left. Hildamay was eight years old. He left her with a dream. A dream of something great and solid and wonderfully glamorous. And her name. He would have no truck with Hilda. 'Why!' he would exclaim to Maggie, 'look at the girl. You can see she's no plain Hilda.' And Hildamay she became, despite her mother's quiet but stubborn persistence. 'Hilda,' she would say, correcting people when they asked her about her daughter. 'Hilda,' she would repeat in her small, quiet voice. When she was very small it did not occur to Hildamay to contradict her mother and at home she always answered to both names, depending on who was doing the calling. But on the day her father disapppeared she changed her name, clinging fiercely to the only thing that he had left her. Hildamay.

It became a source of considerable tension between mother and daughter, although Johnnie Smith suffered not even a whisper of reproach. Maggie refused ever to hear a bad word said against her husband and regarded herself as married right up until the day she died, although he had been long gone. She cherished him with a fierceness that was strange to see in a woman so gentle and mild. It was strange to her daughter, who wanted a father and could not bear to live with a departed saint. 'Oh, fuck my father,' screamed Hildamay when she was just sixteen. Her mother had looked at her and said, very quietly, 'I just wish that I could.' Hildamay never mentioned him again.

Hildamay spent her eighteenth year amongst the smell of antiseptic and unemptied bed pans and death. The scent of gardenias was to make her gag for the rest of her life.

'Mother,' she said again, 'why don't I call the nurse to give you something for the pain?'

'Yes, Hilda dear,' said her mother. 'Perhaps you should.'

Hildamay looked at her with alarm. 'She really is dying,' she thought as she ran to find a nurse. And suddenly, she did not want her mother to die. She very badly did not want her mother to die, although she had taken little notice of her when she lived.

'She is a woman of no imagination,' reflected Hildamay as she stared at the worn face lying on the hard hospital pillow, now peaceful, drug-clouded and free from pain. She did not know from what source her mother drew her hope. She seemed always happy, bright with optimism, full of cheerful clichés. 'Be thankful for small mercies,' she trilled to her small daughter. 'Every cloud has a silver lining,' she said, smiling brightly.

Hildamay was not thankful for small mercies. She wanted the big ones.

One day, during her mother's last week in hospital, she had woken and said, 'Will you do something for me?'

'Yes, Mother.'

'Learn to love, Hilda. You did not seem to learn from me. Try, Hilda. It is not good to be so alone.'

Hildamay had looked at her, too astonished to speak. It was only years later that she remembered her words. About being alone. She had never found that love stopped you from feeling alone.

Love had not stopped Liz from feeling alone. She was bitterly and terribly alone. One evening she had got violently drunk and had shown a part of her so bloody, so scabby with picked-over sores that Hildamay had recoiled at the pain. She knew that Liz was not yet healed from her divorce, although it had been five years since John left.

'I felt like a child when he left,' Liz had said, tears pouring out of her unblinking eyes. 'Like a child,' she repeated so softly that Hildamay did not know whether she was aware of her presence. 'As though someone had turned out the light and had put me out in the cold and I wandered around crying, "Oh, please tell me what I did wrong? Was I bad? Did I do something terrible? What did I do? What did I do? What did I do?"' She had sat there rocking and singing that line until Hildamay grew frightened and moved to put her arms around her. 'WHAT DID I DO?' she screamed, grabbing Hildamay so hard that she had fallen.

'You did nothing,' said Hildamay.

'Yes, that must be it. I did nothing,' said Liz, picking up the song, 'nothing, nothing, nothing, nothing,' until suddenly she stopped and looked at Hildamay in bewilderment. 'Why does nobody love me?'

'They do, Liz,' said Hildamay. 'I do.'

Liz stopped crying and smiled at her. 'Yes,' she said, then looked down and shook her head. 'But it's not. It's not . . .'

'I know,' said Hildamay, who really didn't. But she hugged her anyway and said, 'I know. It's not.'

Hildamay thought about romantic love. Sentimental love. It did not seem to last long. It went as quickly as it came, but that was its nature. She had watched her friends, bewildered and confused after the storm of passion had passed. It was, they said eagerly, particularly when they were in the grip of the obsession, 'true love'. Hildamay did not believe them.

'Just you wait,' they said. 'It will happen to you.'

Hildamay doubted it just as she doubted that was the love her mother had meant. None of her friends seemed to experience that love. Partnership, friendship, companionship, yes; all those, if they were lucky. But the love that says you are not alone? Not likely. Thus doubting, Hildamay arrived at Piccadilly Circus.

CHAPTER THREE

GEORGE Brown stood in Hildamay's office. In his hands he held a small bunch of pale pink roses. George had worked for Hildamay for five years and two weeks. He was her secretary and his devotion to her was dogged. He looked like a dog; a small breed, hairless and tail-less. He was very small. His face was round and smooth, his skin very pale and his eyes so light a blue they were almost white. He had no eyelashes or eyebrows to speak of and so blinked a great deal. Hildamay knew nothing about him other than that he lived alone in Streatham. She supposed him to be somewhere in his early forties.

George went out every day in his lunch hour to buy a lamb chop for his supper. For lunch he ate pickled herring and cucumber sandwiches which he brought, neatly wrapped in silver foil, to the office each morning. He spread a napkin on his desk, white damask and perfectly ironed, unwrapped his sandwiches and ate them. Then he ate a pear. 'Lamb and pears,' he said, 'are the least allergenic of all foods.' He did not explain the virtues of pickled herring.

He was never late in the morning and left punctually at six o'clock.

He wore only brown suits and starched white cotton shirts but had a weakness for brilliantly patterned and coloured ties. Hildamay had at first wondered if he was gay but had decided that he had no sexual nature.

He insisted on calling her Miss Smith. At the end of his first week with her, she had insisted that he call her Hildamay. Monday was a black day. George had managed to stammer out her name twice, but for the rest of the day had hovered about her desk so obviously unable to speak that no work was done at all. They were both relieved when, the next morning, he reverted to the more formal address.

'Good morning, handsome,' said Hildamay, walking into her office.

'Good morning, Miss Smith,' he said, thrusting the roses clumsily at her. 'Happy birthday.'

'Thank you, they're divine,' she said, looking at him holding them. 'They suit you, George. You should carry them more often.' He blushed and put his hand to his head. What sparse strands of sandy hair he possessed were cemented firmly into place across his white scalp. Bitch, thought Hildamay immediately and with regret. He hated to be teased and she was very fond of him.

No man was less handsome than George. The first time she had jokingly addressed him as 'handsome', he flushed a pink so brilliant she was astonished he had that much red blood in his milk white skin. She was also concerned that she had offended him, but the smile she caught told her it was the colour of pleasure. The other secretaries picked up the nickname but when Sheila in accounts dared say it to his face, George looked at her and said, 'What might I do to help you, Miss Oliphant?' with such deadly contempt that she flounced out of the door, quite forgetting about the letter she had come to ask Hildamay to sign.

Nobody dared try it again except Jack Rome, Stone & Gray's marketing director. George blinked at him in silence for a full minute until Jack, who prided himself on his way with people – 'I like to think,' he often repeated, 'that I can charm the birds out of the trees' – had been forced to apologise. George did not mention the incident again but never after referred to Jack as anything other than 'that man'. And nobody ever again called George anything other than George; except behind his back.

Stone & Gray was a small textiles company which dealt only in the very best cashmere and tweed and whose motto, 'Quality Above All Else', had not changed in the hundred years since it was founded. Hildamay was its managing director, a position she had held for six years since Young Mr Stone, son of Old Mr Stone – who had personally sold tweed to Gabrielle Chanel and was rumoured to have been so passionately in love with her that he had almost squandered the company's fortunes on rafts of white camellias – had retired. There were those who said that Young Mr Stone suffered from the same affliction that had plagued his father; the love of a fine pair of ankles. Why else should Hildamay Smith now be sitting in his seat? Hildamay blessed her ankles often for, although she knew it was not they that had made her good at her work, she also knew that, did she not possess them, she might never have been able to prove it.

Young Mr Stone was indeed susceptible to a fine pair of ankles. He was of the opinion that they indicated good breeding and high intelligence. 'A clever woman, that,' he would thunder as he watched a pair of shapely legs across a restaurant. Young Mr Stone liked to sample all the newest and most fashionable restaurants and would take Hildamay out to lunch at regular three-monthly intervals. At lunch Hildamay was careful to produce all six of her smiles for him, because she knew it pleased him. And once every three months she bought a pair of silk stockings. 'You book,' he would roar down the telephone, for he was very deaf. 'Let's go somewhere different for a change.' As they never went to the same place twice, this was an unnecessary suggestion, but Young Mr Stone liked people to think that he was a man of society. In truth he only ever ventured out of his club to eat with Hildamay.

Hildamay liked Young Mr Stone and he liked her and asked her to call him 'Si', a privilege which she was careful never to abuse outside their lunches. He was one of those men, rare in his generation, who truly believe that women are good at business, and talked to her as his equal. 'Look at Gabrielle,' he would thunder at Hildamay. 'Ran rings around my father. Clever woman. Best pair of ankles I ever saw.'

Other than their lunches, Hildamay had no other contact with him except at the annual general meeting. He saw the profits and saw that they were healthy. He never asked 'How?' but only 'How much?' In Hildamay's case, 'How much?' was one hundred per cent, for she had doubled the profits since he had made her managing director. Si Stone was more than ever convinced that a woman's brain was in her ankles.

*

Hildamay sat in her office, crossed her legs and ignored those same fine ankles. She was considering a scrap of silk tweed from their new line. Out of the corner of her eye she saw Jack Rome approach the glass door marked 'Managing Director'. He walked in without knocking. He was a man who believed that whatever a woman was doing, it could be interrupted. Hildamay kept her head bent over the fabric. Eventually, Jack coughed. She looked up.

'Good morning, Jack,' she said. 'I am sorry. I didn't hear you knock.' His brilliant smile dimmed but did not falter. Jack had been told by so many women that his smile would get him everything that he was defenceless without it. Hildamay considered it. It was a good smile, but not a great one. It lacked nuance.

'You look very smart today, Hildamay,' he said, adding with a roguish wink, 'very sexy.'

'So do you, Jack. So do you. It's that adorable tie. It makes you look so – so – what's the word?' She ran her tongue over her lips. 'So – wanton.'

'I say –'

'What do you say, Jack?' said Hildamay, smiling her most dangerous smile. 'I'd just adore to know.'

His smile flickered. 'I had thought I might buy you some champagne. It is your birthday and I know how you girls like a bit of bubbly,' he said boyishly. Jack had also been told by so many women that he needed looking after that he had quite forgotten his age, which was forty-two. He narrowed brilliant green eyes; a green so vivid it was impossible to believe that they were real, which they were not. His coloured contact lenses were the joke of the office, as was his hair, tinted an improbable black, and his dazzling white, artificially enamelled teeth which he kept on permanent display. He had a big, loose mouth, the lips bulbous, reddened and permanently slicked with saliva. Hildamay thought his mouth repulsive but she did not mind the teeth. She understood that so much financial investment deserved a fair return. Nor did she object to the contact lenses, although she found them disconcerting. No, it was not the teeth nor the eyes nor even the vanity she minded. It was the complacency. Moreover, each time she lunched with Si Stone, he reminded her that he thought Jack 'A good sort of a chap'. She knew about the bottles of claret exchanged every Christmas. She also knew that Jack's father was a member of Si Stone's club. So she kept silent. It was the way of the world and Hildamay had no desire to disturb it for the sake of men like Jack.

'Jack,' she said, 'how perfectly sweet of you, but I'm afraid I can't.' His smile disappeared altogether. 'My mother,' she added, shrugging helplessly. The smile returned. 'Your mother,' he said, nodding complicitously. 'Is she not well again?'

Hildamay had once, in a fit of contrition, gone out for a drink with Jack. She had hoped that familiarity might ease her contempt. It had not. He had taken her to a crowded bar, full of red-faced, sweating men. Pushing his way through the crowd, he had wedged her against a stool and pressed himself hard against her. The more she squirmed, the harder he held her. Hildamay realised that he thought her movements a sign of pleasure so she went limp in his arms. He enjoyed this still more and made a great show of ordering a bottle of Bollinger.

'Bolly, my good man,' he called to the barman who, by his demeanour, did not consider himself either Jack's, nor good, nor, particularly, a man.

'Keep it down, big boy,' he shouted, in loud contemptuous tones. This proved too much for Jack. He thrust his erection hard against Hildamay's bottom, whispering loudly, 'They know me here,' and then spent the next hour enraptured by a monologue about his wife, the whole of which he addressed to her breasts. 'She doesn't appreciate me,' he told them. 'She says she's bored,' he said, gazing at them in bewilderment. 'And now she says she's going to take evening classes in women's studies,' he finished, looking pained. 'What can she mean?'

'I can't imagine,' said Hildamay, her voice dry as paper.

'I knew you'd understand,' said Jack to her breasts, studying them as if they might contain the answer to his wife's mystifying behaviour.

'Is there something wrong with my blouse?' asked Hildamay, to shame him.

'What?'

'My blouse,' she said, peering down at her breasts. They both stared at them for some time.

'It looks perfect to me,' he said. Beads of sweat glistened in a watery moustache above his upper lip. 'Shall I take a closer look for you?'

'I must go,' she said in tones as cold as any she had ever uttered.

'But you can't.' He snaked an arm around her waist and brandished a half-empty bottle of champagne in the air. 'I know you don't really want to,' he added, bending his mouth to her neck. She felt sweat and spittle on her skin and, returning her head, bit him on the cheek. He jumped.

'Why did you do that?' he asked, looking as confused as a six-year-old boy whose family pet has suddenly snapped at him.

'Do what?' she asked, widening her eyes.

He looked at her, then smiled understandingly.

'Oh, you like that, do you?' he said grinning.

'I must go,' she said. 'I should have been home hours ago. It's my mother. She's ill. Very, very ill.'

His arm was back around her waist. 'Don't be embarrassed,' he whispered. 'I like a bit of the rough stuff myself. I'm a man of the world.'

'Dying,' she shouted, and left.

He had asked her out again, on many occasions. Hildamay always refused, explaining that she had to get home to her mother. Jack understood a woman who loved her mother, for he loved his intensely, and so enquired constantly and solicitously after her health.

'She's quite comfortable, thank you,' Hildamay always replied, with a smile.

She smiled again. 'Was there anything else?'

'Only old Bonham,' he said easily, stretching lazily in his chair. 'Playing silly buggers again. Says he's considering switching the account. Says our deliveries are always late and that we charge over the odds. Says he'll go somewhere else. Don't worry. I can handle him. I'll take him out for a good lunch. Buy him a bottle or two.'

'Charles Bonham doesn't drink,' said Hildamay quietly.

'Well, that sales director of his does. She's quite a woman, Adele March. We have lunch. On a regular basis.' He smiled. 'She's very relaxed. Very relaxed.'

'About the late deliveries, too, no doubt,' said Hildamay, smiling pleasantly.

'She's a very understanding woman.' Jack's teeth flashed white with the memory of her sympathy.

'How late are they?'

'Are what?'

'The fabrics.'

'Oh, slightly. Very slightly.'

'Days? Weeks? Months?' asked Hildamay impatiently.

'Daa – Well, the last batch was a couple of weeks late but nothing to get too alarmed about.' He smiled indulgently at her. 'Don't worry so much,' he said, stretching his arms behind his neck.

'Oh, I don't,' said Hildamay.

'That's good,' said Jack, grinning. 'It's about time you learned to relax. Stop taking the job so seriously. Loosen up a bit. You could learn a great deal from Adele March.'

'Oh, I have,' said Hildamay sweetly. 'In fact I've learned so much, I'm taking over the account.'

'I don't quite understand,' said Jack yawning, his hands clasped behind his neck. 'As sales director, I think that's rather my preserve.'

'Not in this case,' said Hildamay innocently. 'Charles Bonham insists that he deal with me. And as one of our most valuable and long-standing customers, I could hardly disagree.'

'He's an old fool,' said Jack harshly, then gave a low, dirty chuckle. 'Miss March and I were handling things very well. Very well indeed.'

'Miss March,' said Hildamay with her most charming smile, 'has been fired. Something about mixing business with pleasure.'

George watched Jack leave Hildamay's office then took her telephone messages in to her.

'What did that man want?' he asked.

'A cup of tea, I expect,' said Hildamay. 'It is usual to offer one during a meeting, George.'

George blinked rapidly but did not speak. Nothing on earth, not even Hildamay, could have induced him to make Jack Rome a cup of tea.

Hildamay looked fondly at him.

'My job, George. He wants my job.'

Then she smiled. George had seen the look on Jack Rome's face as he left her office. And although George had no sympathy for Jack Rome, he had a great deal of sympathy for men, for he knew them to be the weaker sex.

'You can be very cruel sometimes, Miss Smith,' he said quietly.

Hildamay thought that he was probably right.

She walked to Luigi's, the restaurant where she and Liz met for lunch every week. They had been going there for nearly six years.

The first time had been a business lunch. Liz, who worked as an editor at a small publishing house, had been working on a book about textiles and had called Hildamay to ask her some technical questions. She had offered to buy her lunch in return for some advice. They spent the first half hour discussing fabrics but by the end of lunch had somehow ended up talking about sex. They had got very drunk. It was then they had made the arrangement to meet every Wednesday for lunch.

That was in the days when Liz was still married. She was also having an affair. It was not a serious one but her husband John found out. He was, said Liz, 'destroyed. He simply fell apart and I've promised him it will never happen again. And it won't.' She talked endlessly about 'working at the relationship'. She was so busy working at it and so convinced by the dream of happy ever after that she did not notice that John was also working at one, but with someone else.

'How could I not have noticed?' said Liz at lunch. 'How could I have been so stupid?'

It was the night John left and during the following months that they became really close friends. Hildamay remembered that night well. Liz had called her at about nine o'clock.

'He's left,' was all she said. She sounded very calm.

'Come over,' said Hildamay and went out and bought a bottle of brandy. Liz drank half of it that night and kept telling and telling and retelling the story.

'I'd been in Frankfurt at the book fair over the weekend. I called him as soon as I got back, in the afternoon. We arranged to meet at home at seven-thirty. I got home, early for a change, and went into the kitchen and made dinner. The jar of coffee was in the cupboard. I remember thinking how strange that was because John never put anything away and the thought that he was having an affair flashed through my mind. I remember thinking I was being absurd. We were happy. It was nearly eight-thirty by the time he got home and the minute he walked in I knew something was wrong. He put his arms round me and hugged me hard for minutes. I could feel his heart beating really fast and I knew then that something terrible had happened. I thought he must be ill, that he was going to tell me he had some fatal disease. "I've got some bad news," he said. I didn't say anything. "I'm leaving you." I felt as if he had hit me in the stomach although I'm sure he didn't. I asked him why. He said that he was having an affair, that he had wanted to leave me for months. I asked him if he still loved me. He said "no". Just "no". So I said that he had better leave. He walked out. It took two minutes. Two minutes to end six years of marriage. I took the dinner out of the oven, threw it away and called you.'

Eventually the brandy knocked her out. Hildamay put her to bed, woke her in the morning, fed her breakfast and took her to her office. Liz did everything she was told, like a child. They had lunch as usual the following Wednesday.

'I saw him,' said Liz, her eyes guarded. 'He came round to talk things over, or so he said. He talked, I listened. For an hour. He told me that he didn't love me, that he didn't find me attractive, that I was boring, that our life together was dull and getting duller. He said he wanted some glamour, some excitement. When I finally asked him what that meant, he just shrugged.' Liz took a deep breath. 'I wish I understood what he meant.'

'He meant revenge,' said Hildamay.

'Do you think so?' she said miserably. 'I don't care what he meant. I just know it hurts like hell.'

She had eaten nothing. Suddenly she put down her fork, put her elbow on the table and her hand to her forehead so that it hid her face. Hildamay knew she was crying.

'I'm sorry,' said Liz after a few minutes. 'I seem to do this rather too much at the moment.'

'I like salt with my food,' said Hildamay.

Liz giggled and took her hand away. Tears dripped slowly down her face. She made no move to brush them away but sat staring over Hildamay's shoulder.

'Maybe I am dull. I suppose I'm not very appealing,' she said quietly.

Hildamay looked at her friend's face. She had a big, naturally red-lipped mouth, a funny, crooked nose, and brown eyes fringed by lashes which Hildamay had at first thought were false. It seemed so odd to wear false lashes and no other make-up that she had regretfully decided they must be real. She leaned across the table and ruffled Liz's short, dark, curly hair.

'You're the most appealing girl I know,' she said.

Liz looked at her and grinned. 'Do you know anybody else?'

'Up your bum,' said Hildamay.

'No, sweetie,' said Liz. 'That's what boys do. We're girls, remember?'

'So we are,' said Hildamay. 'So we are.'

CHAPTER FOUR

LUIGI was standing by the door of the restaurant when she walked in. 'Hildamay!' he exclaimed, his black eyes twinkling with pleasure and his big, handsome face collapsing into a smile. 'My waters, they are good today,' he added, patting his round stomach over which a long apron of starched white linen stretched and crackled. 'I knew you were coming. I made *tortelloni con salva* especially.'

'It's Wednesday, idiot,' murmured Hildamay affectionately as she kissed his smooth, scented cheek.

'An exceptional day!' he exclaimed, beaming, and then steered Hildamay over to the table where Liz sat waiting. Having deposited Hildamay in her chair and patted Liz's curly hair, he put big white napkins on both their laps, tucking them around them as if they were children.

'I'm hungry today,' declared Hildamay, because she knew it pleased him.

'*Bella!*' he exclaimed, beaming again and, rubbing his hands, hurried off to attend to his *tortelloni*. Hildamay watched him weave his way through the tightly packed tables; she never stopped being surprised that a man who carried so much bulk could be so light on his feet. Liz looked at her expectantly, her face shining with excitement.

'Well?' she said.

'Well?' said Hildamay.

'Oh, Hildamay, be pleased. It's what I want.'

'Why?'

'Why do you want to have a child?' said Hildamay patiently.

'Because I'm thirty-four years old.'

'So?'

'So, Down's syndrome,' said Liz, and ordered mineral water.

Hildamay looked at her aghast. 'Mineral water?'

'For the baby.'

'You don't have a baby,' said Hildamay dubiously. 'Do you?'

'No, of course not. Not yet,' said Liz, smiling. 'But the three months before you conceive are as important as the nine months you're carrying. I'm preparing myself. Beginning the ritual of purification.' She smiled beatifically across the table.

Good grief, thought Hildamay and opened a packet of cigarettes.

'I don't suppose you want one, do you?' she asked, waving the packet vaguely in Liz's direction.

'No. Thank you,' said Liz, and looked at her again in that shining way that made Hildamay's stomach turn over.

'Are you perfectly sure that this is a good idea?' she asked.

'Perfectly,' said Liz.

'It might be a better idea to have a husband as well as a child.'

'Hildamay Smith, what on earth are you talking about? I thought you didn't believe in men?'

'Don't be absurd,' said Hildamay. 'What does that mean? How can you not believe in something that exists? I like them well enough but I'd rather not live with one. The compromises are too great. But I don't have a child, and nor do I intend to have one.'

'But I don't want a man, I want a child,' said Liz tersely.

'And what about the child?' said Hildamay. 'It'll grow up disturbed, off balance. It'll only have one example, one sex from which to draw its conclusions. God knows, men are different from women. How will it ever understand the male? We live in a patriarchal society. That's difficult enough to cope with as it is. You're going to give the child an added disadvantage. And what if it's a boy?'

'I don't want a boy,' said Liz crossly.

'Well there's a strong chance you might have one,' said Hildamay.

There was silence broken only by Luigi bustling over with steaming plates of food. When they failed to exclaim over their *tortelloni*, his black eyebrows beetled with paternal concern but he performed the ritual of grating Parmesan in sympathetic silence.

'You're not disturbed,' said Liz finally. 'And you had no father to speak of. No role model to illuminate this patriarchal society.'

'Yes, I am,' said Hildamay. 'I'm very disturbed.'

Liz just looked at her.

'Well, I'm not exactly what you would call normal, am I?'

'No,' said Liz. 'And nor are most so-called normal marriages. Most of the world doesn't exist in happy little nuclear units with Mummy and Daddy forming a perfect balance for the kids in the middle. Most kids grow up in the rough and tumble of what we choose to call relationships. How many happy relationships do you know?'

'Delilah and Ned? They seem contented enough together.'

'I guess passive is another word for contented, or a fair enough substitute in a relationship. If you like that sort of thing,' said Liz. 'Ned just wants an easy life so he sits back and lets Delilah do all the pushing and shoving. She's incredibly frustrated at times but she's made up her mind that's the best there is; especially after all the trauma she went through for years with Dan. I think Ned's about as stimulating as a dead light bulb, but then I wouldn't choose to live with him. If he's supposed to be the blueprint for the masculine role I wonder what his children will grow up believing men actually do?'

'They'll simply believe that women run the world; which is as it always has been. At least they won't believe that to be a man you have to drive big cars, earn pots of money, drink beer and shove your cock into every orifice that moves. Ned's OK. I'd rather have him than Ben, any day.'

'Well you could have Ben any day. Couldn't we all? I don't know why Kate puts up with him.'

'Because she believes, deep in her heart, that men should be like that.'

'No pride,' said Liz gloomily.

'Well, none of what we call pride. For Kate pride doesn't matter. Having a man does. I sometimes wonder what he does to her self-esteem but I really don't think she looks at it that way. Her self-esteem exists in having a man, not on what he does when she's got him.'

'Well,' said Liz. 'You've just painted a glorious picture of why I don't want a man around.'

'I'm not suggesting you get either Ned or Ben to father it,' said Hildamay. 'I just think kids need mothers and fathers.'

'I hadn't realised you were so old-fashioned,' said Liz.

'Don't be unkind,' said Hildamay. 'I'm not old-fashioned. Women are far too emotional. They apply sentiment where logic would be appropriate. You're being sentimental and, I think, selfish.'

'I am not being selfish!' shouted Liz.

'OK, OK, I'm sorry. But tell me why you want a child.'

'Because I do.'

'There's cool logic for you.'

'You wouldn't understand.'

'Why not?' said Hildamay coldly.

'You just wouldn't,' said Liz. 'I don't know why I told you in the first place.'

'Because I'm your closest friend. What you actually mean is you don't know why you told me in the second place. The arguments about whether or not it's fair to have a child alone are secondary to the decision to have one. You want a child and no matter what the arguments are, you're going to have it anyway. Because that's what you want and bugger the consequences, or the child. And because I actively want to live alone, and I don't want either a man or a child, that means I'm incapable of understanding how you feel?'

'Yes,' said Liz sharply.

'Oh, don't be absurd, Liz,' said Hildamay equally sharply. 'I've made my choices and you've made yours. I thought you wanted to discuss this. You obviously don't. You want me to agree with you.'

'Is that so difficult?' said Liz. She was shaking and her eyes were suspiciously bright. Luigi arrived with plates of grilled fish and chips, which he placed in front of them in a show of exaggerated silence. Liz bent her head, her eyes fixed on the napkin which she kept twisting around her fingers.

Hildamay watched her for a while. 'Not if you could tell me why,' she said eventually, her voice gentle.

'I don't know why. It's as if I have to. Have to give birth, I mean. I know what my child looks like. I can see it walking beside me, feel it holding my hand. I can hear it speak. It's real. I feel so alone because it's not with me. I feel a physical pain whenever I pick up a baby. I just want to devote my life utterly and completely to some other human being. I suppose you could call that selfish, but I don't see it that way.'

Her voice was strained and low and she kept her head bent as if she were speaking to the table. Hildamay sighed and stared at the top of her curly hair, watching how it sprang in a vigorous but perfect circle from the crown of her head. Eventually she reached across the table and took her hand.

'Liz, are you sure a child is the answer you're looking for? It might not make you happy. What then? It just seems so hard, having children. I know they're supposed to bring you love and joy and all that shit, but they also take a great deal and it can be very isolating. I think you feel lonely enough already. From the minute they're born it seems you spend the next eighteen years teaching them to leave you. It's hard enough with a husband around to give you emotional support, but without one? All I'm saying is, are you absolutely sure you know what you're taking on?'

Liz snatched her hand away and looked up. 'I'm not lonely,' she said furiously. 'And I'm not using the child as a substitute teddy bear. If you don't want to know, that's fine by me.' She stabbed at the french fries on her plate, scooping them up with great gobs of ketchup. Hildamay watched her defiantly stuffing food into her mouth.

'Oh, Lizzie, don't be like that. I want to know, I'll be around. I just have to know that what you want is a child and not something else.'

Liz put down her fork and wiped the ketchup from her mouth. 'A child,' she said, her voice low. 'All I want is a child. I can't imagine you've ever been broody in your life, have you?'

'No,' said Hildamay. 'The thought's never even crossed my mind, to be honest. Children are something that happen to other people. Maybe I'm just jealous.'

She smiled her most appealing smile. Liz smiled back uncertainly.

'Jealous? But you don't want children.'

'Jealous of the child, you idiot. It'll make everything different. At the moment there's just you and me. You're my closest friend and we're the same, or at least, we're fairly alike. Suddenly you'll move into another world. A special club for which the only membership is a child. I don't even want to join but sometimes I talk to Kate and Delilah and feel like a Martian. They can be so horribly complacent, although I know they really don't mean to be. Kate's the worst. She sits there being a mother, all cosy and warm and exclusive in her little nest. She smiles at me pityingly sometimes as if to say, "Look at me. Look at what I've done. I'm a *real* woman." And society rushes around her, patting her on the back. It changes everything, children. I like things just the way they are.' She looked down at her hands and then back up at Liz and grinned. Her real, normal, natural grin; not one of her Hildamay smiles. 'Now who's being selfish?'

Liz grinned back. 'I won't change,' she said. 'You just get junior, too. So, will you help me, Hildamay?'

'Yes. On one condition.'

'What?' said Liz, looking at her dubiously.

'That you don't devote your whole life to that child. It will not thank you and you will not thank it.'

'OK,' said Liz.

'OK,' said Hildamay and, leaning across the table, kissed her. 'Now let's order some really fat pudding and talk about men.'

'After,' said Liz, 'you've opened this incredibly rich gift I bought you.'

'A straight nose,' said Liz rubbing hers. 'And a great body.'

'Thin,' said Hildamay and ate a piece of strawberry tart.

'No, you idiot,' said Liz. 'I'm thin enough for two.'

'I hate you,' said Hildamay automatically. 'Clever, then.'

'Piss off.'

Hildamay narrowed her eyes. Liz laughed.

'Oh, OK, clever then. And an even temperament. That's more important.'

Hildamay looked bored.

'I said even, not placid. And good legs. He must have good legs.'

'And a good cock,' added Hildamay.

'Don't be vulgar.'

'Suit yourself,' said Hildamay, 'but you're the one who's got to fuck him.'

'That's where the problems start.'

'Since when has fucking been a problem?'

'Since when I don't want him to use a condom.'

'Oh, that,' said Hildamay.

'Yes, that,' said Liz. 'What do I do? Show him an HIV certificate and say, darling, your worries are over. I'm a disease-free woman. Let's do it with our clothes off tonight?'

'Well tell him.'

'Tell him what?'

'Tell him you don't want him to use a condom.'

'He'll just think I'm a raving lunatic. An HIV positive raving lunatic.'

Liz looked at Hildamay who was busy licking strawberry jam and cream off her fingers.

'I don't believe your heart's really in this.'

'It is, it is, my little sweet. I'm not going to be wicked godmother to just any old baby. So you're not going to tell Daddy who he is?'

'No.'

'Why not?'

'What if he suddenly turns all paternal on me and decides he wants visiting rights? Men do, you know. They see the fruit of their loins turn into a real little peach and suddenly it's "Hey, that's mine!" Men are far more emotional than women give them credit for and just as primitive when it comes to kids. When they suddenly see their one-night stand get up and stagger shakily around they think, "Hang on. That's a part of me over there. Is she feeding it right? What school's she going to send it to? Does she let it watch video nasties?" They can't help it. Those great big egos of theirs just get up and roar.'

'Well it seems a bit unfair,' said Hildamay. 'You just saunter up to some poor guy, act all lovey-dovey then run off with what's rightfully his and lie to him when he says, "That's mine. I want half of it."'

'It's only a sperm, Hildamay. One tiny little cell of his body. He won't even know. Not if I don't tell him.'

'I suppose not,' said Hildamay dubiously, but it made her feel very uneasy. Was it stealing? She wasn't sure. But she was sure she'd think it stealing if some man removed a cell of hers and took it off somewhere to grow into a small version of herself. She'd want it back. But men seemed indifferent enough to the consequences of sex. They seemed indifferent enough, much of the time, to children. Her own father had proved that both to her and to her mother. Hildamay remembered thinking, even as a child, that she never wanted to feel the pain her mother tried so hard to hide. And she never wanted to feel as alone again as she had felt the year after her father left. Then there was Marcus, a friend of hers who had never had a father. 'I am illegitimate,' he would say. She wondered what kids said these days. 'I am a single parent child'?

Marcus said he had never recovered from the shock of his mother marrying when he was eleven. The anger at what he saw as her betrayal had, he claimed, nearly destroyed him. He was still in therapy although that seemed to have little effect. 'Look at me,' he said; rather too proudly, she thought. 'I'm a textbook case. I'm gay because I don't trust women. I can't sustain relationships because I test people to see if they will abandon me. And of course they do. Nobody can handle that amount of need. They wouldn't be human if they could. I don't want them to be human. I want them to be superhuman; the way my mother was when I was a kid.'

She sighed. Why did anybody want children? The mess was horrendous, however you looked at it. All those ghastly stretch marks and loose, emptied breasts. She wondered if placenta cream would help. She'd seen a new brand. 'Miracle Mark: guaranteed to prevent obvious signs of stretching', on her last visit to Harrods' beauty hall. She had debated whether to buy some for herself – you never knew when it might come in handy, thighs being what they were – and now determined to buy some for Liz. Then she caught Liz's eye.

'Are you ever going to speak again?'

'Sorry,' said Hildamay. 'I was just thinking.'

'What did you decide?'

Hildamay looked at her. Liz was going to have this child, whatever she said. So she grinned.

'I guess there are enough big bastards running around who've made little bastards and can't be bothered either with them or the women left holding them. Every time a man masturbates, there's the potential for the population of London in his hand. And what does he do with it? Wraps it in a handkerchief and leaves it there to die. Flushes it down the loo. What's one little sperm mean to them? Anyway, it's about time women took control.'

'Right,' said Liz, her face flushed with excitement. Her voice dropped to a whisper and she leaned across the table. 'So who's the man? And what are we going to do about the condom problem?'

'Buy a packet and make pin holes in all of them?' ventured Hildamay cautiously.

'It might not work. We've got to be sure first time. I could be fucking like a rabbit for months and nothing happens. Anyway, I've completely forgotten all my hard-learned seduction techniques. I'm not sure I could pull it off more than once.'

'All we want is one little sperm,' said Hildamay. 'We don't need the whole thing.'

Liz burst out laughing. Her laugh was very loud; the sound halfway between a hiccup and a sob. She couldn't stop. She was crying with laughter.

'Jesus,' thought Hildamay, 'what is it with babies? One lousy joke and I get an Oscar.'

Luigi came hurrying over to their table.

'Hildamay, Hildamay, what is the matter. Is Lizzie all right?'

Hildamay treated him to her most dazzling smile. 'She's fine, Luigi. Fine. It's just labour pains.'

'Some hot water, then,' he said and called to one of his waiters. 'Some coffee. At once. For the ladies.'

'Some ladies,' said Hildamay.

CHAPTER FIVE

'TO the ladies who drink!' Hildamay pushed open the door of The Globe and walked in to find Cassie standing in the middle of the room, a champagne glass in each hand. Her full body was contained in purple, or violet as Cassie preferred to call it.

'Violet is my colour, darling. Violent violet! Vivid violet! Vesuvius violet! I only wear purple when I'm passionate. When I'm prone, darling. When I have something gorgeous and big and purple beside me in my bed. A member of the opposite sex, you might say.'

Cassie was often drunk. Too often drunk, thought Hildamay, as she was enveloped in an overpowering embrace. Cassie kissed her full on the mouth.

'Darling!' she said, holding Hildamay's face in both hands and kissing her again on the mouth. 'Darling, darling Hildamay. Happy birthday. How pretty you look. So pink and pert and pretty. So pretty!' she sang. 'Oh so pretty, oh so pretty and witty and gay!'

She started to waltz on the spot, hugging Hildamay to her. After a few moments Hildamay pushed Cassie gently away.

'I need a glass of champagne,' she said.

'Oh, darling!' said Cassie. 'Of course you do. Silly old *moi*. Jack? Jack! Where's that bottle? We've finished it? Well, let's have another. It's Hildamay's birthday. You know Jack, don't you, Hildamay? Jack's the best barman in London. The nicest and the kindest and he makes wicked martinis. Are you married, Jack?' she added archly, leaning against the bar and fluffing up her long curly hair. It was dark brown but rinsed with a very deep violet. 'You think my hair's gorgeous, don't you, Jack? This colour's called "Wicked Lady". Isn't it to die for?' She giggled. 'It makes me feel so naughty. You're not married? How perfectly divine.' She picked up his hand and, putting it against her breast, stroked it as if it were a kitten. 'I don't suppose you're straight, then, are you?'

'Yes,' he said, taking his hand away.

'Well, hallelujah!' shrieked Cassie and lifted her glass. 'A toast, a toast everyone,' she called. 'To the last handsome, single, straight man in London. Let's drink to his health. God knows he must need it.' She downed the contents of her glass in one and danced off to talk to somebody sitting at one of the small tables in the far corner of the room.

'Hi, Jack,' said Hildamay, although she knew he was called Thomas. He grinned good-naturedly and shrugged. Cassie often changed people's names if she thought they didn't suit them. He was handsome in a tame, domesticated sort of way. His hair, which was bright blond and dead straight, fell in a shiny spray over his eyes causing him to toss his head a great deal like a flirting girl. Hildamay wondered if it was an affectation but, after considering him for a few minutes, decided that it was not. He simply needed a haircut. She wondered how many women had tried to give him one. His eyes, which were brown, crinkled at the corners, possibly because he was constantly blinded by his hair. She examined his nose, for noses were of particular interest to Hildamay. She considered it rather fine, being perfectly straight and neither too large nor too small. His lips were slightly too thin but otherwise it was a nice, if unremarkable, face.

She produced her most dazzling smile. Thomas looked amazed. She noticed the look. Men rarely thought that Hildamay was pretty until she smiled and then they began to think she was beautiful. He was not really her type. She liked her men dark and well worn; glamorous in a crumpled sort of a way. Thomas was too boyish for her taste, but she decided to flirt with him anyway. Hildamay liked to flirt. She flirted with men, women, children; with inanimate objects if she felt in need of some practice.

Cassie appeared suddenly at her shoulder.

'Darling!' she said. 'I know Jack is just dying to get to know you but he's so busy. Aren't you, Jack?'

She picked up Hildamay's champagne glass.

'I've organised a lovely table for us, right over there in the corner. Come. Come. Your present's over there. You're going to love it.'

She pulled at Hildamay's arm. Thomas picked up the bottle and began to move from behind the bar as if to follow them to the table.

'Don't worry, Jack, darling,' called Cassie over her shoulder. 'I'll come back and get it. And we need three more glasses.'

Hildamay winked at him as she turned to follow Cassie. As she left the bar she pulled in her stomach, straightened her back, thrust out her breasts and then stalked to the table. Sitting down she crossed her legs and pulled her skirt up high over her thighs. She looked over to the bar. Thomas was watching her. Hildamay turned and smiled at Cassie.

'Such a shame about linen, isn't it, darling,' said Cassie. 'It does crease so. Terribly unsexy.'

Hildamay looked down at her linen skirt and burst out laughing. Cassie grinned at her. 'You mustn't tease poor Jack,' she said. 'He's only young. Well, he's only about twenty-five. He doesn't understand about older women. He'll think you're being serious and he'll get his knickers in a twist, poor lamb. What that boy needs is a good woman. He's so confused. He tells me everything, of course.'

'What's he confused about?' asked Hildamay.

'Well, he trained to be a solicitor while all the time he wanted to act but his father was dead against it. So he worked as a solicitor until he decided he couldn't stand it a moment longer. Now he's at drama school and works here at night to earn money. He says he's got no time for a relationship; he's got to get his career sorted out first.'

'He doesn't sound too confused to me,' said Hildamay.

'Oh, yes, darling, because he's lonely. He adores women but he can't get involved with anybody because he says he couldn't give them the time they deserve. Have you ever heard anything more *divine*?' she sighed. 'That's why I tease him about being married. He fucks though, darling. There's nothing wrong with him. He's a regular boy. He's even had an HIV test. Says one must be responsible. Isn't that adorable, darling? I said I'd be rather more worried about somebody giving it to me but he says we can be carriers just as easily as we can be receivers. It was negative, of course. I mean you can tell just by looking at him. He looks so, well, *clean*. They're frightfully grown-up, darling, those young ones. Much more grown-up than we ever were. It's absolutely fascinating. We often sit and chat in the evenings.' She paused. 'Not that there's anything between us, of course. I just listen to his problems. He thinks I'm one of the boys. Most men do,' she added bitterly.

'You don't look much like a boy to me,' said Hildamay reassuringly. Cassie was voluptuous. Some people unkindly called her fat. She ate too much, just as she did everything else too much. Cassie smoked, drank, ate and lived to excess. And was always vowing to give everything up.

'I'm giving up drinking tomorrow,' she said.

'What?' said Hildamay. 'Again?'

'Don't be horrid, darling. I know I said I was giving up last week but then we had that ghastly presentation and I was just under too much stress to cope with a little drink in the evening. This time I'm going on a cleansing regime. I read about it in a magazine. You drink water and just eat brown rice and vegetables for ten days. And no smoking, of course. Just imagine the sheer bliss of it. A spring in the step, a sparkle in the eye, a shine to the skin. Within minutes, you feel eighteen again.' She looked hopeful.

'God forbid,' said Hildamay. 'I can't imagine anything worse than being eighteen again. I spent my youth longing to be old so I could do just as I liked and people would stop assuming they had the right to tell me what to do.'

'Oh, darling, I couldn't imagine anything better than being eighteen again and having breasts that point to the heavens and a mind that points to the stars. That's the awful thing about age. Everything stops defying gravity. Breasts, mind, stomach; they all start heading for the ground leaving your dreams up there somewhere.'

'What do stomachs have to do with dreams?' asked Hildamay.

Cassie looked down at hers. It was very pronounced. 'Masses, darling,' she said ruefully and then giggled.

'I'm so *sorry*!' Hildamay and Cassie looked up from Cassie's stomach. Kate was standing over them looking, as she nearly always did, hot and flustered. She had that pale English skin which turns pink at the slightest provocation. It must be why Max Factor call it Hectic Pink, thought Hildamay as she stood up to kiss her.

'What are you sorry about?' she asked, curious.

'Oh, for being late. Ben says it's my most irritating habit. He says I've got lots, but being late is the worst. I suppose he's right, I do always seem to be late. He says women have something wrong with their brains. Some chemical imbalance which makes them incapable of keeping to a logical time scale. He'd be so irritated if he were here.'

'He's not, is he?' asked Hildamay, looking around with mild alarm.

'No, no, of course not. It's just if he was, he'd be irritated. He hates to be kept waiting and I do know what he means. It is so annoying, especially when one is terribly busy. And Ben's always so busy. He works so hard, poor darling.'

'It must be dreadful for him,' said Hildamay drily. 'All those evening meetings and weekend conferences. He was just telling me the other day how he regrets not being able to spend more time with the children. And with you, of course,' she added, smiling at Kate.

'Oh, Hildamay, did he? He's such a darling. I know it worries him. He's always telling me how much he misses them. Us. But school fees and houses do have to be paid for. Although quite why we need two such big houses, I don't really understand. And Harrow! I'm not sure that Harry and Simon are really all that keen to go. Ben says I'm talking nonsense. He says that with the extra tuition they'll be perfectly ready and that they can't wait to get away from me. From home, I mean. They do seem so awfully little to be away from home, but Ben says it's what boys need. He adored it, of course. And I do get to have little Katie at home with me. He says girls don't. . . .'

'He's such a fabulous husband, darling,' said Cassie quickly, glaring at Hildamay who was paying no attention but was wondering what size Thomas's penis was. It wasn't true what they said about performance. A small penis is a small penis.

'Fabulous,' she said, and poured Kate a very large glass of champagne to make up for the size of Ben's cock, which she suspected was very small. In her experience, the greater the interest a man took in his cock, the smaller it was. Ben's must be tiny.

'And how is your fabulous husband?' she asked, smiling sweetly at Kate.

'Oh, he's well. Very well. He says I'm looking tired. Do you think I'm looking tired?' she asked, frowning slightly.

'No, darling!' said Cassie. 'You look adorable. Blooming and rounded and happy. It must be so lovely to have a man like Ben to look after you, and those three wonderful children. That must be what gives you that pink glow. It's the flush of contentment. All that love,' she added wistfully.

'Yes,' said Kate, looking pleased with herself.

'You do look a bit tired,' said Hildamay, who thought that Kate looked ill. She was enormously overweight and her face was swollen with exhaustion, her eyes red-rimmed and constantly weeping. They seemed to have sunk into the flesh of her face which was reddened here and there with scaly patches of skin. 'Hardly surprising,' she added more gently, 'with three children and no help. And now that second house as well.' She wondered if Kate would take it badly if she gave her a pot of eye cream. She'd just found a new one: 'Removes fine lines. Permanently'. It was so pretty, a translucent pink gel flecked with strands of gold. She decided that she would probably take it very badly so said instead, 'Is the house in the country nearly finished?'

'Yes,' said Kate, her smile brave. 'It's so lovely, really. You must come down for the weekend, Hildamay. Both of you, I mean,' she said, hurriedly including Cassie, although Hildamay knew that the last thing Kate wanted was Cassie staying for the weekend. Even an evening with Cassie was a liability if Ben was around. She didn't so much flirt with him as climb all over him. Ben loved it. Hildamay had found them in the kitchen, Ben's tongue down Cassie's throat. Cassie had telephoned her the next day.

'It wasn't my fault, darling, really it wasn't. He grabbed me in the kitchen and started kissing me. I was as surprised as you were.'

'Cassie, you were drunk,' said Hildamay coldly.

'Well, maybe I was a tiny bit, darling, but I didn't encourage him. Really I didn't.'

'Really, Cassandra! Better men than Ben might have been fooled. You had your hands all over him and that was at the table. Before we even started to eat.'

'Oh, please don't call me Cassandra, darling. You know it's unlucky. I didn't think he'd take me seriously,' said Cassie miserably.

'Cassie, it's not you he takes seriously. It's himself. And it's Kate you should be calling, not me.'

'Oh, darling! You don't think she suspects anything, do you?'

'Is there anything to suspect?' asked Hildamay.

'Oh no, darling! Of course not!' Cassie sounded shocked.

'Kate might be slow, Cassie, but she's not stupid and she's not blind. You were climbing all over her husband. And whatever I might think of Ben, she adores him. I'm amazed she sat there and said nothing last night.'

'Because she's got him, hasn't she?' said Cassie bitterly. 'She's got a husband so she can afford to be sweet and quiet. She doesn't know what it's like out there.'

'Out where?' asked Hildamay, confused.

'Out on your own,' said Cassie. 'If I had a gorgeous husband I wouldn't behave like me either.'

'Well, if you keep on behaving like that you won't get a husband. Or have any friends, either.'

'Oh, darling, I wasn't that bad! It was just a little fun. Anyway, I've kissed Ben before. It's nothing serious.'

'You've done what?'

'Oh, darling, do stop being such a prude. It doesn't suit you. I've kissed Ben before. So tell it to the *Sun*.'

'Kissing other people's husbands isn't something I'd wish to advertise,' said Hildamay with asperity.

There was silence followed by a sigh. 'No, darling, I suppose you're right. I'll call Kate and apologise for being a drunken harlot. She'll be fine, honestly. She thinks Ben is the most faithful of men.'

Hildamay looked at Kate and wondered if that was true. Could she really believe that Ben was faithful to her?

'I said, shall we make a date now? Hildamay, are you listening? Ben made me promise I'd make a date with you for a weekend. He says he's dying to see you, doesn't see enough of you. He's so fond of you.'

Hildamay knew that Ben was not fond of her. She also knew he wanted her approval. Hildamay hated the country. The idea of spending a whole weekend in it with Ben and three screaming children for company did not appeal. But she missed seeing Kate.

'When the weather's warmer?' she suggested.

'That would be lovely! I'm going to take the children down on Monday and spend two weeks there finishing the painting. It's Ben's idea. He says I need a good rest and the fresh air will do me good.'

'It doesn't sound much like a rest cure to me,' said Hildamay, looking at her dubiously.

'What doesn't?' asked Liz. Her eyes were still shining.

'Lizzie, darling!' said Cassie and threw her arms around her. 'What on earth have you done to yourself? You look fabulous. Is it love, darling? Have you found a divine man? Is that sperm glowing in your cheeks? Best beauty treatment ever, a good fuck.'

'No, Cassie,' said Liz, sitting down. 'It's not a man. It's just that I've finally made up my mind about something.'

'Your mind?' asked Cassie, handing her a glass of champagne.

'No thanks,' said Liz. 'I'll have a mineral water.'

'Mineral water, darling? Have you found religion? Is that what you mean? Oh dear, and there I was talking about fucking. Sorry, darling. Religion and fucking aren't quite the same thing really, are they?'

'They are to some,' said Hildamay and Delilah walked in.

'Talking dirty again?' she said, smiling, and took a glass of champagne. 'Oh, don't stop, please. I love girls' talk.' She pushed back her black, shiny hair and narrowed her dark grey eyes. Thomas appeared at the table with another bottle. She flashed him her most brilliant smile but he was watching Liz, who was fending off Cassie's questions.

'Oh, darling, do stop being so horrid and tell me what it is you've discovered. Your eyes are so bright and your cheeks so pink, it must be something wonderful. It can't be God. People always look smug when they find God. It must be something much more exciting. Do tell, do tell. I know you're dying to.' She stroked Liz's arm cajolingly.

Cassie touched people constantly. She always kissed Hildamay on the mouth, which Hildamay did not mind for she thought that a kiss was a kiss, whichever sex it came from.

Cassie had once insinuated her tongue into Hildamay's mouth and put her hand to her breast. Hildamay had removed the hand and turned her head away from the kiss, and Cassie had smiled fuzzily at her. 'Sorry, darling, but you do have the most beautiful breasts. I just couldn't resist them. Tits feel awfully nice, darling. Delicious, really. Do you want to try?' she had added, cupping her own breasts in her hands.

'No,' said Hildamay. 'Thank you.'

Cassie giggled drunkenly. They were lying on the sofa in Cassie's flat, drinking champagne and gossiping. Cassie had her head on Hildamay's shoulder.

'Don't you like girls, darling?' Cassie asked.

'Yes,' said Hildamay, who was also fairly drunk. 'But not right now.'

Cassie scrambled up to a sitting position. Her eyes were wide with excitement. 'Sexually, darling?' she squeaked. 'Do you mean you've done it with girls?'

'Yes,' said Hildamay, her voice cool. Why hadn't she kept her mouth shut? Fool. She knew what was coming next. In her experience, most women wanted to make love to another woman at least once in their lives, and every woman was intrigued by the idea. Once they found out that you had, their reserves broke down. Women had this odd idea that they wouldn't know how to make love to another woman. Quite what the difference was, Hildamay had never discovered. Sex was sex. But women always seemed to want to be initiated. It must, she reflected, be all those years of conditioning, being taught to be passive, being taught that it was their partners who took the initiative. It must be such a bore, being a man. Then the other question that women always asked was, who led? As if they were learning to waltz in the school gym. She laughed.

'What are you laughing at, darling?' said Cassie.

'Oh, nothing,' said Hildamay, and turned to smile at her. Cassie's pupils were dilated and her lips were very pink and very wet. Hildamay's heart sank. The girl was on heat.

'Will you do it with me, darling? Oh, please, please. I've always wanted to.'

'Have you never done it?' asked Hildamay, playing for time. She was also faintly surprised, for she had always assumed that Cassie, who was physically so demonstrative with both sexes, would have few inhibitions and must have experimented with her own.

'Not since I was about fourteen, darling, but that doesn't really count. Will you?' she pleaded.

'No,' said Hildamay. That way madness lay. With Cassie one kiss would be a lifelong commitment. And the end of a friendship. 'Absolutely not,' she said vehemently.

Cassie looked stung. 'Don't you think I'm attractive, darling,' she said quietly.

'Yes,' said Hildamay honestly. 'Yes, I do.'

Cassie swung round and, grabbing Hildamay's breasts, forced her tongue into her mouth.

Oh shit, thought Hildamay, springing violently to her feet so that Cassie tumbled on to the floor. She looked down at Cassie sprawled on the carpet. 'Sorry.'

'Then why won't you?' wailed Cassie tearfully. Hildamay sat down and took her hand.

'Cassie, I don't go to bed with every man in the world and I don't go to bed with every woman. I love you very much and this would just interfere with our friendship. You're a little drunk and in the morning you might feel ashamed.'

'How could I?' Cassie whispered. 'How could I ever feel ashamed of you?'

'Oh, you could,' said Hildamay and kissed her on the cheek. 'You most certainly could,' she added as she walked out of the door.

She watched Cassie stroking Liz's cheek. Delilah was also watching her.

'Strange as it may seem, Cassie, not everyone likes to broadcast their personal life to the world,' she said coolly as she watched the beginnings of irritation show in Liz's face.

Cassie looked at Delilah and grinned lopsidedly.

'But most people love to hear it, darling. You should know that. You make a living out of it.'

'How's Ned?' asked Hildamay, interrupting before Cassie became aggressive. Her mascara was already smudged in circles around her eyes. Drink blurred Cassie and she was not a happy drunk. She became loud and sometimes vicious. Hildamay wondered how unhappy she really was. It was hard to tell. Cassie believed that you weren't doing your bit for humanity unless you were perpetually cheerful. She understood her role in life as entertainer. Hildamay suspected she was terribly unhappy. She sighed. After a first date Cassie was talking about marriage. Most men thought of her as a good-time girl. Good for a laugh. Good for a drink. Good for a fuck. But good forever? And every time another came and then went, she smiled bravely and drank another drink.

'Fuck 'em,' she would say with a great big smile. 'They just don't know what they're missing.'

Hildamay knew what Cassie thought she was missing. Love. She was more desperate for love and more incapable of finding it than anyone Hildamay had ever known.

'Be cool this time, Cassie,' she would urge. 'Don't rush at him like that. Give him time.'

'Yes, darling, I will. I promise. It'll be different this time, you'll see.'

But it never was.

Delilah was speaking. 'Oh, Ned,' she said with a sigh of exasperation. 'He's . . . he's, Ned. He's working hard on the book, he's painting like a demon and is very committed to his students. Actually he's terribly pleased because all his pressure groups, the environmental issues he's been banging on about for so long, are suddenly fashionable and he's in great demand as a speaker. I hardly see him at the moment. It's fine,' she added quickly, 'but the kids miss him. They've got so used to having him around.' She shrugged. 'I do sometimes wish he'd pay less attention to the universe and more to his own little world. But it makes him happy so –' Her voice tailed off.

Hildamay raised her glass. 'Here's to the grass widow,' she said, smiling.

Delilah grinned at her. 'Oh, it's not that bad, although I sometimes wonder whether environmentalists ever remember there are people on this planet. All they seem to talk about is whales and waste. Ned's got this obsession with disposable nappies. Hates them. He went out and bought a huge pile of terry towelling. I refused to even look at them. Sarah, the nanny, burst into tears and went and packed her suitcase and he just stood there shouting about the goddamn planet. I told him I was more concerned with keeping our household together and that he could soak and boil them himself every night if he felt like that. He did. Once.'

'Are terry-towelling nappies better?' asked Liz eagerly.

Delilah looked at her and raised an eyebrow. 'For whom?' she replied acidly.

'For the baby,' said Liz.

Cassie gave a whoop of joy. 'You're pregnant!' she shrieked and threw her arms round Liz's neck. The women crowded around Liz, kissing her. 'No, I'm not,' she said, but her eyes shone.

'Who's the father?' asked Kate.

'That's what we'd all like to know,' said Hildamay and hummed the masturbation song.

CHAPTER SIX

HILDAMAY sat on a plastic bench on the tube platform at Oxford Circus and wondered what idiot had designed the seats. 'Someone who never travels on the underground,' she said aloud as she shifted uncomfortably on the pre-formed vacuum-moulded seat. 'Nobody's got a bottom this shape,' she exclaimed, again aloud, but fell silent as she noticed a child turn to stare and then smile. She stared back, her face set in a mocking challenge, but the child turned away, tugging a baseball cap low over its eyes. 'Spoilsport,' muttered Hildamay and then sighed, wondering what to do with the evening. There was nothing on television and nobody she wanted to see.

It was six-thirty. She sat for a time admiring her new bottle green suede shoes. They had very high heels. 'Proper fuck me heels,' she said, this time quietly, and sighed again. What she really wanted to do was get laid. She began mentally to tick off the men she could telephone. She could think of nobody. Until last month she had had two lovers. But they had both, quite suddenly, started to talk about love. Philip, with whom she had enjoyed six months of glorious weekly sex, had taken her out to dinner and embarked on an earnest monologue about the nature of commitment. His grey eyes were earnest, beseeching. He had finally left his girlfriend. It had never, really, been right. They had met too young. She had become too clinging. What he was looking for now was a mature relationship. Hildamay had opened his eyes to the real, the very real, possibility of that. She watched his mouth forming the words – he had a wonderfully shaped mouth – with a growing sense of loss. After dinner he pressed his marvellous lips to hers and murmured into her eager mouth that he felt that now, at last, he understood the nature of love. It was a mature, a seriously adult emotion. Sex had been very good that night. It was the last time she ever saw him.

Then there was Bob. Bob with the hooded, dark brown eyes and a dick made in heaven. Bob who thought sex was as natural as breathing and wanted to do it just as often. And was young enough to do exactly as he wanted. Too young, thought Hildamay, to talk of love. Except. Except that the last time she had seen him those hooded eyes had drooped in mournful petulance. 'You're so cool,' he said and the corners of his mouth tugged down.

'Cool,' she said carefully, kissing the corners of that spoiled mouth, 'is what you like.'

'You only like me for my dick,' he complained, pulling out of her.

'Is there any other reason for liking you?' she teased, ruffling his hair.

'Yes.' He turned away from her. 'You think I'm too young, don't you?' he asked, his voice muffled by the pillow.

Hildamay watched his hurt, reproachful back. 'Past puberty,' she said lightly, 'there's no such thing as too young.'

'Women!' He leaped out of bed and pulled on his jeans. 'All you think about is sex. You're all the same.' His lips quivered, pale and rejected. She watched sadly as he covered his heavenly cock, zipping it carefully away in his faded, tattered Levi's.

'When you want this,' he said, stabbing at his heart with his forefinger, 'instead of this,' he added, cupping his cock with a careful, protective hand, 'call me.'

She did not call.

Hildamay was so deep in thought that she did not notice a small pair of feet stop directly in front of hers. A slight movement caught her eye as the feet shuffled impatiently. Still she did not look up until a hand shook her gently by the shoulder.

'I said excuse me!' said a high, pained voice. Hildamay looked up. The child with the baseball cap stood gazing at her with curious eyes.

'Were you asleep?' she demanded.

'Thinking,' said Hildamay, examining the child. It had a small, heart-shaped face; very pale and out of which stared eyes of a blue so dark it was almost navy. The black leather baseball cap it wore was too big, forcing it to keep its chin up to see from under it. It was a small, determined chin in which Hildamay could see a faint cleft, the shadow of a dimple.

'Are you a boy or a girl?' asked Hildamay.

The child twisted around so that Hildamay could see the pony tail which hung down the back of her padded, khaki nylon jacket. 'Boys don't have pony tails,' she said contemptuously.

'No.' Hildamay's tone was agreeable.

'Well?' said the girl, staring at her curiously. 'Can I?'

'Can you what?'

She sighed in exasperation. 'Borrow your *Evening Standard*. I've asked you three times already.'

'Sure,' said Hildamay, handing it to her.

'I'll give it back.' The girl settled herself on the bench next to Hildamay and began to flick furiously through the pages. Eventually she seemed to find what she was looking for and began to read with small impatient sighs. Hildamay glanced down at the paper and saw that she was reading the small ads.

'What are you looking for?' she asked eventually.

'Divorce,' replied the girl, without looking up from the paper. 'Stuff about divorce.'

'Bit young, aren't you?' said Hildamay.

'Funny ha ha,' said the girl, but she smiled slightly under her cap. She sat up, lifting her chin to get a better look, and examined Hildamay carefully. 'Are you divorced?'

'No,' said Hildamay.

'Separated?' asked the girl, hopefully.

'No.'

'There's a difference, you know.'

'Yes.'

'Pity,' said the girl, and then sighed; a sigh which seemed too big for her person.

'Trouble at home?' asked Hildamay sympathetically.

The girl glanced at her sharply. 'A long time ago,' she said, putting down the newspaper and pulling the baseball cap lower over her eyes. She sat in silence for a time, kicking her sneakered foot against the leg of the bench. Eventually she looked up at Hildamay.

'Will you come home with me?'

Hildamay stared at her in astonishment.

'Well?'

'Why?'

'Because,' said the girl truculently. There was silence. 'Well, I suppose I'd better tell you why,' she said eventually.

'It is the usual way,' said Hildamay.

The girl looked at her carefully. 'I'm not supposed to be out on my own. I told my grandmother I was going to see a friend and that her mother would bring me home.'

'And what if you hadn't found me?' asked Hildamay, curious.

The girl shrugged and looked away but not before Hildamay noticed her shiver slightly.

'So where have you been?'

'To the library,' muttered the girl.

'Surely your grandmother wouldn't mind you going to the library?' The girl stared up at her and in her blue eyes contempt briefly flickered. Hildamay smiled apologetically and they both sank into silence.

'My name's Sky,' said the girl eventually.

'I'm Hildamay.'

'Will you?'

'Yes.'

'Good,' said Sky, watching the electric rail intently. It began to quiver and hum. 'That means the train's coming.'

The train arrived and they got on it, sitting side by side in the long, narrow carriage. Sky sank back in the seat, her legs dangling so her toes nearly, but not quite, touched the floor. She kept her baseball cap pulled down low over her eyes and her arms folded protectively over her narrow chest.

Hildamay watched her for a while in silence. 'How old are you?' she asked, shouting above the roar of the train.

'Nine.' Sky turned her face to yell in Hildamay's ear. 'Nearly ten. It's a difficult age.'

'Is it?' said Hildamay, twisting her head to look at her, her eyebrows raised in comic surprise.

'So they tell me at home,' shouted Sky and then smiled conspiratorially. The smile lit her thin white face, transforming it with a warmth so unexpected that Hildamay smiled back and they sat, for a few seconds, grinning silently at each other.

'What a good smile,' exclaimed Hildamay in admiration. Sky flushed, then shrugged and looked away.

Hildamay looked down at the top of her black leather baseball cap and felt a sudden desire to hug the thin shoulders and bring another smile to the small, pale face. The thought took her in turns by surprise and embarrassment so she turned her head away to stare at the advertisements facing her. Hildamay had no experience of children and did not know whether the emotion she felt was an emotion that everyone felt towards them, so she pondered on it for some time, and in some astonishment. She was not used to feeling kindness towards strangers.

'We have to change here,' said Sky as the train pulled into King's Cross, 'and get the Northern line.'

'Where are we going?' asked Hildamay.

'Woodside Park.'

'Where the hell's Woodside Park?'

'Home,' said Sky, her mouth tightening in a line of grim, adult resignation.

They walked down the street together. It was a narrow street in which the houses jostled for space; their tiny, rectangular gardens neat with laurel and privet. To the side of each front door, all of which were made of buttery, shiny oak veneer, hung baskets trailing with salmon pink geraniums. Every house was identical, although some had brass door knockers and others curly wrought-iron signs or slices of wood cut from the bole of a tree and charred with a name. Hildamay liked 'Seaview' best. She thought it showed a fine sense of irony.

She walked along, looking in at picture windows hung with fancy ruched net curtains, cluttered with porcelain figurines, plastic flowers and pot plants. It was surprising that any light filtered through to the people behind them. She imagined them, pale and slow, sitting having tea by the blue, flickering light of the television.

They turned a corner and entered an even narrower street where the laurel grew wild and the nets covering the windows were grey with age. Sky stopped suddenly and, jerking her head, indicated to Hildamay to follow her into a shop. It was a small newsagent and post office cluttered with boxes of chocolates wrapped with bright shiny ribbons, stacks of notebooks, balls of string and boxes of Biros. To one side stretched a long counter laden with sweets and at the end of the shop was a wire grille with holes like large mouseholes cut in it.

Behind the sweet counter stood a man, of Indian origin. His thick, black curly hair grew in perfect, sweeping waves from a high forehead and his dark skin, stretched across high cheekbones and a big, straight nose, shone like polished mahogany. At his neck gleamed a white cotton shirt, brilliant against the dark brown wool of his collarless jacket, but brightest of all were his teeth. 'It's arrived,' he exclaimed, smiling proudly.

'It looks very nice, Haadji,' said Sky nodding at the counter.

'It's new,' he explained, turning his brilliant smile to Hildamay.

'Very nice,' she agreed, admiring the smile. Sky seemed to be waiting for something and Haadji, sensing her impatience, ducked down behind the counter. He emerged carrying an old Marks & Spencer's plastic carrier bag which he handed to her. From the bag Sky extracted a shabby navy blue wool jacket and a pair of brown leather sandals. Placing the jacket carefully on the counter, she kneeled down, unlaced her white trainers and buckled the brown sandals on to her feet. She put the trainers carefully into the bottom of the bag and, pulling off the baseball cap and nylon jacket, rolled them up into a neat bundle and tucked them reverently into the bag which she handed back to him. Then she shrugged on the navy blue jacket and stood in the middle of the shop, carefully brushing the front and shoulders with her hand, while the two adults watched her. Haadji beamed happily, his teeth white with complicity, while Hildamay watched in astonishment.

'Grandmother,' explained Sky, glancing up and catching her eye. Under the jacket she wore a blue and white checked Viyella blouse with a little rounded collar trimmed with braid. The jacket matched exactly her navy blue pleated skirt and thick wool tights. In her new clothes she looked like quite another child.

'Any letters today?'

'No,' said Sky, scrubbing with a dirty hand at the lapel of the jacket. 'But she was writing one when I left this morning,' she added, looking up at him. 'So I can come and see you again tomorrow,' she said, smiling shyly.

'I'd like that,' he said gravely and walked to the door to open it for them.

'So would I,' said Sky and gently patted the hand which held the door.

Hildamay followed her out of the shop, back into the narrow street, up to the corner and back into the neat and shiny street down which they had first walked. She glanced at Sky curiously from time to time but did not say anything.

'Grandmother never goes to that shop,' said Sky eventually. 'She doesn't like coloured people,' she added, her tone matter of fact. 'Haadji's my friend, though. He comes from Bombay. He says it's nicer here. Bombay must be terrible,' she added thoughtfully. Then her voice dropped to a loud whisper. 'This is where I live.'

'Why are we whispering?' whispered Hildamay.

'Grandmother,' hissed Sky and stopped to open a low, wrought-iron gate. She was fumbling in her pocket to find a key when the door of the house opened.

'You're late,' said a flat, harsh voice. Hildamay looked up to see a woman barring the doorway. She was in her early fifties, very thin, and wore a beige artificial silk blouse tied with a bow at the neck. Over this was buttoned a black and beige patterned knitted waistcoat, the black matching the wool of her skirt and her low-heeled patent shoes. 'You're late,' she repeated, staring at Hildamay out of small, suspicious eyes. 'The tubes –' explained Hildamay.

The woman acknowledged the explanation with a shrug. 'I'm Mary Matthews,' she said, nodding curtly. 'Sky's grandmother.'

'Hildamay Smith,' said Hildamay, holding out her hand. The woman put her hand into it, letting it lie limp and slack like an empty glove.

'You'd better come in, I suppose,' she said, snatching her hand away in an abrupt, nervous gesture. Then, turning, she disappeared into the house. Sky watched Hildamay silently, her face anxious. Hildamay was astonished by the woman's cold indifference but, seeing the child's worried stare, arranged her face into a reassuring smile and stepped into a cold, narrow corridor in which a light gleamed palely. A strong smell of Vacu-Fresh rose from the brown carpet on which the tracks left by a vacuum cleaner were still visible. The only furniture in the corridor was a low pale wooden table on which sat a telephone. On the telephone was a lock and by it lay a small gilt notepad. There was nothing else in the hallway; no bits of paper by the phone, no coats, no umbrellas, no pictures on the walls.

Hildamay hesitated by the front door for Mary Matthews had stopped in front of the first of four closed doors which led off the corridor. As her bony hand fumbled for the door knob she turned to give Hildamay a quick, assessing glance and, apparently changing her mind, dropped her hand and walked towards the back of the house. Hildamay followed her into a small, square room in which stood a hard-backed sofa and three straight-backed chairs. On each chair, placed precisely in its centre, was a hard, square cushion and by each chair and to either side of the sofa were low wooden tables, each covered with a mat embroidered with bright, coloured wools. The wall facing the door was bare save for a square of yellowish ceramic tiles into which was set a new gas fire, its stainless steel surround bright and shining. On the ledge above the fire stood a collection of porcelain animals, all dressed in some semblance of human dress and each engaged in a domestic activity. A mouse brushed, a hedgehog polished, a cat cleaned. There were no other ornaments in the room, nor even any of the other clutter people usually accumulate; no photographs, no magazines, no books, not even, Hildamay noticed with surprise, a television. The fire was not lit. Hildamay shivered slightly, although not from cold, and Mary Matthews glanced sharply at her.

'Cold?' she asked in her harsh voice, but made no move towards the fire.

Hildamay smiled faintly. 'No,' she said. 'Just a feeling.'

Mary Matthews looked at her curiously. 'You'd like a sherry,' she said abruptly and left the room, walking with quick, anxious movements. 'Do sit down,' she called over her shoulder, and scarcely had Hildamay done so than she reappeared carrying a small, round gilt tray with a glass bottom on which was placed a cut-glass decanter and two small glasses. While Mary Matthews busied herself pouring the sherry, Hildamay examined her. Her hair was a bright chestnut brown, dyed judging by the evenness of the colour, cut short and arranged in tight springing curls except for the very front, which was brushed forward in a short childish fringe, incongruous above the long, bony face. Sparse eyelashes were clumped around tiny hazel eyes and these she had beaded with black mascara, startling against the pale turquoise of her eyeshadow. Her thin mouth was painted with a slash of brilliant vermilion lipstick pasted thickly above and below the natural line of her lips and her nose was so pronounced that even the powder with which it was caked could not disguise the bone which shone white through. At either side of her nose were pronounced grooves, etched down to a mouth which curved still further down at the corners.

'Cheers,' said Mary Matthews, a smile emerging through the thin red line of her lips, sharply unexpected. 'I'm afraid it's a small one,' she said, raising her glass with a slight gesture. 'But I'm expecting my ladies. They'll be here any minute.' Hildamay raised her glass slightly and then, noticing Sky standing silently in the doorway, smiled at her.

Mary Matthews turned her head sharply in the direction of the smile. 'Run along, Sky,' she said with an abrupt, dismissive gesture of her hand. 'Go and wash your hands. I'll be getting your tea any minute now.'

Sky melted into the shadow of the hall and then a faint squeak was heard as she climbed the stairs. So little noise, thought Hildamay, for a small child to make. Mary Matthews looked at her expectantly. Hildamay smiled but said nothing. She could not think of anything to say.

'My ladies,' said Mary Matthews eventually, with a slight, deprecating shrug, 'are from the local council. I'm a councillor.' She looked quickly at Hildamay, her small eyes taking in the high-heeled shoes, the cashmere suit. 'Tory, of course.'

'Naturally,' murmured Hildamay.

Mary Matthews' long face softened slightly and her eyes sparkled with sudden animation. '*She* came to see us. Said we were of more value to the community, to the country, than words could express. It was a crime, making her go like that,' she added in a low voice. 'A crime,' she repeated more loudly. She stared at Hildamay challengingly. 'Oh, of course, the new man is all right. In his way. But he has none of her spirit!' The tiny eyes flashed with indignation and the nostrils of her great bony nose quivered slightly. 'He's coming to see us. Not that we expect much,' she said darkly and sank into a brooding silence.

'He may be better,' said Hildamay and Mary Matthews glanced at her sharply.

'Better?' she asked, her voice incredulous.

'Better in the flesh, I mean,' added Hildamay.

'You mean than on television?' asked Mary Matthews, relaxing visibly.

'Yes.'

Mary Matthews brightened. 'Maybe you're right,' she said, almost gaily, and sipped at her sherry. 'Your daughter,' she continued, 'is she the same age as Sky?'

'Daughter?' said Hildamay, frowning. Mary Matthews looked at her curiously, the tiny eyes made even tinier with doubt. 'Daughter!' exclaimed Hildamay with a little laugh. 'Sarah! How could I have forgotten?'

'I thought her name was Jane?' said Mary Matthews, frowning.

'That's what Sky calls her.' Hildamay smiled and dropped her voice until it was low, confidential. 'You know how young girls are. They love to give each other nicknames. Make up all sorts of extraordinary things. She's only just given up her imaginary friends.'

'Imaginary friends?' repeated Mary Matthews, a frown twitching her thin, pencilled eyebrows into sharp lines.

'Maybe Sky didn't have them,' said Hildamay reassuringly.

'I should hope not. Imaginary friends indeed! They get such odd ideas about things. And pick up dreadful habits,' she added, her face darkening. 'Dreadful,' she emphasised. 'One must be constantly on one's guard.'

'Guard?' said Hildamay doubtfully.

Guard,' repeated Mary Matthews firmly. 'Children need a firm hand,' she explained.

'Sometimes,' murmured Hildamay, thinking of Sky's careful, silent ascent up the staircase. 'She's very – Sky's very well-mannered,' she asserted.

'Ah, yes,' said Mary Matthews, finishing her sherry and putting the glass down on the table beside her with deliberate emphasis. 'Manners,' she said abruptly, 'are important.' She looked at Hildamay expectantly. She seemed about to say something else and Hildamay waited, patiently, until she realised that Mary Matthews was not waiting for her to say anything at all, but instead waiting for her to finish her sherry and go. She emptied the rest of her glass with one swallow. The sherry was sweet and very warm. 'I really must be going,' she murmured.

'Yes,' said Mary Matthews briskly. 'Yes, of course, and I must be getting the hors d'oeuvres ready for my ladies.' Hildamay made a silent movement, as if to get up from her chair, at which Mary Matthews sprang to her feet with quite astonishing agility and almost pushed Hildamay in her seeming impatience to get her out of the room.

'I make it all myself, of course,' said Mary Matthews as she ushered Hildamay into the hall. 'None of that shop-bought stuff. Not in this house.' Hildamay turned an obedient attentive face to her. 'Not like some of them around here,' she added, her voice suddenly sharp. 'Mind you, there aren't many of them eat what we would call food. Foreign, you see,' she explained, her voice dropping to a loud whisper. 'Not that I've got anything against foreigners. Even coloured people. I don't mind them. Really I don't. Even seeing what they do to the neighbourhood. Each to his own, that's what I say. The good Lord made us all in many colours. So long as they keep themselves to themselves –' She shrugged. 'And don't expect us to run round after them. They tried to have the Lord's Prayer stopped in school assembly. We soon put a stop to that,' she added, her stare defiant. 'Go back to where you belong, we said, or stay and learn the right way. They couldn't argue with that, now, could they?' The small eyes glittered triumphantly.

'Only in Urdu,' said Hildamay, with her most ingenuous smile.

Mary Matthews frowned in confusion and an uncertain, answering smile hovered on the thin lips. 'Well . . .' she said, with an abrupt, motioning gesture of her hand towards the front door. 'It was kind of you, Mrs Smith,' she added briskly, 'to bring Sky home.' She turned and Hildamay heard her call, her voice sharp, 'Sky! What are you doing?'

'Waiting to say goodbye to Hildamay, grandmother,' said Sky in a small voice.

'Well, don't lurk in the shadows like some animal!' exclaimed Mary Matthews. 'Come here, child, and let us see you!' Her voice had taken on a sharp, unpleasant edge. Hildamay shivered suddenly as Sky crept into the pale pool of yellow light thrown by the overhead bulb. 'Very well,' said her grandmother in a slightly gentler tone as Sky's face peered up at her, pale and anxious. 'You may see Mrs Smith to the door. Do it properly, now.' She turned and held out her hand to Hildamay who took it, feeling the cold clamminess of the woman's flesh against her palm. 'Goodbye,' she said brusquely and, turning, disappeared back into the room which they had just left.

'May I have your business card?' whispered Sky, standing on the front step and pulling the door nearly closed behind her.

Hildamay looked at her in astonishment.

'I collect them,' she explained.

'I hope I've got one on me.' Hildamay frowned and scrabbled around in her bag. Eventually she found a dog-eared card with a number scrawled in pencil on the back. 'Do you want a new one?' she asked, examining it doubtfully, but Sky shook her head. 'It's got something written on the back. My home number,' she explained, handing it to her.

'May I ring you up?' Sky's face was suddenly bright with hope.

Hildamay looked at her, frowning. Under the frown, Sky's face seemed to close; the blue eyes darkened and, lowering pale eyelids over them, she stared at the ground.

'Of course you can,' Hildamay said gently, seeing the child's distress.

Sky looked up, smiling brilliantly, and held out her hand.

'I have always depended,' she said gravely, 'on the kindness of strangers.'

'What did you say?'

'I have always depended –'

'I know what you said,' said Hildamay abruptly. Sky looked at her in confusion. 'I meant, where did you learn it?'

'I heard it on the radio. So I went and looked it up. A person called Blanche used to say it,' said Sky confidingly. 'So I taught it to my mother. Her name's Blanche. She says it lots because it annoys my grandmother. Blanche votes Labour,' she explained helpfully.

Hildamay smiled. So there is a mother, she thought. 'Does she live here, too?'

'Oh yes.'

'With your father?'

Sky looked down and kicked her foot against the step. 'He left a long time ago,' she whispered. 'He got a divorce,' she added suddenly.

'People do,' said Hildamay reassuringly. 'How old is your mother?'

'She's twenty-four. But grandmother says she looks older because she smokes, and drinks so much gin. Blanche likes gin. She says it's "mother's ruin" and when she's drunk some she dances around the house singing "it's mother that ruined me".'

Hildamay laughed.

'She laughs, too,' said Sky. 'Some of the time.'

'And now I must go,' said Hildamay firmly. 'Will you be all right?'

Sky looked at her sharply, the navy blue eyes narrow with suspicion. 'Why shouldn't I be?' she asked.

Hildamay smiled at her. 'No reason,' she said lightly and patted her gently on the cheek. 'No reason at all.'

CHAPTER SEVEN

HILDAMAY sat up in bed, picked up her magnifying mirror and examined her face. She looked, she thought, pretty much as usual, until she noticed the shadow of a frown tugging at her eyebrows. 'What's this?' she wondered and then remembered Liz and felt unaccountably depressed. She smiled her most encouraging smile. It did no good. 'No good at all,' she sighed. She looked at the sky outside her bedroom window. It was a perfect morning. The sky was a fine blue; pale and hesitant and new. It was a blue that ordinarily would have cheered her. She was optimistic about mornings and gladdened by blue. But it did no good. This was no ordinary morning. She sighed again and set about the task in hand.

Condoms. There was a story about condoms which continued to elude her. She concentrated hard. She imagined a condom stretched over an erect penis and began to enjoy herself. No, no. That was not the task in hand. She wrenched her mind back with some effort. And then she remembered. She picked up the mirror and examined her face. 'It might just work,' she murmured thoughtfully and smiled at herself, pleased. After deliberating for some minutes she picked up the telephone and dialled Liz's number.

'It's me.'

'Hildamay, it's seven-thirty on Saturday morning.'

'That's not important.'

'To whom?' said Liz waspishly.

'To you.'

'Well it feels it,' said Liz grumpily. 'It feels very, very important.'

'Shut up. I've solved the condom problem.'

'How?' Liz sounded suddenly very alert.

'I remembered this story. It's a true story about two lesbians who wanted a child. They go out to a bar and pick their victim. He's tall, attractive, amenable. Nothing special but nothing dangerous. One of them flirts with him then invites him back to the flat. They make love. When they've finished she says she's got to go to the bathroom, takes the condom and gives it to the other woman who's waiting in another room. She goes back to bed and the other woman empties the contents into a champagne glass and puts it in an incubator. He goes off the next morning, suspecting nothing. That night they have an impregnation ceremony and nine months later are delivered of a healthy bouncing boy.' Hildamay was triumphant.

There was silence.

'Liz?' said Hildamay.

Still there was silence.

'Do you only ever get boys from champagne glasses?' said Liz eventually.

'Yes,' said Hildamay. 'Nice big, bouncy, bubbly, good-natured ones.'

'It might turn out to be alcoholic.'

'Almost definitely.'

'Where do we get hold of an incubator?'

'A minor detail,' said Hildamay confidently, although she did not feel it.

'And what about the man?'

'I've found him. Thomas. In the bar. The other night.'

'A barman?' said Liz gloomily. 'Poor little bugger doesn't stand a chance. They say it's hereditary.'

'What?'

'Alcoholism.'

'Liz Valentine, do you or do you not want a fatherless child?'

'I do,' said Liz.

'Good. Then meet me at The Globe at six.'

'Can you get hold of an incubator by then?'

'No, and I'm not going to try. You're the one who's got to get a hold.'

'On what?'

'On Thomas.'

'Which bit of him?' asked Liz, laughing.

'His heart. They say that usually does the trick,' said Hildamay and put down the phone.

Sighing, she walked into her bathroom, locked the door and, sitting on the little wooden stool, scrubbed at herself with determined vigour. As she scrubbed she thought about Liz. Nine months of growing bellies and ripening breasts. It would be as impossible to share Liz's delight as it was impossible to share somebody else's pain; however much we might want to. She would try to, because she loved Liz. Yet she hated the idea. Two years of feeds and nappies, of focusing eyes and exploring hands, of developing teeth and limbs. She thought perhaps it might be fascinating if it was your own cell growing before your eyes but she doubted it was interesting in any but the most purely selfish way.

She knew she was thought to be selfish. There was a part of her that she could not, would not, share. She wondered if that mattered. It appeared to matter a great deal to other people. Even friendship assumed proprietorial rights.

'You are my friend. You are mine.'

'I am not anyone's,' said Hildamay aloud as she climbed into the bath and lay soaking in the hot scented water. She knew that was part of her charm; that she would not give all of herself. She did not think selfishness a vice, any more than she believed selflessness to be a virtue. Selflessness she assumed to be a fantastic arrogance. Who could believe that the world wanted that much, all, of them?

People tired her. They took parts of her, grabbed pieces big and small until she thought that there was no more that they could take. She had a dream sometimes. A nightmare in which she stood naked in a room, surrounded by people. They grabbed at her flesh with their hands, plucked great chunks off her body and stuffed them into their mouths, their jaws working hungrily, blood and sinew spilling out of their lips, grease shining fattily on their chins and cheeks.

It terrified her, that dream. It woke her at three o'clock. Always at three, the hour of death. 'Give it back,' she sobbed in the darkness. 'Give me back.' And they would hand her some part of themselves. 'No, no,' she sobbed. 'I don't want you. I want me, I want me, I want me.'

'They might take it away. Take me away,' she said as she climbed out of the bath and wrapped herself in towels. She looked at her face in the mirror. 'And then where would I be?' Alone. But alone is all right. Alone is good. It is being exposed, vulnerable, that is frightening. If they could, they would take her, all of her, and she would be gone, subsumed in somebody else's identity, gobbled up in their ego, dispersed in their being.

'Alone,' she whispered, looking around at the clean white walls of her private kingdom, 'it is better.'

She gave until anyone tried to assume possession. Then she withdrew into some cool and clever part of her that laughed and teased until they moved away again. Liz wanted her. Messy, emotional, needy Liz. She wanted what she thought she saw in Hildamay; the strong and shining part of her. She wanted that distance, that cold logic, for herself. She wanted it and she hated it. She wanted to break it down, to push away the male and nurture the female. Hildamay suspected that was why Liz had solicited her help, her complicity with the child. 'You are to be godmother,' she said and would hear no argument. Liz, by giving her the child, even at conception, was binding Hildamay irrevocably to her. If Hildamay had a part of her, she would have a part of Hildamay.

Her solitariness hurt Liz, as it did all her friends. Sometimes, when she could bear it no longer, Hildamay put away her public face and retreated. For days she would not answer the telephone but listened to disembodied voices floating through the answering machine and echoing around the flat as she sat, alone. She spent most of the time in her bathroom lying wrapped in towels on the cream carpet in the sparkling white and glass room. When she emerged she felt purified, her mind scrubbed as clean as her body. At work she told George to tell everyone who called that she was in a meeting. Sometimes weeks went by.

'Where have you been?' they cried.

'I've been so busy.' She would shrug in apology.

'Too busy,' said Liz acidly, 'for your friends.'

'I'm sorry,' sighed Hildamay. 'But there it is.'

'Take care the wind doesn't change,' said Liz darkly.

'What, and leave me selfless and loving and giving?' teased Hildamay. But Liz did not smile.

'Your friends,' said Liz, 'are all you have.'

'It's not good for you, darling,' said Cassie. 'You need people. We all need people.'

'Do we?' asked Hildamay idly.

'Yes,' said Cassie, quite crossly for her. 'We do. You do. You may not know it yet but someday you will. I just hope it's not too late.'

'Is that a threat?' asked Hildamay, smiling.

'Yes,' said Cassie, who was not smiling at all.

'It is difficult,' said Delilah, 'to live alone and be emotionally healthy. A few people achieve it. But very few.'

'Perhaps,' said Hildamay, 'I am not emotionally healthy.'

'Perhaps,' said Delilah, 'you are not,' and peered at her curiously as if she, Hildamay, were one of her patients.

'Oh, good grief,' said Hildamay.

'I understand,' said Kate. 'It must be such bliss to be alone.'

'You'd loathe it,' said Hildamay.

'I'd miss them,' said Kate, her eyes misting over with tears.

Hildamay heard the telephone ring distantly. She did not go to answer it but lay on her bathroom floor, wrapped in towels, cocooned in her own invention. In her bathroom she did not exist, for in the world her bathroom did not exist. She was not unhappy. She liked her life. She liked it that way.

Liz was waiting when she arrived at The Globe. Hildamay stood and watched her from the doorway. She sat alone at one of the smaller tables, her back straight against the black steel of the little upright chair. A glass of mineral water stood on the table and she had shredded the mat on which it had been served. Little twists and curls of white paper littered the surface on which her fingers now tapped, impatiently. She kept looking curiously over at the bar where Thomas stood, then ducking her head if he tried to catch her eye. Once he smiled and Liz caught the smile full on. It trapped her, momentarily. She shook her head as if to brush it away and stared out of the window, deep pink staining her cheeks.

Hildamay made her way through the over-stuffed armchairs and angular black steel chairs and the laughing people bright with Saturday night. Liz looked up, her eyes dark and shining with fear. Hildamay bent to kiss her, then wrapped her arms around her and hugged her, rocking her gently.

'Are you all right?' she asked, releasing her and sitting down.

'No,' said Liz, getting up. 'Shall we go now?'

'No,' said Hildamay, putting a hand out to stop her. She kept her hand on Liz's arm and stroked her as if calming a frightened animal.

Liz shook her head. 'I can't do this. Not like this. Not now.'

'You don't have to do anything now,' said Hildamay. 'Except flirt a little.'

'Flirt?' said Liz, her voice squeaky with nerves. 'Flirt? I can't do that. I don't know how. Hildamay, this is ridiculous. Let's go. Please.' She was begging.

'Of course you can flirt,' said Hildamay implacably. 'You're a master of the art. Or should that be mistress?'

'Weak,' said Liz but she smiled faintly. 'Very, very weak.'

'Yes,' said Hildamay. 'Well, what do you think?' she added, jerking her head in the direction of the bar.

Liz glanced over quickly. 'He looks like a nice boy,' she said, sounding far from convinced.

'He is a nice boy. I have it on the best authority.'

'Whose?'

'Cassie's.'

'Since when was Cassie an authority on men?' demanded Liz. 'The woman's a walking disaster.'

'She hasn't slept with this one,' said Hildamay.

'Ah,' said Liz. There was silence as the two of them gazed consideringly at Thomas who, sensing their stares, began to shift uncomfortably. 'Why not?' she added.

'Maybe he's got great taste?' said Hildamay.

'Maybe you're a bitch,' said Liz, grinning.

'No maybe about it,' said Hildamay cheerfully. 'Now, some champagne.'

'What about the baby?'

'There is no baby. Yet,' said Hildamay firmly. 'And I hear that nervous adrenalin is a great deal more toxic than champagne.'

'What a good theory,' said Liz.

'Well?' said Liz briskly on the telephone the next morning.

'Well what?' said Hildamay grumpily. A hangover at least

deserved a reward and she could not see even the tiniest sign of one.

'Well, do you think he liked me?'

'No. That's why he was sitting on your lap at one o'clock in the morning. Or were you sitting on his?'

'Both,' said Liz happily. 'He's got very nice ears.'

'What about what's between them?'

'Passable.'

'Muscle tone?'

'Above average.'

'Disposition?'

'Fair.'

'Cock?'

'I wouldn't know.'

'Liar.'

'Responds to attention,' amended Liz.

'Well at least it works,' said Hildamay. 'There's a start.'

'Nothing starts until you get your incubator.'

Hildamay felt vaguely resentful. This was not her child. 'Oh, I see. This is suddenly my incubator?' she said, trying to keep her voice light.

There was a silence.

'Oh. It's just that – well, it was your idea, Hildamay.'

Hildamay said nothing.

'Please help me, Hildamay. You said you would. And I've no idea how to get hold of an incubator. You're so good at those sorts of things. I can't do this on my own. Anyway, I'm going to ovulate soon.'

'You're going to what?'

'I'm at my most fertile soon. This weekend, in fact.'

'How do you know?'

'Oh, Hildamay. Sometimes I don't think you even know what sex you are. By taking my temperature, of course.'

'Is that why they call it hot to trot?' said Hildamay giggling.

'Oh, shut up. There's no reason to fuck unless you're going to get pregnant, is there?' said Liz impatiently.

'I can think of a few,' said Hildamay laconically.

'I'm being *serious*,' insisted Liz.

'So am I.' There was silence. Hildamay sighed and wondered what it was about babies, even the idea of them, which engendered such lack of humour in women.

'OK,' she said eventually. 'But don't get your knickers in a twist just yet. And if you should happen to see Thomas next week, keep those pretty little legs of yours crossed, however hot you get.'

'Don't be rude,' said Liz. 'It's Sunday.'

'I'm leaving the rude bits to you,' said Hildamay. 'Goodbye.'

CHAPTER EIGHT

'GEORGE,' said Hildamay. 'I need to get hold of an incubator. Just for one night.'

It was Monday morning. George blinked mildly at her.

'Could I,' he said, 'ask what it's for?'

'Ummm,' said Hildamay. She did not look at him but studied, with a show of grave concern, the letter he had just put in front of her.

George peered myopically at her.

'What sort of function,' he continued gently, 'would it be expected to perform?'

'The usual,' said Hildamay. She had not thought she would have to tell him that.

There was silence.

George shuffled the bunch of letters on the desk in front of him. Neither of them spoke. He glanced curiously at her from time to time. She continued to read the letter, which she had been staring at for five minutes.

'There is another letter here,' he said finally, 'which needs your immediate attention.'

'Yes,' she said, glancing abstractedly at it. 'Yes,' she added, a great deal more decisively, 'take a letter, George. Dear Monsieur Chanot,' she continued, scarcely drawing breath, 'Thank you for your letter and for drawing to my attention the matter of the stained bolts of cashmere full stop. I have contacted the factory concerned and have discovered. Is that the right word? Discovered? It'll do. Discovered that comma despite their usually rigorous safeguards comma they had inadvertently.' She broke off. 'It needs to keep something. A substance.' She searched for the right word. 'A fluid,' she said emphatically, 'a fluid which needs to be kept at body temperature.'

George looked up from his notebook. 'I see,' he said. 'And would that be blood, Miss Smith?'

Hildamay started. 'Had inadvertently allowed a few bolts of the spoiled cashmere to be shipped to Paris full stop. We are all at Stone & Gray very distressed that this could have happened particularly – sperm.'

His pen stilled.

'Particularly,' continued Hildamay, 'to such a valued client full stop. I have ordered our shippers to deliver four more bolts as soon as possible full stop.' She paused.

'Human?' said George.

'Yes,' said Hildamay, and added. 'Please accept our sincere apologies for any inconvenience full stop. Yours sincerely etcetera etcetera.'

'I see,' said George and, gathering together his papers, notebook and pen, left the room.

'Oh dear,' said Hildamay to the closed door. 'I think I may have upset him.'

She was pondering on the awfulness of this when George walked back into the room with a cup of tea.

'A nice hot drink,' he said. 'Strong and very sweet.'

Hildamay winced. She did not take sugar in her tea. George put sugar in it when he was cross with her. She took a sip. It was not sweet. George blinked at her.

'I have a friend,' he said gravely, 'who works for a medical supplier. I shall telephone him.'

'Thank you, George,' said Hildamay and smiled brilliantly at him. He coloured slightly.

'Your telephone calls,' he said, pushing a list across the desk.

'George,' said Hildamay. 'Not only are you the most handsome man I know, but you're also a complete treasure. What would I do without you?'

George blinked rapidly. He did not speak. Then, very quietly, he said, 'I bet you say that to all the boys, Miss Smith,' and walked very quickly to the door. The back of his neck was fiery pink and Hildamay thought she heard him laugh as he shut the door.

She thought about Liz and decided that she had perhaps not been as kind as she might have been. She determined to be nicer during lunch and was just practising her conciliatory smile in the mirror which hung on the wall of her office when George walked in. She tested it on him. He blinked slowly and gazed at her with concern.

'Are you quite all right, Miss Smith?'

'Yes, George. Why?'

'You look most – most unusual. Not yourself,' he amended hurriedly.

Hildamay frowned. Conciliation was not one of her strong points. Maybe the smile needed more attention? She stopped smiling. George relaxed visibly, shut the door and hurried over to her.

'I've spoken to my friend,' he said, so quietly that Hildamay had to bend her head towards his to hear. 'He says it can be arranged. He says if it's only for the one night, then we could do it, ah, on the quiet.'

Hildamay looked confused. George looked at her gravely.

'Otherwise,' he continued earnestly, 'it would cost you a great deal of money. To buy it, you see.'

'Oh, I wouldn't want to buy one,' said Hildamay.

'I thought not. So if you could let me have a date.'

'A date?'

'Arrangements must be made,' he whispered. 'My friend says a Friday would be preferable.'

'I see,' whispered Hildamay. 'This Friday, then.'

'This Friday?' said George in a normal voice. It sounded so loud they both jumped. 'I'll ask my friend,' he added as he inched his way towards the door. 'But he says it must be returned the following day. By six. At the latest?' He blinked urgently. He was just shutting the door when Hildamay called out to him.

'George?'

'Yes, Miss Smith?' His shining face peered around the door at her.

'Just one more thing.'

The hairless eyebrows peaked like circumflexes over his round, blinking eyes.

'Could you possibly ask your friend if he could add a syringe to the list? Not a hypodermic. One of those big syringes which they use to – oh, I don't know what they use them for. The sort that spurt fluid out of them. I'm sure your friend will understand.'

'A syringe,' said George faintly. His milk-white skin was ashen.

There was no sign of Liz when Hildamay arrived at the restaurant. Luigi, though, was waiting, his big face beaming and his hands clasped comfortably over his great stomach. 'I look forward all morning, Hildamay,' he said, kissing her enthusiastically as he tucked her into a corner table, at the same time gesturing abruptly to one of his waiters to fetch her a glass of champagne.

She was just taking the first sip of her drink when she saw Cassie across the room. She waved and smiled. Cassie stared at her then turned her head away. Hildamay's hand stopped in mid-air. How extraordinary, she thought, and craned her head to see whom she was lunching with. She could see only the dark head of a man, as his back was turned to her. She got up and began to make her way towards their table when she saw Cassie's eyes. They were narrowed to slits and her mouth was pursed in a warning 'no'.

Hildamay began to veer off in another direction, towards the opposite corner of the room. She was not sure what she would do when she got there, other than turn around and come back. She was marooned and searched frantically for someone she might vaguely know. As she looked the man sitting with Cassie turned his head to follow her riveted gaze. Hildamay caught the unmistakable glint of artificially enamelled teeth and was so surprised, she stopped dead.

'Hildamay,' he called, rising to his feet. 'Hildamay. Over here.'

Hildamay groaned and walked over to their table. Jack Rome took her outstretched hand in both of his. 'Hildamay,' he said, pressing her hand warmly, 'how lovely to see you. What are you doing here?'

'I come here sometimes,' she said, looking down at Cassie.

'Very occasionally,' she added. Cassie's eyes were so dark, they were almost black. Hildamay realised, with a shock, that she was very angry. She looked back at Jack.

'Do you two lovely ladies know each other?' he asked.

'Yes,' said Hildamay.

'No,' said Cassie.

'Vaguely,' said Hildamay. 'We know each other terribly vaguely.' She smiled abstractedly. 'Almost not at all, really.'

'Cassie Montrose –' said Jack.

'Cassandra,' said Cassie.

'Cassandra Montrose, meet Hildamay Smith. Hildamay and I work together,' he added, beaming cheerfully at Cassie whose eyes widened with shock and sudden recognition. She opened her mouth but no sound came out.

Idiot, thought Hildamay. She's never been able to remember the name of the company.

'At Stone & Gray,' she said loudly, enunciating the words slowly and with great care. 'Where I am the managing director.' She sounded as though she was talking to an idiot. Jack's smile froze.

'Well, quite,' he said a shade too heartily. 'Splendid, splendid!' he added, and the two women looked at him, curious to see what was splendid. 'To have a woman as a boss,' he explained, the smile back on his face and gleaming powerfully.

'A great admirer of the fair sex. Women run the world. As it should be,' he said, winking at Cassie.

Hildamay felt a pang of contrition. He thought she was trying to upstage him.

Oh, dear, she thought with dismay. He's going to tell us he's a feminist next.

'I'm a sort of feminist myself,' he said, beaming.

'Delighted,' said Cassie.

'Don't be ridiculous,' snapped Hildamay automatically.

'To meet you,' finished Cassie.

Jack looked crestfallen. And ridiculous. He was still standing and shifted uncomfortably between the two women. Hildamay felt sorrier for him than she would ever have believed it was possible to feel for Jack Rome.

'Feminism,' she said, smiling winningly at him, 'is women's only claim to freedom. We don't like it when men, who have so many, claim it too.' Jack looked confused. 'But we know you meant it as a compliment,' she finished with her most dazzling smile. 'Don't we, Cassandra?' She fixed Cassie with her smile. Cassie ignored her.

'Oh, yes, yes,' she said, gazing at Jack in frank admiration. He seemed to swell before them. 'The world needs more men like you, Jack. More men who really appreciate women.' His chest had more than doubled in size.

Oh, good grief, thought Hildamay, recognising the look on Cassie's face. 'Appreciate me,' it said.

'Like it needs global warming,' said Hildamay.
'What?' said Jack, staring at Cassie.
'Warming,' said Hildamay.
'Warming,' repeated Jack, his eyes following the curves of Cassie's breasts as she reached for her champagne glass and lifted it to her mouth. She licked her pink-stained lips and looked up at him and Hildamay realised, with a sinking heart, that Cassie was not even drunk.

'Who's that with Cassie?' asked Liz, when Hildamay got back to the table.
'A business acquaintance,' said Hildamay. 'They're discussing a new advertising campaign. Cassie's writing the storyline. Something about birth control, I gather.' She took a large swallow of her drink.
'Birth control?' said Liz, laughing wickedly. 'Let's tell them our idea. Brings a whole new meaning to control.'
'Let's not,' said Hildamay hurriedly. 'How are you feeling?'
'Fine.'
'Nervous?'
'Not at all.'
'Good, because Friday's the night.'
'This Friday?' The freckles on Liz's face stood out in stark relief against the pallor of her skin. Hildamay peered at her.
'You've gone pale,' she said accusingly.
Liz's hands went up to her face. 'Of course I've gone pale,' she said unsteadily. 'It's not every day you become a mother.'
'You'll be fine,' said Hildamay reassuringly.
'Will I?'
'Yes. George is going to get an incubator on Friday night.'
'George?' said Liz, aghast.
'Oh, don't worry. George doesn't know what it's for and, even if he did, he'd never tell a soul. He's got a friend who works for a medical supplier. He's getting us a syringe, too.'
'A syringe?' Liz was staring at her in horror.
'To get the stuff up you. There are various ways of doing it but a syringe is best. I called Anna, a doctor friend of mine. She said you could even leave it in the condom and sort of shove it back up you, but you'd need to do that quickly. And do a shoulder-stand at the same time, I imagine. The timing and temperature are crucial. Apparently you can get incubators in pet shops. The sort that kids

keep gerbils in. She said that would probably do the trick but it seemed rather dodgy to me. Sperm lasts for about three or four hours unless you keep it at a controlled temperature, in which case it'll last, at full strength, for about sixteen. So I decided we needed a proper incubator. To be sure.'

'Sure,' echoed Liz.

'You don't want to go through this again, do you?' asked Hildamay.

'No,' said Liz faintly and was silent. 'Not unless I decide to have a really large family,' she added, starting to laugh. 'Of gerbils.' She giggled hysterically.

'Oh, shut up,' said Hildamay, laughing too. 'Are you sure about Thomas?'

'What do you mean, sure?'

'Sure he wants to fuck you?' said Hildamay.

'Yes. Yes, I'm sure.'

'Well, you'd better put in some night work in the next few days. We want to be sure we've got him at the right temperature.'

'God,' said Liz. She stopped laughing and looked apprehensive.

'No,' said Hildamay, still smiling. 'Thomas. As far as the world's concerned, this is an immaculate conception. But as far as you're concerned, we need Thomas. The Virgin Mary you're not.'

'I don't think you're taking this seriously at all,' said Liz, suddenly irritable. 'And what about HIV?'

'What about it?'

'Well, it's all very well using a condom but what about the child? If he's positive, the child will be born with it.'

'He's negative.'

'How the hell do you know?'

'Cassie told me. He told Cassie.'

'Oh. Well, how can we be sure?'

'We can't. Just as we can't be sure he doesn't suffer from some hereditary disease, like schizophrenia or diabetes or God knows what else.'

'Thanks.'

'Liz,' said Hildamay gently, 'I had assumed you'd thought all this through.'

'I have,' she said defiantly. 'It's just that −'

'That what?'

'Wanting and getting are different things.'

'Yes,' agreed Hildamay, watching her curiously.

Liz's face suddenly softened. 'A baby,' she breathed. 'Very soon,

I'll have my very own baby.' She lapsed into silence, a half smile playing around her mouth.

Hildamay watched Cassie across the room. She could see her mouth. It looked pink and large and hungry. Hungry to bed a fool. Desire makes idiots of even the sane. Hildamay turned to look at Liz and watched her for some time in silence. She looked at her eyelashes and wondered if the child would have them. She thought of Thomas's eyes and wondered if the child's would crinkle at the corners, its hair grow straight and shiny, or whether it would be curly and springing to the touch like Liz's. Could anything, given such ludicrous beginnings, grow strong and brave and proud? What would Liz say to it when it asked, 'Mummy, Mummy, where do I come from?' Would she tell the child that it came from two women fumbling in a kitchen and a man, oblivious to the stirrings of new life, lying in ignorance in a crumpled bed? That it was conceived cynically and without love? That it had no father?

'I'm going to have a baby,' said Liz suddenly, her smile triumphant, her eyes hard with assurance. Hildamay looked at her and wondered if she even cared about the child. Soft, vulnerable, needy Liz. She looked suddenly so determined, so single minded. Did the soul, the psyche, the spirit that she was even now creating really matter to her?

Liz looked at her curiously. 'What's the matter?' she asked.

'Nothing.'

'There is. I can see it in your face. What is it? Tell me,' she demanded urgently.

Hildamay sighed and stared down at her hands. Eventually she looked up at Liz. 'I don't like playing with lives,' she said quietly. 'With Thomas's, with yours, with the child's. I'm not cut out to play God.'

Liz jerked her head in irritation. 'You'd think it was you who was going to give birth,' she said. 'You're not playing God. You're simply helping me to have a baby. You're not the creator, simply an accomplice.' Her mouth was hard. 'I want this baby and I'm going to have it. Whether you help me or not.'

Hildamay stared at her. Then she reached out and picked up her glass. 'Well, God bless mothers everywhere,' she said quietly.

Liz smiled.

CHAPTER NINE

GEORGE walked into Hildamay's office.
'It's here,' he hissed.
'What is?' asked Hildamay.
'The thing,' he said in a loud whisper. She looked at him, bemused. He was blinking excitedly and little pearls of sweat beaded his upper lip. She had never seen George sweat before. She had not thought him a person bothered with excretions. He seemed to have his flesh so rigorously under control; as perfectly behaved, washed and pressed as his starched white shirts.

'What?' she said slowly, 'thing?'
'The incubator. Adrian just brought it.'
'Well, ask him to bring it in here.' Hildamay was curious to meet George's friend. She imagined him, small and hairless. She thought there might be an army of small hairless men who all knew George; who from low positions in high places controlled London. All George's friends seemed to be useful.

'How do you know that? How did you manage that?' she would ask.

'I have a friend,' he would say, as if getting hold of the Department of Trade's clothing export figures before they were officially published was a matter of mundane achievement.

'How many friends do you have?' Hildamay asked curiously one day.

'Enough,' said George.

'He's gone,' he said, producing a perfectly ironed white handkerchief which he dabbed tentatively at his upper lip.

'Shame,' said Hildamay. 'I wanted to thank him.'

'You might not when you see the size of the thing.'

'Is it very big?' she asked, getting up to walk to the door.

'Very,' said George gravely and they stood in the door of her office gazing at a large cardboard box stamped in red, 'Medical Supplies. Urgent.'

'Well, we can't leave it here,' said Hildamay. 'We'll have to put it in my office.'

The two of them were struggling to move it, leaning forward and pushing hard to slide it through the door when Hildamay felt a warm sensation in her rear. Someone was watching her. She felt eyes burning into her buttocks and, straightening up, she turned around. Jack Rome was standing behind them.

'Can I,' he said, a leer and a smirk fighting for best position on his face, 'be of assistance?'

'No,' said Hildamay, 'thank you. We can manage.'

She leaned against the box and folded her arms, trying to hide it from him.

'It was very nice to see you the other day,' he said, the leer winning. 'It's not often we lunch in the same establishment.'

'It's cheap,' said Hildamay, 'but terribly unfashionable. I go there very rarely.'

'I think it may become one of my favourites,' he said, the leer now convulsing his face. 'Your friend seemed to like it. She liked it very, very much,' he added, winking.

Hildamay looked at him with disgust. 'I wouldn't know,' she said, her tone indifferent.

His eyes were bloodshot, the redness rimming them accentuating the fraudulent green of his eyes. 'I've been away,' he said, lowering himself into George's chair and putting his feet on the desk. 'Took a few days off and went to the country. A small, charming hotel.

Superb food and wine. Four-poster beds. With a friend,' he added, looking pointedly at Hildamay. She thought he might lick his red, bulbous lips, and stared at him with dismay.

'Was the weather good?' she asked with freezing politeness.

'Didn't see much of it,' he replied, smirking.

'That's the trouble with those bourgeois little English hotels,' she said sharply. 'They're so festooned with chintz and blinds, you never see the light of day.'

His smile broadened. 'Oh, I don't know about that,' he said. 'Very cosy, it was. Intimate.' His eyes swept lazily over her body and came to rest on her breasts. Hildamay, embarrassed in front of George, shifted uncomfortably and, flushing, looked away.

George coughed. 'Paris has been calling all week,' he said suddenly. 'It seems that pile of papers on which your feet are resting need your immediate attention.'

Jack smiled and shrugged. 'They can wait,' he said, leaning back easily in George's chair.

'They seemed to think they couldn't,' said George mildly. 'I told them you had taken a sudden holiday and that unfortunately you had failed to inform Miss Smith of your whereabouts. I told them you seemed to have left no telephone number so that there was no way we could get in contact with you.'

'You told them what?' said Jack, his voice sharpening with alarm. He stared at George in outrage.

'I always think the truth is best,' said George, blinking. 'When one has nothing to hide. Don't you?'

'Naturally, George. Naturally,' said Jack, sitting up and scrabbling at the papers on the desk.

'Allow me,' said George while Hildamay leaned against the box and smiled. She knew that there had been no call from Paris.

'George,' she said when Jack Rome had gone. 'You're wicked.'

'Wicked?' he echoed, his eyes round and unblinking.

They drove to Liz's flat with George crouched backwards on the front seat, his arms wrapped around the box balanced in the back.

'Is that absolutely necessary?' said Hildamay.

'I think it might be rather fragile, Miss Smith,' he said in strangled tones. They drove for a while in silence.

'George,' said Hildamay. 'I'd appreciate it if you would tell no-one about this. No-one at all.'

There was a hurt silence.

'I wouldn't dream of it,' he said eventually, his voice muffled but ringing with dignity.

'I'm sorry, George. I shouldn't have mentioned it.'

'No,' he said.

It took them some time to manoeuvre the box up the stairs but eventually it was done. They both sat down for a moment to catch their breath but Hildamay felt too agitated to sit still, so she got up and began to prowl around the room. George watched her. She wished he would go so she could unpack the box. It seemed wrong to do it in front of him, obscene; like unwrapping a condom.

'Shall I make you a nice hot drink, Miss Smith?' he asked gently.

'No. No, thank you. I'll, er. I'll . . .' She looked distractedly around.

'Well, I'll be going then,' he said and picked up the paper bag containing his lamb chop for supper. It had got squashed in the move and blood seeped out of it, staining the white paper a dark, rusty brown. They both looked at it and their eyes slid to the incubator.

George put the package behind his back.

'Adrian and I will come and get the, uh, machine at five o'clock tomorrow,' he said.

'Oh! Is that really necessary? To come here?'

He looked at her, blinking quizzically.

'I don't see how you'll move it otherwise,' he said mildly.

'But it's your weekend, George.'

'Adrian must have it by six,' he said firmly. 'Otherwise he might get into trouble. We'll be here at five.'

Hildamay opened her mouth. George lifted his hand warningly then patted her on the shoulder.

'It'll be fine,' he said kindly. 'You'll see.'

After he had gone Hildamay thought about his hand on her shoulder. It had felt surprisingly large and firm for so small a man. She thought of George as she unpacked the box and felt oddly reassured.

Liz posed in the doorway. Hildamay looked up from the newspaper and whistled.

'Is it you?' she said. 'You look so glamorous. Do you know, I don't believe I've ever seen you in a frock. A little black frock at that.'

'Do I look all right?' Liz walked nervously to the middle of the room and did a shaky pirouette.

Hildamay started to cough.

'Jesus, Liz, how much perfume have you got on? You're trying to seduce him, not asphyxiate the poor man.'

'Oh dear. Do you think I've overdone it?'

'Only very slightly,' said Hildamay, her eyes watering. She went over to kiss her on the cheek. 'Maybe he's got shares in Chanel.'

'Bitch.'

'You look completely gorgeous,' said Hildamay, taking her by the shoulders and marching her to the front door. 'Now go and do your worst. Be your baddest.'

Liz stood in the door. She looked terrified.

'No,' she said and ran back into the sitting room. Hildamay followed her. 'I can't do it,' she said, flopping down on the sofa.

Hildamay sat down next to her.

'Why not?'

'I haven't fucked anyone in over a year. I really don't know how to. I can't remember what to do.'

'I'll show you,' said Hildamay, and got down on to the floor. She lay with her legs apart and a huge smile on her face. Then she started to pant; at first quietly and then louder and more urgently, moving her hips up and down in time to her breathing.

'Enough!' said Liz, trying to cover her eyes and her ears at the same time.

'I won't stop until you go,' panted Hildamay.

'What about a sperm bank?' said Liz. 'Maybe that would be better. Nice and clean and straightforward.'

'You've got a sperm bank waiting at The Globe,' said Hildamay, sitting up. 'Now move your butt.'

'I'm serious,' said Liz.

'So am I. Anyway, they're talking about changing the law. Soon the child will have access to the donor's identity. And I thought that's exactly what you didn't want to happen.'

'It is,' said Liz, gnawing at her lower lip. 'It just seems a bit unfair on poor Thomas.'

'Well, it is,' said Hildamay and they looked at each other dubiously.

'Oh, sod it,' said Liz. 'I'm going. I can't let him down now.'

She left Hildamay sitting alone in a cloud of Chanel perfume.

'No,' she said softly. 'You can let him down tomorrow.' She knew Liz would have nothing to do with Thomas once she thought she was pregnant. Hildamay felt sorry for him, although she did not know quite why.

She went into the kitchen to check on the incubator. Then she filled a kettle, ready to boil. She got a champagne glass out of the cupboard, washed it and put it together with the syringe in a big saucepan which she had washed and scoured. Once Liz and Thomas had disappeared into the bedroom, she would creep out here and boil and sterilise everything. Then she would wait. She hoped Thomas wasn't one of those men who prided themselves on taking hours to come, pounding away as some poor woman lay impaled and trapped beneath him. She rather hoped he was a hit-and-run man.

Hildamay sat at the table and read the instructions for the incubator. It looked quite simple. She checked the temperature control dial and turned it on to make sure the red light came on. 'Oh, shit,' she said out loud. She had forgotten the precise temperature at which sperm should be kept. What was blood temperature? She flicked through all Liz's cookery books. 'Beef,' she read. 'Beef, lamb, chicken, goose, turkey. Bread, cakes, pastry. Shit. This is no good. Where's sperm?'

She ran into the sitting room to see if Liz had a medical dictionary. 'Sperm, sperm, sperm,' she muttered like an incantation. She picked up the phone.

'Anna, thank God you're there. What temperature did you say you keep sperm at?'

'I got it wrong,' said Anna. 'I've been trying to call you. I spoke to a colleague who specialises in IVF. I thought it was blood temperature or slightly below but in fact it's twenty-five degrees centigrade, which is about the temperature of a centrally heated room.'

'Oh, shit. You mean we don't need an incubator?'

'Well, it's probably better you've got one. At least it'll keep the temperature steady, particularly at night when it's a bit colder. Set it at twenty-five degrees and it'll keep for three or four hours. At full strength. It'll go on for about twelve, but it'll be a bit weak by then.'

'Three or four hours?' shouted Hildamay. 'That's no good. He'll still be here in the flat, asleep.'

'Well, you'll have to get rid of him. Or you could get hold of some culture medium. From a pharmaceutical suppliers. You can't just get it at a chemist.'

'You amaze me,' said Hildamay through gritted teeth.

'Really? Well, you have to separate the sperm from the semen. Then it'll keep for a week.'

'Perfect,' said Hildamay and hung up.

She was lying on the sofa, half asleep, when she heard the sound of a key in the front door. She sat upright and waited. She could hear Thomas crashing around in the dark hall shouting drunkenly, 'Where's the light? Where's the fucking light?' and Liz murmuring, 'Why don't we just go straight to the bedroom? Thomas? Thomas!' The door of the sitting room was flung open. Hildamay vaulted over the back of the sofa and inched her way under it.

'Let's sit in here,' said Thomas, 'and neck. I love necking. Makes me so horny.'

'No,' said Liz firmly. 'Let's go to bed, Thomas. Now. I can't wait.'

He laughed. 'Wild woman,' he said. 'Are you wild, woman? Come here.'

Hildamay felt the sofa give. Her nose was pressed against a wooden leg.

'You're so gorgeous,' said Thomas. The sofa bulged still further towards the floor. Hildamay lay trapped under the weight.

'Leth's go tho the –' said Liz, sounding as though she had something in her mouth. There was a loud sucking noise then a silence of sorts. A silence punctuated only by the click of teeth against teeth, the squeak of saliva against skin.

'So lovely,' said Thomas.

'Let's go and lie down,' pleaded Liz.

'Not yet. Give me your hand,' said Thomas. 'Here. Here. Oh yes, there.'

'Oh!' said Liz.

'Oh, good grief,' said Hildamay.

'Later,' said Liz.

'Lower,' said Thomas. 'Onhnhnhnhnhn.'

'The bedroom,' said Liz.

'Your breasts,' said Thomas. 'So beautiful.'

'Mmmmmmmmmm,' said Liz.
'Oh, no,' said Hildamay.
'This curve. So pretty. Nipples. So hard. So soft. Do you like that?' said Thomas.
'No,' said Hildamay.
'Stop,' said Liz.
'Please,' said Hildamay.
'I know, I know. Down here,' said Thomas. 'Like this?'
'Please,' said Liz.
'So wet,' said Thomas.
'No!' said Hildamay and grabbed Liz by the leg.
'Aaaagh!' said Liz.
'Did you come?' said Thomas. 'Oh, darling. Darling.'
The sofa bulged violently.
'No!' shouted Liz. 'Not yet!'
'Oh, dear,' said Thomas.
'Oh, shit,' said Hildamay.
There was a long, still silence. Then suddenly the weight of the sofa was no longer on her. They had gone.

Hildamay crawled out from under the sofa and sat cross-legged in the middle of the floor, waiting. Eventually Liz tiptoed into the room and sat down next to her.
'Sorry,' she mumbled, her head turned away.
'Glad to see the sperm bank's operational,' said Hildamay, after a while.
'Unhhh,' said Liz.
'Can he do it again?'
'He's only twenty-five,' muttered Liz defensively.
'I wasn't asking for his birth certificate. We need some sperm. It only lasts four hours.'
'You said sixteen!'
'I was wrong.'
'What are we going to do?'
'Fuck him and get rid of him.'
'I can't do that.'
'Why not?'
'It seems so – so unkind,' said Liz softly.
'OK. I'm going.'
'No!'

'Get rid of him.'

'Can't we let him sleep?' pleaded Liz.

'I thought he was just a donor,' said Hildamay crossly. 'Not a human being.'

'Don't be unkind. He's . . . he's . . . sweet,' said Liz defiantly.

'Well why don't you just fuck him and have a baby, then?'

'No!' said Liz. 'I'm sorry. I got carried away. I'll go in there now and get the sperm.'

'You're not milking a cow, Liz.'

'Shut up. I'll bring the condom out and you do whatever you have to do. Then, when he's asleep, I'll come back out again. And we'll, uh, do it.'

'Can't wait,' said Hildamay.

She was asleep when she felt something tugging at her shoulder. She opened her eyes to see a condom dangling in front of them.

'Eeeugh,' she said. 'It's all slimy.'

'Well, what did you expect?' hissed Liz. 'Tinsel and balls?'

'Only if it's Santa Claus you've got in there,' giggled Hildamay weakly.

'Take it!'

'Must I?' said Hildamay, gazing at the shrivelled bit of rubber in front of her nose.

'Take it!' hissed Liz.

'Some girls have all the fun,' said Hildamay and gingerly picked up the condom between finger and thumb. 'Why me?' she said as she walked towards the kitchen, her arm held stiffly in front of her.

Liz woke her again. The sitting room was bathed in a pale, pearly grey light.

'What time is it?' she mumbled.

'Five o'clock.'

'Five! That's four hours.'

'He wouldn't go back to sleep. I had to hear the story of his entire childhood. His adolescence. Why his father hates him. Why he loves his mother. I'm shattered.' Liz lay down next to Hildamay on the sofa.

'Get up. There's no time for this.'

'Tyrant.'

Hildamay went into the kitchen and got the champagne glass out of the incubator. Then she took the boiled syringe out of the pan and carefully filled it with the sperm. Liz was asleep.

'Wake up!' she hissed, handing her the syringe.

'What am I supposed to do with this?'

'Stick it up you and then empty it by pushing the top bit down.'

Liz undressed and knelt down on the floor. She put the syringe between her legs and tried to push in the plunger.

'It won't go. God, it's hard!'

'You wish. What do you mean, it won't go?'

'I can't get the angle right,' said Liz giggling.

'Act your age!' hissed Hildamay.

'I can't. You'll have to help me.'

'No chance.'

'Oh, Hildamay, please. I can't do it. It's getting late. Please!'

'Good grief,' said Hildamay and got down on the floor.

She had her hands between Liz's legs, who was lying naked on the carpet with her knees drawn up and her head pointing to the door, when Hildamay heard a noise. She looked up and in the grey light of dawn saw Thomas standing in the doorway. She was so startled she pushed the plunger violently down.

'Ouch!' said Liz.

'Oh my God!' said Thomas.

'It's not what you think,' said Hildamay as Thomas rushed out of the room. She pulled the syringe out of Liz, who struggled to get to her feet.

'Get down. I said get down! It won't work otherwise. No, Liz, don't.' She pushed Liz on to her back. 'Do a shoulder-stand. I said do a shoulder-stand! I'll take care of Thomas.' She ran into the bedroom. Thomas had a bundle of clothes in his arms.

'Get out of my way,' he said. His face was a livid, angry red.

'Thomas –' she said.

'I don't want to hear,' he said and, pushing her violently away from him, he rushed out of the room. She ran after him but he was already out of the front door and running down the corridor.

'It was perfectly innocent!' she yelled after his naked back. 'We were only playing mummies and daddies.'

CHAPTER TEN

'DO you really think you should?' said Ben, watching a spoonful of trifle heading towards Kate's mouth. Kate jerked her hand back. A quivering heap of raspberries, custard, cream and chocolate slid slowly from the spoon and fell with a dull splatter on the white damask tablecloth.

'Oh, Katie,' said Ben impatiently. 'Must you be so clumsy? It's the fat that does it, you know. It coats all the cells in the body. That's what makes you so slow and tired all the time. Disgusting, when you think about it; all those oily white molecules clustering around good red cells. I'm only saying it for your own good,' he added, slapping his lean midriff. 'Fat's so bad for your health. We have special low-calorie meals at the bank now. And a gym for all the staff. Amazing, the results. Output and productivity right up. You should see the change in the figures. Especially the female figures,' he said, laughing.

There was silence. Henry, who at nine was the eldest of the three children, ducked his head and gazed miserably at his trifle. Simon and Little Katie stared with hostility at their mother. Kate had not moved. She held her spoon at shoulder height above the table, and was staring at the drops of raspberry juice which were dripping on to the white tablecloth, staining it with tiny but perfect circles of brilliant pink. Dull red blotches of colour dappled her neck and cheeks.

'It's not so much a cottage,' said Hildamay into the silence, 'as a mansion. You've made it look so pretty, Katie. You have such a talent for these things.' Kate did not acknowledge her but stared mulishly ahead, the blotches on her cheeks now a livid red. Nobody else spoke.

Delilah sprang suddenly to her feet. 'I'll get a cloth,' she said, walking lithely across the big stone-floored kitchen to the sink. She was wearing tight white jeans and a black, scooped-neck fitted T-shirt. Her feet were bare save for a coat of lustrous scarlet polish, gleaming on each perfectly shaped toenail. They sat in silence and watched her walk across the room, her shiny dark hair swinging in time to the motion of her hips. She bent to look in the cupboard under the sink and, legs apart, presented her perfectly shaped bottom. After searching for some time, she put her head between her legs and called through to them, 'Terrible mess in here, Katie. Where did you say you kept the cloth?'

'I didn't,' said Kate. Her voice was thick.

'What?' shouted Delilah.

'I didn't,' repeated Kate as she pulled herself up from the table. A splotch of colour had travelled up from her cheek and settled over her eye, giving her a curiously rakish look. Her blouse was too tight and through it showed the outline of her bra. It cut into the flesh which bulged out on either side then settled in two quivering rolls above the waistband of her skirt, the zipper of which was broken and held together with safety pins. Her fat, pale legs were bare and stubbled with dark hair and on her feet was a pair of battered old leather shoes, the heels trodden down to expose raw, red blisters. She shuffled across the kitchen and stood over Delilah, who was still bent over the cupboard. Ben watched the two of them, a curious half smile on his face.

'It's right at the back,' said Kate. Delilah stooped lower and pushed the upper part of her body into the cupboard.

'No, further,' insisted Kate. 'You'll have to get down on your hands and knees. It's to the right.'

They waited and watched in silence. Suddenly, Delilah screamed and reversed out of the cupboard on her hands and knees, banging her head. She got to her feet, her face red with effort, the knees of her clean white jeans scuffed with dirt. She had torn her T-shirt.

'Disgusting,' she spat vehemently.

'What?' asked Kate, her eyes round with innocence.

Delilah held up her hand which was covered in a thick coating of dirty green slime.

'Oh!' said Kate. 'Did I say right? I'm so sorry. I meant to say left. I haven't cleaned at the right yet. There's years of dirt and damp back there. Horrid, isn't it?' she asked sympathetically.

Ben walked over and put his arm round Delilah's shoulders.

'Are you all right? Nasty, was it?' he crooned as if talking to a small child. Taking Delilah's hand he held it under the tap and washed it for her, lathering soap over her fingers and massaging them with his. 'It's disgusting, Katie,' he said over his shoulder. 'Leaving stuff like that in the back of a kitchen cupboard.'

'It's an old house and we've only been here a few weeks. I haven't had time to get to that lot yet,' said Kate quietly, scrubbing viciously at the stain on the tablecloth. 'Nothing wrong with a bit of good, honest dirt. Or fat,' she added under her breath.

'Can I have your trifle if you're not going to eat it?' said Hildamay, reaching for Delilah's untouched plate but watching Kate's tears drip on to the stained tablecloth.

Ben had finally finished drying Delilah's hand. 'I think I'll take Delilah for a walk round the garden. Steady her nerves,' he shouted as the two of them walked out of the kitchen door. It slammed behind them.

'Are you OK?' asked Hildamay, putting her hand on Kate's arm.

Kate pulled it away. 'Why shouldn't I be?' she said, clearing away the dirty plates and pulling the tablecloth off the table.

Hildamay lay on her back and sighed with pleasure. All she could see was the sky which was tinged with coral and faint white streaks, like the ghost of chalk on a blackboard. It was a perfect evening; the air was soft and fresh, charged with a sense of expectation. She pressed her head back against the springy grass and stretched her arms in a circle, feeling with her fingertips for the leaves which marked the perimeter of her hiding place. It was a perfect little grotto, marked at the edge by small heaps of charred twigs. She supposed the children must have made it their private place. They were indoors with Kate, having their supper. Ben and Delilah had gone off to the pub.

Hildamay thought suddenly of Sky and wondered if she would like this place. She thought of her often, as she had last seen her, her hand outstretched, a little, solemn look on her face. 'I have always depended on the kindness of strangers.' She sensed that Sky had need of kindness, and thought of her in that chill house with that thin, cold woman and shivered slightly. She wondered about the mother, pictured her dancing, drunk, around the house, then gave up trying to put a face to her and fell again to wondering about Sky. It was strange, the way in which the child had affected her. She felt, again, that same sharp longing she had felt, sitting on the tube, to put her arms around the thin shoulders and hug her until she smiled. Well, she reasoned, I shall probably never see her again, and so she put Sky from her mind and thought instead about Delilah, wondering why she had suddenly turned up at the cottage late the evening before. As she pondered, she heard Ben's voice.

'It's fine. They're all inside,' he said soothingly. 'Don't worry, nobody will see us.'

Delilah was giggling.

'You like that, don't you?' said Ben. 'Just there. And there. And there. And here.' He let out a small groan. 'I thought we'd never get away,' he said. 'I've been looking at you all day. I kept getting an erection and having to hide it. It's stiff as a board. Feel it,' he panted.

Hildamay supposed they must be immediately to her left, around the back of the summer house. She waited for five minutes. She doubted whether Ben was much of a man for preliminaries. Then she got up and walked towards the place she thought they must be standing.

Delilah was naked from the waist down, her T-shirt pulled up to expose her breasts. She had her eyes closed and her back supported by the summer-house wall, her legs wrapped around Ben's hips. Ben's trousers were around his ankles; his white buttocks jerked spasmodically.

'Nice evening,' said Hildamay conversationally.

Delilah opened her eyes and snapped her head back, cracking it against the wall. Ben dropped her and turned to run, forgetting that his trousers were tangled around his ankles. He fell face-first into a rose bush and screamed in pain then scrambled out, blood running from the scratches on his face. Delilah was lying in a heap, dazed, against the summer house. Hildamay walked over to her and sat down and the two of them watched Ben rolling on the grass, wrestling with his trousers. Eventually he pulled them up, stuffed his shirt into them and half fastened his flies, leaving a tail of fabric hanging out of them.

'Ben,' called Hildamay as he started to hurry away from them. 'Your cock's turned blue.' He stopped, startled, his hands flying protectively to his penis. In silence he unzipped his flies, stuffed the shirt back in, and moved at a half run in the direction of the house.

Delilah made no move to dress but lay half naked on the grass, staring mutely at the place where Ben had been.

'I wondered why you were here,' said Hildamay. 'Kate never seemed quite your type. Well, at least you're consistent. Consistently cruel.' Delilah did not speak. 'Oh, for God's sake, put your trousers on,' said Hildamay eventually. 'You look ridiculous.'

Delilah sighed and got up to look for her jeans. She wandered listlessly around for some time before she found them and pulled them on. Hildamay noticed that she wore no underwear and that she had perfect breasts.

'Bitch,' she said quietly.

Delilah started but still did not speak.

'You could have walked away. Pretended not to know,' she said, after some time. She did not look at Hildamay.

'Yes. I could.'

'Then why didn't you?'

'I don't know.'

'Hateful,' said Delilah.

'Who?'

'Because now it's dirty. Dirtied.'

'It always would have been. Eventually.'

'No. I love him,' said Delilah. 'I love him,' she said again, her voice heavy with tears, and she turned to look at Hildamay. Her face was twisted, as if in pain. Hildamay stared at her with astonishment.

'Oh, Delilah,' she said, inspecting her friend's face closely. 'How could you?'

'I don't know what to do.' Delilah's face crumpled. 'I don't know what to do.' She buried her head in her arms and sobbed.

Hildamay made no movement but, as the sobs increased in anguish and volume, she eventually leaned over and patted her clumsily on the head. 'I'm sorry,' she said. Eventually Delilah looked up. Her pale skin was tinged with pink across her high, sculpted cheekbones and her eyes, glittering with tears, shone. Her mouth was swollen and reddened with kissing. Hildamay was momentarily irritated by her beauty. She wondered, briefly, why physical perfection was so mesmeric.

'Why are you sorry?' asked Delilah, suddenly curious.

'Pain makes me sorry.'

Delilah looked away.

'You could stop the pain,' said Hildamay eventually. 'You don't need him. Kate does.'

'So do I,' said Delilah harshly.

'You have Ned.'

Delilah sighed, a long drawn-out breath. 'I don't love Ned,' she said quietly.

They watched a butterfly float like a dry leaf, borne aloft by a warm current of air, tossed to and fro across the crushed rose bush.

'Why choose Ben?' said Hildamay in exasperation. 'It will make you unhappy. Unhappier still,' she amended.

Delilah shrugged. 'He makes me feel alive.'

Hildamay looked at her curiously. 'Do you need pain to know that you live?'

'No. Yes,' said Delilah softly.

'I don't understand.'

'No.'

'But, Delilah,' said Hildamay in exasperation, 'all three of you. All three in pain. You'll all be unhappy.'

'That's not unusual.'

'But it needn't be. Not if you stop it now. I thought you were supposed to know about these things,' exclaimed Hildamay.

'What things?' said Delilah sharply.

'Love, pain, happiness, misery.'

'Hildamay?'

'Yes?'

'Grow up.'

There was silence.

'What? Like you?'

Delilah laughed. A sharp, hard laugh that carried no expression of joy.

'No,' she said. 'Not like me.'

They sat together, their backs warm against the stone of the summer house, as the light faded and gloom settled like dust over the garden. Hildamay watched the leaves leaking their brilliance into the evening, all their greens softening to the colour of old silk velvet. Delilah sighed occasionally with the hoarse, exhausted gasps of a person who has not yet cried enough. Hildamay patted her hand distractedly. She thought about pain, but felt only exasperation. She thought about the three of them, about Delilah, Ben and Kate, but could picture them only in isolation. She saw only their deliberate, almost wilful desire to hurt one another – which she supposed was part of their pleasure. Even Kate, Kate who participated by silent consent. Hildamay longed suddenly for the quiet and solitude of her bathroom; for the shining bottles and pots of lotions and their cool, clean, soothing scents. She imagined herself in the white tiled room. She saw the sharp gleam of glass and chrome and felt towels, clean and rough on her skin. But more than anything she longed for the hard, cold, solitude of the place.

Still, she was curious, and from time to time glanced at Delilah, who stared into the gloom of the garden as if she were waiting for something. Sometimes an errant tear slipped down her face but she did not stir.

'Delilah,' said Hildamay, her voice strange in the stillness, 'can you not stop this?'

'No.'

'But it seems so foolish.' Hildamay hesitated. 'To go on when you know there is only suffering there.'

'But I am here. There is only forward. I can't go back.'

'Why?' exclaimed Hildamay in fury.

Delilah looked at her, her pale face shining through the fading light. 'Have your bones and your blood never screamed out for need of someone?' Her voice was thin and wispy, as faint as an echo.

'No.'

'Then be kind and shut up,' she whispered.

Hildamay thought about screaming blood but only felt hers bubble gently through her veins.

Delilah stood up. 'I think it's supper time,' she said in a normal voice.

Kate met them at the kitchen door.

'There you are!' she said, her round face beaming. 'We were about to send out a search party. Come and have a drink. Ben's going to open a bottle of champagne.' She threw an arm around each of the women's shoulders and drew them into the warmth of the lighted, cheerful kitchen. She was wearing an old navy blue silk dressing gown. The front gaped open to reveal a slip of dirty white lace, and the dark crevice of her abundant cleavage. Her fine hair was bundled haphazardly on her head, wisps of it floating and curling around her flushed, happy face. She looked almost pretty.

'Darling!' she called. 'Darling, the girls are back!'

Hildamay and Delilah blinked, their eyes unused to the clattering light after the silent, perfumed gloom of the garden. Ben was lolling in an over-stuffed armchair. As they came in he sat bolt upright on the edge of his chair and looked at Delilah with the abashed, apologetic air of a little boy who has done something wrong. Delilah squinted at him and at Kate and then stiffened.

'Benny's got some bubbles for you,' trilled Kate. 'Haven't you, darling?' she said, going over to him and stroking his hair. He made a gesture, as if to get up. 'No, no, darling. Don't you move. I'll do it!'

She bustled around the kitchen, smiling and chattering, collecting glasses and pouring out a glass of champagne for each of them. Delilah did not move but stood staring at Ben.

'Isn't this lovely!' said Kate. 'Just the four of us. All such good friends.'

'Friends,' echoed Delilah, taking a glass from her.

'Are you all right, Delilah?' asked Kate sympathetically. 'You're terribly quiet. Have you got a headache?'

'Yes,' said Delilah faintly. 'A headache.'

'It's all that wine we had at lunch. I had a headache earlier, too,' said Kate, giggling. 'But it's gone now, hasn't it, Benny?'

Ben looked away and flushed, his mouth crooked with embarrassment. The women stared at him. Nobody spoke.

'Well, I'll go and get you some aspirins,' said Kate eventually. They heard the slow, heavy tread of her footsteps as she climbed the wooden stairs.

'Bastard,' hissed Delilah.

'She was suspicious!' protested Ben. 'I had to do something.'

'Bastard,' repeated Delilah.

'Delilah!' said Ben, beseeching. 'Darling!' he added in an undertone, trying to reach across the table and take her hand. 'You know it doesn't mean anything. You know it doesn't!' he implored as Delilah pulled her hand away.

'Bastard,' she said, refusing to look at him. A tear slid down her face.

'Oh, don't, darling, please don't,' whispered Ben urgently.

'You said you never made love to her. Never!' exclaimed Delilah to her plate.

Hildamay stared at him.

'What are you staring at?' he demanded in a hoarse whisper.

Hildamay said nothing but continued to look at him.

'Oh, just look at little Miss Perfect,' he said, his voice low. 'Look at her, Delilah. Sitting there, holier than thou. She wouldn't do something nasty like fuck somebody else's husband, would she, Delilah?' His eyes glittered. He turned to look at Delilah who was still staring fixedly at her plate. He jerked his head in irritation and glared venomously at Hildamay.

'Never felt the urge, have you, Hildamay? Never felt the urge for a piece of married cock? Or has it never felt the urge for you? Wouldn't be able to penetrate that cool exterior. You've never been trapped in the heat of emotion, have you? Have you?' he demanded, his voice rising. 'Love is an emotion, Hildamay. It's hot and it's hard and it takes you by surprise. You don't choose it. It chooses you. But at least it's normal.' He laughed suddenly, a sharp, bitter sound. 'Never heard of normal, have you, Hildamay? You never get involved in anything normal and nasty like a bit of human contact, do you, Hildamay? Do you?' He had started to shout, his face red with exasperation and guilt.

'Does she what?' said Kate from the doorway.

'Ben was just asking me if I liked to fuck,' said Hildamay, staring at him.

Kate giggled. 'Oh, everyone likes to do that, don't they, Benny?' she cooed, pulling his head back to nestle against her large breasts. He jerked his head forward, leaving her standing behind him, her arms still outstretched, a look of confusion on her face.

'Anyone who's normal,' he said mutinously.

Kate looked down at his head and then across at Hildamay.

'Hildamay, why are you staring at Ben like that?'

'He's got spinach in his teeth.'

'Has he!' Kate laughed with delight. 'Oh, darling, you're such a messy boy. Let me look.'

'No!' said Ben, pushing her roughly away as he scraped his chair back from the table. 'I'll do it myself. I'm going to the bathroom.' He stormed out of the room.

'Wash your mouth out with soap,' called Hildamay after him. 'Gets rid of all those nasty, clinging bits.'

'Does it?' said Kate, looking interested. Then she stared down at the table at the remains of their dinner. 'But we didn't have any spinach.' There was silence. 'Oh, well,' she said brightly, 'must have been the parsley.' She looked across the table at the two women. 'Well, you're a couple of bright sparks tonight.' Delilah groaned and put her hands to her head. 'Oh, Delilah, I'm sorry! Your aspirins. Here you are. They'll make you feel better in no time. And you haven't eaten a thing. Would you like to lie down? Yes, come along. There's a good girl. I've got a bed all made up for you upstairs. You'll be much more comfortable there. It's this heat and the wine. You're probably exhausted. You work too hard, you know. All those problems. All that misery you have to deal with day after day.' She led Delilah out of the room, her arm around her shoulders.

Ben walked back into the kitchen.

'You still here?' he said harshly.

'I'm afraid so. Ruining your cosy little *ménage à trois*.'

'Oh, shut up. It's not like that. It's. . . . Oh, you wouldn't understand.'

'No,' said Hildamay. 'I wouldn't.'

'Ever tried three in a bed, Hildamay? You never know, you might like it.'

'I prefer my pleasure concentrated,' said Hildamay mildly. 'Anyway, I thought three in a marriage was more your style.'

'Oh, leave me alone,' groaned Ben, sinking into a chair.

'It would be a pleasure.'

He looked at her. 'Will you tell Kate?'

'Tell Kate what?'

'You know. About Delilah.'

'Why should I?'

'Why shouldn't you?' he said sharply.

'Other people's affairs don't interest me.'

'Other people don't interest you,' he said, closing his eyes.

'Some do.'

'But not me?' he said, opening his eyes and looking at her. In his glance was both curiosity and hope.

'No.'

'Bitch,' he said and shut his eyes again.

Hildamay got up and went to look for her handbag. When she returned to the kitchen Ben was still sitting slumped in the armchair, his eyes closed. She looked at him closely for a minute.

'Tell Kate I had to go.'

He looked up at her. 'It's dark and lonely out there,' he said, his handsome face suddenly lit by a smile.

'That's the way I like it.'
His face darkened. 'You would.'
'Yes.'
'She'll be unhappy.'
'Then make her happy.'
He looked suddenly tired. 'I'll try.'
'Good.'
'Kiss me goodbye?' he asked, smiling again.
'Goodbye,' she said and walked out of the house into the night.

'George,' said Hildamay on Monday morning. 'This week I'm disappearing.'

'From here?' he asked. 'Or from there?' He jerked his head at the window.

'From there. I'm in a meeting all week.'

'Would you like to talk about it?'

'Not unless you can tell me why people cause each other pain.'

George looked at her in silence, his head cocked to one side. 'No. No, I can't tell you that,' he said, after a while.

'Then there is nothing to say.'

'No.' He walked to the door of her office and then stopped. 'Miss Smith?'

'Yes?'

'Pain is not always bad.' He hesitated. 'Sometimes it brings life.'

Hildamay looked at his round, kind, shining face for a long time. Then she turned away.

'I'm in a meeting, George.'

CHAPTER ELEVEN

HILDAMAY sat up in bed, picked up the magnifying mirror, looked at her face and frowned. She put it down again, pulled the covers over her head and sat, hugging her knees. She had spoken to nobody for two weeks. Not even Liz who, undeterred by Hildamay's silence, called with regular progress reports of her pregnancy.

'Now for today's baby bulletin. At fifteen hundred hours GMT on this the third day of the month the limb buds are clearly distinguishable as arms and legs,' said her voice echoing through the answering machine. 'Or at least, that's what the book says. The heart has started to beat and the brain is coming along fine. Have you started reading the Bible yet? You've got six months to get through it. I threw up three times today. Just thought you might like to know. Bye.'

'Hi, it's me. Junior's now three centimetres long and weighs approximately two grammes. The eyes are fully developed and a nose has now appeared. I'm feeling great although I get quite tired. The consultant says I'm a fine specimen although he seems to think

I'm ancient. He keeps calling me an elderly primagravida. He's about two years old.' A sigh of irritation hissed through the machine. 'How long are you going to hide for this time? I do wish you'd come out, Hildamay. The kid wants to take a look at you now it's got eyes to see. I hate this bloody machine. Goodbye.'

Delilah had called every other day. There were five messages on the answering machine. 'Call me sometime,' was all she said in her cool, quiet voice. She did not ask for help, nor did she demand forgiveness. Hildamay wondered if she wanted either. Forgiveness, anyway, was not hers to give and, as to help, she did not know how. Hildamay sat under the tent of her bedcover and sighed. She needed one of George's nice hot drinks. She did not get up to make one but rocked gently in her bed.

Delilah liked men who treated her badly. 'It's my weakness,' she admitted. Dan, with whom she'd had a relationship for ten years – 'if you can call it that,' said Hildamay gloomily to the underside of her quilt – was an emotional sadist but the more badly he behaved, the more Delilah seemed to love him. It was Dan, or rather Delilah's response to Dan, that had sent her into therapy. After two years in analysis, she decided to become a psychologist. And as she embraced psychology, so she abandoned Dan, much to Dan's surprise.

'You are unkind, Delilah,' said Hildamay. 'You've just destroyed that man's whole philosophy of life. What's he to do now that the one tenet he held to be true has been proved invalid?'

'I offered him discount,' said Delilah.

Hildamay thought about the lover who had told her, with a smile on his face, that women liked men who treated them badly.

'We're only having an affair,' said Hildamay. 'Just a tiny little enjoyable affair. Can't we have a good time instead?'

'But it's true,' he protested. 'Women love it. I'll prove it.'

'Not with me, you won't,' said Hildamay, and left him there and then. At first he had not taken her seriously but then, to her horror, became obsessed with her. He left flowers strewn on her front door step, rang her at all hours of the night, sent telegrams and letters. One night he appeared at her door, weeping, a bottle of whisky and a bunch of deep red roses clutched in his hand.

'Oh, go away,' she said. He stood there, whimpering. 'I thought it was women who liked to be treated badly,' she added crossly.

'It's OK, Hildamay, it's all right. I give up. You've proved your point.'

'What point?' she asked, bemused.

'That you won't put up with being treated badly.'

'I wasn't making a point.'

'I understand,' he said, opening his arms wide as if to receive her in a forgiving embrace. 'I understand,' he said, smiling. 'Come here. I love you.'

'Are you mad?'

'Aren't we all, a little?'

'Oh, good grief,' exclaimed Hildamay in exasperation and beat him with the roses.

She told Delilah, who merely shrugged and said, 'Well, what did you expect?'

'I expected him to understand plain English when I told him I didn't want to see him again.'

'He probably thought you were just saying that.'

'I was saying just that.'

'No, you idiot. He thought it was a mating ritual. A game.'

'I don't play games.'

'Well, how's he supposed to know that? You'd already discussed the rules.'

'And I told him I didn't want to play.'

'Well, he thought you did. People often say no when they mean yes. They play games with each other all the time.'

'And life's a ball, I suppose.'

'No. Life's a bitch.'

'Do you like your job, Delilah?'

'I do it, don't I?'

Sunshine streamed into the room, patterning the carpet with squares of buttery yellow light. Hildamay sat on the edge of her bed, looked out of the window and for a time admired the pale, fresh green of leaves silhouetted against the blue of the sky. She felt suddenly cheerful and decided to go out and buy some deep blue irises to put in her apricot ceramic vase. No, cream tulips. Fat, luscious, blowsy, double cream tulips. 'Delicious,' she said and went singing into the kitchen.

'Life's a bitch,' she sang as she waited for the kettle to boil, 'and ain't that right. But if there weren't no hitch, it wouldn't be –' She was trying to decide what rhymed with right and at the same time admiring her pyjamas, which were soft white cotton poplin piped in navy blue, when the telephone rang.

'Hello, this is the residence of Miss Hildamay Smith and this is a recorded message,' she said into the telephone. 'Miss Smith is unable –'

'Oh, dear,' said a small voice. 'And I've got no more money.' There was a slight sigh. 'Well, I'll have to call again, I suppose?' it added dubiously.

'Who's that?' asked Hildamay. The voice sounded familiar but it was very high, like a child's.

'Oh! You're not a machine at all,' said the voice accusingly. There was a pause. 'It's Sky Matthews.' There was another pause, longer this time. 'You said it was all right for me to telephone you?' she added hesitantly.

'Quite all right,' said Hildamay slowly, surprised by the pleasure she felt at hearing Sky's voice.

'I wondered if I could come and see you? It's just . . . it's just that I need some advice on something and –'

The small voice tailed off. Hildamay waited patiently. 'And?' she prompted eventually.

'And – well, I thought you might know, you see.'

'Well, I might,' said Hildamay doubtfully. 'I won't really know until you ask me, will I?' she added and waited, expectant. There was silence. 'I see,' she said after a while. 'Well, when would you like to come and see me?'

'Today?'

Hildamay said nothing.

'If that's all right,' Sky hurried on, 'because I could always come another time. If you're busy. I mean, if you don't have time.'

'Today is fine.'

There was silence.

'Sky? I said today is fine.'

'Oh, good.' Sky's voice lightened. 'Where shall I meet you?'

'Get the tube to King's Cross St Pancras and when you get there, go up to St Pancras main-line station and stand by the main ticket office and I shall come and get you. At three o'clock.'

'Three o'clock,' repeated Sky. 'By the ticket office.'

'Goodbye, Sky.'
'Goodbye, Hildamay.'

Sky stood by the ticket office. Hildamay stood, some distance away, and watched her. She was wearing the same khaki nylon jacket which she kept, stored in a plastic bag, in Haadji's shop, and which Hildamay noticed suddenly was much too big for her. The knitted cuffs were folded back so many times over the quilted lining that they formed lumpy bracelets around her thin wrists. Her baseball cap was pulled low over her eyes and she stared down at the ground while she kicked at it with her trainers; first the toe, then the heel, then the toe, in an impatient but deliberate rhythm. She looked very small and, Hildamay thought suddenly, very lonely, a thought which caused her to hurry across the station. She had almost reached her when Sky looked up, peering out from beneath the peaked brim of her cap.

'Hello,' she said, smiling shyly.

'Hello,' said Hildamay, stumbling to a halt some feet away and feeling suddenly awkward. How do you talk to children? she wondered in a moment of fleeting panic. Children had always seemed to her like an alien race, and this child seemed utterly foreign; a disconcerting mixture of childish vulnerability and adult reserve. Sky stopped smiling. She had about her that curious manner which marries aggression with diffidence; a manner which ordinarily comes only with experienced pain. Hildamay looked at her in silence for a few minutes. She looked so self-contained and yet so defenceless that Hildamay did not know whether to step forward and hug her or to hold out her hand. She felt nervous; Sky's pink mouth was a firm adult line in the round, childish face and her blue eyes were wide with excitement, yet wary. Eventually Hildamay held out her hand, as one does to a timid animal, and when Sky did not flinch or step away she raised her hand still further and pushed Sky's baseball cap back off her face with an affectionate, gentle, fumbling gesture.

'So I can see your face properly,' she explained.

Sky frowned and looked at her curiously for a moment. Then, with a sudden, brilliant smile, she readjusted the cap so it sat properly on the back of her head and took Hildamay's hand.

'I'm very happy to see you again,' she said in a quiet, pleased voice.

'Me too,' said Hildamay, reassured by the feel of the small hand in hers. Relaxing, her nervousness quite forgotten, she smiled down at Sky and they stood for a few minutes gazing at one another in pleasure.

'I suppose we should go somewhere so we can talk?' said Hildamay.

Sky shrugged, a slight, contemptuous gesture which seemed to say that the question she had come to ask Hildamay was not so important after all, and that all that was important was that Hildamay was there.

'What do you usually do on a Saturday afternoon?' Sky demanded suddenly.

'I go down to Portobello. To the market, to buy food and flowers.'

'Food?' asked Sky, bemused.

'I like food.'

Sky smiled at her. 'Well, that's what we'll do, then,' she said in an amused, affectionate voice which caused Hildamay to wonder for a moment who was the child and who the adult. And when Sky added, her tone firm, 'We'll talk on the way,' she wondered even more.

The market was very busy so Hildamay held Sky's hand tightly as they threaded their way through the crowds. Sky stopped whenever she saw something that interested her, which was frequently. Hildamay kept looking down to see that she was all right. She was worried that she might get trodden on or whisked away by a surge of people. She did seem very small. Sky, however, appeared utterly unconcerned. It was a very warm day; the sun, trapped behind a wall of cloud, made the sky glow a dense, leaden white and the heat pressed down on them like a weight. Sky's nose was peppered by a faint beading of sweat, her cheeks very flushed.

'Do you want to take off your jacket?' asked Hildamay.

'Of course not,' said Sky quickly, her hands creeping protectively to the zip at the neck of her jacket.

'It just seems rather hot,' explained Hildamay.

'Hot?' echoed Sky stupidly.

'Hot,' said Hildamay firmly. Sky shrugged and suddenly jerked the baseball cap back down over her eyes, staring down at the ground, shifting miserably from one foot to the other. Hildamay watched her in surprise and then sighed, wishing she understood children better. Then she wondered why she wished she understood children better or, rather, this child in particular. Why should this child affect her so strongly? She gazed speculatively at the top of Sky's head. Even her baseball cap looked unhappy and Hildamay watched it in silence for some time before it suddenly dawned on her that the cap and the jacket were Sky's protection; her talismans against the child her grandmother wanted her to be. And whom she obviously hated. Making her take off her cap and jacket was like insisting another child strip naked.

'Actually,' she said, taking Sky's hand, 'I think you're right about the jacket. It's suddenly got much cooler.' And with her other hand, she pushed back the baseball cap so it was once more sitting on the back of Sky's head.

Sky looked up at her and shrugged again but she left the cap where Hildamay had pushed it and where it balanced precariously, bunched over the knot of her pony tail. Only when they stopped to buy some vegetables and she thought that Hildamay's attention was distracted did Hildamay notice her surreptitiously tug it into place.

'Thought you'd left me, love,' said the man on the flower stall as Hildamay picked out a huge bunch of tulips. 'Thought you'd gone off and bloody left me for some other bloke with a bigger show.'

'Bloody ought to,' said Hildamay, smiling. 'The prices you charge. What kind of mortgage do I need for those?' she added, pointing at a tub of delphiniums.

'Precious as gold dust this time of year,' he said, shaking out a bunch of deep blue spires and presenting them to her with a flourish. 'But I'll let you have them for a tenner.'

'Don't be daft,' said Hildamay and gave him a fiver. He shrugged good-naturedly and added the delphiniums to the pile of tulips and irises. 'Give us another fiver, girl, that makes a tenner for the lot, and we'll call it a day.'

Hildamay searched around in her bag for the money while he waited patiently, the bunch of flowers cradled tenderly in his huge hands. 'Pretty girl, your daughter,' he said. Hildamay looked up at him in surprise. 'Pretty,' he repeated, nodding his head in Sky's direction. 'Though why you let her run around in that gear beats me. Pretty girl like that. Seems a shame.'

'Like a girl in a frock, do you?' said Hildamay, taking her flowers.

'Flowers, frocks, girls. Make the world go round,' he said, grinning.

'There's a theory it's flat,' said Hildamay.

'What?'

'The world.'

'Well, if they all ran around dressed like that,' he said, jerking his head over at Sky again, 'it would be. Flat, I mean. Stands to reason, don't it?'

Hildamay laughed.

'Give her these, will you, love?' he said, handing her a small bunch of anemones. 'Pretty flowers for a pretty girl.'

Sky was standing staring at a group of Rastafarians, who sat on the pavement outside the pub, drinking beer out of cans and laughing and singing in their rich, dark voices.

'Hey, man!' they called when they saw her watching them, 'you want some beer?'

Sky flushed and shook her head but she did not look away.

'You want to come and sit with us, man?' called one who wore a scarlet wool knitted hat. She did not move. 'That's a cool cap, man, a very cool cap. The coolest, man!' called another, who also wore a baseball cap, but it was orange and very big, being full of hair. Sky touched her hand slowly to the peak of her cap and smiled shyly. 'What yo'all called?' shouted another.

'Sky,' called Sky, in a clear high voice.

'Man.' They whistled in unison. 'Now ain't that the coolest name?'

Sky blushed and smiled and continued to examine them steadfastly. 'Can I feel your hair?' she asked eventually.

'Man!' exclaimed the one with the red knitted hat. 'That's the best offer we had all day. Having our hair stroked by a lady!'

Sky smiled and then inched forwards with her hand outstretched. He pulled off his hat and, shaking his head, tumbled his hair into her outstretched palm.

'It's hard!' she exclaimed, patting at it gently.

'Hard!' he echoed. 'Of course it's hard, man. We're hard men!' At which the group burst into wild cackles of laughter and whistles while Sky stood among them, watching them with grave blue eyes.

'Hey, Sky. Sorry. Sky!' said one of them, catching sight of her face, and they all fell silent and smiling.

'Thank you very much,' she said politely, looking around at them. And then she looked up and caught sight of Hildamay. 'I have to go now,' she said. 'I might come and see you next week.'

'We'll look forward to it, man,' said the one who wore the red hat, bowing in a fluid, gracious movement.

Hildamay stood some distance away, watching this exchange. Sky ran over to her, smiling eagerly. 'They're my friends,' she said, in explanation.

'Good,' said Hildamay, examining her curiously. She wondered why a child with such an obvious propensity for making friends, for inspiring affection and sympathy, should strike her as so singularly lonely.

'These are for you,' she said, handing Sky the bunch of anemones.

'For me?' repeated Sky, gazing at them in astonishment.

'From the man at the flower stall,' said Hildamay, shaking the bunch gently at her.

'Why?'

'He thinks you're my daughter,' said Hildamay, before she could stop herself. Why had she told her that? Sky looked at her carefully, but in her eyes was a bright eagerness. 'Do you mind?' she asked cautiously. Hildamay shrugged, indifferent. Sky turned away. 'I don't want the flowers,' she said in a small voice.

They left the market and caught the bus to Bloomsbury. Sky sat in the seat next to the window, her face averted as she watched the people passing by. Hildamay watched the soft curve of her cheek and the way her hair grew in a fine, clean line, from her temple where the skin was creamy, traced faintly with blue veins, then up around her ear to dissolve in a faint gold fuzz at the nape of her neck. It looked so vulnerable, her neck, that Hildamay sighed and wondered what she should have said. That she would have liked to have been her mother? Sky sensed the sigh and, turning slightly, said, 'How do you find divorced people?'

'Who?' asked Hildamay.

'My father.' She sighed suddenly. 'Maybe he might want me,' she said in a voice low with doubt. 'He gave me my name.'

'Your name?'

'Sky. It's a stupid name, isn't it?' She turned to Hildamay and grimaced. 'A really stupid name. That's what they all say at school. But I like it,' she added stoutly. 'Because Blanche says he gave it to me so I'd have something to reach for. Although she doesn't think that'll make much difference.' She looked up at Hildamay. 'Blanche says that the world is a hopeless place.'

Hildamay considered this for a moment. 'An optimistic view,' she said drily. 'Can't you ask her? Where he is, I mean?'

Sky shrugged. 'She doesn't know.'

'Your grandmother?'

Sky turned away and looked out of the window again. 'She says he was a bad man,' she whispered. Her shoulders sagged. 'I don't even know what his name is,' she added mournfully. 'Matthews – it's not even his name.'

Hildamay sat in silence, watching Sky's neck. She put out a hand and stroked it gently. Sky did not move.

'So you don't know how to find divorced people?' she said finally.

'No,' said Hildamay sadly. 'I'm afraid I don't.'

Sky heard the sadness and turned her head. 'It's all right,' she said, smiling reassuringly. 'It was just a thought.'

They sat in Hildamay's yellow kitchen. Sky wandered around examining everything minutely. When she had picked up everything in the room, turned it over, looked at it and put it down carefully, she sat down and said, with a satisfied sigh, 'I like it here. It's nice. Nice colours.'

'Nice colours?'

'Yes,' said Sky, pointing at the yellow glazed walls and then at the apricot vase in which Hildamay was carefully arranging the tulips. 'Nice colours.' She gazed solemnly at the flowers. 'Hildamay?'

'Yes?'

'Are those flowers living or dying?'

Hildamay looked at them hard. Then she looked at Sky.

'They're dying.'

'Oh.' There was silence.

'Hildamay, do you like flowers?'

'Yes.'
'Well, if you like flowers, why do you let them die?'
Hildamay just looked at her.

They sat at the table drinking tea and eating Garibaldi biscuits. Sky had chosen them because she liked the name.
'They're a bit disappointing,' she said, picking at the raisins.
'We used to call them squashed fly biscuits.'
Sky giggled. 'Why?'
'Well, look at them.'
'Maybe they're not so disappointing,' she said. She put one in her mouth and buzzed like a fly. Hildamay laughed so Sky buzzed louder.
'What's Blanche look like?' asked Hildamay when the buzzing had quietened.
'She's got blonde hair. Not like yours. Hers is whiter and stiff.'
'Stiff?'
'Yes, it's sort of hard.'
'Oh.'
'She's very pretty, though,' said Sky wistfully. Hildamay said nothing.
'But she's not like a proper mother.'
'What are proper mothers like?'
'She doesn't do housework or anything. She just listens to music and writes letters or something. She doesn't come and get me from school, either. And she doesn't cook my supper. Grandmother does that. She says she's too young to be a mother. She hates being called mother. She likes people to think we're sisters.'
'Does she work?'
'Oh, no.'
'Oh.'
Sky looked up at her.
'Can I go and look at your books now?'
'Sure.'
Sky got down from the table, walked over to the sink and washed her hands and face. Then she disappeared into the sitting room. Hildamay stayed in the kitchen, where she listened to the radio and chopped vegetables. She was making soup. She made a huge pot every weekend. This Saturday it was roasted pepper with saffron mayonnaise. It was an American recipe.

Sky reappeared. In her hands she was clutching a book, *The Rituals of Death*.

'An interesting choice,' said Hildamay.

'It has pictures in it. I'd like to go to Italy and see the graves,' said Sky, flicking through the pages of the book and stopping at a particularly lurid illustration of a tomb. 'They're so pretty. They have flowers in little vases sticking out of the wall. They seem to bury people standing up. I thought you had to die lying down.'

'I don't suppose it matters much. Once you're dead, that is.'

'Where do I go when I die?'

Oh, no, thought Hildamay. How the fuck do I know? She went on chopping vegetables.

'Into a tomb, I suppose,' she said eventually.

'I know that,' said Sky scathingly. 'But where do I *go*. Where does *me* go?'

Hildamay said nothing but put some olive oil in a heavy pan and scooped in the finely chopped garlic and red chillies. She was considering the question.

'Hildamay!'

'Yes?'

'Where do I go when I die?'

She turned the heat down low and walked over to the table where she sat and looked at Sky. The smell of garlic filled the room.

'Do you remember where you were before you were born?'

'Yes.'

'Good. Then you know where you go when you die.'

There was silence. Sky sat and picked at the toe of her sock. She began to make a hole and picked at it more eagerly.

'Sky, don't do that. Socks don't grow on trees, you know.'

'Of course they don't,' said Sky agreeably and then smiled at her with an expression of such pure, uncomplicated affection that Hildamay caught her breath and shook her head, momentarily startled. Sky, frowning with concern, got up from her chair and walked over to put a small hand to Hildamay's face.

'Are you all right?' she said worriedly.

'Quite all right,' said Hildamay, but for some unaccountable reason her eyes filled with tears.

CHAPTER TWELVE

'IT'S me and I think I'm going to die. No. I think I have.'
'Oh dear,' said Hildamay.
'Oh dear?' exclaimed Liz. 'Surely death deserves something more memorable than "oh dear".'
'A wreath?'
'Shut up. But if I go I want pure white arum lilies. Sheaves and sheaves of them and nothing else.'
'I'll order them now.'
'Good.'
'I wish there was something I could take to stop me feeling this sick,' grumbled Liz. 'I bet if men had babies, there'd be hundreds of remedies for morning sickness. The whole of medical science would be quite different. Contraception would be safe and effective, being pregnant painless and sickless and aftercare would be a dream. Executive crèches, supermarket crèches, cinema crèches, opera crèches, theatre crèches. It's only when you get pregnant that you begin to understand what being a woman in this society really means.'
'What does it really mean?'

'It means you feel like shit.'
'Nice.'
'Not nice. God, I feel sick.'
'How about a double brandy?'
'The foetus, the foetus,' groaned Liz in exasperation. 'I'm never going to stop being sick,' she wailed. 'Never. I had to get off the tube at every stop this morning to throw up. Can you imagine anything worse?'

'No,' said Hildamay, with feeling.

'No,' agreed Liz, cheering up. 'It was revolting,' she added happily. Liz only seemed happy when she was talking about her pregnancy. She was never more animated than when she was discussing, in lurid detail, her body's physical changes. That Hildamay was incapable of joining in the conversation seemed not to matter to her. She would talk, Hildamay would listen. Their conversations had become a monologue. Hildamay knew better than to interrupt or contradict.

Liz, despite her endless complaints about sickness, was pleased with her body. She exercised it every morning, anointed it with special oils, fed it on healthy foods, although she did indulge its cravings. 'It knows what it needs,' she said. 'We should listen to our bodies more. It's just one of the things I've understood since I became pregnant.' She took it off to weekly ante-natal classes and generally treated it like a new lover; a lover still strange enough to be fascinating. She dressed it in very tight black Lycra dresses and thrust her growing breasts and belly at anyone who looked remotely interested. She was pleased with her new breasts and fondled them absent-mindedly but constantly; as if she were surprised to find them attached to her body.

She stroked them as she sat across the table from Hildamay. It was Wednesday. Luigi, who was serving the antipasto, did not seem particularly surprised. '*Bella*,' he said paternally, patting Liz's curly hair with a basil-scented hand.

'They've got quite big. Nearly as big as yours,' she said to Hildamay, her hands splayed on her breasts.

'Yes,' said Hildamay abruptly. She did not like to talk about breasts, she did not even like to think about them. Imagine them pregnant! Large as melons, the skin taut and white, shiny and distended, patterned with pale blue veins, and crowned with hard, swollen purple nipples bursting out of their centres. She shuddered.

'Are you cold?' asked Liz, peering at her.

'No.'

'Well, why are you shuddering?' Being pregnant made Liz aggressive. Hildamay had thought it would make her happy. It did not seem to, at least not in a way that Hildamay would have recognised as happiness in the old Liz. Hildamay did not like the change.

'I was thinking about pregnant breasts.'

'Pregnant breasts are beautiful,' said Liz loudly. 'Pregnant women are beautiful. What's disgusting is the way society treats pregnancy. As if it's something to hide. We're supposed to go round pretending that sex doesn't exist, or anyway that the consequences of it don't. Fuck? Me? Oh, no, sir. This is just some nasty deformity which is why I cover myself with a shroud and tie bows and ruffles around my neck to distract attention from my belly. It offends you? Sorry about that. Won't do it again.' Liz looked at Hildamay, her eyes hard. 'Don't you like my breasts?' she asked, thrusting them across the table over her plate of rare liver. The nipples stiffened and poked through the thin fabric of her dress.

Hildamay looked away. 'Very nice,' she said faintly.

'You don't!' said Liz, accusing, her eyes filling with tears.

Not again, thought Hildamay wearily. These days the slightest thing made Liz cry. Hildamay supposed it was all those hormones hurtling around in her body. Suddenly freed, they did not know whether to laugh or cry.

'I think they're perfectly lovely,' she said, leaning over to pat her on the shoulder.

'Don't you patronise me,' muttered Liz. She stared at Hildamay with hostility then, with a shrug, began to eat again. There was silence as she scraped up brown, liverish blood and spooned it noisily into her mouth.

'How's Ed's book doing?' asked Hildamay carefully.

'Oh, it's fine.' Liz seemed indifferent, bored even. Ed Krane's book, which she had edited, had once been a matter of enormous pride to her. He had spent years living rough and would still do so for weeks at a time, although his first novel had made it to the bestseller lists, staying at number one for weeks, and had made him a considerable amount of money. 'He's nearly finished his second,' she added, shrugging.

'Is it good?' asked Hildamay, who was fascinated by Krane.

'It's OK. Yes, yes, it's very good,' said Liz impatiently. 'Did you know that the foetus has fingernails already? I'm sure she's going to have blue eyes. I thought I might paint the spare room green.

I'm going to turn it into the nursery. It's supposed to be psychologically the most calming colour.'

Hildamay sighed and tried to think of something interesting to say about green.

'Eau de nil sucks,' she said eventually and Liz burst into tears.

That had been the last Wednesday lunch they had together. Liz said it was too much for her, going into Soho on the bus. Anyway, she said, she couldn't bear the smell of garlic in Luigi's. She preferred to sit at her desk and eat cold plain boiled chicken and puréed vegetables. 'All that rich food,' she said complacently, 'it's so bad for you.'

Hildamay did not mind. They seemed to have so little to say to each other and anyway, the guilt she felt over her boredom with Liz's pregnancy gave her terrible indigestion. The daily telephone calls had stopped, too. Liz called once a week. Hildamay did not call at all.

'It can't last much longer,' Hildamay murmured into the telephone.

'What do you know?' said Liz sharply. Hildamay said nothing. 'The doctor said it would stop at fourteen weeks. Like clockwork. that's what the books said, too. Mind you,' she added with a complacent sigh, 'I don't think the textbook pregnancy exists. There's a theory it's all to do with vitamin B levels but I've been pouring pills down my throat, so that can't be right. Then there's another theory,' she continued, her voice thin with irritation, 'that it's all to do with emotional balance; psychological and not physiological. Another hysteria complex loaded on women by a medical profession, male of course, which can't find a rational answer. Bloody marvellous, isn't it?'

'Marvellous,' said Hildamay. 'How many are you now?' Her voice was slow with boredom. Once, she would have pretended interest for Liz's sake, but now she knew that Liz would not even notice. No emotion, other than her own, interested Liz these days.

'How many what?'

'Weeks.'

'Fifteen. And three days.'

'Really? That long?' said Hildamay politely.

'Yes, isn't it amazing?'

'Amazing.'

'That's what the girls at the ante-natal class say. Oh, I know that really I don't need to go to classes yet. But how else are you supposed to get any information about pregnancy? That's what I'd like to know. It's only women who know anything. They're so nice, the women at the class.' Liz sighed with satisfaction. 'It's extraordinary how children bring people together. I feel like a real woman, for the first time.'

'How wonderful for you,' said Hildamay drily.

'We all go out and have herbal tea after class,' continued Liz, ignoring the irony. Or perhaps she hadn't heard? Hildamay closed her eyes and longed for the old Liz, for her friend. 'I'm the novice. I just listen to everything they have to say. Most of them are on their second. Or third. They say the time just rushes past and before you know it you've got a toddler on your hands. Or under your feet.' Liz laughed. 'Can you imagine?'

'No,' said Hildamay.

'They keep telling me to treasure the time. These weeks of new life are so precious. And morning sickness really isn't that bad. I can't wait for the fifth month, though. Twenty weeks that is,' she added, with perfect seriousness.

Good grief, thought Hildamay. Now we are six.

'Pregnancy,' explained Liz earnestly, 'is always counted in weeks. Anyway, they say that after the twentieth week you start to feel wonderful. Blooming and full of energy. Your hair looks great and your skin gets really clear. Even your fingernails grow. I've started to have a weekly manicure.'

'You? A manicure?' said Hildamay faintly.

'Yes. I'm going to paint my nails scarlet and wear huge gold hoop earrings. It'll look great with black, don't you think?'

'Fabulous,' said Hildamay.

'The girls at the clinic think I'm terribly brave. "Avant-garde," one of them said. For showing my bulge. I said I didn't care what anybody thought; that we ought to celebrate pregnancy. Pregnant women are so sexy. And they feel fabulously sexy. I know I do. Horny as hell. In between throwing up, anyway. Such a waste, really. Men seem to find it difficult enough to look at a woman when she's pregnant, let alone fuck her. I can't see much chance of picking up a gorgeous stranger in my condition. I masturbate, though. It's great. When you're pregnant your tits get really sensitive.'

'Fascinating,' said Hildamay.

'Yes, isn't it. Well?'

'Well what?'

'What have you been doing?'

'Nothing.'

'That's nice. I want to hear all about it. And I want to show you my bulge. It's got even bigger. You'd be amazed at the difference in just a couple of weeks. I'm really starting to show. Shall we have lunch next Saturday?'

'No. Not Saturday,' said Hildamay quickly.

'Why not? What are you doing?' demanded Liz, suddenly interested.

'Don't be so nosey,' protested Hildamay, laughing.

'Sorry. Well, what are you doing? What's more important than seeing your best friend? Your pregnant best friend. Mother of your unborn godchild.'

'I'm – I'm just busy, that's all.'

'You've got a lover!'

'I have not got a lover.'

'You have. I can tell. You've got your "I want to be with somebody else and I'm not going to tell you who it is" voice on. Which is quite different from your "I want to be alone" voice. There is somebody,' insisted Liz.

'Piss off,' said Hildamay, but she laughed again.

'I will not. Who is it?' demanded Liz.

'It's nobody. I've just got things to do.'

'What things? It can't be work. That's against your code of ethics. "Business and pleasure don't mix," said Liz, mimicking Hildamay's voice. 'And certainly not on weekends.'

'Housework,' said Hildamay.

'Rita does that. Don't tell me she's left?'

'No, Rita's still there.'

'Well, what housework have you got to do? That woman does everything. She'll go to the unions if you start messing around with her work.'

'I don't,' protested Hildamay. 'I buy flowers.'

'Flowers? How long does it take to buy a bunch of flowers?' demanded Liz.

'I've made Saturdays my organising day,' said Hildamay firmly. 'Buying flowers. Going to Portobello to buy food. Giving myself a facial. That sort of stuff. It's my day of pleasure.'

'Oh,' said Liz. 'Well, how about the pleasure of my company for lunch between all those little delights? I'd appreciate a fresh-faced person over a plate of pasta. We could eat the Portobello offerings.'

'Solitary pleasures,' said Hildamay firmly.

'Oh, trust you,' said Liz, an edge to her voice.

'Always,' said Hildamay. 'I'll call you tomorrow. To see how you are,' she added, her tone cajoling.

'Oh, don't bother,' said Liz, and burst into tears.

'Don't –' said Hildamay, but Liz slammed the phone down. She stared at the buzzing receiver and wondered why she had not told her that she spent Saturdays with Sky. And then she stopped wondering and concentrated on her indigestion.

CHAPTER THIRTEEN

'HE'S gone.'
'Who?'
'Why, Ned, of course. Who else am I married to?'
'I had simply thought,' said Hildamay mildly, 'that you might have meant Ben.'
'Oh.'
'It goes on, then?'
'It goes on,' said Delilah flatly.
'And Kate?'
'Kate's Kate. A wife. I love him.'
'And she doesn't?'
'She is him. There's a difference.'
'You mean a wife has no identity.'
Delilah sighed then stood up, walked over to the fridge and got out a bottle of white wine. She made spritzers, splashing soda water noisily into glasses. It was too hot to eat and so they drank, sucking on ice cubes to cool themselves. They were sitting in Delilah's kitchen. It was a big, cheerful room, airy and white, littered with

toys and hung with Ned's paintings; great, bold, splashy abstracts. Hildamay lay on the sofa which was covered in scarlet canvas. The colour made her feel hot. Delilah, thin and cool, sat at the table scratching at some blobs of old candle wax with long, restless fingers. She wore a faded grey T-shirt and a pair of tattered Levi's. Occasionally she pushed her hair back from her face, catching it in both hands and pulling at it viciously, stretching the skin on her face.

'In five years' time,' she said, 'I'll have a face lift.'

'Why?'

'Oh, why not?' she said sharply. There was silence. 'Sorry. I'll be forty, that's why.'

Hildamay looked at her face. 'You'll grow old gracefully,' she said.

'Not a chance,' said Delilah. 'I see no grace in age. Only resignation.' She sighed and took a long swallow of wine.

'Acceptance?' ventured Hildamay.

'Resignation,' said Delilah shortly. 'The wifely emotion. He'll go back to her, of course.'

'Who?'

'Ben.'

'As far as I know, he hasn't left her.'

'In spirit,' said Delilah, 'if not in body.'

'And the spirit is weak?'

'Yes. Very.'

'Then why do you love him?'

'Don't be so rational,' said Delilah, smiling one of her rare, unexpected smiles. 'That's my role.'

'Because you know you can get him?' said Hildamay, staring at her beautiful face.

'Because I know I can't,' said Delilah, getting up and walking barefoot to the fridge. She stopped in front of one of Ned's larger canvases, so large it took up most of the wall, and stared at it reflectively.

'Where is he?'

Delilah shrugged thin shoulders. 'With friends,' she said abruptly.

'Does he know about Ben?'

'No,' she said quietly. 'I'm not that unkind.'

Hildamay raised an eyebrow.

'Oh, I'm not,' said Delilah, irritable. 'Confession absolves only our own consciences. We simply hand the burden on to somebody else.'

'And what about your burden?'

'It is mine. I chose it.'

'What does Ned know?'

'That I don't want to be married to him. At least, not right now.'

'Does that make it easier?'

'Nothing makes it easier.'

'But he has hope,' protested Hildamay. 'If he thinks there is nobody else.'

Delilah turned and stared at her. Then she walked back to the table and sat down. 'Hope is not destroyed by infidelity. Hope is a remarkably resilient emotion. All a name, a body will do is give him knowledge with which to damage himself.'

'And you?'

'I have done that already,' said Delilah, bitterly. 'He wants to go and have counselling. Says we can work it out together. He won't, or can't understand that I don't want us to be together. He thinks we can talk it through. Talk!'

'I thought that's what you did anyway. Talk. Don't you counsel couples?' asked Hildamay, curious.

'Good advice is rarely personal,' said Delilah and tears spilled out of her cool grey eyes.

'Perhaps,' said Hildamay gently, 'you should be on your own for a time. To think. To decide what you need. Leave Ben be. Leave him to Kate.'

'I can't,' said Delilah, the tears sticky on her smooth white skin. 'Not everybody is good at being on their own, Hildamay. Just because you are doesn't mean we all have that ability.'

Hildamay shrugged. 'It just seems better.'

'You mean easier,' said Delilah and cried into her glass.

Hildamay was silent. Did she mean easier? She had always thought that she meant better.

Hildamay sat in her car outside Delilah's house. It was unseasonably hot for early June; already the trees in the avenue looked dusty and worn. She could feel sweat trickling down between her breasts. A small boy kicked a football disconsolately against a wall. She watched him for a while then switched on the engine and drove off, very fast, heading for the cool marble of Harrods' beauty hall.

A brown Cortina pulled up alongside her at some traffic lights. A white stripe ran along the side of the car, and on either side of it were painted luminous orange flames. Above the flames, near the engine, were emblazoned the words, 'Hot Rod'. The driver was young and, he thought, handsome. He had jet black hair, combed back off his face and held in place with so much oil that Hildamay could see the teeth marks the comb had left. 'Hey, baby,' he shouted, 'that's me. I'm Rod. Hot Rod!' And he laughed, a loud, screeching laugh that ended in a whistle. 'Hey, baby,' he shouted again, 'you like my *machine*?' He made wild, masturbatory gestures with his hand.

Hildamay watched him in silence until the lights changed and then she drove off, moving slowly. He revved his engine aggressively, speeding past her and then, realising that she was way behind, slowed down until he dropped behind her. She watched him in her driving mirror, his fat, fleshy tongue lapping at his thick lips. They were dark pinky brown, the colour of fresh liver. She shuddered. 'Another prick with his brain in his dick,' she muttered. They stopped at the next set of traffic lights. Hildamay stared ahead. Suddenly, she felt a jolt as her car was bumped forward. 'Dickhead!' she yelled and slammed her hands on the steering wheel. She did not look back at him. Her car was jolted again. He was nudging hers forwards with his.

'Oh, good grief,' she said aloud and, turning in her seat, stared at him with exasperation.

'Go away!' she shouted, motioning with her hand for him to leave. He made wild gestures in return, and shouted something, but what it was, Hildamay could not hear.

The lights changed and she moved off slowly. He was right behind her, revving his engine furiously. She slammed on her brakes, forcing him to swerve sharply to avoid hitting her. He drove halfway on to the pavement and stalled. She watched him thoughtfully for a moment then got out of her car, walked over to the passenger side of his and leaned through the window. His thick-fleshed face was slack with shock.

'Hi,' she said with her most brilliant smile.

'Well, hello, little lady,' he said, relaxing, and leaned back against his seat, pushing his pelvis up against the steering wheel, rubbing his penis against it, up and down, up and down, as he ran a hand slowly though his black, well-oiled hair.

She walked round to the back door on the passenger side of his car and opened it. Leaning in, she smiled seductively. He turned around and smiled at her, his face bright with interest, his fleshy tongue moving over his smiling lips. 'Don't be a prick all your life,' she said and, leaving the back passenger door wide open, walked back to her car. By the time he had got out to close the door, she had driven off.

She inched her way through the traffic in Knightsbridge. The air was metallic with heat, the noises of the street tinny as they bounced off the concrete buildings. A languor had settled over the city; men and women wandered along the pavements in bright, unsuitable clothes, their faces dazed and blurred in the unfamiliar sun. Hildamay watched a woman cross the road. She wore a tight white skirt, creased with sweat around her thighs. Her bare legs, blotched pink and white with heat, looked vulnerable, as if newly unwrapped, the pockets of fat above her knees joggling uncertainly. Her feet, crammed into a pair of bright blue plastic high-heeled shoes, had swollen so that the flesh spilled over the sides. She walked with legs stiffened, trying to avoid lifting her feet so that the cruel plastic would not bite any harder into the red welts already carved into her heels. Her jacket was a cheap, bright navy wool, ballooning out from shoulders stiffened with foam pads, the fabric then gathered and pulled sharply into a wide band which strained over her hips. Under it she wore a white polyester chiffon blouse with a high, frilled neck. Her face was red and sweating from the heat.

'Why?' shouted Hildamay in exasperation out of the open window. She had not meant to say the word out loud but the woman, who was standing on a traffic island, simply turned and looked at her dully.

'Why do you have to dress like that?' said Hildamay who had drawn up alongside her. 'It's too hot,' she added, as if in apology.

'My boss likes me to look smart,' said the woman, peering in at the open window. Hildamay looked at the kind face, which wore a sort of bemused expression as if the woman were surprised to find her warm, tender flesh marooned in the sharp, judgmental city. The woman looked lost, a child in an office suit, her fine, blonde hair stuck to her scalp in patches, leaving tufts of hair standing in little, surprised clumps.

'And so you do,' said Hildamay gently, suddenly ashamed.

The woman's face seemed to dissolve at the tenderness in her voice. 'He doesn't love me,' she said breathlessly, her small eyes hot with tears. 'He says he'll leave his wife, but I know he won't.'

'Why don't you leave him instead?' said Hildamay, watching the woman's face crumple with misery.

'Because I can't. Don't you understand?'

'No,' said Hildamay.

'Lucky you,' said the woman. 'I wish I didn't.' And she stood on the traffic island, in the middle of the roaring, hooting cars, hugging her plastic quilted fake Chanel bag to her chest, and cried.

'Madam's skin is dry,' said the girl behind the counter, stacking dry skin products in front of her with extraordinary speed.

'I have an oily centre,' said Hildamay patiently, watching the pile grow.

'Madam may,' said the girl sympathetically, 'once have had an oily panel, but her skin is dry now.'

'Combination,' said Hildamay.

'Dry,' said the girl, her smile tight.

'It's my skin,' said Hildamay, suddenly tiring of the game.

'The computer,' persisted the girl with infinite patience, 'does not lie. It was developed in Switzerland using the highest Japanese technology. It is programmed to detect the condition of the skin in a manner that the human eye cannot see. We at Shanebo are proud of our achievements. This is the most advanced skin-care programme in the world.' She sounded like a child reciting long, difficult words which she had learned parrot fashion.

Hildamay looked wearily at her. 'Combination,' she said quietly.

'If Madam,' said the girl slowly, 'would care to look at her computer printout.' The syllables of the word computer spat like bullets from her mouth. 'If Madam could possibly take the time to examine her printout, then she would see that she is mistaken.' She looked at Hildamay as a mother would a small and tiresome child. 'One's skin changes.' She gestured sharply at nothing. 'One's skin changes in this heat.'

Hildamay stared at her stonily.

The girl smiled impatiently at her. 'The computer,' she said, 'does not lie.'

'When did it tell you that?' said Hildamay and walked off, leaving the girl with two hundred pounds' worth of dry skin products stacked in a shimmering, metallic pile on the counter in front of her. Hildamay sighed and looked around the hall. Normally she would have enjoyed the exchange but today she felt only a listless irritation. Half-heartedly she fingered a sample of liposomes, packaged in peach and gold, which stood on the counter nearest her. 'Scientifically proven to reduce the effects of ageing,' said the card propped next to it. It was printed in fine gold letters, designed by some expensive expert to look as if a computer had formed them.

Why do we believe machines more than we believe people? thought Hildamay wearily. Because people are such messy, unpredictable creatures.

She looked at the cool, clean package and thought about the woman crying stickily on the pavement. She wondered where she was now. Sitting on the top of a bus, her Marks & Spencer's single person portion, low-calorie, cabinet-chilled, oven-ready meal in a plastic bag on her lap, cooling the empty warmth between her legs as she dreamed of her boss's kisses. And then Hildamay thought about Delilah and the defeated slope of her thin shoulders. She wondered what she could do, but knew that nothing was to be done. She watched a man, over at the perfume counter, and wondered if he had ever told a woman that he would leave his wife.

'No,' he said loudly, blustering at the painted girl. 'I told you. I want the most expensive perfume you have.'

'But sir,' she protested, 'this is the newest. Absolutely the *dernier cri*.' She said it as if it were a stocking, her long coral nails flashing with sincerity as she twirled the etched glass bottle seductively before his nose. 'A light, floral fragrance, perfect for the day.'

'I don't want it for the day,' he said, smirking. Her mascara-stiffened lashes did not quiver. His mouth tightened.

'What was the one Marilyn Monroe wore?' he asked suddenly.

'Chanel No 5,' said the girl in a tired monotone.

'She wore that in bed,' he said. 'With no clothes on.' His voice had dropped to an undertone so Hildamay had to move nearer to hear. She busied herself testing some eyeshadows. 'Bet you didn't know that, eh?' he said, pleased with himself.

'No, sir,' she replied, obedient.

'Well? What about it, then?' he demanded.

'A light, floral fragrance,' intoned the girl.

'Oh! But I thought. . . .'

'Yes, sir?' she said, her smile sharp with boredom.

'Never mind.' He looked downcast. 'Is it very expensive?' he added, suddenly hopeful.

'No, sir. Well –' The girl hesitated. 'It's not the most expensive we have,' she said finally.

'Well, what is?' he barked.

'This, sir,' she said, holding out a discreetly lettered box. 'But from what you've told me about Madam, I don't think –'

'Madam will like whatever I give her,' he said abruptly. 'I don't think it's your place to tell me my business. Or her likes and dislikes.'

'No, sir,' said the girl quickly, dropping her eyes to hide the contempt which flickered so suddenly in them. Her lowered eyes revealed lids frosted tangerine, pink and violet. 'So you'll take this one?' she said carefully, not looking up.

'I just said I would,' he said, irritated.

She wrapped the box in silence while he swaggered impatiently, drumming his fingers on the counter. She slipped the box into a shiny green and gold bag and handed it daintily to him, twirling the ribbon handles in long polished nails. He snatched it from her.

'That will be five hundred and twenty-three pounds, sir,' she said.

'What!'

'The most expensive, sir,' she said, smiling sweetly.

'I'm not sure –'

She ignored the plea and continued to hold out the bag, jerking it at him in little impatient gestures.

'And how would you like to pay, sir?' she said, her voice very loud.

Hildamay went off and bought sixty pounds' worth of dry skin liposomes from the girl with the computer. As she paid, she watched the man from the perfume counter sign his American Express form with a shaking hand. She felt a sudden twinge of compassion for him and then she thought of the woman for whom it was destined. She imagined her opening it carefully, untying the ribbons, peeling off the sticky tape with patient, gentle fingers as he stood over her, thrusting his stocky body impatiently. The woman would dab it at her wrists, spill a drop into her cleavage, fumble at her ears with it; her face soft with love and gratitude. 'The most expensive,' he would brag, impatient lest she should believe it to be simply a perfume. 'The most expensive,' he would boast, emphatic with pride. 'See,' said his strutting walk, 'see how much my love is worth.' And she would wear the damned stuff day after weary day; each scented drop a potent reminder of his love for her. And if she should ever mention his wife? Should ever hint that this much was not, was nowhere near, enough? 'You smell delicious,' he would say, his hand closing possessively around the tender, scented column of her neck.

Hildamay stood naked in her bathroom, carefully unwrapping the little pale blue pots from their shiny apricot boxes, unscrewing their gilded tops and breathing in the scent of them. The cool, clean fragrance soothed her and, as she tenderly arranged them on the gleaming glass shelves, she looked around her at the slim, shining bottles and stout ceramic pots and on her face was a look of devotional satisfaction. As she sluiced buckets of cool water over herself and rubbed away with a bar of rose geranium soap, she felt the sticky emotions of the day dissolve and run away to nothing. Sighing with pleasure, she wrapped herself in towels and lay on the floor and let her mind go blank. When she roused herself it was late but she did not hurry, dressing with care, clothing herself with cotton and silk which she buttoned and arranged about her cool skin with sensual pleasure. Then, seeing the face of the small silver clock which stood by her bed, she exclaimed and hurried out of the door. Cassie was sitting in the bar at The Globe talking to Thomas when she walked in.

'Darling!' exclaimed Cassie, as if she had not seen her for months, instead of weeks. 'How completely wonderful to see you. Now, isn't this simply perfect?' she added, planting pink kisses on each of Hildamay's cheeks. 'Just you and I and a whole blissful evening to ourselves.' Hildamay smiled fondly at her then turned to say hello to Thomas. He stared hard at her in silence then flushed and walked away, busying himself shaking cocktails at the other end of the bar. Cassie stared after him, puzzled.

'Whatever is the matter with him?' she said and then turned suddenly to look at Hildamay. 'Darling, what have you done? You haven't!'

'No,' said Hildamay, 'I haven't.'

'Well, you've certainly done something, darling,' said Cassie, watching her carefully. 'He's normally such a well-mannered boy.'

'I embarrassed him in front of Liz,' said Hildamay, feeling suddenly ashamed.

'How?' demanded Cassie, curious.

'I made him feel unwanted.' Hildamay shrugged and looked away. Cassie stared at her averted face for a few minutes and then said,

'Oh, never mind, darling. But do try to be more careful. You know how fragile the male ego is. Like Venetian glass,' she added pensively.

'Reinforced concrete wouldn't have helped,' said Hildamay, looking over at Thomas.

'What?' said Cassie vaguely and lapsed into silence. She looked tired. Violet make-up was caked around her eyes, clinging in patches as dust does to damp paint, sticking here and there in drifts of violent colour. The skin beneath was dry and papery, like chamois wrung out and left to harden in the sun. She had tried to hide the circles beneath her eyes by pasting over them with concealer; its waxy surface catching the light and throwing into relief the sharp grooves etched in the fine skin.

'I know I look tired, darling,' said Cassie suddenly. She put her hands to her face and made little patting movements at her eyes.

'Are you all right?' asked Hildamay gently.

'Oh, darling, I'm fine! Honestly! Couldn't be better. Really I am. It's just that we've had to do three presentations this week. Three terribly important ones, darling. It's essential that we get the accounts. Times are hard, darling. Desperately hard –' Her voice trailed off.

'How's Jack?' asked Hildamay casually.

Cassie looked sharply at her. 'He's all right,' she said cautiously. Hildamay did not speak but sat and stared at her. Cassie flushed. 'Oh, I'm sorry about the other day, darling. No, no, it was weeks ago. Whatever – I'm sorry, truly I am. I hadn't realised you both worked for the same company and when I saw you walking over to the table and the way he took your hand in both of his, I thought perhaps he was an old flame. Jealous, I suppose.'

'Jack Rome!?' said Hildamay incredulously. 'An old flame?'

'Well, why not?' said Cassie sharply. 'He's a very attractive man.'

'If you like that sort of thing,' said Hildamay, without thinking.

'Well, it just so happens that I do, darling,' hissed Cassie. 'I don't know why you're being so unkind. He's never had anything but praise for you. "Hildamay this and Hildamay that." He thinks the sun shines out of your ass, and moonbeams of wisdom flow from your mouth. Fuck knows why,' she added sulkily.

'Charm, intelligence, dazzling good looks,' murmured Hildamay.

Cassie giggled suddenly. 'He says you're a demon at work. "Iron knickers," he calls you.'

'Charming,' said Hildamay. 'A closet sweetheart. I'd always wondered.'

'Oh, darling!' protested Cassie. 'He only means it affectionately. He's a very nice man. Really he is. He's just one of those men who's difficult to get to know.'

'You don't seem to have had much trouble.'

'The meeting of true minds,' said Cassie primly.

'Good grief,' said Hildamay, to her drink.

'What did you say?' demanded Cassie.

'Good for you.'

'Well, actually it is. His wife's an invalid. She doesn't get out of the house at all and he has to go to so many business do's.'

'Business don'ts,' murmured Hildamay but Cassie ignored her.

'So he's always on his own. That's where I met him, actually. At some drinks thing for the launch of a photography book. He says it's part of his job, to keep an eye out for good creative ideas. He's fascinating on the whole subject of textiles and the creative ideas behind them.'

'A fascinating talent for ligging,' said Hildamay.

'What's ligging?'

'A technical term,' said Hildamay quickly. 'Ask Jack. He'll explain.'

'I told you I'd met him. On the telephone.'

'When?'

'The man with mean green eyes.'

'Does he take them out at night?'

'Take what out?'

'His eyes.'

'Oh!' exclaimed Cassie, her eyes bright with amusement. 'His contact lenses. Aren't men funny, darling? They will go on so about women being vain but I honestly think there's no competition.'

'Good sex?' said Hildamay brightly.

'The best,' breathed Cassie. 'But it's much, much more than that. We have an understanding. A very real understanding. He tells me all about his problems at home. With his wife. They haven't been able to do it for years. Poor lamb. I was the first woman he'd slept with in eight years. But it's not just the sex,' she added quickly. 'He says our communication is extraordinary. We have an understanding that's almost spiritual.' She clasped her hands together and looked at Hildamay with shining eyes.

'Hence the bread and water?' asked Hildamay, looking at the mineral water in front of Cassie.

'Just a diet, darling. A tiny little diet. You know, the one that makes you feel eighteen again.'

'And do you?'

Cassie looked down. 'No, darling,' she said regretfully. 'I think it might take more than vegetables and water to feel like that, let alone get a body like that. Not,' she added, her voice harsh, 'that my eighteen-year-old body was anything to write home about.'

'I'm sure it was,' said Hildamay soothingly.

'Don't you mean present tense, darling?'

'Slip of the tongue. Silly old *moi*.'

Cassie smiled but tears glittered suddenly in her eyes.

'Do you think I'm fat?' she asked.

'No,' said Hildamay quickly. Too quickly.

Cassie looked at her consideringly for a moment, then patted her hand. 'Oh, it's all right, darling,' she said. 'I know I could do with losing a few pounds. It's the stones that are so hard. So sharp and unyielding.'

'Like words?' suggested Hildamay.

'Like words, darling,' sighed Cassie. 'I disgust him.' A tear slipped gently over the waxy surface of her thickly painted skin. 'Or that's what his eyes say,' she added miserably. 'His mouth says he's going to leave his wife.'

'Oh, that,' said Hildamay.

'Yes, that. Oh, fuck it, darling, shall we have some champagne? A bottle?' she added hopefully.

'Two,' said Hildamay and gently rubbed at the track the tear had left on Cassie's face.

CHAPTER FOURTEEN

HILDAMAY and Sky met every Saturday. At three o'clock, by the ticket office at St Pancras station. Then they caught the bus to Portobello. Then they went home for tea. The routine never varied. They both liked it that way.

Every Wednesday evening, at seven o'clock, Sky telephoned, her voice high and anxious.

'Hildamay?' she would ask, sounding slightly surprised. 'It's Sky Matthews.' Always Sky Matthews, never plain Sky.

'Hello, Sky,' Hildamay would say in a grave, pleased voice. 'How are you?'

'I'm very well,' said Sky, in a rush. 'Is it all right to meet on Saturday?'

Once Hildamay had said that yes, Saturday was fine and that she was looking forward to it and she thought they ought to go to Portobello because she needed to buy some flowers, then Sky's voice would slow to its usual rhythm and they would talk of other things. Usually words, for Sky had a passion for new words and collected them much as other children do bubble-gum cards or the toys out of cereal packets.'

'What does ruined mean?'

'It's – You know what an old house looks like when there's no glass in the windows and weeds all over the garden and all the paint has peeled off the doors?'

'Yes.'

'That's a ruin. It's ruined. It means spoiled or destroyed.'

'Poor Blanche,' said Sky quietly.

'Is Blanche ruined?'

'No,' said Sky sadly, 'only her life. She's depressed today. She and grandmother had a quarrel and she shouted that the frigid old bitch had ruined her life.'

'The what?'

'That's what Blanche calls her. The frigid old bitch.'

'I see,' said Hildamay, smiling down the telephone.

'Then grandmother calls her a whore and a slag and they don't speak for a week. They often don't speak,' added Sky with a small sigh.

Hildamay stopped smiling.

'But Blanche is better now because she got a letter from Spain. She hadn't had one for two weeks, which is why she was depressed. I went and got it from Haadji's. He's bought another new sweet counter. He says it's very marvellous.'

'I'd like to meet Blanche,' said Hildamay.

There was silence.

'I have to go now,' said Sky, and put the phone down.

'A person called Sky Matthews called,' said George the following day. He looked at her curiously. 'She said that she was sorry that she couldn't talk to you for longer on the telephone last night but she suddenly remembered that she had something to do. She said she hoped it was still all right for Saturday. She sounded very anxious. I told her that I was sure, if you'd made a previous arrangement, that you'd be there.'

'Good,' said Hildamay automatically. Then she looked at George in astonishment. 'She called here?'

'Indeed she did,' said George, with a slight smile. 'She asked to speak to the managing director, Miss Hildamay Smith. When I told her that you were out at lunch she wanted to know who I was and when I told her that I was your secretary she wanted me to explain what I did. She seemed perplexed by the idea that men could type. She insisted on knowing how I learned to do so.' He looked at Hildamay expectantly but she said nothing. 'She also asked me to explain the meaning of various words. She explained that it was the only way she could learn as her grandmother refused to buy her a dictionary because she says that too many words are a dangerous thing and that little girls should be seen and not heard.' At this he hesitated and frowned slightly but then appeared to remember something and smiled. 'She was very pleased with the word vocabulary which she said she would recite to herself a hundred times so she would not forget it. Apparently she lies in bed at night and repeats words until she falls asleep.' He paused and Hildamay opened her mouth as if to say something but George, nodding enthusiastically, went on. 'Sometimes, if she has learned a great deal that day, it means that it's hours before she can go to sleep. When I commented on her already extensive vocabulary she said she was very pleased to hear about the word extensive and added that to tonight's list.' He stopped, breathless and glowing slightly.

'George,' said Hildamay grinning. 'That's the longest speech I've ever heard you make.'

'Ah. Yes.' He flushed, embarrassed, but continued to look steadily at her, smiling shyly. 'She was very entertaining,' he said, inching towards the door of her office. Then he hesitated. 'Is she very young?' he asked.

'She's nine,' said Hildamay, still smiling.

'Nine,' he said, his voice wistful. 'Is she very pretty?'

'Pretty?' repeated Hildamay, frowning. She never thought about Sky being pretty. She was a child. She was just, well, Sky. Then she thought about her navy eyes and her pale, heart-shaped face. 'Yes, yes I do believe she is. Very pretty.'

'Is her hair blonde?'

'Reddish blonde. What they call strawberry, I think.'

'I see. Is she your niece?' he ventured.

'Nor have I ever seen you so curious,' said Hildamay, but she smiled. 'She's my friend, George.'

'Well,' he said gravely. 'I can quite see why.' And then he closed the door of her office and went to sit at his desk.

Hildamay watched him through the glass partition. Ordinarily, George was always occupied, busy typing or entering meticulous notes in shiny black ink in a series of red hard-backed books which he kept piled on his desk. But now he sat, staring into space. Hildamay peered through the glass. She could not be sure but she thought she saw an expression of longing on his face. She looked at him and wondered if anyone other than George would understand why she had befriended a nine year old child. She very much doubted it.

'Miss Smith?'

'Yes, George?' said Hildamay, not looking up from the letter she was trying to compose. It was a difficult letter concerning currency exchanges and tariffs which an Italian client was obdurately refusing to pay. She wondered whether to tell them to go to hell, and then wondered how to phrase that politely in Italian. Perhaps it was easier to explain import duties to the Italians after all than to explain a drop in profits to Si Stone. She sighed and looked up.

George's milk white skin was pink and his eyes were almost completely round.

'Umm,' he said, blinking rapidly.

'Yes, George?' said Hildamay gently. When George was excited or alarmed, it was sometimes difficult for him to form words. His hands were clasped behind his back. Slowly, and without speaking, he inched them round his body to reveal a small package, wrapped in plain brown paper. He put it gingerly on her desk.

They both looked at the parcel. Hildamay kept her eyes fixed on it to allow George time to speak.

'For Sky,' he stuttered.

'For Sky?' repeated Hildamay, glancing up at him.

'A dictionary,' he whispered, his voice breathless with embarrassment. 'Tell her it's small, so she can keep it hidden. Will you give it to her tomorrow?' he asked, his face pleading.

Hildamay rose from her desk and planted a firm kiss on each of his cheeks. His skin was very warm. 'She'll love it. Thank you, George.' She kissed him again. 'This one's from Sky,' she said, smiling. His pale eyes filled with tears, but then he blinked more rapidly than ever, and they were gone.

'Thank you,' he stammered, moving away from her hands which still rested on his shoulders. 'Have a good weekend,' he called as he scuttled out of the office.

'What are you doing this weekend?' called Hildamay after him but he did not reply and so she thought that he had not heard her.

*

She was walking to the tube when she saw George's slight figure some way in front of her. He had moved to the right of the pavement to escape the press of people who eddied around him. His body was close up against the window of a shoe shop, and he had his forehead pressed against the glass. His back was half turned away from her and his shoulders were hunched, as if he were cold. She had just raised her hand and opened her mouth to call out to him, when he turned slightly. She could see, even from where she was standing, that his face was contorted and that the stoop of his shoulders came, not from cold, but from pain. She sensed at once that he was not in physical distress but suffering from some unspeakable emotional pain. And so she did not call out but dropped her hand and stood for a moment, silent. People surged around her, pushing at her, but she did not move. Then she turned and walked back down the street crossing it and taking another route to the station, so that George should not see her. Or see that she had seen.

She worried about him all the way home and by the time she reached her flat had decided to telephone him. It was only when she had the receiver in her hand that she realised she did not know his telephone number or even the name of the street where he lived. She called directory enquiries.

'Which name?'
'Brown,' said Hildamay.
'With an e?'
'No.'
'Initials?'
'G. George.'
'Address?'
'I don't know.'
There was an incredulous silence. 'Then I can't help you,' said directory enquiries finally.
'Oh, do please try,' said Hildamay. She smiled her most beseeching smile until she remembered that he could not see her and so she stopped.
'There are four thousand six hundred and forty Browns without an e,' said directory. He had a nice voice. Warm and friendly, although Hildamay could detect a squeak of irritation in it.
'George,' she said, to remind him.

'There are two hundred Browns with a G,' said the warm voice, cooling rapidly.

'Somewhere in Streatham,' cajoled Hildamay.

'The computer does not understand "somewhere in",' said the voice. 'It has to have the name of a street. It can manage without the number but it must have the name of the street.'

'Oh dear,' said Hildamay and then was silent.

'Well, goodbye then,' said the voice, hesitating. Hildamay spoke before he could put the phone down.

'He really was very upset. It looked as if he was crying,' she said. 'On the street,' she added in explanation.

'Oh!' said the voice, startled. Hildamay could see that it would mean something to a man; the idea of another man crying on the street. Through the silence she could see him trying to picture George Brown without an e, weeping.

'Was it a death?' he asked eventually, unable to contain his curiosity.

'No,' said Hildamay. 'At least I don't think so. It's something to do with a child. I didn't like to ask him, you see. I don't think he would want me to know. That I saw him at all,' she explained.

'No,' said the voice, understanding. 'But then what could you say to him now?'

'Oh, I could just ask him how he was,' said Hildamay confidently. 'You know. Whether he was going to have a nice weekend. Stuff like that.'

'Wouldn't he think that odd? If you've never called him before. I mean,' he hesitated, 'it sounds as if you haven't called him before. You might have lost the number?'

'No,' said Hildamay. 'No, I've never had it. But he's a friend,' she added reassuringly. 'He's really a very good friend,' she said, surprised.

'But you don't have his number?'

'No,' said Hildamay, mystified. She thought about that for a few minutes. She wondered how she could have spent so much of her life with George, five years' worth of eight hours a day, and not even have thought to ask for his telephone number. She felt sick with regret.

'Maybe he has a friend you could call? Someone who might know his number.'

'I don't know who his friends are,' said Hildamay sadly. 'Except Adrian.'

'Well, what's his surname?'

'I don't know. Jones, I expect,' said Hildamay gloomily.

'I'd better go,' said the nice voice, sounding very warm now. 'You know what people say about never being able to get through.'

'Yes.'

'I'm sorry about George.'

'Yes,' said Hildamay. 'So am I. Thank you for being such a nice man.'

'Ohh!' said the voice. 'That's perfectly all right. I enjoyed it. Oh, I don't mean I enjoyed being nice. It's not often people tell us we're nice, you see. I haven't always done this job. I used to have my own business. I was in computers. Did very nicely, too, until that woman went and messed everything up. Society is made of individuals, she says. Stand on your own two feet, she says. And when you do, then what does she do? Pulls the rug out from under your feet. It was that business poll tax that really did me in. And thousands like me. Not much good them changing their minds a year later, either, was it? The damage was done.'

'I'm sorry.'

'So am I.' There was silence. 'Well, there you go. My wife left. Said she couldn't stand it. I cried on the street then, too. I wish somebody had telephoned me. I hope you find him.'

Hildamay poured herself a glass of wine and went and lay down on her sofa. In her hand she held the brown paper wrapped dictionary. She lay on her back, staring at the ceiling and thinking about George. She knew so little about him. She had never really tried to find out; he was a private man and did not seem to welcome questions. Still, she could have asked. She wondered why a child and a dictionary should cause him so much pain. It could have been anything that had distressed him. But she understood, without knowing why, that it was all to do with Sky.

'For me?' said Sky, looking first at the parcel in Hildamay's hands, then up at her face. 'For me?' she repeated, incredulous.

'For you,' said Hildamay, smiling. Sky's face was pink and her navy blue eyes so darkened with pleasure that they were almost black. 'It's from George,' she said as Sky took the package reverently from her.

Sky looked up at her. 'He's very nice,' she said. 'Everything you have is nice,' she said, looking pleased.

'I don't own George, Sky.'

'Nooo,' said Sky doubtfully, frowning a little. 'But he's yours.'

Hildamay shrugged. 'Open it, then,' she said.

'In a minute,' said Sky, turning the small brown parcel over and over. She looked around her. 'Over there,' she said, pointing across the station.

'What?'

'I want to go over there,' said Sky, looking up at Hildamay, 'and sit on that bench. I want to open it properly.'

'All right. Do you want a Coke?'

'A Coke!' said Sky looking as if she might faint with pleasure. 'We're not allowed Coke at home. I've never had a Coke before.'

Hildamay looked down at her, startled, but Sky looked so pleased that she did not want to disturb her happiness by asking her why not. 'Would you like a chocolate biscuit, too?' she asked. 'Or perhaps a cake.'

'A cake!' breathed Sky. 'I've never had a shop cake before. Grandmother,' she explained, taking Hildamay's hand. 'Do you think there'll be a pink one?'

'Well why don't we go and see? We could sit in the restaurant,' said Hildamay, pointing at the shabby café opposite platform three.

They stood in the queue with Sky clutching firmly on to the tray, her parcel clasped awkwardly in one hand. She was frowning with interest at the sandwiches, cut into little triangles and lying damply beneath clingfilm, their contents and prices neatly typed on white labels, stuck haphazardly on their tops. She read every one then looked for some time at a stale croissant and inspected a currant bun minutely. Then they passed the counter which held pieces of hardening cheese; halves of grapefruit, their surfaces crinkled and drying, their centres stained with maraschino cherry; and little aluminium bowls on stands in which puddles of prawn cocktail glistened pinkly. Sky's face was dark with disappointment.

'What's the matter?' asked Hildamay, suddenly noticing her silence.

'Nothing,' muttered Sky, looking away.

'The cakes are further on,' whispered Hildamay and Sky's head shot round to stare at the end of the queue.

'There's a pink one!' she exclaimed. 'I've always wanted a pink cake. And now I shall have one,' she sighed, her eyes closing in the bliss of anticipation.

Sky opened her eyes. In her mouth was the first bit of pink cake and on her face was a look of confused disappointment.

Hildamay examined the remains of the cake. Underneath the brilliant pink icing were two thin layers of white sponge, sandwiched together with a sticky, pale cream.

'I thought it would taste like strawberries,' said Sky, glaring at it.

'Things quite often look nicer than they are,' said Hildamay consolingly.

'Yes,' said Sky reflectively. 'Like people.'

Hildamay glanced at her sharply but Sky was poking at the pink icing.

'I'll get you a chocolate cup cake,' said Hildamay. 'At least they're reliable.'

'What's reliable?' said Sky.

'Open your parcel and see.'

'My parcel?'

'Open it.'

Sky looked at her in confusion for a moment and then began, very slowly, to ease the sticky tape from the edge of the paper. She was so absorbed that Hildamay left her at it and went off to get the cake. When she got back Sky was just teasing off the last piece of tape. She looked up at Hildamay. 'It's a book,' she whispered, peering through the sides of the paper. Hildamay said nothing.

'I've never had a book before.'

'Don't you get presents?'

'Well –' said Sky, hesitating. 'Yes,' she said, trying desperately to be honest. 'It's just that I always get the same thing so they're not really presents. Socks for Christmas and handkerchiefs for my birthday.'

'Very useful,' said Hildamay, her voice heavy with irony.

'Very,' said Sky matter of factly, and then she let a low moan of pleasure. 'It's a dictionary,' she breathed, her voice faint with excitement. 'A dictionary, a dictionary, a dictionary,' she murmured, almost comatose with joy. Her whole body was rigid and she moved very slowly, like a little old woman who is frightened of jarring her brittle bones or, thought Hildamay, like a sleeper who, half awake, dare not itch his nose lest it should rouse him from a delightful dream.

'He says,' said Hildamay, smiling, 'that he's sorry it's such a small one but he thought it might be better. So that you can keep it a secret,' she explained.

Sky bent her head to the little book and breathed in the smell of it. Then she looked up. 'Oh, isn't he *nice*,' she said, her eyes shining with happiness.

'I'm sure you can do better than nice,' said Hildamay, looking grave and nodding at the dictionary.

'Undoubtedly,' said Sky, and looked up nice.

'She made a good impression on her grandmother,' said Sky gravely.

'His body left an impression in the sand,' said Hildamay.

'He was under the impression that –' said Sky, looking around her, 'that all the people wore brown coats.'

'My impression is,' said Hildamay, looking at the clock on the wall of the station cafe, 'that we'd better hurry if we are to go anywhere else today.'

'Your impression is false!' shouted Sky, giggling.

'Sadly not,' said Hildamay and smiled at her.

'It's not late, is it?' said Sky, looking appalled. 'Not time to go home?'

'No. But it is four o'clock. So we can either go to the flat or to Portobello. You can't do both. Which is it to be?'

'Do you need flowers?'

'I always need flowers,' said Hildamay.

'Well let's go to Portobello,' said Sky. She looked thoughtfully at Hildamay. 'Would it be all right,' she said uncertainly, 'if I telephoned George? I want to tell him what an, an *admirable* man he is.'

'Quite all right.'

'Was that the right word?' she asked, taking Hildamay's hand.

'Can't think of any better,' said Hildamay absently. She looked down at her. 'Sky,' she said hesitantly, thinking of the lock on the telephone in the chill house in Woodside Park. 'Where do you get the money to make all these telephone calls?'

Sky peered up at her and then frowned. 'I don't steal it,' she said, carefully removing her hand from Hildamay's.

'I didn't mean that,' said Hildamay, although she had, on occasion, thought it. 'What I meant was, would you like me to give you some money? After all, you seem to spend most of it on me.'

Sky shook her head. 'No, thank you,' she said, with dignity. 'It's quite all right. I earn the money.'

Hildamay looked at her curiously.

'Blanche gives me ten pence every time I go to the post office for her. You see, her letters to Spain are a secret from grandmother. Like my jacket and cap,' she explained, twitching at the peak of her baseball cap. 'Blanche gave them to me. To make up for being a lousy mother, she said. She's quite good like that,' she added thoughtfully, taking Hildamay's hand again and patting it reassuringly. 'She understands how awful it is to look stupid at school.'

'Have you many friends at school?'

Sky looked at her with old eyes. 'If we don't hurry,' she said gently, 'we'll miss the best flowers.'

CHAPTER FIFTEEN

'GEORGE,' said Hildamay on Monday morning. 'Sky liked the dictionary very much. She said that you were an admirable man.'

'Admirable!' said George, his face turning pink with pleasure. 'Admirable,' he repeated, blinking rapidly. 'How gratifying,' he murmured, as if to himself. 'How very gratifying to be considered admirable.' Still murmuring, as if in some sort of trance, he walked out of Hildamay's office and went and sat at his desk. Hildamay watched him through the glass. His face was still pink and a small smile played around his mouth. He looked, she thought, as if he were enjoying a delightful daydream. Or perhaps it was a memory? She frowned. She knew, she realised suddenly, nothing about him. Neither his present nor his past. Impetuously, she called out to him.

'George? George, could you come in here a minute?'

He appeared in the doorway, blinking owlishly, the dream still fading from his face.

'Do you have much experience of children, George?' she asked, her voice measured, neutral.

'Children?' He frowned at her, then flushed. 'Children?' he repeated, growing flustered.

'It's just,' said Hildamay carefully, 'that you seem to know what they will like. You were so clever about the dictionary. So I thought –' Her voice tailed off. George was staring at her, mild outrage rounding the features of his face. His eyes and mouth were perfect circles. This is no good, thought Hildamay. If I am to know anything about him, we must put this relationship on a different footing. And then it occurred to her what to do.

'I thought,' she continued more firmly, 'that we might have lunch.'

'Lunch,' he echoed, gazing at her in horror.

'Good grief, George,' said Hildamay, her tone slightly peevish. 'Anyone would think I was suggesting we had sex together instead of a simple, innocent lunch.' Even as she said the word, she wondered how innocent her motive really was. Still, a faint smile flickered across George's face.

'We've never had lunch,' he said. 'Not in five years.'

'I know,' said Hildamay firmly. 'And I feel perfectly awful about it. Other people have lunch with their secretaries. Other people take them out on a regular basis. As a sort of thank you or on their birthdays. I've never even known when your birthday was, George.' Her voice was almost wistful.

George looked at her sharply but ignored the question. 'I have no need of thanks, Miss Smith,' he said stoutly. 'I am paid for what I do. Is what I do not sufficient?'

Oh, dear, thought Hildamay. This is going very badly. It suddenly seemed the most important thing in the world that they should have lunch together. How else would she find out more about him?

'More than sufficient, George,' she said, and quite suddenly turned on her most dazzling smile. He blinked at the force of it. 'Much, much more than sufficient. Which is why I'd like to take you out to lunch. Just a small one. Nothing grand, if you don't like the idea. A small lunch. A tiny, tiny little lunch. You could have lamb chops!' she added triumphantly.

'I have those for dinner,' he pointed out.

'Oh,' she said, downcast. 'So you do. Well, how about a nice bit of fillet of lamb? With *pommes dauphinoise*? It's the most delicious combination. It's what I have whenever I go to Paris. With a *tarte citron* to follow. At Angelina's. They do the best *tarte citron* in Paris. I've spent years researching them. They do quite a good one at Chez Georges, too. In the Rue du Mail. When it's on the menu. Which it often isn't. They change the menu often, you see. But there's always the Rum Baba. That's always on the menu. Sticky with sugar, fragrant with alcohol, smothered in cream.' She was almost leering. 'The best Rum Baba in Paris. Without a doubt.'

She was gibbering like an idiot in her eagerness to convince George to go out with her. She realised suddenly how perfectly awful it must be to be a man and always have to offer the invitation. No wonder men talked to women as if they were speaking to retarded children. Or greedy ones.

George looked at her curiously but in the depths of his blinking, milky blue eyes was the ghost of a twinkle. He seemed to be trying not to smile.

'Well,' he said, when she seemed quite calm again. 'It seems rather irregular. But if it would please you, then certainly we can go out for lunch.'

'Oh *good*!' breathed Hildamay, her smile brilliant. 'When? How about today?'

'Today? Today seems a little hasty,' said George calmly. The Rum Baba seemed to have quite restored his composure. His limbs were back in their usual, neat arrangement. 'How about Wednesday?' He got up and moved to the door, hovering by it in his usual way. 'It'll give me time to organise a restaurant. Where would you like me to book?'

'You choose,' said Hildamay gleefully. 'Somewhere nice.'

'I shall do my best,' he said drily. 'One o'clock suit you?'

'Oh, I think so, George, don't you?'

'Why break the habit of a lifetime?' he said and disappeared.

The rest of the day passed without incident and at six sharp Hildamay began to pack up her bag. Just as she had finished, George put his head around the door.

'We are to go to Langan's,' he said, beaming. 'They've managed to find us a table. It's an old favour – I mean, I've always wanted to go there.'

'An old favourite, George?' said Hildamay, puzzled.

'It's everybody's old favourite, isn't it?' he said brightly. 'You do want to go there? Would you rather go somewhere else? I can change the booking.' He frowned at her.

'Oh, no! No, don't do that. I'd love to go there. And they do a very good *gigot*. I'm going home now,' she said, heaving her enormous bag on to her shoulder.

'Bad for your posture,' he said, nodding at the bag.

'Sorry?'

'I have a friend who's an osteopath. Most back problems in women are caused by handbags. They unbalance the delicate musculature of the body and put the spine out. You should try a rucksack. Better balance. They hang off both shoulders,' he explained.

'Very fashionable, George.'

'Ah, yes,' he said. He had now manoeuvred his body round the door of her office and stood there, hovering. 'A nice hot drink?' he asked hopefully.

'More like a nice cold one,' said Hildamay. 'It's six, George.' He did not move but gazed at her beseechingly. She waited.

'Sky telephoned me,' he said eventually.

'Yes,' said Hildamay, watching him. 'She said she would.'

'She sounds like an extraordinary child,' he said, his voice wistful.

'She is,' said Hildamay. 'Perhaps you'd like to meet her?' Her voice was casual, and she busied herself with some loose papers on her desk. George frowned. Hildamay looked up at him. 'Why don't you come to Portobello with us on Saturday?'

'This Saturday?'

'Yes, the one in five days' time.'

'I'm not sure . . .' he said hesitantly.

'Well, think about it. You should meet Sky. You'll like her.'

Some of his previous agitation returned. 'She may not like me,' he said quickly. 'You know how children can be.'

'No,' said Hildamay. 'I don't. How can children be?'

He ignored the question. 'I think you should ask her first and then I'll think about it.'

'No,' said Hildamay, equally firmly. 'I'll ask her and then you must say yes. You know how children can be.' She smiled at him then and he returned the smile, shyly, and with such a look of pleading that Hildamay went and kissed him on the cheek.

She called out to him as she stood by the lift. 'Good night, handsome,' she cried as the doors opened. He did not hear her nor see her wave but stood, motionless, at the door of her office. On his face was a look of both pleasure and despair. Hildamay stepped into the steel cage of the lift. As the doors closed she glimpsed his face once more and the thought struck her, quite forcibly, that George had a daughter.

*

She walked into her flat, closed the front door and kicked off her shoes. Her aim was expert. They landed in the corner, by the old tin umbrella holder which was painted a deep Venetian yellow and decorated with blowsy cabbage roses, or some plant approximating them. 'To the Victorians,' said Hildamay as she passed, 'every flower was a rose. Fat, blowsy and easily bruised. Like their women.' Her shoes landed upright, quivering on high, slender heels, as if astonished to find themselves so suddenly at liberty.

'It was so nice!' sang Hildamay, 'I did it twice!' and tangoed barefoot down the hallway and into the kitchen wondering if there was any champagne in the fridge or if she had drunk the last bottle. In truth, there was always champagne in Hildamay's fridge; champagne and plenty of food. Cheeses, smoked meats, fresh pasta, three sorts of tomato (plum, cherry and yellow), four sorts of salad leaves (radicchio, mâche, oak leaf and plain round English), half-used jars of pesto and sun-dried tomatoes and bowls covered in cling-film, filled with the remains of homemade soup. She could not understand people whose fridges contained nothing but a pot of plain yoghurt and a bottle of water. She could neither understand nor befriend them for she felt no empathy with those who did not like food. She uncorked the bottle with a flourish and poured it into a slender crystal glass. Hildamay collected champagne glasses. 'So useful,' she said to her friends when they presented her with yet another. She had twenty-five and none of them matched. She thought that part of their charm. She had chosen a particularly fine example, Georgian and etched with grapes and vines, which Delilah had given her.

'My, my, my, Delilah!' she sang as she danced through to the bedroom. 'Why, why, why, Delilah?' she chorused as she turned on the answering machine. She turned the volume up very loud and stood there humming, swaying gently in time to the music in her head as she listened to the messages. There were three. The first was blank. Nothing but the sound of a sharp intake of breath as somebody put the phone down. Liz, thought Hildamay automatically. Liz hated the answering machine. 'I know you sit there and listen to me talk. Babbling away like an idiot and yet you don't pick it up. It's so cruel.' Liz had tried every tactic she could think of to persuade Hildamay to pick up the telephone – cajoling, laughing, crying, shouting – but as she could never be absolutely sure that Hildamay was actually there and listening or whether she really was out, her performance lacked conviction.

'Hildamay? Hildamay, are you there?' A voice burst suddenly out of the machine. She did not recognise it, all she knew was that it belonged to a woman. It was hesitant and breathless with a rasp to it; a voice rough with pain and longing. Hildamay shivered and the room was filled with the sound of sobbing, a high thin wail of pain, going on and on, like an animal caught in a trap. Hildamay put her hands to her ears and knelt down, then fumbled to find the volume control. The voice quietened, but still it called, 'Hildamay! Hildamay!' and the sobbing carried on, but growing deeper and more human. It went on and on, for minutes, as if the caller had forgotten that she was holding a telephone, or as if she was holding a lifeline. Gradually it quietened and a voice, the words interposed with great hiccups of breath, said, 'I'm sorry. I'm sorry.' Then the sobbing started anew but ended with a click as the telephone was put down.

Hildamay sat on the floor and stared at the machine, her chest tight. She felt panic, the frightened panic of impotence, and tears pricked at her eyes. 'Who are you? Who is it? Who is it?' she cried, banging the machine with her fists. It stopped and then suddenly started again. Delilah's voice echoed plaintively through the room. 'It's Delilah. It was me, crying. I rang back to say how sorry I was to do that to you. I didn't mean to cry but when I heard your voice, I couldn't stop. I simply couldn't stop . . .' Her voice, still breathless with tears, tailed off, but then echoed out again; the tone cool, well modulated, indifferent almost. 'So I thought I'd take the children to the park because it's my day with them. I wondered if you'd like to come? We could go up to the round pond and swim. And we'll take a picnic, of course. Call me if you feel like joining us. Call me anyway.' Hildamay shook her head, confused, until she realised that the first message had run on into a second, older one. She grabbed the telephone. Delilah's number was engaged. She kept trying, calling every five minutes, but the number was permanently unobtainable. In the end she called the operator. She felt breathless and panicky. Delilah had sounded so strange.

'I'll call you back,' said the operator.

'Hurry,' pleaded Hildamay. 'Please hurry.'

'I'll do my best,' said the voice slowly. 'But we're very busy here. It's the flu, you know. So many funny illnesses around. It's the weather, of course. It's not right. Not surprising everybody's sick with all the seasons being the wrong way round. Anyway, all this sickness around means we're very short staffed which means we're busy. Very busy. Might take a while.' Hildamay was jumping from one foot to another in agitation, her panic turning to anger.

'Well, I'm busy, too,' she said through gritted teeth. 'Busy working my butt off to pay British Telecom the vast amount of money it demands for so-called public services, so I suggest you pull a finger out and unbusy yourself.' She slammed the phone down. 'Oh, shit,' she cried to the empty room, 'now they'll never call me back.' The telephone rang.

'Look,' she said, 'I'm sorry about that. About losing my temper, I mean. But I have this friend and she sounds –'

'Hildamay?'

'That was clever. I'm only listed as H. Not even as "Miss". How did . . . ?'

'It's Ben.'

'Ben?'

'Yes, Ben. Remember me? The penis on legs?'

'How could I forget?' she said acidly. 'What do you want?'

'It's Delilah.' His voice was urgent. 'She's in a terrible state. You must go round there and see her. She won't stop crying. I'm worried that she'll do something terrible.'

'What do you mean, terrible?' said Hildamay slowly.

'Oh, I don't know,' he said irritably. 'I just know she needs somebody and I can't go round there.'

'Why not?'

'Oh, for God's sake. You know why not. It's over,' he added sulkily. 'I've finished it.'

'You told her on the telephone?'

'Yes.' The word was almost inaudible.

'Why, you little shit. You nasty, cowardly little shit. You'll fuck her in your own garden but when it comes to finishing something you haven't even got the guts to go to her house and tell her to her face.'

'I thought it was better,' he pleaded, 'for everyone.'

'Asshole.'

'Please, Hildamay. Please, please go round there. I'm worried about her. I love her, really I do. But Kate . . .' His voice tailed off.

'You want me to go and clear up the nasty little mess you've made. How like a man to run and hide and let the women tidy up afterwards.'

'She slammed the phone down on me. She's taken it off the hook.' His voice was sullen.

'I know. I've been trying to call her. Honestly, Ben, what did you expect? An ode to the glories of your penis?'

'I tried to explain –'

'Oh, go away, you silly little man,' said Hildamay, suddenly exhausted, her anger gone. 'I'll go round and see her.'

151

Delilah's house was dark. Hildamay rang the doorbell. Nobody came. She rang it again, three short rings and then silence, followed by another three short rings. Still nothing. She scrabbled in her bag, looking for paper and a pen. She found a stub of pencil then ripped the back off her cheque book.

Standing under a street light, she wrote a note, 'It's only me, Hildamay,' which she pushed through the letter box, and then sat on the step to wait. She heard a slight sound and a match being struck. Then the light in the hall went on and the door opened. Delilah stood there, an arm shielding her eyes. She wore an old T-shirt, the front ripped and dark with tears. Her mouth, as much of it as Hildamay could see, was swollen and bloodied. 'Come in,' said Delilah in a low, hoarse voice, chewing on her bleeding lips. She dropped her arm and peered at Hildamay. Her eyes were swollen and half shut and her skin a deathly white.

'Oh, Delilah,' said Hildamay and put her arms round her.

Delilah did not move but allowed herself to be hugged. Then she pulled away, walked into the sitting room and sat on the sofa in the dark. Hildamay went round switching on all the lamps until the room was cheerful with light.

'I thought you might be Ben. I don't want to see him. Not like this.' Delilah shrugged her shoulders helplessly and then rubbed at her eyes.

'He called me,' said Hildamay, watching her warily. She did not sit down but stood, irresolute, in the middle of the room.

'Did he?!' Delilah's face was suddenly radiant with hope and she started to chew frantically at her mouth. 'What did he say?' she asked eagerly. 'Did he talk about me?'

'All he said was would I come round and see you,' said Hildamay apologetically. 'To make sure that you were OK.'

'That was nice of him,' said Delilah, starting to cry.

Hildamay looked at her and shook her head. Nice?

'Shows he loves me really,' said Delilah, hiccuping with sobs.

'Loves you,' said Hildamay, incredulous. 'This,' she said, pointing at Delilah huddled on the sofa, 'this means he loves you?'

'Shut up Just shut up! You don't understand. You don't understand anything!' screamed Delilah, pulling herself to her knees. She threw a cushion across the room, then a glass and then another cushion. 'Ben was right' she howled, drumming her fists on the arm of the sofa. 'He said you didn't understand. Don't you remember?' Her voice was hoarse with tears and anger. 'He said you didn't like or understand anything normal and human and messy like love. He was right, he was right, he was right!' She kept drumming her fists in a mad rhythm.

'OK!' said Hildamay, shouting to be heard. 'OK, so he was right. Maybe I am an emotional retard but right now it's not me we're concerned with. It's you. Look at you!' She lowered her voice until it was almost a whisper. 'Oh, Delilah, just look at you.'

'Oh, leave me alone,' said Delilah viciously. 'Leave me alone. I'm always left alone. What difference does it make now? Go away,' she shouted. 'Go away! You hate him anyway. You think he's an asshole. Why are you here? To gloat? To say "I told you so".' Her voice dropped into a mocking tone. 'Poor little Delilah. Silly little Delilah, to think that horrid old selfish Ben could possibly love her. To think that he said he would leave his wife for her. And she believed him. She believed that she could get away with it and be happy.' She started shouting again. 'Happy? I'm happy! I know he loves me, I understand how much he loves me and I know why he's left me and none of it makes it any better. So will you please go home.'

'No,' said Hildamay.

'Well, fuck you!' screamed Delilah and threw herself on the floor.

There was silence for a while. Hildamay was still standing in the middle of the sitting room, her arms hanging helplessly by her sides, her head bowed as she watched Delilah who had her arms wrapped around her chest, and was rocking herself, sobbing quietly. Oh shit, thought Hildamay despairingly, I'm no good at this. Maybe Ben's right. I don't understand this kind of pain.

'Have a brandy,' she said.

'I've had one,' said Delilah sullenly, like a child.

'Well have another,' said Hildamay in exasperation.

'I don't want another!'

'It'll make you feel better,' said Hildamay, her tone wheedling. She bent down and put her arms round Delilah, rocking with her as she sat on the floor. After a while, the sobbing subsided. 'Oh, all right,' said Delilah, whispering. 'But just a small one.'

Hildamay went and poured them both a very large brandy. She persuaded Delilah to get back on the sofa where she lay, her feet in Hildamay's lap, and rambled on about Ben. Hildamay said nothing. She did not know what to say. Delilah's pain seemed to her ludicrous, comic almost. Very little of what she said made any sense.

She kept going over and over the same points. What Ben had done. What Ben had said. How much Ben loved her, when everything she said seemed evidence to Hildamay that Ben did not love her, did not want her, did not want to destroy his marriage because of her. How could she interpret that as that? she thought despairingly as Delilah mumbled on. Why does she think that? Still, she said nothing but poured brandy and stroked Delilah's feet and eventually persuaded her to go up to bed.

'I don't want to be alone again,' whispered Delilah, clutching at Hildamay's arm. Hildamay winced at the strength of her grip. 'Please don't say I have to be alone again.' Tears slipped out of her eyes, ran gently down the side of her face and leaked into the pillow.

'Alone is not so bad,' soothed Hildamay.

'Alone is living death,' said Delilah in a flat monotone. 'I'm so frightened. So frightened.' She curled up in the bed. 'I don't want to be alone,' she sobbed.

'Maybe Ned will come back now,' said Hildamay, stroking her hair.

Delilah wrenched herself away. 'I don't want Ned to come back,' she said in a harsh voice and rolled over to the other side of the bed. 'Ned makes me feel even more alone.' Her voice was muffled by the pillow. 'Ben,' she sobbed. 'I want Ben. I love Ben.' She sat up and stared hopelessly at Hildamay, tears squeezing out of the cracks of her swollen eyes and dribbling down her face, mingling with the congealing blood on her bitten lips. 'Why has he left me so alone?' she whispered, 'when I need him so much?'

Hildamay said nothing but sat on the other side of the bed watching her in a sort of despair, and wished never to find this thing they called love.

CHAPTER SIXTEEN

DELILAH lay on her side, curled in a ball, and occasionally her thumb would steal into her mouth. But then she would quickly withdraw it as though, even in sleep, she could hear a voice telling her to take it out of her mouth. She looked so fragile lying there, so defenceless, that Hildamay wondered how this could be her friend; so cool, so capable, so contained. She wondered at Delilah's fear of being alone and, sighing, bent over and gently eased a strand of dark hair which lay across her face, stuck to the tears which had dried on her cheek. 'But Delilah,' she said softly, 'we are anyway alone.' Delilah stirred in her sleep and, taking the hand which she had felt on her face in hers, pulled it down to her neck and clasped it tightly. Hildamay let her hand lie there and stretched awkwardly against the pillows. As she closed her eyes she wondered at the emotions which allowed facts to become so distorted. She tossed them this way and that in her head, but still she could find no answer. That Delilah, normally so calm, so rational, could distort the evidence so badly seemed to her a sort of cruelty. She knew that she was in pain, but it seemed to her a monstrous pain because it was self-inflicted. Sighing, Hildamay eventually fell asleep.

Her flat felt cold and grey, all the colours in it ghostly and deadened in the early morning light. Even the sunny yellow of her kitchen seemed tired and jaundiced. Hildamay walked into her bedroom and switched on the answering machine. The red light flashed showing five messages. Each one was from Ben. She sighed with irritation and suddenly felt the great dead weight of Delilah's grief. Quickly stripping off her creased clothes she almost ran into the bathroom. She closed and locked the door, and filled the bath with boiling water and eucalyptus oil, running the hot water until the room was clouded with sharply scented steam. She breathed it in deeply, pushing each breath out from her diaphragm and filling her lungs with air. She continued to breathe deeply until she felt calmer and then she scrubbed herself all over, stinging her skin with the hard little wooden brush. The water was so hot she had to lower herself into it, inch by inch. She lay in the bath for a while then climbed out and, after she had dried herself, automatically slipped into the ritual of applying her lotions and creams; a dot here, a dab there. She could not shake the thought of Delilah from her head and when the telephone rang she ran to answer it. It was Ben.

'How is she?'

'She's OK,' said Hildamay, sighing. 'At least she had nearly stopped crying when she finally fell asleep.'

'That bad?' said Ben softly.

'Worse.'

'I've been awake all night, worrying.'

'Join the club,' said Hildamay abruptly.

'What a mess.' Ben sighed, a long breath that hissed down the telephone.

'Could have been worse.'

'How?' His voice was startled.

'She could have cut her wrists, taken an overdose, hung herself.' There was violence in her voice.

Ben did not speak. 'Thanks,' he said eventually, his voice thick with tears. Tears? thought Hildamay. Tears now?

'I didn't think she'd take it this badly,' he said, his voice shaking.

'You thought she'd behave like a good girl and say "thank you very much, that was lovely"?' Hildamay was incredulous.

156

'No. No, of course I didn't think that. But she knew the score. She knows I'm happily married.'

'Happily!' Hildamay's voice echoed through the telephone.

'Yes. Happily,' he said irritably. 'As a matter of fact, very happily. Delilah knows that. When the affair began it was just about having a good time, a good fuck, a good laugh. We agreed on that. And then – then it changed. That's when I realised I'd have to stop it.'

'You might have realised that when she left Ned.' Hildamay was scornful, her voice thin with anger.

'She told me she left him because she didn't love him. She swore it had nothing to do with me.'

'And you believed her?'

'I should accuse her of lying?'

'No. No, I'm sorry. I didn't mean that.'

'She knew,' he went on, almost to himself, 'she knew I'd never leave Kate.'

'You told her that?'

'Well of course I told her that,' he said, his voice sharp with irritation. 'I told you, it was an affair. We were having a proper grown-up affair. No ties, no hard feelings.'

'You told her you loved her?'

'Oh, love,' he said abruptly. 'Love can mean many things. Mostly it's just shorthand for "I want to fuck you", or "I think you're gorgeous", or even, "You make me laugh".'

'You make me *laugh*?'

'Yes, yes,' he said impatiently. 'It's just code for "You're special". It doesn't mean you want to grow old together and go through the real process of life with each other. That thing called reality.'

'That thing you have with Kate?'

'Exactly.'

'So you never told her you'd leave Kate?'

'What is this, a hearing test?'

'Sorry. Just checking.'

'No, I never told her I'd leave Kate,' said Ben slowly, spelling it out. 'Not that that seems to have made much difference.' There was a pause. 'Will you call me?' he added, 'and let me know how she is?'

Hildamay hesitated. 'I'm not sure.'

'Just over the next few weeks. Think of it as an act of charity.'

'Sweet,' said Hildamay.

'Thank you,' said Ben, sounding relieved. 'And thank you for your understanding. In normal circumstances you're the last person

I would have thought of turning to. I've underestimated you.'

'Oh, little big man,' said Hildamay and put the phone down.

Hildamay sat in her office and felt depressed. Jack Rome put his head round the door.

'Go away.'

'There's something –'

'Go away.'

She looked so strange without her smile, which she normally put on with her make-up before she left the house, that Jack went away. She had forgotten her smile that morning and, having forgotten it, did not seem to be able to find it again. George looked at her curiously from time to time and kept her supplied with a constant supply of nice hot drinks but did not speak to her except to give her her telephone messages.

She kept remembering Delilah's bitten lips. She put down her pen and, gazing out of the window, sat and thought about her. The leaves were beginning to turn. It would be autumn soon. 'Death,' she sighed, for she hated the winter and dreaded the long dark evenings. The telephone rang.

'It's me.' The voice was hoarse, scarcely more than a whisper.

'Telepathy,' said Hildamay. 'How are you feeling?'

'I just woke up,' croaked Delilah and groaned. 'Thank God for nannies.'

'Oh, the children!' said Hildamay, for she had forgotten all about them.

'They'll be home soon. I'm going to have to pull myself together and smarten up. Thank God for children. They're one reason to stay alive, at least.' Delilah laughed, a short, bitter laugh. 'Can't think of any other.'

Hildamay was silent. 'I didn't ring to bore you,' said Delilah after a while. 'I rang to say thank you and sorry.'

'Sorry for what?'

'Sorry for calling you a cold, heartless bitch.'

'Oh, that,' said Hildamay.

'Yes, that. I didn't mean a word of it. I was in pain and you weren't. I wanted you to hurt – like me. Oh, not you. Ben, I suppose. It's very lonely, pain,' she said musingly.

'Skin like a rhinoceros,' said Hildamay brightly, although she did not feel it.

'You wish. You know your trouble? You won't let anybody in because you're so frightened that you'll never be able to let them out again.'

'It's a bit late in the day for potted psychology,' said Hildamay wearily.

'There's nothing potted about that,' said Delilah sharply. 'There's five years of hard labour in that sentence.'

'Perhaps you're right.'

'What do you mean, I'm right? Is this the Hildamay we all know and love?' said Delilah with some of her old briskness. 'Come, come, girl. Don't go soft on us now.'

'Well, fuck off, then. Is that better?'

'Much,' said Delilah with relish.

'Shall I come round and see you after work?'

'No, no, you don't have to do that. But I might call you later if the demons start biting.'

'Whenever. Goodbye.'

Hildamay sat and thought about Delilah, who protected her vulnerability so effectively with a waspish indifference. Which made her think about Liz. She felt a sharp stab of indigestion. Perhaps Liz's aggression was a mask for fear? She had not been kind to Liz. She was pregnant, alone, perhaps frightened. With a sigh she picked up the telephone.

'Hello, it's me.'

'Who?'

'I know it's been a while but surely you're not senile yet.'

'Well, well, well, it's Miss Hildamay Smith,' drawled Liz. 'To what do I owe the pleasure of this call?'

'I wondered how you were,' said Hildamay abruptly.

'Fine.'

'Good.'

There was silence.

'You called me,' said Hildamay after a time.

'No.' Liz's tone was flat, expressionless.

'The answering machine,' explained Hildamay. 'There was a blank message. I thought it must have been you.'

'No.'

There was another silence, longer and more charged than the first.

'Has your lover left? Is that why you've got the time to ring me?' asked Liz, her voice harsh.

'Lover?'

'Your Saturday lover.'

'What Saturday lover?' asked Hildamay, bewildered. 'I don't do anything on Saturdays.'

'Thanks,' said Liz bitterly. Hildamay remembered suddenly their last telephone conversation and felt a violent stab of indigestion.

'Sorry, Lizzie,' she said, taking a deep breath. 'I've been a selfish cow.'

There was a long silence then Liz let out a sharp sigh, her breath hissing down the wire. 'Oh, shit,' she said. 'I was going to be really angry with you, but I can't. It was my fault, bleating on about babies. I'm sorry, really I am.'

'No, it was my fault.'

'Oh, shut up. I'm claiming the blame and therefore the glory. It's OK. I understand. I know it's boring hearing me go on about being pregnant and babies and ante-natal classes but it is pretty exciting and I thought you'd want to know. I guess I overdid it with the expectant mother routine.'

'Slightly,' said Hildamay cautiously.

'Well, you know me. Never one for moderation. Can't drink a glass of champagne, have to have a bottle. Can't be a vegetarian, have to be a vegan. I'm trying to learn balance.' Her tone was serious.

'God forbid,' said Hildamay fervently.

'Oh, don't worry. He will,' said Liz and laughed.

'You sound better,' ventured Hildamay.

'Better than what?'

'More like you.'

'I always was me,' protested Liz, her tone sharp. 'Oh, Lord preserve us from the childless, from those in control of their own bodies,' she exclaimed. 'And minds. I think my hormones must have settled down at long last. I can get through a whole hour without crying.'

'How about three hours?'

'Dodgy.'

'Supper?'

'Sure,' said Liz cautiously. 'When?'

'Next week. Shall I cook? I could make steamed fish and puréed vegetables.'

'No way. I want out. I've had enough of treating myself as an invalid. All these early nights and steamed food, it's enough to turn any right-minded girl into a weeping idiot. Anyway, I've moved into the disgustingly carnivorous stage now. Red meat dripping with blood. French fries shining with grease.'

'You've stopped being sick?'

'My, my, what diagnostic ability. They graduate from medical school on less.'

'Up your bum. Luigi's? Eight-thirty?'

'OK, and just wait until you see my new earrings. They're knock-out.'

'I'll duck.'

'Piss off.'

'I love you too.'

'Hildamay?' said Sky's small, anxious voice. 'It's Sky Matthews.'

'Hello, Sky,' said Hildamay, her voice flat with exhaustion. 'How are you?'

'I'm very well,' said Sky, the words tumbling over each other. 'Is it all right for Saturday?'

'Fine,' said Hildamay quickly.

'Are you all right?' Sky's voice was hesitant.

'Yes. Why shouldn't I be all right?'

'You sound – funny.'

'Do I? I'm sorry, Sky. I'm just a bit tired. I was awake most of the night looking after a friend.'

'Is she very ill?' asked Sky gravely.

Hildamay smiled. 'Critical but stable.'

'That sounds horrid. Is it catching?'

'I sincerely hope not. No, don't worry. It's not catching and I'm about the last person who'd ever catch it. I have a well functioning immune system.'

'What's functioning and immune?'

'Functioning means working, immune means – immune means you'll have to look it up. Which reminds me. Is it all right if George comes out with us on Saturday?'

'Dictionary George?'

'The very same.'

'Yes,' said Sky consideringly. 'I think that would be very nice.'

'Good. Then I shall invite him. And now I must go to bed and get some sleep.'

'It's very early,' said Sky doubtfully.

'And I am very tired.'

'Are you quite sure Saturday's all right?' asked Sky, anxiety making her voice shrill.

'Quite sure.'

'Oh, good. I look forward to Saturday all week,' said Sky, relieved. There was a long pause and then her voice dropped to a confiding whisper. 'I miss you, Hildamay.'

Good grief, thought Hildamay in astonishment, I think I'm going to cry. It must, she supposed, be all the emotion of the previous night. All that free-floating pain.

'I miss you too,' she said, her voice unsteady.

'Are you *quite* sure you're all right?' asked Sky.

'Perfectly. Good night, Sky.'

'Good night, Hildamay.'

Hildamay switched off the light by her bed and lay in the dark. She wondered why Sky affected her so much and understood, quite suddenly, that she loved her. She lay and thought about her small, sturdy body and shiny eyes and shiny hair and smiled at the thought of her. But as she lay in the drugged stupor that marks the borders of sleep some half forgotten memory pushed at her mind. 'Pain,' she murmured, 'love.' And she woke completely, startled, and sat up in bed and wiped the dream from her eyes. The image had gone but an emotion remained; small and cold and solitary, a feeling crying in the dark. She turned on the light again and blinked as the room settled into its familiar shapes and colours. But still she felt restless, and tossed and turned until, knowing that she would not sleep, she got up and walked into the bathroom, locking the door behind her.

CHAPTER SEVENTEEN

'Now that this thing with Delilah's finally over,' said Kate, 'Ben will be wonderful for a few months. Full of shame and contrition. He'll be nice to the kids. He'll buy me presents, make love to me, call me his precious flower and then. . . .'

Her voice tailed off and she looked down at her hands. The skin was cracked and reddened, the nails torn and rimmed with dry paint. She held them up and stared at them. With a defiant twist she turned the diamond of her engagement ring back to the centre of her finger. The ring was loose, the stone usually nestled in her palm. Her wedding ring was too tight and embedded in her finger, the flesh puffing out on each side of the gold.

'And then?' prompted Hildamay.

'And then it'll start again.'

Kate sighed and looked out of the restaurant window. Hildamay poured her another glass of champagne.

'You knew about Delilah?' she asked gently.

Kate looked back at her. Her round, open face was creased with fatigue and her eyes a dull, wintry grey.

'Not at first.' She shrugged. 'Not when she came down for that first weekend. You were there. You must remember? In the summer?'

'I remember,' said Hildamay drily.

'I was so pleased.' Kate's mouth twisted. 'I thought she liked me. I thought if Delilah was interested in me, then perhaps I wasn't so dull, not just a fat wife and mother, after all.' She looked at Hildamay. 'I hated her, too. Parading around my kitchen that day, so cool and perfect. Leaning under the cupboard and waggling her bottom in the air for Ben to admire. She was always so bright and shining. Like you. I was always in awe of the two of you when you were together. You seemed to have everything so –' she hesitated – 'so under control. You made the world look easy. So when she started to ring up and be friendly, really friendly, I thought it was because of me.' She shrugged again and her mouth twisted down at the corners. 'Stupid,' she whispered, as if to herself. 'It took me a while to realise, but by the time I had, it was too late. They were well away.' She sighed. 'It was my own vanity, of course, which allowed it to happen. I didn't know what to do. He'd never –' she grimaced – 'he'd never done it so close to home before. In the end I decided I just had to sit back and wait.'

'Didn't you mind?' asked Hildamay.

'Don't be ridiculous,' said Kate. 'I could cheerfully have killed her. And him. I thought about it,' she added dreamily. 'I went to the chemist and bought rat poison. A huge great bag of it. I mixed it up and made ginger spice biscuits. I thought the ginger and spice,' she said, lowering her voice and bending her head towards Hildamay's, 'would be strong enough to disguise the taste of the poison. I made a great big batch of them, with real root ginger, the way Ben likes them. Not with that powdered stuff. It's so insipid. Then I packed them up in a Tupperware box to keep them fresh. They're in the larder.' She smiled. 'They've been there for weeks.'

Hildamay gazed at her in awe. Round, gentle, simple Kate, cooking up poisoned biscuits in her cosy kitchen.

'Did you know?'

The question took Hildamay by surprise. Her mouth opened, but no sound came from it. She sat looking stupidly at Kate, her mouth still open.

'Oh, of course you knew.'

Hildamay still did not speak. Kate looked at her then looked away.

'You didn't laugh at me, did you?' she whispered. 'You didn't laugh at me?'

'No,' said Hildamay. 'Nobody ever laughed.'

'You think I'm stupid, don't you?'

Hildamay shrugged. She thought Kate's only stupidity had been in marrying Ben.

'Oh, I may be simple, Hildamay,' said Kate, looking at her with irritation, 'but in the end I'm not stupid. I know when my husband's fucking around. It may take me a while but I always figure out who he's fucking. Always.' Her mouth twisted with regret. Hildamay was shocked. The word sounded so obscene in Kate's mouth.

'I wish I didn't know.' She sighed then took several deep breaths. 'No. No, that's not true. I'm glad I know. I need to understand the nature of the beast I'm dealing with.'

Hildamay frowned.

'Then I know what I'm up against,' explained Kate, her round face shining and earnest. 'I can make the right plans.'

'Why don't you just leave him?' asked Hildamay.

Kate looked at her consideringly.

'I know it's difficult for you to understand.' She patted her hand maternally. 'But he's my husband. For better or for worse,' she added harshly, although her tone was not bitter. 'I need him,' she said simply.

'For what?' asked Hildamay, curious.

'For my being. To be. To live. To survive.'

'Wouldn't another kinder and more faithful version be better?' asked Hildamay.

'Better for what?' Kate shook her head. 'He wouldn't be Ben. I know Ben. I understand him. Oh, he likes women like Delilah. Or Katie. She was the last one. Before Delilah. Tactful of him, wasn't it? To fuck another Katie. I guess it made it easier when he came. When he comes he calls out my name,' she added, her face pink with pleasure. Hildamay felt nauseous. 'He likes women like that. But only in his imagination. He doesn't really like them. Not *really*.' She drew out the word. 'That's why he leaves them. They tire of him, you see. They don't understand what he needs. They're brilliant and glamorous and hard.' She shook her head. 'Very, very hard. They have no centre into which he can sink when he's tired. He likes a soft centre. And he gets tired. Very tired, poor darling. He's sweet, really, Hildamay. Don't be hard on him.'

'Sweet,' echoed Hildamay.

Kate looked at her consideringly for a moment.

'Oh, yes. He's sweet. He's just a boy, really. He's very gentle inside. It's hard for them. Men, I mean. They've been taught that they've got to be big and strong and macho and go out and prove themselves so they rush around waving their dicks in the air. Ben needs to show us all that he's a man. If he thinks every woman wants a bit of his dick, he's happy. He comes home swaggering, like a hunter from the kill. He comes in and puts two bottles of champagne on the table or gives me money and tells me to go out and buy a good joint of beef. For a treat. For his family. He's just proving he can do it. All.'

'And what about you? What about your identity?' asked Hildamay. She sat there in appalled fascination.

'My identity?' Kate looked confused. 'Oh, that identity. It's all bound up with Ben. We've been married since I was twenty. Identity!' She laughed harshly and gulped at her champagne. 'What you mean is pride. Pride is a luxury, Hildamay. A luxury for women like you who've never found something, someone, they want enough to keep. It's a fine idea, Hildamay. Fine. But that's all it is. An idea. It doesn't mean anything, him fucking around. I know he'll be back. You see, he needs me. If I left him and took the kids he'd fall apart.' She smiled at Hildamay with compassion. 'Fall apart,' she repeated, banging her ringed hand on the table for emphasis.

'But what if he falls in love with somebody else?'

'Love?' said Kate scornfully. 'What's love got to do with anything? What men really understand by love is a full belly, a spent cock, a comfortable bed and an easy heart. He thinks he's in love. He thinks it quite often actually. He once told me. Said he was leaving. I told him not to be so silly. That it would pass. I said he'd never see his children again. I said, if necessary, I'd leave the country, take the kids so he'd never find us. I'd make him give me half of his income for support. No court in the land would have refused. Then where would he be? He likes money. Comfort, really,' she added reflectively. 'And how could he have a decent life with no money? What could he give his woman then? Living in a small, cold flat with only his love to keep him warm. And how long would that last? With the boys at work too embarrassed to invite him to all those business dinners without a wife. It doesn't go down well, you see. It doesn't go down well in the City at all.'

'What doesn't?'

'Walking out on your family. Shows you've got no spine. No loyalty. They don't like that. Playing around is one thing but abdicating your responsibilities is quite another.' She speared a piece of steak and chewed on it in silence for a while.

'They think they love him, of course.'

'Who?'

'His tarts,' said Kate. 'They're fools. Women who've forgotten how to be women. They want to compete. The last thing that a man like Ben wants is competition. His whole life is a competition. Usually with himself. Those tarts haven't an ounce of sense in their heads. If they had, they'd keep him. That's why I have to know who he's fucking. In case he chooses one of the clever ones. No,' she continued, heaping potatoes into her mouth, 'they all fall in love with him because he always leaves and goes back to his wife. To me. He came back, after the last one, after Delilah. He buried his head in my lap and he cried. Like a child. Said he'd hurt her. Said she was distraught. Said he hurt. He made me rub his heart. To take the pain away. "Only you, Katie," he said. "Only you can take my pain away."' Kate's face softened. Her eyes brimmed with tears.

'I expect she was distraught.'

'Who?'

'Why, Delilah, of course. We always love the ones that leave us.'

'Do we?' asked Hildamay, fascinated.

'Well of course,' said Kate comfortably. 'Or, at least, we think we do. It has nothing to do with love. Not real love. Real love isn't wine and roses. It's acid and shit. Acid and shit,' she said and cleaned her plate, scraping the knife over the surface to pick up the last fragment of cream and cheese and potatoes. Hildamay looked at the blood coagulating in the cream. Kate spooned it up expertly with the blunt side of her knife and licked the blade.

'That,' she said burping gently, 'was delicious. Thank you, Hildamay.' She patted her hand. 'It's good to see you again. Just the two of us. A real girls' lunch.'

Hildamay pushed her uneaten plate of food away.

'Is Delilah a tart?'

'Well, what do you think?' said Kate and smiled at her. She had bits of bloody meat stuck between her teeth. She picked at them absently with her cracked nails. 'No bitch,' she said quietly, staring out of the window, 'is ever going to take my husband away from me.'

Kate. Gentle Kate.

CHAPTER EIGHTEEN

'LET'S meet at The Globe.'
'Must we?'
'Yes, darling,' said Cassie briskly. 'We must. I loathe pubs. All those ghastly men with distended bellies. Anyway, what's The Globe done to you that it's suddenly out of favour?'

'Nothing. It's just – it's just that it'll be full of people we know and they'll insist on coming over to talk to us. It's so difficult to have a private conversation there.'

'Nonsense, darling. We just tell them to fuck off.'

'An elegant solution,' said Hildamay. 'Now why didn't I think of that?'

She found herself a small table in a dark corner, as far away from the bar and Thomas as possible. She willed Cassie to appear. She could not see Thomas anywhere, so began to relax slightly. It must be his night off. Well, she didn't mind seeing him, he was really rather nice to look at, but she did not want to talk to him. She would feel forced to offer him some sort of explanation. Poor bastard. She sighed and stared into her drink.

'Oh, let him think we're a couple of dykes,' Liz had said. 'What's the harm?'

'No harm in that,' Hildamay had replied, 'but even a nice straight boy like that might think it a little odd, two dykes doing it in the sitting room while he's unconscious in the bedroom. Strange way to get your kicks.'

'So there are some strange people around. He's probably in shock. At least it means he won't talk to anyone about it.'

'Still,' Hildamay insisted, 'I think you should call him and give him some sort of explanation. He must think it weird that you were so keen and then turned on the big freeze.'

'I haven't even seen him to freeze him,' protested Liz. 'Anyway, that's where the dyke scene comes in. If he thinks I'm a lesbian, he'll expect the red light.'

'I still think you should call him.'

'No.' Liz was obdurate. 'This is my child. It has nothing to do with him. Let him think what he likes. It was an immaculate conception.'

Not so immaculate, thought Hildamay gloomily, as she sat and sipped champagne. It bothered her that the plan had gone wrong. She felt an indefinable sense of unease. Oh, how would he find out anyway? Nobody was about to tell him. But what if it looks just like him? The thought startled her. Babies did have a habit of looking like their parents. Perhaps Thomas had a particularly strong genetic identity kit stashed away in that blond head of his. She was thinking so hard about Thomas and his genes that when she looked up and found him standing over her, she missed her mouth and emptied her glass down the front of her silk T-shirt.

'Aaaagh!' she said.

'I might well say the same to you,' he said, briskly rubbing at her breasts with a clean white handkerchief. He walked off and returned a minute later with a fresh glass of champagne.

'Cold and dry,' he said, 'for shock.'

'You surprised me,' she said accusingly.

'And I thought you were just pleased to see me.' He sat down at the table. 'Twiglet?' he said, putting five into his mouth at once.

'I've given them up,' said Hildamay, gulping at her champagne.

'Wise woman. How's Liz?'

Hildamay took another gulp of champagne and put on her most dazzling smile. He did not respond. 'She's fine,' she said, increasing it in size and sincerity, 'really very well. Blooming. Roses in her cheeks, a sparkle to her eye, a spring in her step.'

'And a bun in her oven,' finished Thomas, matching her smile.

She stopped smiling. 'What I want to know is, where did you figure in it all? Why did you have to be there at conception? It is mine, I take it?'

Hildamay stared at him, expressionless.

'Come, come, Hildamay. You can tell me I'm a father. I'm man enough to take it. You were woman enough to help create a child. Surely you're woman enough to tell the truth?'

'I don't know what you're talking about.'

'Oh yes you do!' He grabbed her wrist and held it, twisting it hard as he pulled her across the table, so that her nose was almost touching his. His face was contorted with anger. 'That's why you're skulking over in this corner. Trying to hide.' Hildamay blushed at the truth. 'You two set me up,' he hissed. 'Thought I was some stupid little sucker who didn't have the nous to work out the truth, and if I did have the nous, wouldn't have the guts to confront you with it. Where do you get off? Life isn't that cheap for some of us, Hildamay. If that's my child then I want to know about it. I want to take care of it. You thought you'd got away with it, didn't you? Didn't you?' He tightened his grip, pulling her further across the table. 'Thought that little lesbian scene would send me screaming back to Mummy, not daring to say a word. At first it did, but then I got to wondering and when I heard that Liz was pregnant, then I got to thinking. And this is what I thought. I thought, that's my baby. I don't know how you did it because I used a condom. All I know is that you did.' He stopped suddenly and smiled, a smile contorted by pain. 'I liked her. I really, really liked her.'

Dear God, she thought, shocked. He still likes her.

He stopped smiling and his eyes narrowed. 'So you can tell Liz when you see her that I want my child.' He released his grip.

She sat back and looked at him, but did not speak.

'And you can also tell her that I'm going to marry her.'

'Who?'

'Liz. I want her.' He looked at Hildamay sharply. 'I want her very much. And I want my child. We're going to be one nice, happy little family.'

'You're mad.'

He shrugged and laughed harshly. 'Perhaps. Perhaps I am mad. That crazy little thing called love.'

Then he stood up and walked away.

'Hildamay Smith,' she murmured to herself. 'You really fucked up this time.' He was right. She had thought him a sucker. She had chosen him for precisely that reason. Had even convinced Liz that he was 'a nice sort of boy'. The sort who would never cause trouble. Well, he was a nice sort of boy, exactly the nice sort of boy you'd want to be the father of your child – caring, committed, responsible. If, that was, you wanted a father for your child. She felt a sharp stab of sympathy. After all, it was his child. Or half of it, at any rate. How do you give half a baby back? She imagined the head with Liz, the torso with Thomas, the smile with Liz, the eyes with Thomas. What a mess. She groaned and bent her head to her glass, letting the cold bubbles fizz and sparkle over her face. When she looked up there was a bottle of champagne on the table. Standing by it was Thomas.

'I'm sorry if I hurt you,' he said softly, nodding at her wrist which she had been unconsciously rubbing. 'This is from me.' She opened her mouth to protest but before she could speak he said, 'I know Cassie's joining you. She'll drink it, if you don't want it. And I should move tables if I were you. She won't be pleased to be stuck out here in no man's land.'

'Cooee, darlings!' They both heard her at the same time and turned to look. Cassie waved enthusiastically. Even from where they sat, which was quite some distance away, they could hear her bracelets clattering. 'Won't be a tiny minute, darlings,' she called, sweeping down on a group of people and kissing them loudly. She was dressed entirely in deep purple velvet: a tailored jacket, cut sharply in at the waist and trimmed at the neck with shocking pink ostrich feathers, under which she wore a full skirt which swept almost to her feet. A sparkling violet scarf was draped across her shoulders and from her ears hung small chandeliers of violet crystal. Her mouth was painted a brilliant pink, her hair tinted aubergine and around her eyes glittered smudges of frosted lilac.

'Darling!' she said, kissing Hildamay on the lips.

'Cassie,' murmured Hildamay, discreetly wiping lipstick from her mouth. She loathed that particular shade of pink.

'Darling!' said Cassie, enveloping Thomas in a bear hug. He sneezed as the feathers tickled his nose and she released him, laughing, then dabbed at the luminous pink lipstick marks which glowed on either cheek.

'Oh goody, darlings. Champagne!' Cassie clapped her hands like a child. 'Just the thing for divine inspiration.' She flung herself down on the chair opposite Hildamay. 'I'm writing a novel, darlings,' she said with a dramatic wave of one arm, the other busy tilting a champagne glass to her lips. She swallowed half the contents and wiped her mouth with relish. 'Well, darlings. Aren't you pleased for me?'

'Yes,' said Thomas. 'It's the great British public I'm worried about.'

Cassie giggled and wrinkled her nose at him. 'They'll adore it, darling. It's stuffed with sex. Nice sex,' she added quickly.

'Mary will be pleased,' said Hildamay.

'Barbara won't,' said Thomas.

'Darlings?' Cassie frowned. 'What are you both talking about?'

'Whitehouse,' explained Hildamay. 'Cartland,' added Thomas.

'Oh, those two old bitches,' said Cassie, flapping her hand dismissively. 'Why are we sitting here?' She gazed about her in outrage.

'Hildamay will tell you,' said Thomas. 'Bye, sweet.' He bent and kissed Cassie and nodded at Hildamay.

'Well, aren't you going to kiss her, darling?' Cassie demanded loudly. Thomas stiffened. Neither of them moved.

'Lord, but you're bossy tonight,' said Hildamay eventually.

'Oh, sorry, darling.' Cassie was immediately contrite. Like most exuberant people, she was used to being told off. She blew a kiss at Thomas who went back to the bar.

'Now,' said Cassie, gazing around, 'let's find ourselves a proper table.' The bar was full but in no time Cassie had summoned up a team of waiters who somehow produced a table and two armchairs out of nowhere.

'Put it there,' she said imperiously and herded all the people at the surrounding tables into cramped little groups. 'You don't mind? You are sweet! So charming!' she exclaimed, dropping blessings on every head. Hildamay watched her with a kind of envy. For somebody who professed to find life so difficult, Cassie had a remarkably assured way of handling it.

'There we are, darling.' Cassie settled into her chair and gazed at Hildamay. 'That's better. Now why were you sitting in that corner? And what does it have to do with Thomas?'

'I was hiding,' said Hildamay. 'Life's been a bit trying recently.'

'Oh, you mean the Delilah affair?' Cassie clasped her hands together. Her eyes shone with complicity. 'Delilah and Ben!' she exclaimed. 'Too thrilling, darling.'

'I don't imagine Kate's too thrilled,' said Hildamay laconically.

'Oh, Kate!' said Cassie in exasperation. 'The woman's too silly for words. A husband like that, and what does she do? Gets herself up like a perfect frump and then goes off and buries herself in the country. I wouldn't let him out of my sight if I was her. Anyway, darling, she must know.'

'Must know what?'

'That her husband fucks like a rabbit, darling,' said Cassie, sipping delicately at her champagne. 'Anyway, I hear you've been a perfect angel. Playing nursemaid to Delilah.'

'Who told you that?' said Hildamay sharply.

'Ben. He said Delilah's in a terrible state. So's Kate. Mind you, darling, he doesn't sound too rosy himself, poor lamb.'

'Delilah's fine,' said Hildamay abruptly.

'That's not what I heard, darling,' said Cassie, looking at her expectantly. 'Oh, don't be a bore, darling. Do tell. I hear she's left Ned.'

'There's nothing to tell,' said Hildamay firmly. 'Delilah's perfectly all right. And she left Ned weeks ago. Are you very thin under all those clothes or am I imagining it?'

But Cassie was not to be deflected. 'I hear she took some pills, darling!' She loved to hear about grief; she said it made her feel so much better about life. Hildamay raised an eyebrow but did not speak. 'Lord, you're a bore sometimes, darling. So sniffy about a tiny bit of gossip.' She pursed her lips in a pout of discontent. 'Well, if you won't tell me, darling, I shall simply go to my other sources.' She looked at Hildamay slyly and then tossed her head so that the purple glass chandeliers in her ears tinkled. 'Thin, darling?' she continued, after a momentary pause. 'Why, I've positively wasted away. Weeks and weeks of vegetables. Raw. Such a bore, darling. My breath smells like manure.' She giggled. 'So it's probably a good thing there are no admirers flocking around me at the moment.'

'What's happened to Jack?'

Cassie's face darkened. 'That bastard,' she said bitterly. 'Liar, cheat, charlatan.' Her voice began to rise.

'I know all that,' said Hildamay impatiently, 'but what exactly did he do?'

'Well, if you knew, darling, why didn't you bloody well tell me? I thought that's what bloody friends were for?' Cassie's voice was loud with indignation.

Hildamay shrugged. 'You'd never have believed me.'

'Oh, I suppose you're probably right, darling.' Cassie sighed. 'He was wonderful at first. Marvellous! Then he started going on and on about my weight. He said I was disgusting. Not that it stopped him fucking me, or telling me that he was going to leave his wife. It was a sort of power play, I think. The minute I felt relaxed or happy, he'd start. He'd sneer and withdraw and once he had me gibbering on the carpet, a jelly-roll of insecurity, he'd start the charm-school number, pick me up off the carpet again, dust me down, stick me back on the pedestal and I'd relax. A few days later it would start all over again. So, darling –' she took a deep breath – 'I decided to get thin and stop all that nonsense. I stopped eating, except for the odd carrot here and there. The funny thing was, the thinner I got, the nastier he became.'

'Nice,' said Hildamay.

Cassie nodded. 'Oh, a regular sweetheart, darling. It was then that I realised what a little man he *was*.' She spat, like a cat cornered. 'So I told him to go and of course as soon as he thought I didn't want him, thought I was indifferent . . .' She paused and looked at Hildamay proudly. 'God, I was good, darling. Never had a woman been colder. Anyway, once he saw that, he went mad. It started all over again. The charm, the champagne, the tears, the dinners, the sex. He couldn't live without me. He was going to leave his wife. The works. And I believed him, darling.' She shook her head. 'Such a sucker. Trouble is,' she smiled sadly, 'I'm so insecure that if somebody tells me they love me I simply can't resist them.'

She lapsed into a brief silence but then her eyes gleamed again with indignation and she sputtered with outrage, spraying Hildamay with champagne. 'Oh, sorry, darling,' she said, dabbing at her face with a silk velvet sleeve. 'Then,' she continued, her voice high and thin, 'I found out he was fucking someone else as well! He didn't care about fat meat, or lean meat, he wanted fresh meat. All that crap about me being the first person he'd slept with in eight years! It got me thinking he was a liar and so off I went to see his wife, Beth.' She nodded at Hildamay. 'You know, the invalid.' Cassie smiled suddenly. 'Some invalid, darling. She's charming. A marvellous woman but completely bewildered as to what she's doing married to that creep. I could see that straight away, darling.' Cassie's voice was rounded with complacency but in it Hildamay could hear the bitter whine of revenge. She shifted uncomfortably in her chair, for while she had no love for Jack Rome, she hated the triumphant cruelty shining in Cassie's eyes. She seemed to her like a child, tearing the legs off spiders one by one, and smiling as she watched their hopeless stagger.

'We've got him set up, darling,' said Cassie with relish. 'We're both pretending that we think the sun shines out of his cock and we're making plans.' Her face was shining with excitement.

'What plans?' asked Hildamay, despite herself.

'We've decided to set up a women's commune in the country. Just a small one, darling. Her, me and the kids. The house in Surbiton belongs to her, you see, and she's already sold it, without telling him, and has bought a house in the country. And I've got my redundancy money which means I've plenty to live on. The country doesn't cost much, does it, darling?' She peered at Hildamay. 'Well, I don't think it does. Not compared to London. All you do is go out for walks and they're free. Just about. Oh, didn't I tell you, darling?' she said, noticing Hildamay's questioning frown. 'The agency made me redundant last week. Gave me a year's salary to piss off. And so they should, darling,' she added indignantly, 'after ten years' hard labour. I'd been dying to leave, anyway, and write a novel. There were only two problems: no money and no plot. Then along came darling Jack with the perfect plot and, of course, darling . . .' She paused dramatically and flashed Hildamay a triumphant smile . . . 'a perfect revenge!

'Beth's going to help me with the male character. We're going to build him flaw by flaw. God knows, she's got enough material and God knows, darling, so have I after all my years of fucking. I've fucked a few flaws, I can tell you. Imperfect, every last one of them. It'll be dynamite, darling. Explosive. It'll be the feminist's *Hollywood Husbands* except I'm going to set it in Surbiton. Don't frown like that, Hildamay, it's very unbecoming. And Surbiton's a brilliant idea, darling. Pure genius. Everybody'll identify with it. The whole world lives in Surbiton or somewhere like it. They'll all be able to spot their neighbours or the people they live with. What the punters want, and I should know after all those bloody research groups I used to have to sit through, is a bit of real life. It's time for dirty realism, darling.' She giggled. 'Very dirty.' She clapped her hands and picked up the bottle of champagne with a flourish. It was empty. She frowned at it and gestured to a waiter to bring another then turned and looked at Hildamay expectantly. 'Well, darling?'

'Well –' said Hildamay, at which Cassie raised a laconic eyebrow. 'I hope it all works out,' she added feebly.

'Oh, no doubt about it, darling. I'm going to keep my flat in London but spend most of the time living with Beth in the country. I shall have my own room and a study in which to write and she's wanted to move to the country for years, darling, so it suits us both perfectly. She'll have company and she can use my flat when she needs it. And Jack Rome will find himself homeless, sexless and, with your help, jobless.'

Hildamay laughed uneasily. 'Cassie!' she exclaimed. 'I do believe you're serious.' Cassie looked at her in astonishment, a little frown of reproof tugging at her eyes.

'Well, of course I'm serious, darling. I've never been more serious in my life.'

'And what's Beth going to do, sitting in the country?'

'Restore antiques. She's been doing evening classes for years. She's really very good but there's never been that much call for it in Surbiton. Anyway, she wants the kids to be brought up in the country. She's been fighting with Jack about it for years. He refused to move so he could carry on going out catting every night. So we've made the decision for him. Amazing really, darling,' she murmured with a smile, 'how easy life is once you've made up your mind.'

'Amazing,' echoed Hildamay, who thought life was rather more likely to make up minds than the other way around. She had a sudden vision of life – it would be a woman, she reflected – running around and sticking her hands into people's minds, making them up. She shook her head. It must be age. Age affected the mind much as it did the body; softening it, blurring the outlines. Youth was so hard and definite. She remembered it, smooth and elastic, always snapping back into the same determined lines. She sighed and Cassie looked at her, her frosted violet eyes twinkling with concern.

'Darling, what is it?'

Hildamay smiled briefly. 'Intimations of mortality.'

'Sounds horrid, darling. Have some more champagne. If that doesn't make you feel immortal, nothing will.'

'I'll miss you, Cassie,' said Hildamay, laughing.

'Don't be silly, darling. I'm writing a novel, not my epitaph. Anyway, we both know perfectly well that I'm sweeter in small doses.'

CHAPTER NINETEEN

L ANGAN'S Brasserie was busy on a Wednesday, it being considered by the advertising and publishing community a good day to lunch. Men in dark suits and bright striped shirts, women in pale jackets and fluttering silk blouses talked and laughed and drank champagne and called each other names. Sugar and Sweetie crowded up against George and Hildamay as they waited at the bar for their table, while any number of Darlings were hailed as they wandered, blinking, into the brightly lit room.

As they sat, perched on the shabby, plush-covered stools, Hildamay wondered what George thought of all this. He looked an odd, solitary figure in his plain brown suit and starched white shirt although he had, Hildamay noted with amusement, picked out a particularly magnificent tie that morning; violet and emerald silk splashed with an intense royal blue. George kept his face averted from the chatter and bustle of the restaurant and was sunk in a deep, brooding silence. Hildamay, worrying that he felt uncomfortable, had at first tried to put him at his ease but after a few forced attempts at bright conversation, which he toyed with in a desultory fashion and then abandoned, had sunk into an equal silence. As she lit a cigarette and thought of the hours stretching ahead, she felt vaguely alarmed. He had not seemed excited by the prospect of lunch with her and now he seemed, if anything, dismayed by the idea.

She was deep in thought, preoccupied with the idea of George's daughter – it did not occur to her to doubt her instinct and she was busy fleshing out the child's pale features – when a woman stalked into the room, pushing aside the heavy velvet curtains which cloaked the door in a massive, impatient gesture. Her face was heavy, bordering on handsome, save for lines of discontent carved on either side of her sticky red lipsticked mouth and scored in a permanent frown between black, pencilled eyebrows. She raised her hand imperiously to Joe, the restaurant's greeter, walked right up to him until their noses were almost touching, and jabbed two fingers in the air. Then, without a word, she turned her back on him and shrugged a heavy, full-length mink coat from her shoulders. It slid to the ground in a hiss of silk and fur and she looked down at it, then up at him with a look of intense, supercilious irritation. He bent to retrieve it and said, with a tight, pained smile, 'Table for two, Madam?' The woman brushed past him without a word and swept into the restaurant, causing him to trot, like an obedient dog, in her wake.

Hildamay marvelled at the woman's indifferent insolence and wondered at the turns her life must have taken to have leached her of all human warmth. As she mused, she glanced at George and saw on his face a look of such contemptuous distaste that she murmured, 'Quite a performance.' 'Arrogant bitch,' he exclaimed in a manner so unlike his own that she glanced again at him, startled, but he retreated once more into silence.

They were both deep in thought and were thus momentarily startled by the head waiter who, as he approached, patted George affably on the shoulder and exclaimed, 'Why, Mr Dogwood! It has been so long since we saw you. Such a pleasure to have you back, sir.' Hildamay watched George with interest. He coloured and waved a hand abruptly at the man.

'Brown,' he said brusquely. 'The name is George Brown.'

The waiter looked perplexed and glanced quickly at Hildamay, then back at George. 'I'm sorry, sir,' he said smoothly. 'You look so like a gentleman who used to come here that I thought –'

'You thought wrong,' said George, his smile fixed like a warning. 'Is our table ready yet? It's booked in the name of Smith. For two.'

He turned away from the man and, placing his hand lightly on the small of Hildamay's back, propelled her in front of him towards the main dining area. The slight gesture conveyed such authority that Hildamay instinctively complied and allowed herself to be led to a table by the window. They sat down but were immediately surrounded by such a flurry of activity, with napkins being laid on their laps, menus being brought, and bread and butter manoeuvred into place on the small and crowded table, that there was no minute in which they were alone to talk.

When the last waiter had gone, Hildamay leaned forward slightly in her seat and opened her mouth to speak, but George, anticipating the gesture, said, 'Shall we decide on our order now? Then we can relax and talk.' They studied the menu in silence, but Hildamay could not help glancing at George obliquely from time to time and in some puzzlement. For a man who, to her certain knowledge, only ever lunched on herring and cucumber sandwiches and suppered on a solitary lamb chop, his grasp of restaurant etiquette was remarkably assured. After they had discussed their choice of food, which they did for some time and in great detail, since Hildamay was greedy by nature and therefore indecisive with menus, George picked up the wine list. He read it in silence and with evident enjoyment, a slight smile playing about his lips, before he became aware that Hildamay was watching him closely, at which he put it down, blinked furiously and blushed a brilliant red.

'Would you like to choose the wine?' he stammered. 'I really don't know very much about it. I was just enjoying the sound of the names. I sometimes think the names are more enjoyable than the actual wines.' He pushed it across the table and Hildamay took it from him with a slight, questioning frown. He shook his head slightly and turned away, apparently engrossed in the room in which they sat while Hildamay, puzzled, bent her head to the wine list. She had been watching him make his way through it with a familiarity which suggested he knew a great deal about wine, and good wine at that.

'Do you like white burgundy, George?' she asked eventually, looking at him carefully.

'Very much,' he said, and then quickly added, 'that's what they always say in the wine columns in the Sunday newspapers, isn't it? That burgundy is the king of white wines. Whatever you suggest,' he added with a deprecating shrug of his shoulders.

They ordered their food and, while they waited for it to arrive, Hildamay entertained him with office gossip and urged him to drink his wine, hoping it might relax him. He drank slowly, scarcely sipping at it as he listened carefully to Hildamay's nervous chatter. She felt suddenly ashamed, both of her curiosity about the child which, by this time, was as real to her as if she had met her, and the mannner in which she had bullied George into coming out for lunch with her. She liked George and did not wish to see him made uncomfortable. Certainly not by her. That had not been her intention but she began to see that perhaps her intentions had not been as honourable as she had, lying on the floor of her bathroom, pretended them to be. Still, once they were safely distracted by their food, she could not resist asking him whether he had any children.

'No,' he said, without looking up from his lamb. 'None.' His tone was so guarded that Hildamay was silenced.

'Odd that the head waiter mistook you for somebody else, wasn't it?' she said curiously, after a time.

'I must have that sort of face,' he replied quietly, which caused Hildamay to reflect that he did not have that sort of face at all. He had a quite unmistakable face, being so pale and his eyes so light a blue that he was like a photographic negative of a person.

'Would you like children?' he asked suddenly. Hildamay stared at him in astonishment.

'Do I strike you as the sort of person who would like to have children?' she demanded.

'You strike me as the sort of person they would like to have,' he said, and smiled. 'Which is not necessarily the same thing, of course. But I imagine that's why Sky likes you so much.'

'Why does Sky like me so much?' she asked, curious. It was a question she had often asked her bathroom mirror.

'Because you treat her as a person and not as a child. It must be so frustrating being a child. All those adults talking to you like an idiot. They don't like it, you know.'

'Don't they?'

'No.' He shook his head. 'They find it very frustrating, which is why some of them, many of them, behave badly. They are treated badly and they reply in equal, usually double, measure. Children are of course very extreme in their reactions for they know nothing of the so-called civilising influences.'

'You seem to know an awful lot about children,' said Hildamay, glancing at him curiously.

'I have studied them in great depth. I go to a park on Saturday and sit and watch them.' He flushed and looked away. Hildamay had a sudden vision of a slight, solitary figure sitting in a park and watching the children play. George seemed so excluded from life;

she imagined it, chattering around him and felt such pity that her voice momentarily shook.

'Are you lonely?'

'Lonely?' He seemed surprised by the question and frowned at her. 'No, not lonely. I like to be alone. Like you.'

'It is better,' she said, nodding in sympathetic agreement.

'No,' he said, quite sharply, she thought, for George was generally so mild in manner. 'It is merely easier.'

Hildamay looked at him intently, but he turned his head away. She thought of Delilah. It was what she had said.

'Does that make it bad?' she asked, curious.

'I meant no judgement. For some people,' he said with a shrug, 'it is the only way.'

It had been, decided Hildamay that afternoon, a very unsatisfactory lunch. She had intended it as a gesture of friendship – or so she pretended, for she had conventionally forgotten her real intention which was to find out about George's past – but it had served only to drive him further into secrecy and the formal, enigmatic manner he had maintained for so many years. And which he had seemed recently to be relaxing. And then she thought, for Hildamay's failing was not a lack of honesty, that if she had driven him away it was entirely through her own scheming. She determined to pry no further, realising that she had upset George by doing so and that his discomfort in the restaurant was less to do with his surroundings than with her unwelcome curiosity. Any intimacy between them must be one established on his terms. She sighed, feeling ashamed. She, like him, was intensely private and disliked uninvited questions and she knew he had trusted her enough to believe that she would not inflict them on him.

Still, she mused, there was that odd incident with the head waiter mistaking him for somebody else. 'Dogwood,' she murmured. She was sure she had heard that name somewhere before. She thought for a while but could not place it and so she began to muse instead on George's daughter. A small, pale child with red gold hair and pale blue eyes. Rather like Sky. Perhaps that was why he was so affected by Sky? But he had not even met Sky. Perhaps that did not matter. Perhaps all the children in the world affected George. It must have been something terrible, something tragic. Perhaps the wife had simply disappeared, taking the daughter with her? Poor

George. Hildamay sighed. And then she sighed again as she remembered the evening ahead. It was a day for difficult meals. Tonight she would have to tell Liz about her encounter with Thomas. She suspected she would take it very badly.

'It's mine!' Liz's voice rang out through the restaurant. It was so loud that everybody stopped eating and turned to stare at the tall, thin girl who stood, clutching her pregnant belly and crying. Her curly dark hair sprang out around her head like an electrified halo and her eyes were large and wild. 'It's mine,' she howled, staring at Hildamay who reached out to take her arm, tugging at it gently in an effort to get her to sit down again.

Luigi came rushing over to the table. 'What is it, *bella*? What's the matter?' he soothed. 'Has somebody tried to hurt you? I kill them and it will all be better.'

'They're trying to take away my baby!' sobbed Liz, throwing her arms around his neck. Luigi was used to pregnant women, having had seven children, all of whom worked in the restaurant on a shift basis. 'One for every day of the week!' he often joked.

'It's all right, *cara*. It's OK,' he said, stroking Liz's hair and looking over her head at Hildamay, his eyebrows raised in question. Hildamay shook her head. 'Come, sit down and we talk about it quietly. Nobody is going to take away the baby.' Liz let herself be sat down and lolled, mute, against the back of her chair, her eyes fixed on Hildamay.

The silence in the restaurant was at first punctuated only by the hiss of whispers but then the noise quickly swelled as voices laughed and joked and the clatter of knives and forks once more filled the room. Luigi sent one of his waiters to get a glass of brandy while he knelt by Liz, stroking her hair and whispering soothing Italian noises in her ear.

'The baby,' murmured Liz, pushing the glass of brandy away.

'*Bellissima!*' exclaimed Luigi, 'how many children have I got? You think I don't know about pregnant women? What's good for the mama is good for the bambina. You're calm, it's calm.' He pushed the brandy back at Liz who picked it up and took a large swallow while Hildamay marvelled at his impeccable logic. Once Liz was completely calm he gathered up their menus and announced that he would bring them pumpkin ravioli seasoned with fresh sage and a rucola salad. 'Very comforting, *bella*,' he said, smoothing

Liz's hair. Liz, who seemed to have entirely forgotten her lust for bloody meat, smiled weakly and nodded her head in dumb agreement. Then she looked at Hildamay.

'How did he find out?' she demanded.

Hildamay shrugged. 'He guessed.'

'How?' Liz's face was dark with anger.

'Instinct?' said Hildamay. 'Intuition? Oh, I don't know.'

'You didn't confirm it, did you?' Liz's voice was sharp.

'Of course not!' said Hildamay impatiently. 'Unless silence is consent. I told him he was mad.'

'And what did he say?'

'He said that he was crazy,' said Hildamay quietly. 'Crazy in love with you and that he was going to marry you. Be one small happy family.'

'Marry me!' cried Liz, outraged. 'Marry me? The man's insane.'

'So he says,' murmured Hildamay with a slight smile.

'Why are you smiling!' exclaimed Liz. 'I see nothing to smile about.'

'The sperm bank answers back,' said Hildamay with a shrug. 'The toy boy playing us at our own game.'

'I told you that men aren't what they used to be,' said Liz, but she did not laugh. 'He's not having it.' Her mouth was set in a thin, obstinate line.

'Perhaps you should talk to him?' suggested Hildamay.

'Talk to him!' shouted Liz. 'Are you mad? I'm surrounded by lunatics,' she moaned, slumping back into her chair and covering her face with her hands. 'What's talking going to do?' she said, sitting upright. 'It's my child. What's he done to earn it? Fuck all. Well, fuck once.' Hildamay smiled but Liz merely glared at her. 'He hasn't had to suffer throwing up and having his body swell and swell till he feels like it's going to explode. He hasn't been to antenatal classes or learned breathing routines or stuffed his face with Bombay Mix when he doesn't even bloody like the stuff. Has he?' she shouted, her eyes wide with indignation. 'What's he done to earn this child? What right does he have to it?'

'In that sense,' said Hildamay mildly, 'no right at all. But it is his cell and that gives him a right.'

'Oh, great!' said Liz contemptuously. 'He's done nothing for it but he can stroll up, point a finger at my pregnant belly and say, "That's mine" just as he can go and choose a hand-knitted sweater in Harrods and say "That's mine". He didn't put any of the sweat or labour or pain into its creation but he can still demand to have it.'

'Sweaters aren't grown from sperm.'

'I know they're bloody not! But the principle's the same.'

'We're talking about life, here, Lizzie. Not designer sweaters.'

'Stop being so bloody righteous! It's all your bloody fault anyway. "A nice boy," you said. "No trouble," you said. "An infallible plan," you said.' She crossed her arms and stared mutinously at the people at the next table who quickly began to take an intense interest in their meal.

'I never said it was infallible,' said Hildamay quietly. 'And when it went wrong that night, there was a chance that he would suspect. OK, so we fucked up. But the point is, you took a gamble and it went wrong and now you have to face up to the consequences.'

'I have to!' Liz stared at her with disbelief.

'Yes,' said Hildamay firmly. 'You do. This is your baby. It's not mine. The only person who can make a decision about Thomas is you. Not me. Not even us.'

'Thanks,' said Liz bitterly. 'I feel alone enough already, without that gesture of support.'

'Well, maybe you'd like to have a father around then. To make you feel less lonely.'

'No!'

'Come on, Liz. Be fair. The child is partly his. It's his sperm, his genes, his chromosomes. What happened was, in effect, stealing. How would you feel if he'd nicked one of your cells and taken it off and grown it into a baby? Men do have rights as well.'

'Men,' said Liz through gritted teeth, 'have no rights whatsoever. And Thomas can go on claiming this child till judgement day but he's not bloody having it. And whose fucking side are you on anyway?'

'I am not on anyone's side!' shouted Hildamay. 'This is not a question of sides. This is a baby, not a fucking tennis match.' She took a deep breath. 'Will you call him?'

'I just told you. No!'

'It might be sensible,' said Hildamay more calmly.

'Since when were you so bloody sensible?' said Liz furiously.

'Just think about it, Liz. At the moment the issue is more or less academic. But when that bump turns into a real baby, it's going to get messy. And you are going to have to decide what you're going to do about it. For the child's sake, at least.'

'If you think being pregnant is academic,' spat Liz, 'you know nothing! There's nothing academic about what's happening to my body. This bump, as you call it, is real. It's a baby.'

'All the more reason for deciding what you're going to do. All I'm saying is that once you have the baby, can hold it in your arms, then the emotions are going to get a whole lot messier than they already are. Thomas might decide to take legal action. Perhaps you should at least try to avoid that and come to some agreement between yourselves.'

'Legal action?' said Liz slowly, staring at her.

'He can prove, through genetic fingerprinting, that the child is his. And if you have to give evidence under oath you'll be forced to describe the questionable circumstances in which the child was conceived. The legal issue is deception and perhaps theft. There's not, at least I don't think there is, any precedent for a case of this sort but Thomas seems like a very determined man and is determined that the child is his.'

'Oh, fuck Thomas!'

'I wouldn't if I were you,' said Hildamay with a slight smile.

Liz suddenly burst out laughing. 'Oh, shit!' she moaned, giggling, 'what a mess.' Then she looked at Hildamay and shrugged. 'I'm sorry I shouted at you. I promise to think about it. Really I will. But I'm not going to call him. If he wants the child he can come and claim it.'

'You have over a month to decide.'

'I've made my decision,' said Liz, her mouth set in a mutinous line. 'And I'm not going to bloody marry him. If he thinks I am he really is certifiable. What kind of arrogance is that, anyway? Men really are the pits sometimes.'

She grumbled on while Hildamay kept quiet and ate her pumpkin ravioli, which she thought was perfectly delicious and probably the best thing that had happened to her that day.

When she got home that evening there was a message on her answering machine from Sky who said that Blanche had left London for good and gone to live in Spain. She sounded very small and very lonely.

CHAPTER TWENTY

THE following Saturday, Sky was very subdued. She scarcely spoke on the bus on the way to Portobello and, when they arrived at the market, trailed disconsolately through the crowds holding tightly on to Hildamay's hand as if she were frightened that she, too, would disappear. She would not even talk to her friends, the Rastafarians, who were sitting in their usual place on the pavement outside the pub on Portobello Road, laughing and drinking beer.

'Hey, Sky,' called one when he saw her, 'come over here, man.' But Sky shook her head at them and held on to Hildamay's hand still more tightly.

'Shy Sky,' they called after her in their rich, full voices. 'Never mind, man. Maybe next week.'

They did not stay long at the market, lingering on the streets, watching the people as they liked to do, but quickly bought flowers and fruit and vegetables and hurried home for tea. Even then Sky did not sit at the kitchen table to talk, as she usually did, but took her mug of tea into the sitting room where she sat on the sofa eating cake crumb by crumb and silently turning the pages of a book about English gardens. When the time came for her to go home they travelled on the bus in silence, Sky staring straight ahead and not, as was her habit, making up stories about the people on the street. It was only as the tube came into the station that she spoke, turning to Hildamay and clasping her arms tightly around her neck, whispering that she was sorry if she hadn't said very much.

'I'm depressed,' she said. 'Like Blanche always was.'

Hildamay looked at her sharply but Sky said nothing else and so she kissed her four times, instead of two, and stood and waved as the train slowly pulled out of the station.

As the weeks went by Sky became more and more withdrawn. Her cheeks lost their blush and her face seemed to shrink, becoming pinched and angular; a white triangle in which the luminous eyes burned, as if with fever. She rarely smiled, although she was always very correct in her thanks when Hildamay planned a surprise for her, which she did with increasing frequency, alarmed by her obvious unhappiness. Even the promised Saturday with George did not seem to cheer her.

'There's something wrong,' said George thoughtfully, watching Sky sitting on a bench in the park. She kept perfectly still, her baseball cap jammed low over her eyes. She did not seem conscious of the other children, laughing and playing around her. When one approached her and spoke, she shook her head mutely and then picked up her dictionary and studied it carefully. But when the other child shrugged and went away, disconsolately kicking a tin can with its small sneakered foot, she put the book down and sat, her expression bleak, and watched the children play. She looked, from a distance, like a little old woman lost in the fog of memory.

'She is quite different from the child I spoke to on the telephone,' said George, shaking his head worriedly.

'Perhaps she still misses her mother?' said Hildamay.

'No,' said George, so quietly he seemed to be speaking to himself. 'No,' he said again. 'It's not that.'

'Why do you say that?' demanded Hildamay. He looked at her, as if surprised to see her standing next to him.

'I'm sorry,' he said quickly. 'I didn't mean to alarm you.'

'Well, what did you mean?' she said insistently.

'Was she close to her mother?' he asked, frowning.

'Not that I know of. She seemed to be more like a sister. She called her Blanche and once told me that she was not like other mothers. But what else could it be?'

'What's her grandmother like?'

'Arid,' said Hildamay slowly. 'Dry, like an old bone.' She shrugged. 'She's not very likeable but I don't think she wishes Sky any harm.' She looked over at Sky and shivered suddenly, wondering if she was right. She shook her head. The woman was unpleasant, not unkind. 'Sky did say, when I first met her –' She hesitated. 'She asked me how easy it was to find divorced people. Said something about her father wanting her. As if nobody else did. . . .' Her voice trailed off as she watched the small, solitary figure on the bench.

George followed her gaze. 'I think,' he said quietly, 'that she is suffering from a lack of kindness.'

'Kindness?'

'Love. Kindness. Call it what you will.' George smiled briefly at her and walked over to sit with Sky. Hildamay stared after him. Love, George had said. She wondered how much love existed in Mary Matthews' house. She doubted it floated freely in the air; it was a chill, brooding house, clean and shiny as a skeleton from which the warm, living flesh has long since melted. She sighed, thinking of Blanche. She could only suppose that she had run off to Spain with a lover, a lover to whom she wrote those endless letters. Bored with him, she would no doubt eventually return.

There was something terrible in Sky's polite, docile obedience. She was like a clockwork toy which, when wound, ran its proper course, a smile painted on its bright, smiling face and then stopped and waited patiently until some careless hand wound it and sent it on its journey once more. When Hildamay asked if everything was all right at home, Sky turned her head away and answered in a small, precise voice that everything was fine, thank you very much, but if Hildamay persisted she would invent something to distract her attention. Once, when Hildamay asked her if she missed her mother, she looked at her thoughtfully and said, 'I miss her singing. And she laughed lots.' Hildamay, who suspected that there was precious little laughter in the Matthews' house, nodded in understanding. One Saturday, when Sky was paler and quieter than ever, Hildamay suggested that the following weekend she should come and stay. 'For a whole weekend?' said Sky, her eyes shining. It was the first time Hildamay had seen her look really happy since Blanche had left.

'The whole weekend,' she promised. 'You can come on Friday at six o'clock and stay till Sunday night.' Sky laughed and skipped around the market for the rest of the afternoon. But when Hildamay asked her to ask her grandmother if she could go and see her, she became suddenly withdrawn.

'Why do you want to see her?' she asked, her eyes narrowed with suspicion.

'To ask her if it's all right for you to come and stay,' explained Hildamay, watching her carefully.

'No!' said Sky and ran into the sitting room where she lay on the floor, hammering her fists on the carpet and screaming hysterically. Hildamay was astonished. She had never even seen Sky cry before. She sat down next to her on the floor and stroked her back and talked to her in whispers until she calmed down. Eventually Sky climbed on to her lap and sat there, like a limp doll.

'What's the matter?' asked Hildamay gently.

'She'll stop me,' whispered Sky. 'She'll make you go away. I know she will.' And then she began to sob again. A thought suddenly struck Hildamay.

'Does she know you come and see me every Saturday?' she said slowly. There was silence.

'Not exactly,' said Sky eventually.

'Not exactly what?' said Hildamay, taking her face in her hand and turning it to look at her. Sky looked away.

'She doesn't know quite a bit about what I do,' she said in a whisper.

'No,' said Hildamay, thinking of the jacket and cap kept hidden away in Haadji's shop, of the secret trips to the post office, of Blanche's illicit letters from Spain. 'No, I can see that.'

Sky looked at her, alarmed. 'You won't tell her, will you?' Her voice was shrill with fear.

'Why?' said Hildamay insistently. 'What will she do if I do tell her? It's pretty harmless, isn't it? Seeing a friend on a Saturday. Wearing a jacket and cap like the other girls at school?'

Sky looked at her as if she, Hildamay, was very, very young. 'Don't tell her,' she said quietly and turned her head away.

'What will she do?' asked Hildamay, feeling a cold prickle of fear at her neck. 'What does she do to you?' she demanded insistently.

Sky would not look at her.

'Sky?'

'She'll make you go away,' she said in a small, defeated voice. She looked suddenly very old and very tired and not like a child at all.

Hildamay was silent for a while, watching Sky's pale, defeated face.

'Will you ask your grandmother,' she said carefully, 'if I could come and see her next Saturday evening? Say that I would very much like to meet her, if it's not inconvenient. I want you to say exactly that. Can you remember?'

Sky nodded. 'I'll remember,' she said grimly.

The following Saturday evening Hildamay drove Sky to Woodside Park and sat and waited in the chill little sitting room for Mary Matthews. The room felt lifeless, dead even, and Hildamay shivered slightly, wondering at the personality of the woman who had made it. Or rather the women, for surely Blanche was as much a part of this house as Mary Matthews? Perhaps, she thought, looking around the room, they saved up all their warmth for other things, lavished their affection on people, not possessions. But then she thought about Sky, about the loneliness which ran through her like a sharp, bright stream, and she knew that if they offered love it was not to the child who lived between them.

Sky sat in one of the hard-backed chairs, her whole body rigid with anticipation, her eyes fixed on Hildamay with an intensity that was disturbing. Does she think I will disappear, like her mother? thought Hildamay, watching the small mouth settle in a line of grim, adult resignation. She smiled at her reassuringly and the set little mouth softened slightly then tightened to a pale pink line as the sound of a key turning in a lock echoed through the cold hall.

Sky jumped out of her chair and went and stood, her back very straight, by the door. Hildamay had spent the week preparing a special wardrobe of smiles for the occasion and quickly put on the first as she turned and took Mary Matthews by the hand.

'It's so kind,' she breathed, 'of you to let me come and call on you.' And as she spoke she shifted her smile imperceptibly from one of greeting to one of warm complicity.

'Well,' said Mary Matthews, her hand lying limply in Hildamay's, soft and pulsing slightly, like a dying creature. The hand was bony, yet covered in skin so thick and white and clammy that Hildamay half expected her fingers to leave dents in it as in the flesh of fish which is no longer fresh. 'Delighted, I'm sure,' added Mary Matthews in a harsh nasal whine. 'Would you care for a small sherry? I do like a small sherry in the evening. So civilised, don't you think?' The sherry, as before, was warm and very sweet. With it Mary Matthews served cheese straws she had obviously prepared especially for Hildamay's visit. 'Homemade,' she said with a complacent smile. 'None of that shop bought stuff in this house.' She smoothed her dress over her waist, sank into one of the hard, over-stuffed armchairs and patted at her stiffly lacquered hair, her hand flat so she did not so much rearrange the curls as bounce them up and down. As she did so her eye caught a slight movement in the shadows. It was Sky, lurking in the doorway.

'Run along now, Sky,' she said sharply with a dismissive wave of her hand. 'Mrs Smith and I wish to talk. You shouldn't be in this room anyway,' she added in accusing tones. That made Hildamay start, the 'Mrs' anyway, until she suddenly remembered that she was supposed to have a daughter. She could not even remember her name. My daughter, she thought wildly. I should have my daughter with me if she is to believe me, and she suddenly bitterly regretted ever having been drawn into the duplicity. But then she thought of Sky, of her pale, defeated face, the blue eyes deadened by despair, and shuddered at the idea that she might let her down. She looked at Mary Matthews' thin, cold face and remembered bleakly how she had imagined, as she sat in her bathroom, that she would charm her with some inconsequential small talk and then gently slide the conversation around to Sky and suggest, laughingly, that perhaps she might like her taken off her hands for a weekend. As she looked at the cold, bright little eyes and the harsh, thin mouth she knew that charm and smiles were impotent in the face of this woman's cold indifference.

Despair caught at her throat and then she felt something hard digging into the small of her back. It brought her back to reality. Why, she thought, she is only a woman. It's absurd to be so alarmed by her. Reaching behind her she extracted a round little cushion covered in beige nylon velvet which had been fashioned into a plaited design and decorated with raised, hard buttons. She held it in her hand; having got it there she did not know what to do with it. Mary Matthews looked at her curiously.

'Charming,' said Hildamay with an admiring smile and with her spare hand indicated the room. 'Charming.'

Mary Matthews nodded complacently. 'Though I say so myself, I have an eye for colour. The girls are always asking me for advice on their homes and I try to oblige but one has so little time for pleasure.' She dismissed the room with a glance and turned her tiny eyes on Hildamay.

'Now, what was it you came to see me about?' she smiled sharply.

The smile did not reach her eyes. They glittered, small and dark, above the beak of her nose.

'It's about Sky,' Hildamay began.

'Ah, yes,' she said, the smile sharpening. 'Sky. What about Sky?'

'She seems,' said Hildamay carefully, 'a little unhappy.'

'Unhappy?' Mary Matthews' tone was disapproving. 'Unhappy?' she repeated on a note of astonished surprise.

'She seems to have very few friends,' continued Hildamay, her voice limp.

'Friends?' Mary Matthews frowned.

'Children,' said Hildamay earnestly, 'set so much store by friendship.'

'Well, I can't help that,' said Mary Matthews harshly. 'She must take life as she finds it. Your daughter,' she added. 'I thought she was a friend?'

'A good friend,' exclaimed Hildamay suddenly. 'Yes, a very, very good friend. She was going to come with me today, of course. But she –' She searched wildly in her mind for some childish ailment. What was it children always seemed to be sickening with? 'Tonsillitis!' she cried. 'That's it! Tonsillitis!' Mary Matthews looked at her curiously. Maybe tonsillitis, thought Hildamay frantically, happens to older children? 'Bronchitis, really. The doctor said she really couldn't be moved. That she must stay, perfectly flat, in a darkened room. For a week. At least a week,' she continued hurriedly as Mary Matthews continued to regard her strangely, the frown sharpening the lines between her small, cold eyes.

Oh, God, thought Hildamay, panicking, she thinks I abandon my own child when she's ill. She'll think I can't be trusted to look after Sky. She'll never let her come for a weekend. 'But she's much better!' she exclaimed. 'Oh, so very much better. My sister's with her now. She adores my sister, of course. Always has done, ever since she was tiny. Not that she's very big now, of course. Well, as big as Sky but she's –' Her voice trailed off and she gazed at Mary Matthews miserably.

'Unhappy, you say,' said Mary Matthews coldly, ignoring her outburst. 'Well, all I can say is that she goes to a good school. The sacrifices I've made for that child! Nobody will ever know –' She paused, as if remembering something, and then she glared at Hildamay. 'And if she has no friends there then I have to say, it must be her fault. She can be a difficult child. Demanding. And I must admit I generally discourage Sky from making friends with the children around here. She gets such ideas in her head. Well, you know how young girls are. And the people around here. . . .' She let the sentence slide into the air and her mouth puckered like an anus.

'I have an idea –' began Hildamay but Mary Matthews cut in angrily.

'I hardly see that it is any business of yours, anyway. Who are you to say that my granddaughter is unhappy? She lives with me and I must say that I think she's perfectly all right. Unhappy! What does happiness mean to a child?' She glared at Hildamay, her bony face illuminated with outrage.

'I'm most terribly sorry. I don't mean to interfere,' said Hildamay miserably. She had let Sky down. She would never be allowed to come for the weekend after this. She gazed at the woman in desperation.

'Well,' snapped Mary Matthews. 'You have.' They stared at each other in silence for a time and then, to Hildamay's astonishment, Mary Matthews' face softened. 'I don't mean to seem unkind. You seem like a nice woman, Mrs Smith, and I'm sure you come from a good family. It must be difficult for you to understand how hard it is to bring up a child in what can only be called difficult circumstances.' She flicked a fastidious hand over the arm of her chair. 'The sort of sacrifices we have had to make for that girl,' she murmured, sighing.

'Difficult,' echoed Hildamay, and on her face she drew a smile, one both admiring and sympathetic.

'We stay in this house,' said Mary Matthews with a dismissive wave of her hand, 'because it is so convenient for Sky's school. So difficult to find a good school in a nice area.'

'Dreadful,' murmured Hildamay.

'Sorry?' Mary Matthews leaned forwards in her chair, her eyes suddenly bright with interest.

'Dreadfully difficult,' said Hildamay, and her expression changed to one of conspiratorial sympathy.

'Oh, yes. Dreadfully,' repeated Mary Matthews, encouraged. 'One can never get it quite right. One can strive, of course. One does. But in the end it always seems to be the same: nice area, terrible school; terrible area, nice school. And as you can see,' she added, her mouth sour with distaste, 'we are forced to live in the latter. But we make every sacrifice for Sky. The sacrifices I have made for that child. Nothing is too good for Sky,' she exclaimed briskly. 'Cheese straw?'

'Delicious,' said Hildamay and felt the pastry, dry as dust, settle in her mouth.

'Nothing,' repeated Mary Matthews, her smile modest with sacrifice, 'is too good for her.' She looked at Hildamay, her gaze assessing. 'She may be right when she says that she has no friends but she must,' her voice rose an octave, 'she must understand that it is for her own good.' Her voice grew more shrill, penetrated by a note of hysteria. 'When a child is young, her mind must be properly controlled, carefully formed. They can get into bad habits so early. Especially these days. I have always taught her manners. Manners and discipline. And of course the right way.'

'The right way?'

'The right way,' said Mary Matthews, the thin mouth tightening. 'Ever since she was a baby, Sky has been taught the correct values. She has not been spoiled. Not like some around here,' she added darkly. 'Running around in the streets at all hours wearing highly unsuitable clothes. And the language! Sky has of course been protected from all that and, though I flatter myself in saying so, I do believe that even at her young age she has learned the right moral values.'

As she spoke her tiny eyes burned with a zealot's ardour and Hildamay understood, with a cold pricking of alarm, that this was no ordinary concern but some infinitely darker thing. She had a sudden vision of Sky, small, vulnerable and lonely, caught in the grip of this woman's obsession. Values, she thought, with a sudden sharp pang of fear. Moral values for a nine-year-old child. What about love? She shivered slightly and stared, speechless, at Mary Matthews who watched her, her face sharp with exasperation.

'Sky is very young,' Hildamay finally blurted out. Mary Matthews' face darkened. 'She seems to miss her mother a great deal,' Hildamay added, her smile warm, sympathetic. 'Which is, of course, absolutely understandable. That she should miss her mother, I mean.'

'Sky's told you about her mother?' said Mary Matthews sharply.

'My daughter,' said Hildamay carefully. 'My daughter explained that Sky's mother had gone away on a prolonged holiday. It was she who said that she thought that Sky seemed a little, well, a little sad,' she continued briskly. 'You know how soft-hearted young girls can be,' she explained.

Mary Matthews frowned. 'She misses her mother?' she repeated, her voice incredulous. And Hildamay understood suddenly that this woman hated her own daughter.

'She has gone to Spain, I understand?' said Hildamay, watching her carefully. Mary Matthews glanced at her quickly, her gaze sharp, suspicious. Ah, thought Hildamay, she is ashamed. The pregnant daughter, the lover in Spain. 'To visit friends,' she added quickly.

'Ah, yes, friends,' sighed Mary Matthews, relaxing. 'Blanche finds the winters here so hard and when her friends suggested that she should go and spend a few months with them, I could hardly say no. We do both miss her very much.' Her expression was pious.

'Of course,' murmured Hildamay. 'Sky was saying just the other day how much she missed her. Missed the laughter and the singing.'

'Laughter?' said Mary Matthews. 'Singing?' She looked suspiciously at Hildamay who merely nodded and smiled encouragingly.

'Oh, laughter!' said Mary Matthews, her voice tinkling like cracked wind-chimes. 'Singing! She's such a gay little creature, my daughter. So like her mother.'

'But not,' said Hildamay, her smile admiring, 'nearly as hard-working.' Mary Matthews frowned and Hildamay thought that perhaps she had gone too far. 'Sky has told me,' she added quickly, 'how much good work you do. From what she says, Mary – may I call you Mary? – nobody could work as hard as you do for others.' The frown suddenly relaxed into a smile and Mary Matthews prodded almost girlishly at the curls which bobbed like singed sausages above her bony face.

'Well, realising how busy you are,' continued Hildamay hurriedly, taking advantage of this sign of mellowing, 'for Sky has told me how many, many councils you sit on, I thought perhaps you wouldn't mind if she came to stay with me, with us, for the weekend. We could go on a few little outings. I thought it might cheer her up, take her mind off her mother being away.'

'A weekend, you say?' The smile faded and the sharp face was rearranged into its habitual frown. 'When?' she demanded.

'I thought next weekend might be a suitable time.' Hildamay paused and smiled her sweetest smile. 'Only if you are entirely agreeable to the idea, of course.'

'Well,' said Mary Matthews slowly, 'I don't know – Sky is not very used to strangers. She has – she has her own ways, you see,' she added, her tone suddenly sharp.

'We're hardly strangers,' said Hildamay firmly, 'and seeing how much you love your granddaughter I know you'd like to see her happy. A weekend might do her some good.'

'Love,' murmured Mary Matthews, in surprise. She looked, suddenly, trapped. She glanced at Hildamay who put on her most sympathetic, reassuring smile. 'Well, I can't see that it would do much harm.'

'No, no,' said Hildamay quickly, 'no harm at all. I'm sure it will do the child a world of good. Take her out of herself. I have so little to do at the weekend myself,' she said modestly, 'not being involved in the sort of work that you give so much of your time for. Not,' she added hastily, 'that I am suggesting for a moment that Sky feels neglected. On the contrary. But when duty calls. . . .' She let her voice trail off and she smiled at Mary Matthews with frank admiration.

'Ah yes, duty,' said Mary Matthews, the trapped look fading to a complacent smile. 'I have to admit that it does take up a great deal of my time. But in an area like this –' she paused and looked at Hildamay meaningfully – 'there is a great deal to be done.'

'How hard you must have to work,' sighed Hildamay.

Mary Matthews smiled suddenly. 'A weekend!' she exclaimed. 'Well, why not!' She drank the last of her sherry, tilting the glass in a quick, almost abandoned gesture. Two spots of colour burned in her cheeks. 'I haven't thought of taking a weekend away, not since I was newly married.' She sounded almost gay. 'Not since I was but a girl myself!'

And Hildamay saw the cold, hard knot of her centre uncurl suddenly in the warmth of her memory, as a flower does in the sun and, watching her curiously, she saw in her expression a glimpse of Sky's eager nature.

'So it is all right?' she asked, suddenly triumphant.

Mary Matthews' face closed at the happiness ringing in her voice and Hildamay saw the centre of her close in on itself until it was like a pebble again: cold, hard, without pleasure.

'I'm sure Sky will enjoy herself,' she said, her voice distant. 'But please be sure that she behaves herself. She understands about discipline, she thrives on it, and I wouldn't want her ruined for the sake of a weekend's pleasure. She can be very difficult when she sets her mind to it. Very difficult indeed. I don't want her spoiled.' She turned and looked at Hildamay, her eyes hard but strangely unseeing. 'You don't like spoiled little girls, do you?'

Hildamay shivered at the venom in her voice and wondered if it was the voice which she used to speak to Sky.

'There's nothing spoiled about Sky,' she said, rather sharply. Nothing, she thought, in sudden surprise, for if there was anyone who would or *could* spoil love, curdle it to sourness, it was this woman.

Mary Matthews started at the tone of her voice and her eyes

focused as if clearing from a dream. 'No,' she said grudgingly. 'No, I don't suppose there is.'

As Hildamay followed Mary Matthews' thin, stiff back down the narrow corridor, she glanced upwards and called in a bright, clear voice, 'Goodbye, Sky. See you when you come and stay next weekend.'

Sky's voice came floating, in a bubble of delight, down the narrow stairs. 'Hildamay!'

CHAPTER TWENTY ONE

THE weekend with Sky had started quite successfully. Hildamay had gone to St Pancras straight after work on Friday evening and had found Sky standing rigidly to attention, a small grey bag at her feet, by the ticket office. She was devastatingly casual in her greeting but Hildamay had looked at her eyes, which were almost black with excitement, and understood. They went first to the video shop, and then to McDonald's where they ordered take-away Big Macs, two large fries, extra size milkshakes, Cokes, and apple pies and then went home. By ten o'clock Sky was pale with happiness and Hildamay exhausted with relief that she had got everything right and so they went to bed; Sky to the small blue room down the hall ('Can this be *my* room?' she asked, belligerent with joy) and Hildamay to her big, cool white bed.

In the morning they had breakfast together at the old wooden table in the yellow kitchen and then they cleared away the plates and crumbs and played five games of Scrabble on the trot, which took quite a long time as Sky insisted on writing down each new word so she could learn them all that night.

For lunch Hildamay had decided that they should go out; she thought something small and delicious and Italian might be nice and Sky had become politely interested until they were walking down the street past McDonald's, at which her feet began to drag.

'Do you think,' said Hildamay, 'that you could *bear* the idea of another Big Mac?'

'I think I could,' said Sky kindly.

When they got home after Portobello, Hildamay was exhausted. She was not used to being so much in another person's company, nor was she used to the relentless energy and enthusiasm of children. 'Do you think you might go and learn your words?' she said hopefully and Sky, obviously disappointed at being sent out of her company, nonetheless nodded wisely and said, 'I think it might be a very good idea,' then disappeared off into her room. Scarcely had Hildamay collapsed on her sofa, which looked so big and blue and welcoming, than the doorbell rang.

'Oh, good grief,' she said, hauling herself up to answer the door. It was Liz. 'Thought you might like some company,' she said, lumbering into the room and heaving herself on to the sofa.

'Lovely,' said Hildamay, wishing that she would go away. Liz half lay, half sat on the sofa, rubbing her back with her hand which made her belly stick out still further.

'You look like a beached whale,' said Hildamay.

'And I love you, too,' said Liz. 'I think my spine has snapped.'

'I'll rub it for you.'

'I definitely love you,' said Liz, struggling to pull herself up. Sky walked into the room.

'Hello,' she said, walking over to Liz and holding out her hand. 'I'm Sky.'

'You're what?' said Liz, who was now balanced precariously on the edge of the sofa and looked like a huge inflatable wobbly toy. Hildamay was tempted to put out a finger and push, just to see if she bounced back.

'My name,' said Sky in the voice she kept for idiots, 'is Sky.' She turned to Hildamay. 'Please may I have some orange juice?'

'Help yourself. You know where it is.'

'Thank you,' she said and walked into the kitchen. They could hear her pouring juice into a glass. Neither of them spoke. Sky walked back through the sitting room carrying the glass and closed the door.

'Who's that?'

'She told you. That's Sky.'

'Yes, but who is she?'

'She's a nine year old child.'

'I can see that. Where does she come from?'

'From Woodside Park.'

'Woodside Park?'

'Woodside Park.'

'Yes, but why?'

'I presume because that's where her mother wanted to live.'

'Hildamay, what's a nine year old child doing in your flat and behaving as if she lives here?'

'She's just staying.'

'Why is she staying?'

'Because she wants to, I imagine,' said Hildamay airily.

'Hildamay, will you stop it! Why do you have a child in your flat?'

'Because she doesn't like her grandmother.'

'Where is her grandmother?'

'Woodside Park.'

'Where is bloody Woodside Park anyway?'

'Somewhere on the Northern line. Where Sky's grandmother lives.'

There was silence. Liz looked at her curiously.

'You don't even like children.'

'I have never said I didn't like children.'

'Yes you did.'

'No,' said Hildamay firmly, 'I didn't. You assumed that because I don't want children, I don't like children.'

'Well, it seemed a fair assumption at the time.'

'I said I had never thought about having one. That the thought had not crossed my mind.'

'Well, that does seem to imply that you don't like them.'

'Wanting and liking are two quite separate emotions,' said Hildamay stubbornly.

'Oh, for God's sake, what does it matter?' said Liz, lying back on the sofa in exasperation.

'It matters a great deal,' said Hildamay.

'Why?' Liz's voice was loud.

'You're making a judgement. You sit there saying that I don't want children, therefore I don't like children, therefore I'm an unnatural woman.'

'I do not sit here and do any such thing!' yelled Liz.

'Yes, you do. All of you. You, Kate, Delilah. Even Cassie. She may not have a child but she believes that having one is the only way to prove that she's a woman. You all sit there with your "I'm a real woman" smiles treating me like some contrary child. I can read your minds and this is what they say: "She doesn't want children therefore she doesn't like children. How can a woman not like children? There's something odd about a woman who doesn't want children. It's not natural. But Nature will catch up with her. She'll change her mind, when she's past child-bearing age. She'll understand what she's really missed. She'll feel barren and alone."' Hildamay spat out the last word. She was shouting. She could hear herself. 'And the only way you can justify it to yourselves, me not wanting children and being free and you all being saddled with a responsibility that you half love, half loathe, is to say that I don't like children. Well I do bloody well like children. And you can go to hell.'

'Fine,' said Liz, lumbering towards the door, still rubbing her back. 'And when I get back perhaps we could sit down and discuss this in a civilised manner.'

'What, over a nice cup of tea? I am bloody civilised. I'm more bloody civilised than you'll ever understand!' shouted Hildamay as the front door slammed shut.

'I don't call stealing sperm civilised,' she yelled to the empty room, then sat down suddenly on the floor and buried her face in her hands. Why had she attacked Liz like that? It wasn't fair of her. Why did she want to keep Sky a secret? She didn't know. But Sky, she thought suddenly, flooded by a fierce wave of possessive love, was *hers*. Was it love? Was that what this was all about? But why should she love a nine year old child? Was it strange of her? They (she meant, she thought, by they, her friends) would think it strange, wouldn't they?

She lit a cigarette and sat on the floor, hugging her knees and smoking fiercely. She didn't want to explain Sky. To herself or anyone else. Sky just *was*. She wanted to keep her life at work, her life with her friends, her life with Sky, her secret life in her bathroom all entirely separate. She felt suddenly marooned, trapped between them all and yet extraordinarily alone. It was an uncharacteristic emotion and she felt a sudden, overwhelming desire to go into her bedroom and lock herself away from the world.

'Sky? Sky! Come here.'

There was no sound. Eventually Sky appeared at the door. She was rubbing her eyes. She looked as if she had been crying. 'Hildamay?' she said, her voice small. 'Hildamay, why were you shouting?'

'Oh, we were just playing a stupid game. To see who could make the most noise.'

Sky looked dubious. 'You weren't angry, then?'

'No. Why should I be angry?'

'It's just that – nothing.'

She looked very small standing in the doorway. Hildamay looked at her carefully. She had intended telling her that she was going out and then she was going to sneak into the bathroom and lock the door. Something made her change her mind and she held out her hand and said, quickly, before she changed it again, 'Come. I want to show you something.'

'What?'

'Come with me and I'll show you. It's my secret and nobody else knows about it. Just you.'

Sky's face lit up. 'Just me? Nobody else in the whole world?'

'Nobody else,' said Hildamay and took her by the hand and led her to the bathroom.

Sky stood transfixed in the open door. 'What is it?' she whispered.

'It's a bathroom.'

'I know that,' she said, still whispering. 'Is it magic?'

'Yes,' said Hildamay.

They both took off their clothes and Hildamay scrubbed Sky all over and then washed herself. Then they got into the bath and lay, toes facing, in the hot, scented water. Sky was giggling so Hildamay splashed her. Sky splashed her back and so it went on, as such things do. When they were both drenched and exhausted, Hildamay got out and dried herself while Sky sat in the bath and read all the labels on the bottles out loud. She lifted Sky out, dried her then rubbed her all over with different lotions, telling her about each one as she did. Wrapped in clean towels and sitting with her back pressed against the wall, she sat Sky on her lap and told her stories. They sat for hours in the warm, scented room with the door shut against the world and just the sound of Hildamay's voice to keep them company. Eventually, Hildamay stopped talking. She looked down. Sky was fast asleep, so she sat, her arms wrapped around her, and looked at the sulky droop of her pale pink mouth and the white skin of her eyelids with its delicate tracery of blue; stroked the shiny hair and breathed in the smell of her. After a while she got up and carried her to the bedroom.

Hildamay was fast asleep when the telephone rang. She was dreaming about her mother. 'Be grateful for small mercies,' said her mother, who held Sky in her arms. 'Be grateful, Hilda,' she said and she turned and stepped off a cliff. She did not fall but remained, floating in thin air, until gradually she dwindled to a dot. The telephone rang again.

'Fire,' said Hildamay, reaching for it. 'Fire,' she said, speaking into it.

'No, just me,' said Liz. 'You know you told me to go to hell? Well, I think I just got there. The pain's awful.'

'What pain?' said Hildamay sleepily.

'Labour pains.'

'Labour pains? That means you're having a baby.'

'Hildamay, did you pass biology O-level?' said Liz drily. 'Of course it means I'm having a baby. I just wanted you to be the first to know.'

'Good grief!' said Hildamay, jumping out of bed and dragging the phone halfway across the room as she started to dress.

'Can you wait five minutes? I'll be there once I've got dressed.'

'I'll tell junior to hang on,' said Liz. 'And Hildamay?'

'Yes?'

'Don't wear high heels. You might need to carry me.'

'Shut up and breathe,' said Hildamay and slammed down the phone.

She left a note for Sky. 'Drink some orange juice and eat some cornflakes. Had to go and see a woman about a baby,' which she left propped up on the kitchen table.

Hildamay walked in and kicked off her shoes. She put the kettle on. The flat was very quiet. She went into Sky's bedroom. She was not there. She looked in the sitting room, her bedroom and the little bathroom. 'Sky?' she called. There was no reply. 'Sky! Sky, where are you?' She looked in all the cupboards, searched under the beds and walked round the flat four times. Feeling sick with panic, she sat on the bed and was riffling through her address book trying to find Mary Matthews' telephone number when she heard a small sound coming from the bathroom.

She went to the door. It was locked from the inside. 'Sky?' she called, knocking on the door. 'Sky, are you in there?' There was no sound. 'Sky?' she shouted, banging with her fists on the door. 'Sky, open this door immediately.' Nothing. 'Sky, open the door!' She was yelling. Still nothing. She went and sat on the bed for a few minutes and tried to think what a nine-year-old child would do in a bathroom. And how do you persuade a child to come out from behind a locked door? 'Sky?' she called, this time more softly. 'Sky, could you come out? I want to talk to you about something.' Still nothing happened.

'Sky? Please?' She heard the key turn and the door opened a crack. She went in. Sky was sitting huddled in a towel on the floor. Creams and lotions were arranged in little piles around her.

'What the fuck do you think you're doing?' shouted Hildamay.

Sky flushed painfully and stared mutely at the floor.

'I'm sorry,' said Hildamay sitting down next to her, 'but this is my secret room and you've gone and messed it up.'

Sky said nothing but hugged her thin arms protectively around her knees. Hildamay started to put the tops on the lotions. She noticed Sky had only used the ones that she, Hildamay, had used on her last night.

'Sky? Sky, I'm sorry. I didn't mean to shout.'

Sky would not look at her. She had disappeared into a tight bundle of elbows and knees, withdrawn into some secret, safe place. Hildamay leaned forward and gently prised her chin away from her knees. She had cream smeared all over her face. Hildamay smiled and gently began to smooth it in.

'I'm not sure you need cellulite reducing cream on your face,' she said.

Sky looked at her warily.

'What's cellulite reducing?'

'It's what you get on your backside. Or rather it's what you don't get on your backside if you use this cream. Or perhaps it's what you don't get on your backside if you're stupid enough to pay enough to believe that you won't get it on your backside if you use this cream. Oh, it's just a stupid cream, Sky. They're all just stupid creams.'

'But I made a mess,' muttered Sky fiercely. 'I made a mess of the magic bathroom. I just wanted to sit in here because you said the magic bathroom would make everything better. Now I've gone and made a mess.' She squeezed her eyes tightly shut as if, by not seeing, she might make everything go away.

'No, you didn't. Open your eyes.' Sky opened her eyes. 'Look, no mess.'

'Where's the baby?' asked Sky suspiciously.

'What baby?' said Hildamay, confused.

'The baby you said in your letter you'd gone to see.'

'Oh, that baby,' said Hildamay.

Sky flushed and looked away.

'Now what's the matter?' said Hildamay.

'You want a baby instead of me,' she said in a hurt, strained voice. 'You want to swap me for a baby. You don't like me any more.'

'I do like you, Sky. I'd never swap you for a baby.'

Sky looked at her warily.

'You do like me?'

'Yes.'

'Very much?'

'Very much,' said Hildamay.

Sky smiled. Then her eyes glittered.

'I thought you'd left.'

'Why should I leave? This is my home.'

'Blanche left. And it was her home.'

'Well,' said Hildamay, 'she'll come back.'

'No, she won't.'

'Why not?'

'She just won't,' said Sky, shaking her head hard.

'Why not?'

'She wrote to grandmother and said that she didn't want to see either of us again. Ever. She said that I had never really been her daughter and that anyway I remind her too much of my father, who she said she hates, and she said she hates my grandmother, too. For ruining her life. She said she had a chance for a new life and that she was going to take it. She said to look after me and not to be too unkind,' added Sky, her voice small, 'because I was a good kid really.'

'And so you are,' said Hildamay, so fiercely that Sky looked up and gave her a small, pale smile.

'Anyway,' continued Hildamay, 'I'm sure she didn't really say all that. Maybe your grandmother misunderstood. Perhaps she was upset and didn't read the letter properly.'

'I can read,' said Sky with dignity.

'You read the letter?' asked Hildamay, shocked.

'My grandmother made me. She said my mother had hated me since I was a little girl. She said she didn't even want me before I was born. Nor did my father. She said my father was horrible. But not as horrible as my mother. She said if I didn't behave properly I'd be like my mother. She said if I read the letter then I'd understand what a – a – a slat my mother is.'

'Slut,' said Hildamay automatically. She hated Mary Matthews.

'Then where did you go last night?' asked Sky. But Hildamay was not listening. She was concentrating on hating.

Hildamay opened her eyes. All she could see was glass and bottles. She blinked. Her bathroom wall moved into focus. Her neck hurt. She was lying on the floor, a towel wedged under her head. She felt cold then realised that the towel draped over her was damp. She must have fallen asleep in the bathroom and Sky must have covered her while she slept. She smiled and sat up. She stopped smiling and shivered, feeling stiff and old. She wondered how Liz was feeling. Then she remembered that Liz had been in labour when she left the night before. No, it had been early this morning. She scrambled to her feet and walked into the bedroom to look at the clock. It was one o'clock. She picked up the telephone and called the hospital. After what seemed like an interminable length of time, she was put through to Liz's ward.

'Ward four,' said a voice.

'I'm calling to see if Liz Valentine has had her baby yet,' said Hildamay.

'Are you a relative?' asked the voice.

'I'm her husband.'

There was a silence. 'I'm afraid I –'

'No need to be,' said Hildamay. 'That's what she was afraid of.'

'What?'

'A husband,' said Hildamay patiently. 'So I'm the next best thing. I'm her closest friend, I'm the one who brought her in last night.'

'Oh,' said the voice doubtfully.

'Well?'

'Well what?'

'Well, has she had a baby yet?'

'Yes,' said the voice. 'A boy.'

'Oh dear,' said Hildamay.

'Oh no, he's fine,' said the voice. 'Mother and baby are doing fine. He's a great big bouncing boy.'

'She's not going to be pleased,' said Hildamay. 'When she finds out.'

'I'm sorry?' said the voice.

'So am I,' said Hildamay. 'But there you are.'

'Where?' said the voice.

'With a baby boy,' said Hildamay.

There was a long silence. Hildamay sat and thought about Liz and wondered how unhappy she would be. Maybe not unhappy at all. People usually weren't. 'Probably so pleased to get it out,' she said aloud.

'I'm sorry?' said the voice again. Hildamay jumped and looked at the telephone receiver. She'd forgotten she was speaking to somebody.

'Don't be,' she said. 'I'm sure she'll like him.'

'She seems quite pleased,' said the voice dubiously.

'Good,' said Hildamay firmly. 'When can I come and see her?'

'Visiting hours are four till eight.'

'Fine,' said Hildamay. 'Polish the champagne glasses. You do have some, don't you?' she added.

'We don't –'

'Never mind,' said Hildamay. 'I'll bring my own.' She put down the telephone receiver and went whistling into the sitting room.

Sky was sitting in the middle of Hildamay's very large pale blue sofa. Her hands were folded in her lap, and her short legs stuck out in front of her. She was wearing a beige dress with smocking all over the front, thick navy blue tights and her beloved trainers.

'What a horrible dress,' said Hildamay.

Sky looked down at it. 'Grandmother,' she said as if in explanation. 'You went to sleep,' she added.

'Yes,' said Hildamay. 'Thank you for covering me with the towel.'

Sky looked pleased. 'I saw them do it on the television once. But I think they were dead,' she added, frowning.

'We're going to the hospital,' said Hildamay. Sky's frown deepened until she was scowling.

'Are you sick?' she said.

'No. We're going to see the baby.'

'Which baby?'

'The one I went to see last night. Except it hadn't arrived. Liz's baby. It's arrived now. Except it's a he and she's not going to be pleased.'

'Oh dear,' said Sky.

'My sentiments precisely,' said Hildamay. 'Shall we have some lunch?'

'What's sentiments?' said Sky.

Hildamay and Sky spent some time searching for Liz. They walked past her many times before they found her lying in a bed in the middle of a vast ward. There was a great deal of noise but Liz was fast asleep, her head lolling to one side, her mouth wide open; a drool of spittle leaking from one corner. Her face was the same colour and texture as the pillow, grey white and papery. There were deep purple circles under her eyes and her skin was puffy. Even her curly, resilient hair looked defeated.

'That can't be her,' whispered Hildamay to Sky.

'Why not?'

'It doesn't look anything like her.'

'Maybe babies change you,' said Sky reassuringly.

'I think you're right,' whispered Hildamay gloomily.

They walked over to the bed. Hildamay stroked her hand through Liz's hair, as much to reassure herself that it was still vital and springing to the touch as to wake her. The hair felt coarse and matted. She took her hand away. Liz opened her eyes and frowned at Hildamay.

'You weren't here. When the baby came.'

'You told me you didn't want me to be.'

'Well, I was wrong,' whispered Liz. Tears leaked out of her eyes and dribbled down on to the pillow.

Sky moved forward and patted her hand.

'Did it hurt?' she asked. 'Very much?'

'Very much,' whispered Liz and, picking up Sky's hand, pulled it up to her breasts and held it in both her hands.

'I'm sorry,' whispered Sky.

'It's OK,' said Liz and stared up at the ceiling.

'Do you mind?' asked Sky.

'Mind what?' said Liz, not turning her head.

'That it's a boy.'

'Oh, that. No. No, I don't mind.'

'At least it's not a champagne glass,' said Hildamay, pulling three out of the carrier bag she was holding. Liz made a faint noise. Hildamay peered at her and then smiled.

'Is she crying?' whispered Sky, trying to look at Liz's face. 'Shall I go and tell the doctor?'

'No. She's not crying, she's laughing.'

'Why?'

'You're not grown-up enough to know,' said Hildamay.

'I hate grown ups,' said Sky crossly. 'They're so rude.'

'Here you are,' said Hildamay, handing her a glass of champagne. 'You can be rude, too.'

CHAPTER TWENTY TWO

THE following Friday, Hildamay came home late in the evening to find Sky curled up in a little ball on her front doorstep. She bent down and shook her gently but Sky just curled up even tighter so, with a sigh, Hildamay picked her up, carried her upstairs and put her to bed.

'I've come to live with you,' said Sky, waking and smiling, a pleased, trusting smile.

'Why?'

'Because I hate my grandmother,' she said conversationally, and then her eyelids fluttered irresistibly over her dark blue eyes, and she was asleep.

'Tomorrow,' said Hildamay, bending to kiss her. 'We'll talk about it tomorrow.' She went to telephone Mary Matthews.

It was morning. Sky sat motionless at the kitchen table, her hands folded serenely in her lap. She was dressed in a sage green pinafore and her baseball cap was jammed down hard over a lopsided pony tail.

'Have you eaten?' asked Hildamay as she walked in, yawning.

'No.'

'Do you want an egg?'

'Yes, please,' said Sky. 'It's Saturday. You don't have to go to work today.' She looked pleased. Hildamay looked at her but did not return the smile. A look of doubt flitted across Sky's face. It was as if somebody had turned out a light. She stared down at her hands. Hildamay sighed, boiled an egg, made toast, buttered it, cut it into fingers and set it down in front of her.

Then she poured herself a cup of coffee, lit a cigarette and sat down. Sky looked suspiciously at the egg. 'Eat it,' said Hildamay. 'It's pure protein.'

'What's protein?'

'Eat.'

Sky tapped cautiously at the egg with a spoon and for the next five minutes picked away at bits of shell until the egg was naked, the white bald and shiny. They both contemplated it for some time.

'Why are you taking so long to eat your egg?' asked Hildamay eventually.

'So I won't have to talk. It's rude to talk while you're eating.'

'Why don't you want to talk?'

Sky glowered at the egg.

'Because,' she said.

'Because you don't want to hear me say no?'

'Yes,' said Sky.

'No,' said Hildamay.

Sky sat and looked at the egg, tracing squeaky patterns with her finger over its bald white dome.

'Why can't I come and live with you?' she asked, her voice trembling. Her mouth kept on turning down at the corners although she fought hard to keep it steady. 'Don't you like me?'

Hildamay watched the corners of her mouth play out their brave, jerky rhythm. 'Of course I like you. Like has nothing to do with it. It's just that I'm used to living alone. I like it that way. I'm a person who is best suited to being alone.'

'Why?'

'Because,' said Hildamay, watching the tears slip down Sky's translucent skin. They made it shine, like a polished apple.

'We can still see each other a great deal,' she added gently.

'I had a quarrel with grandmother,' said Sky, in a small voice. She looked up at Hildamay, the blue of her eyes dark with fear. 'She knows you don't have a daughter. She made me tell her. I didn't want to!' she cried in sudden, shrill alarm.

'It's all right,' said Hildamay soothingly. 'I shall explain to her when I take you home.'

'No!' cried Sky in alarm. 'She won't let me see you again. She said so. Never!'

'She didn't mean it,' said Hildamay. 'She'll change her mind. You'll see.'

Sky looked at her in despair. Then she turned her head away.

'I won't go home,' she said in a low, strained voice. 'I won't go and live with her any more. She hates me. She told me.'

'She was angry,' said Hildamay, gently wiping Sky's tears away with her thumb. Sky jerked her head away.

'I won't live with her,' she repeated. 'I can't. And if I can't live with you then I shall have to go and live with somebody else.'

Hildamay sighed. 'You can't go and live with somebody else, Sky. You're only nine years old. You have to live with your grandmother.'

'I can, too,' she whispered, glaring at Hildamay, eyes brilliant with anger. 'I can too. Anyway I'm ten. Nine years and eleven months. Nearly ten.'

Hildamay smiled.

'I'm ten,' yelled Sky, infuriated, tears of rage and anger pouring down her face. She picked up the egg in her small fist. 'You're just like all the rest. All of them. You don't want me either. You just pretend you like me. Well, I don't like you either. You're horrid. I hate you. I hate you, I hate you, I hate you!' she shouted and smashed fist and egg down on the scarred wooden table. The egg, which was soft-boiled, splattered over the surface. Sky stood, her hand flat on the table, viscous yolk and fragments of rubbery white sticking to her fingers. She looked appalled. 'Sorry, Hildamay,' she whispered. 'I'm very sorry.' She was flinching. Hildamay looked at the fear in her eyes and wondered how often Mary Matthews hit her.

'It's OK,' she said, her voice shaking. She walked over to the sink to get a cloth. She spent a long time rinsing and wringing out the cloth. When eventually she could speak she turned back to the table. Sky had gone. Only the battered egg remained, its smashed yellow eye glistening reproachfully at her.

*

She found Sky sitting huddled on the floor in a corner of the bathroom, her thin arms wrapped protectively around her legs, her head sunk motionless on her bare, bony knees. Hildamay sat down next to her and put her arms around her, awkwardly circling head, arms and knees. Sky did not move.

'Sky? Sky, I'm sorry. Truly I am.'

Sky raised a tear-stained face. 'Can I come and live with you?'

'No.' It was just a whisper.

Sky looked at her steadily. 'Why not?'

'We can't always have what we want.'

'Why not?' she said with a despairing sigh and bent her face back down to her knees.

'God knows.'

'Well why doesn't he tell us, then?' said Sky in a muffled voice.

Hildamay smiled and hugged her even harder, feeling her bony elbows and knees dig into her breast. It was a comforting sort of pain. After a few minutes, with a small sigh, Sky disengaged herself from Hildamay's arms and then clambered up to sit on her lap. She sat facing her, arms and legs clasped around Hildamay's back as a monkey clings to its mother. Hildamay hugged her hard and they sat, rocking in a slow, mournful rhythm. Sky's face was hot and damp, squashed against Hildamay's neck. 'I didn't mean it,' she whispered and Hildamay felt tears wet against her skin. 'I was only pretending. I don't hate you. I love you, I love you, I love you,' she murmured. Hildamay closed her eyes and rocked.

'Hildamay,' whispered Sky, her voice low and urgent. 'Hildamay, do you love me?'

Hildamay hugged her harder, pressing the small body against her own. How, she thought, in a haze of despair, can I explain about love? How do you tell a child that you love her but that she has no real place in your life? Not the place that she wants, anyway. How do I tell her that I love her but by loving her she's messing everything up? Sky would never understand that. To her loving means being. She thinks it's simple.

And so she said nothing.

Sky pulled her head away and pressed her nose to Hildamay's. She giggled, finding their eyes so close together. 'You do love me! You do!' she crowed, triumphant. Hildamay closed her eyes and was silent. 'Don't you?' said Sky after a while, her voice wavering with uncertainty. If she told Sky she loved her, she would not understand why she could not come and live with her. I have to live alone, said a small, defiant voice buried somewhere deep in the heart of her. I am not capable of sharing my life. Everything I love leaves. The thought startled her. I am not capable of sharing my life. She heard her mother's voice. 'Learn to love, Hilda. Learn.' But I do love, I do. 'Not enough, Hilda. Not enough. It is not good to live so alone.' It is for me, thought Hildamay. It is for me.

'Don't you?' repeated Sky's small, uncertain voice. And then she waited, her breath warm on Hildamay's face, her small body rigid with hope. Eventually Hildamay shook her head, very slightly. 'No,' she whispered. She felt tears hot against her skin.

'Oh, please,' moaned Sky. '*Please*,' and sobbed into her neck.

Sky refused to move. She lay flat on her back in the middle of the bathroom floor, a small cold statue crying hot, silent tears. Hildamay stood in the doorway and looked at her in despair. 'Sky,' she said in a low, beseeching voice. 'Sky, we have to go now. I've telephoned your grandmother. She's expecting us.' Sky turned her head away.

Hildamay somehow closed her heart to her, to the heart-shaped face now battered, misshapen with misery, and to the navy eyes dimmed to a paler blue as if all the tears she cried, and kept on crying, had washed them of their colour. She closed her heart and opened her eyes, or so she saw it anyway, to reality, and went and picked Sky up and carried her down to the car. Which was not easy. Sky stiffened every limb until she seemed to have grown to someone twice her size and weight.

Then she started to fight. 'I want to stay in the magic bathroom,' she cried, arms and legs thrashing as Hildamay struggled to control her. 'Let me go to the magic bathroom.' A woman passing by stopped and watched, her mouth thin with disgust. Hildamay, who was concentrating on keeping her balance and not dropping Sky who was by then fighting like a wild cat, did not notice the woman until she called, 'Excuse me, Miss, but I really do think you should let that child go to the bathroom.'

'I am not a miss,' shouted Hildamay, infuriated beyond reason. Sky, seeing the woman, stopped struggling and Hildamay hugged her in a sudden, wrenching spasm of misery. 'And I'd thank you to mind your own bloody business,' she screamed, white-faced with grief. The woman stared at her open-mouthed. 'Go fuck yourself!' bellowed Hildamay and then she bent her head and sobbed into

Sky's neck. After a few minutes Sky gently disentangled herself from the fierce embrace and went and stood silently by the car.

'Sorry, Hildamay,' she muttered and then got into the car and sat, staring straight ahead. Hildamay watched her out of the corner of her eye as she drove through the grey streets of North London. It was drizzling. 'I get so depressed on Finchley Road,' said Hildamay aloud. Sky made no sound. 'Depressed is an understatement,' she said, despairingly. Sky did not ask what an understatement was. Hildamay felt her throat close. They drove in silence.

'It's not that simple, Sky,' said Hildamay eventually. 'You're not old enough to make decisions about where and with whom you live. You belong to your grandmother. It's up to her what happens to you. It's up to your mother, really, but she's not around. So you have to do what your grandmother says.'

Sky turned and looked at her. 'You mean if grandmother says I can come and live with you, then I can?'

Fool, thought Hildamay. Fool, fool, fool.

Sky was watching her carefully.

'No,' she said.

Sky turned and pressed her nose to the window.

'Maybe,' said Hildamay, 'maybe if you could remember that your grandmother is old and that you need to be nice to her and patient because she is older and slower than you, maybe then she would be nicer to you.' She glanced sideways at Sky who turned her face towards her. She did not speak but her small mouth tightened with contempt.

'Yes, all right. It was a stupid thing to say.'

They drove to Haadji's shop where they deposited the cap, jacket and trainers, exchanging them for Sky's shabby navy jacket. She dressed in absolute silence under Haadji's mournful but sympathetic gaze. Then they drove to Mary Matthews' house. Hildamay looked at the plate brass lion's head knocker with distaste. Sky stared straight ahead.

'Are you all right?' asked Hildamay. There was no reply. Hildamay lifted the knocker and slammed it hard against the door.

'All right, all right,' called Mary Matthews' harsh, irritated voice.

'That door's expensive. It doesn't need treating like that.' The door was flung open.

'Well, Miss Smith,' she said, pronouncing the Miss with scornful, deliberate emphasis. 'So you've finally decided to bring my granddaughter home. Very kind of you, I'm sure.' She grabbed Sky by the arm and pulled her past, pushing her into the corridor behind. Sky went silently, unresisting and disappeared into the house without a backward glance. This seemed somehow to please Mary Matthews and a thin smile lit her sharp features. She glanced back at the silent, retreating child and then at Hildamay. 'Sorry to have troubled you,' she said, and a malicious triumph lit her face. 'I don't think we'll be troubling you again.' She started to close the door.

Hildamay put her foot in the way. It was her best pair of suede shoes, but worse than that was the pain. Mary Matthews banged the door hard, thinking that something was stuck in the way. It was. Hildamay gazed down at her foot sadly. The shoe was ruined. The door opened again.

'Good grief,' she said, her eyes bright with tears. 'It looks so easy in the movies.'

Mary Matthews glared at her. 'I don't know what you want,' she said, her tiny eyes made even smaller with anger and the bone in her great nose shining white, 'but I want you to leave my granddaughter alone. I don't want you seeing her ever again. Do you understand? Ever again,' she repeated with careful emphasis. 'She's not been right. Not since she met you. She's either too quiet or she's answering back, sharp as you please, and then suddenly she runs off, not so much as a word, and I get you on the phone. You,' she spat, 'playing the gracious lady. "Sky's upset. Sky's unhappy."' She mimicked Hildamay's voice, parodying her flat, characterless middle-class vowels. 'What do you know about a girl like that? What do you know about what she needs? Got some of your own, have you?' she demanded, her voice thin and high. 'Got a daughter of your own, have you?' she mocked. And then her eyes narrowed. 'It was a lie, you told. Wasn't it? A lie?'

'Yes,' said Hildamay despairingly. 'It was a lie.'

'Thought so,' said Mary Matthews and a curious, bright look of triumph lit her face. 'A liar's not the kind of person people like to see around children,' she added, her expression changing to the hard shine of malice. Her small eyes darted at Hildamay and then over her shoulder as she turned and called into the cold, dark hall, 'Sky! Sky, come here and say goodbye to Miss Smith. Say goodbye, Sky!' Her harsh voice was taunting. They stood on the doorstep, straining to hear the slightest noise. Mary Matthews' smile glittered. 'See? She doesn't even want to say goodbye.'

Hildamay let herself into her flat and walked straight to the bathroom. She closed and locked the door and then turned on all the hot taps until the room was full of the sound of running water. She stood in the middle of the room with her eyes tightly shut. Soon all the mirrors were clouded with condensation. It was only then that she opened her eyes; she could not have borne to look at her own face. 'The magic bathroom,' she whispered. She stood in the steam and the noise for a long time. Then she sat on the floor and cried.

CHAPTER
TWENTY THREE

HILDAMAY stood by the ticket office in St Pancras station. It was fifteen minutes past three. She looked at her watch and sighed. She had thought that perhaps Sky would have forgiven her by now. It was two weeks since their quarrel. It was only a quarrel, thought Hildamay with a slight, impatient tightening of her lips. She had simply told Sky that she could not come and live with her. Surely she could see that it would have been impossible? It had been a whim of the moment. Nothing more. And she had thought that Sky, like most children, would have forgotten within the hour. But Sky, she thought with a sudden quick burst of pride, was not like most children. And then pride became alarm, for Sky was not like most children or indeed most people, being resolute in her judgements and decided in her trust. She will never forgive this, thought Hildamay in despair. She put the feeling from her with a quick, impatient shake of her head. It was not as if she had said that they would not see each other again. She had said, quite distinctly she thought, that they would go on seeing one another. And then she felt a small, cold prickle of fear. She had told her that she did not love her. She could not have believed that? It was perfectly obvious that she loved her. And children forget, forgive things so easily. Even Sky, she thought bleakly.

She had waited, last week, by the ticket office for nearly two hours and had then gone on her quiet, solitary way to Portobello. The flowers had not seemed fresh that day and even the Rastafarians had been silent, drinking beer in deliberate, morose gulps. The loneliness she had felt had caught her by surprise, and she had stood in the middle of the bustling, cheerful market and felt the scratching claw of panic at her throat as she thought of the days without Sky. Alone.

On Wednesday she waited by the telephone all evening, springing to answer it each time it rang. It had never been Sky. She had not called the house in Woodside Park. She knew that Sky would not answer the telephone, that she would hear only Mary Matthews' harsh voice, cruel with triumph as she told her that Sky did not want to speak to her.

Perhaps she should write her a letter? Send it to Haadji who would keep it for her, nestled in the shabby plastic bag with her baseball cap. Perhaps, she thought with a sudden joyful flash of optimism, perhaps there were problems on the Northern line? Then she imagined Sky, her small body slumped low in her seat in a coma of anticipation, her cap pulled hard down over her eyes to contain her excitement. And so she went in search of the station manager, almost running in her eagerness to establish the problems on the Northern line. The misery line, she thought happily. There were always delays on the misery line. She found him tucked away in a tiny room clouded with cigarette smoke and littered with half-empty mugs in which cold tea stagnated, the surface oily with globules of souring milk. There were, he said, no problems on the Northern line. She had been back to ask him so many times that he had finally locked the door on her in exasperation, and refused to open it despite her repeated knocking. She gave it one last kick for good measure and, frowning, left the station to catch a bus home. She had no heart for Portobello.

She let herself into her flat and ran to check the answering machine. No messages. The red light did not blink. Sighing, she went into her kitchen and began to chop vegetables in a slow, deliberate fashion, lingering over each courgette and carrot and onion until she had reduced them all to perfect one inch cubes. She minced garlic, sliced ginger and ground spices, toasting them gently in a little old cast iron frying pan; as the heat began to release the captive oils and essences contained in the shrivelled pods of cardamom and knobbly crinkled seeds of coriander she set to boil a great pan of chicken bones, throwing in carrot, celery, bayleaf and parsley; setting them to bubble until the kitchen was fragrant with smells and the windows ran with condensation. By seven o'clock she had four different sorts of soup simmering on the stove. She looked at them and knew that she would never eat them but the sight of them soothed her. It made everything seem normal.

The flowers which sat in a tubby blue vase on the kitchen table were dying; their leaves yellowed with age and their petals drooping and dispirited. Looking at them, she shivered, feeling sharply alone, and ran through the empty flat in a sudden panic of haste to pick up the telephone. Mary Matthews answered at once.

'Two seven oh, five oh three eight,' she said, strangling the vowels in her harsh, flat voice.

'Mrs Matthews, it's Hildamay Smith. I was calling to see if Sky was all right.'

'What do you mean, all right?' she said suspiciously.

'I haven't heard from her for two weeks,' explained Hildamay patiently.

'Why should you?' Mary Matthews' tone was sharp. 'I told you, I don't want you seeing Sky again.'

'No,' said Hildamay after a while. 'Is she all right?' she added, her voice carefully neutral.

'I have no idea,' said Mary Matthews, sounding tired. 'No thanks to you,' she added, her voice suddenly thin with anger.

'No idea? To me?' echoed Hildamay.

'It was you who said that Sky had turned up on your doorstep because she was unhappy or some such silly nonsense. As if a child who's fed and clothed and housed could be unhappy. I suppose you've filled her stupid head with all sorts of ridiculous imaginings. No wonder the silly little fool's run off,' she said, her voice rough with contempt. 'You filling her with nonsense. It's you we have to thank. The police round here at all hours of the day and night.'

'The police!' said Hildamay, her voice sharp with alarm.

'She's disappeared,' said Mary Matthews roughly. 'Silly little girl, causing all this upset and grief. I had to go to the police and then I had to put a call through to Spain to try and find her mother. Not that Blanche would be much use. She's never been a mother to that child. I've been the only mother she's ever known, poor little thing. And look how she repays that kindness.' She sniffed, a small pinched explosion of disgust. 'By running off without so much as a by your leave. Just like her mother. I don't know where it comes from. Certainly not from me. Must be my late husband. Didn't have a reliable bone in his body. Never turned up when he said he would Always wandering off, in a dream, or sitting around the house with his nose stuck in a book. Just like him, those two. Not so much as an apology. It's a disgrace.'

'Mrs Matthews,' protested Hildamay. 'She's only nine years old!' She could feel panic starting in her chest, a tight knot of it which spun round and round and then started to snake up her arms and down her legs until she could feel the tingle in her fingers and toes. Her voice was loud with fear.

'I know how old my granddaughter is,' snapped Mary Matthews.

Hildamay leaned against the wall and began to take slow, deep breaths to try to calm herself. 'When did she disappear?'

'Two weeks ago. Monday before last.'

'Monday before last?' shouted Hildamay. 'Well, why did nobody ring me to tell me?'

'I wasn't aware that we had to ask your permission,' said Mary Matthews icily.

'Oh, not my permission,' pleaded Hildamay. 'Just so that I would know. So I could help find her. What did the police say? Do they think she's been abducted? Have you contacted the school? When did her friends last see her?'

'Friends?' said Mary Matthews, in surprise. 'Friends? She's not a girl who has friends.' Her voice took on an unpleasant sneering tone.

'And whose fault is that?' yelled Hildamay.

There was a sharp intake of breath. 'Don't you shout at me, young lady. I don't know who you think you are, poking your nose into other people's business, making friends with a nine year old child. It's not right, really it's not.' Her voice sharpened with suspicion. 'Are you sure you don't know where she is? I've always thought it odd, the way you took up with Sky. Want children of your own, then?'

'No,' said Hildamay, her voice flat. 'I don't want children of my own.'

'Something unnatural about a woman who doesn't want children,' said Mary Matthews, her voice whining with spite. 'Not that it seems to bother you, borrowing other people's, I mean. Teaching her all sorts of nasty little manners, trying to make out we're not good enough for her. Lady Muck, you are, with all your airs and graces, looking down your nose at the likes of us.'

'Were the police any help?' said Hildamay, ignoring the hatred she could feel, like a cold, malevolent chill, running down the wire between them.

'As much help as they can be in this situation,' said Mary Matthews sharply. 'Though really, taking up valuable police time because some spoiled little girl has decided that she feels like running off for a week is ridiculous.'

'Did you say a week?' said Hildamay quickly.

'A week, two weeks. I don't know how long it'll be before the little madam decides to turn up, expecting us all to fall over ourselves with gratitude.'

'So you don't think she's been abducted?' said Hildamay slowly.

'Of course she hasn't been abducted,' said Mary Matthews impatiently. 'Who would want to abduct Sky?'

The careless cruelty of that sentence silenced Hildamay and she pressed the receiver hard against her ear until she felt a sharp pain run up through her temple and snake around her head to settle in a throbbing ache over her eyes. Through the silence she remembered Sky's pale, defeated face. 'Don't tell her,' she had said. 'Don't tell her about us. She'll make you go away.' She saw the thin, cold line of the woman's mouth and the zeal burning in her tiny eyes and thought of Sky's terrible, fearful silences. Why had she not believed her? Why, she thought in despair, had she not believed her own instincts? She remembered George's voice. 'She is suffering from a lack of kindness. Love, kindness, call it what you will.' He had known. Why had she not listened? She had not even heard, been so busy convincing herself that everything was fine that she had been deafened to all other voices.

'Will you let me know?' said Hildamay quietly.

'What business is it of yours?' demanded Mary Matthews.

'I am worried about her,' said Hildamay evenly. 'I should like to know that she is safe.'

'Oh, very well,' grumbled Mary Matthews. 'I shall let you know if anything happens.'

Hildamay put the telephone down then quickly picked it up again and dialled George's number.

'Hello?' he said in a gentle, hesitant voice.

'George,' she said, her voice tight, 'it's Hildamay. Sky's disappeared.'

'When?' he said quickly, stammering in distress.

'She's been gone nearly two weeks,' said Hildamay. Fear made her breathless and she stumbled over the words which jumbled together in the urgency of her panic. 'She didn't turn up this afternoon. At three o'clock. You know, which is when we always meet. I waited and waited. Or last week either. She didn't call on Wednesday but I just thought she was sulking. I thought she'd turn up today and we could sort it all out. So I waited and waited and still she didn't come, so I came home. And then I finally rang Mary Matthews and she told me that Sky had disappeared. She must have gone on the Monday morning. The day after I took her home. After we had the quarrel.'

'Why was she sulking?' said George gently.

'Because I told her she couldn't come and live with me.'

There was silence. George seemed to be waiting for her to say something else.

Hildamay took a deep breath and stammered out the words. 'Because I told her I didn't love her.'

'You did what?' His voice was harsh.

'I told her I didn't love her,' she whispered, screwing up her eyes against the pain which thudded in her head.

George was silent for a moment.

'And do you?' he said.

'Yes. Yes, of course I do. I just thought –' her voice tailed off. 'I just thought it was inconvenient.' The word seemed to hang in the air and then it gently rolled away from her, echoing as it bounced down the telephone wire.

'I see,' said George, so quietly that at first she thought he had not spoken. Hildamay closed her eyes again and waited for him to speak. He said nothing else. There was no comfort to be had.

Very gently, she put the receiver back in its place and walked into her bathroom. Locking the door, she turned on the hot tap in the bath and then began to take all the jars and pots of lotions and creams off the shelves. One by one she emptied them into the bath; the creams, coloured apricot, pale pink, cream, ice blue and frosty mint green, swirled in the hot water, forming fat globular patterns, as oil does in water. She watched them forming and reforming, changing shape as she methodically scooped all the creams out of their jars and then carefully shook all the lotions out of the bottles.

As she emptied them she dropped them one by one at her feet until she was surrounded by little pyramids of glass. She looked around her. She had not realised that she had so many. She thought of all the time and love that had gone into those glass jars and all the hours she had spent buying them and smoothing them on her body. Of the silent ritual of secrecy she had performed each day. They looked, she thought as she watched them form their coloured patterns in the hot water, pretty in a useless sort of a way. She looked around her at the bare, shining walls and thought of all the time she had spent in this bathroom, talking to her own reflection, hiding from the world in a room so secret that nobody even knew it existed. Hiding from emotion, she thought, so that she would not have to join in the real process of living. How many walls had she built, she wondered, to protect herself from the mess of life? Protect herself from what? From feeling? Sky had burrowed a tiny hole through those walls, but even as she burrowed, she knew that she, Hildamay, had been shoring up that hole as fast as she could, pasting it over with the cold, hard cement of fear. She had a sudden vision of herself, like a doll encased in a smooth coating of plastic; cold, smooth, inviolable. Perfectly dressed, perfectly groomed, perfectly dead.

She kicked at the pyramids of glass so that the bottles and jars rolled across the floor. 'Empty,' she whispered, staring at them. 'All empty. Like my fucking life.' She kicked a glass jar savagely across the room, so it splintered against the old claw-footed bathtub. 'Hiding from emptiness,' she said aloud to the room.

She hammered her fists on the unforgiving tiles. 'If you're so fucking magic,' she shouted, 'then why didn't you tell me what I was doing? Why did you let her go?' And then she laid her hot cheeks against the cold ceramic and tears ran down her face, for she knew that she had sent Sky away herself, as surely as if she had packed her bag and ordered her out of the house. She knew, too, that she would not come back.

She picked up all the empty glass jars and bottles and began to throw them one by one at the mirrors which lined the walls.

They cracked and splintered with each jar she threw and as she watched her own reflection fragment, she shouted, 'An inconvenient child! She was an inconvenient child! You didn't want her messing up your life, Hildamay Smith. Your perfect, fucking empty life. You didn't know magic when you saw it. Did you?' She aimed a glass jar at a fragment of mirror in which she could still see a portion of her face reflected. 'Did you?' she screamed as her face fell in splinters to the floor.

Finally, when she was standing in a sea of broken glass, she looked around her at walls ugly and patched with globules of greasy lotions and, turning away, walked out of the shattered room. Closing the bathroom door, she locked it securely and dropped the key in a porcelain jar, painted with violets and given to her by her mother, which stood on the chest of drawers in her bedroom.

CHAPTER
TWENTY FOUR

HILDAMAY sat huddled on a bench in St Pancras station and thought about regret; saw it disfiguring the faces of the people passing by. There, in the vertical line that tugged between their eyes, pulling the eyebrows down in a slight, questioning frown. 'What did I do?' the frown seemed to say. There, around the mouth, the slight downward pull of lips that seemed never to smile but always to be asking 'why?' Some faces had harsher lines and she thought perhaps that they were bitterness; the same lines that formed regret but etched even deeper, stern and ineradicable.

'How many regrets does it take to make bitterness?' she wondered and then moaned quietly as she felt regret, like an indigestible lump of food sitting in her belly, weighing her down so that her feet dragged and her shoulders bent. She sighed and stared over to the cafe at platform three. Why had she not listened to Sky? Listened to her terrible silence; terrible as only the silence of children can be. In her mind's eye she watched the luminous navy eyes darken with loneliness, the vibrant, heart shaped face dwindle to a white triangle bruised purple under the eyes, watched it slowly starved of warmth. She thought again of that cold house and then of the day when she had told Sky she did not love her. She felt Sky's tears hot on her neck and felt regret move, like a foetus, within her.

'Hildamay?'
'Yes, Sky?'
'Why do people shout?'
'Because they need more space.'
'Like stars?'
'No. Not like stars. Space as in room around you, rather than in heaven. The bigger and older you get, the more time and space you need.'
'Why?'
'I suppose because it all starts to run out. The space and the time, I mean. Your mind gets fuller and fuller so you need to sort out all that clutter and throw some away. When you don't have enough space to do that, you get irritated and start to shout. And you must have silence. If you have enough space, then you can find enough silence. Constant noise is very aggravating.'
'What's aggravating?'
'Annoying.'
'That's what my grandmother calls me.' Sky's voice dwindled to a sigh. '"An annoying little girl." I try not to annoy her but everything I do seems to.' Her voice sharpened anxiously. 'Do I annoy you?'
'Not so far.'
'You mean I will?' Sky sounded alarmed.
'Everybody annoys everybody, at some time or another,' said Hildamay. 'That's why they need space.'
'I thought that if you liked somebody then they didn't annoy you,' said Sky, her voice wavering. 'Grandmother doesn't like me and that's why I annoy her.'
'How do you know she doesn't like you?'
'She tells me all the time. Does that mean you don't like me?' Her voice was shrill with worry.
'No. I like you.'
There was a long silence while Sky absorbed this.
'Why do you live by yourself?' she asked suddenly.
'Because of the space. And the silence. That's what the magic bathroom's for.'

'Oh. Would you ever live with anybody else?'
'No.'
'Never?' persisted Sky.
'Never,' said Hildamay firmly.
'Oh,' said Sky and sighed.

Hildamay shivered and huddled further into her coat, pulling it around her like a blanket. She was not cold but in need of comfort and scrabbled irritably at the scratchy wool cloth, but it did not ease her. She never felt cold these days. Neither cold nor hunger affected her but she was constantly plagued by tiredness. Whether it was genuine fatigue or simply the enervation of regret, she could not decide. A policeman walked past and smiled cautiously at her. She tried to form her face into a smile but the effect was just a memory. She was out of practice; the magnifying mirror lay under her bed, gathering dust. Still, the young policeman looked pleased to see even the ghost of pleasure on her face and nodded at her encouragingly.

It was now three weeks since she'd heard that Sky had gone; three weeks during which Hildamay went to the station nearly every evening. She came straight from work, rushing to the bench in the middle of the great hall where she sat, balanced like a marionette on the edge of the seat, her body jerking in agitation as she stared wildly at the ebb and flow of the people around her; a tide sucking one wave of people on to a platform, another pushing them off the platform so they burst, in a sudden flurry of grey and brown, spilling out around the criss-cross metal bars of the platform gate. As the crowds thinned and the night wore on she ceased to stare, but slumped back into the curve of the bench and gazed absently around her, her face slowly closing into the blankness of despair. Sometimes she would see a small figure, over in the distance, and jumping off the bench would run across the station calling in a beseeching voice, 'Sky! Sky!' When they heard her call the station guards and ticket inspectors, the policemen and kiosk owners would stop what they were doing and look after her running figure, but when they saw her feet stop and her head drop in a gesture of despair they would purse their lips and shake their heads as the wise do to the foolish.

The man from the Kwik Snak hot dog kiosk brought her over a cup of tea. 'Any luck, love?' he asked, smiling sympathetically. She shook her head and took the tea, gulping at the hot liquid gratefully.

'She'll turn up, love,' he said, patting her clumsily on the shoulder, but his voice sounded hollow. She knew he thought it was hopeless. He had seen, he said, too many parents looking for children, who never came. 'But none so persistent as you, love,' he added brightly, flashing her an encouraging smile. She sipped her tea and nodded, staring over at the platforms blankly. At least he didn't think she was mad. Perhaps I am mad, reasoned Hildamay, sitting on the cold, hard bench. I have a child and a bathroom and nobody knows that they exist. Only Sky knows the bathroom exists. Perhaps the bathroom doesn't exist without Sky. Perhaps Sky doesn't exist without the bathroom. She shook her head. She was tired. So tired. She leaned her head back against the cold, hard wood and closed her eyes.

'But who is she, darling?' Cassie had cried down the telephone. 'A child, you say,' she exclaimed, her voice echoing in disbelief. 'A child? But you've never even mentioned her before. Well, if you say so, darling. But don't you think you'd be better off with the police handling this? I know it's difficult with missing children. Well, where's her mother, anyway? She's run off, too? Oh, darling! I didn't mean it like that! You sound so strange. Shall I come and rescue you? I know you haven't lost your marbles, Hildamay, but honestly, darling, it is all a bit far-fetched.'

Hildamay had scarcely spoken to Liz who was now at home with the baby, Harry. 'Who? Oh, Sky. What do you mean – she's gone?' she had said, her voice slow with exhaustion. 'Where? Oh, you mean she's run off? Why would she do that? Oh, God, the baby's crying. Hang on a minute. Can you hear him? Oh, Harry, stop, please stop.' Her pleading voice came floating down the telephone. 'He won't stop!' she wailed. 'Oh, Hildamay, I don't think I can bear this. Why does nobody tell you? Oh, I know they tell you, but they don't *tell* you. I've never been so tired in all my life. I feel like I'm trapped inside these four walls with a parasite draining my life blood from my body. Hang on a minute, I'm just going to stick him on my tit. Let the little bastard suck some more life out of his mother. Are you still there? But who is she, anyway? You never explained. Oh, I know she lives in Woodside Park and hates her grandmother. She's probably run off in a temper. She'll come back. I've got to go. Come and see me. It'll put you off children for life.'

'Hildamay, what are you doing?' said Delilah's voice. She didn't remember speaking to Delilah on the telephone. She felt a hand on her shoulder and jumped, startled. Delilah was sitting on the bench beside her watching her out of cool, grey eyes. Her dark hair was sleeked like a shining cap over her head and her eyebrows curved in perfect arches, black against the dead white skin. She wrinkled her nose suddenly, giving her the look of an exotic, well kept cat. Hildamay half expected her to start washing any minute.

'George,' she said, 'told me that you might be here.'

'Yes,' said Hildamay and rubbed at her eyes with dirty hands. She pulled her coat tighter to cover the shapeless sweater and skirt she wore and tucked her feet under the bench to hide her scuffed shoes.

'You're a mess,' said Delilah briskly as Hildamay patted clumsily at her hair. 'It is enough,' she added firmly. 'You must stop this now and go back to living your life. You can't wish her back.'

'Why not?' Hildamay's voice was dull with misery. 'What else is there to do?'

'If she wants to come back, she will,' said Delilah calmly. 'She knows where you live.'

'If she knows I want her to come back, she might,' said Hildamay stubbornly. 'You don't know Sky. I told her to go and she went. She won't come back unless I ask her to.'

'What an obedient child,' said Delilah laconically.

'It has nothing to do with obedience,' said Hildamay, her voice flat. 'It's simply that she believes what people tell her. I told her I didn't love her.'

'She may not really have believed you,' said Delilah softly.

'I was cold. And unkind. She knows about that. She was raised on cruelty. She believed me.'

'We all know about that,' said Delilah with a sigh.

'Talking of which, how's Ben?' said Hildamay, remembering, with a sudden shock, that other world she used to live in. 'Have you seen him? And what of Ned? Are you back together? Are you less unhappy now?'

Delilah looked at her for a moment, her face thoughtful. 'Well, at least pain has taught you kindness,' she said and then, seeing Hildamay's face, cried, 'I'm sorry! Hildamay, I'm sorry. It's just that sometimes you seem so remote. Sitting there in your cool, clean, uncluttered life while we messy mortals scurry around beating our breasts and wailing for love; our faces stained with tears and the debris of our lives scattered all around us.' She sighed and lay back against the bench, her shoulder touching Hildamay's. Hildamay was glad of it, feeling the warmth of flesh even through the fabric of her coat. She sat in the cold grey hall and wished, suddenly, for her mother.

'We are none of us immune from pain,' she said quietly, turning her head away.

'But you thought you were,' insisted Delilah.

'No,' said Hildamay slowly, thinking of her bathroom where she had once taken all emotions to be anaesthetised and dissected and then pinned to the wall like broken butterflies, left for dead. 'I just tried to be sure that I was.'

Delilah looked at her curiously. 'Is the pain very bad?'

Hildamay shrugged and looked around her at the stained stone floors, at the sallow faced people, at regret. 'The view could be better,' she murmured.

'Who is she, this child?'

'She's just a child,' said Hildamay, her voice high, her throat tight with tears. She turned her head away from Delilah so that she should not see the tears gathering behind her eyes then dropped her head and rubbed at her eyes hard, pushing her knuckles into the sockets until lights exploded in the darkness. She raised her head. 'She's just somebody,' she whispered, 'who told me about love.'

There was silence for a while. 'It is not usual,' said Delilah hesitantly, 'to find love with a child.'

'Isn't it?' said Hildamay in some surprise. 'I thought that was supposed to be the greatest love of all.'

'With your own,' said Delilah, her tone still hesitant. 'Not with somebody else's.'

'I imagine,' said Hildamay sharply, 'that that's because people like to possess the things that they love. What does it matter,' she added wearily, 'where you find love? It's unusual enough to find it anyway. If you find it you should keep it. Not let it go.' She sighed.

'I had always thought,' said Delilah, 'that you had no time for love. Didn't believe in it.'

'I don't believe in what most people call love,' said Hildamay with a shrug. 'It seems so jealous and unkind.'

They sat in silence. Hildamay watched a couple standing outside the station pub. The man was tall and wore a navy overcoat, grey trousers and shiny black leather shoes. His hair was blond and cut very short at the back; Hildamay could see the red lines the clippers had left on his freshly sheared neck. He was kissing a woman. She had shiny dark hair and wore a green loden coat; her hands, which grasped the back of his navy coat, were very white, the nails painted a deep red. Even as he was kissing the woman, his head bent over her, the man raised his arm to look at his watch behind her back.

Married, thought Hildamay automatically.

He raised his head from the kiss and, patting the woman on the bottom, turned and began to walk towards the bench where Hildamay and Delilah sat. As he walked he pulled out a white handkerchief from his coat pocket and began to scrub at the lipstick stains around his mouth. Something about the gesture struck Hildamay and she looked again and saw that it was Ben. She turned to Delilah. 'Tell me about Ned.' Her voice was low and urgent. She bent her head and leaned it towards Delilah as if ready to share some secret, willing her to drop hers too. But Delilah saw her agitation and lifted her head to look at the place where Hildamay had been staring.

Ben stopped in mid-stride, the white handkerchief raised towards his face. Hildamay could see faint streaks of deep red lipstick still smeared around his mouth.

'Delilah' he said, his pale skin reddening.

'Oh, no,' said Delilah in a low voice and, dropping her head to her chest, sat with her head bowed as if waiting for him to pass. But Ben took one last swipe at his mouth with the handkerchief, twitched his lips into the semblance of a smile and, with one stride of his long legs, arrived at the bench.

'Well, isn't this nice' he said heartily.

'No,' said Hildamay. Delilah did not speak but raised her head to look at him.

'Is this the fashionable place for women to meet?' he asked, attempting a laugh. 'The bench in the middle of St Pancras station.'

'You should tell her to stop wearing that lipstick,' said Delilah in a low, strained voice. 'It's almost indelible. You'll need soap and water to get it off.'

Ben's face seemed suddenly to fragment; the assured mouth trembled and the hard eyes blurred while the smoothly shaved, expensively scented skin paled to leave bright patches of colour shining on his cheeks. 'She has hair just like yours,' he said, his voice hoarse. 'I miss you, Delilah.' He stretched his hand out towards Delilah's shining head but she ducked and he fumbled at thin air.

Hildamay looked from one to the other. Neither of them moved. Ben stood, his hand outstretched, and she saw, to her surprise, that there were tears in his eyes. Delilah sat, her head bent and her thin shoulders raised, as if to protect herself. 'Are you going down to the cottage?' said Hildamay at last.

'What?' Ben turned and looked at her, frowning in confusion, and then looked back at Delilah's bowed head. 'Delilah,' he said, in a low, urgent voice. 'Please. Talk to me. Come and have a drink.

We must talk.' She did not move. 'Well, at least answer my telephone calls. That bloody machine,' he said angrily. 'That horrible, unkind machine.'

Delilah looked up at him. 'How's Kate?' she asked, her voice hard.

He shrugged and looked away. 'She's just the same,' he said in a low voice. 'It's just the same –' His voice trailed off, then he looked at Delilah again. 'She needs me. You do understand? I thought that –' he began. 'I thought it would be –' He stopped and stared at her. 'You're so beautiful,' he murmured. 'Unbearably beautiful.'

'Ben,' said Hildamay gently. 'Go home.'

'Home?' He looked at her curiously for a moment and then stared around him. 'What are you doing here?'

'Looking for someone,' said Hildamay evenly.

'You look –' He stopped. 'You look different, somehow.'

'Must be that sex change I had last week,' said Hildamay but he did not smile.

'Who are you looking for?' he demanded.

'A child.'

'A child?' he exclaimed, his features contorted as if in pain.

'Whose child?'

'Just a child,' said Hildamay quietly and then shrank back into the curve of the bench as Ben squatted down in front of her and pressed his face to hers.

'Why?' he demanded.

'Because I love her,' she said. At that he sighed and, leaning over, clumsily pressed his forehead into the curve of Hildamay's neck. She lay pinned against the bench, too astonished to speak. 'Oh, no,' he murmured in a low, broken voice. He rested there with his head on her shoulder in silence for some minutes. Then, turning his head, he whispered loudly and urgently in her ear, 'Find her!' He pulled his head away and drew himself up until he was standing over the two women. 'Find the thing that you love,' he shouted and walked away.

'Good grief,' said Hildamay and, turning, looked at Delilah who sat, head bowed, staring at her hands which were balled into hard knots in the lap of her skirt. Her shoulders were rigid and she made no sound. Hildamay patted her gently on the back and kissed the sleek dark head, then leaned back against the bench and continued to look for Sky.

'I should have told you,' said Delilah, after a while.

'No,' said Hildamay.

'But I thought you'd be angry with me,' continued Delilah, as if she had not heard.

'Not angry!' exclaimed Hildamay. 'Why should I be angry?'

'I thought you'd despise me,' said Delilah in a low voice. 'For making such a mess. Such a mess!' She began to cry noiselessly, the tears slipping down her face. 'He came back,' she whispered, 'said he couldn't stand to be without me. That he loved Kate but he loved me, too. He was torn apart,' she cried in a sudden passion. 'He was in a terrible state. Terrible! And I loved him, thought that I could make it better, make up for Kate.'

'You mean, replace her,' said Hildamay drily.

'Yes!' cried Delilah. 'Why not? Replace her! Get him away from her. She doesn't love him,' she cried in a low, frantic voice. 'That's not love. It's desperation. She threatens him. Says that if he goes she'll never let him see the kids again. Says she can't exist without him. She told him that she'd die.' Delilah laughed. 'Kate? Die! She's stronger than any of us. Men are so feeble. And they haven't much in the way of duplicity,' she murmured softly. 'They can't believe that a woman's apparent weakness is her strength. Kate would do anything, anything!' she cried passionately, 'to keep him, even see him bitterly unhappy. Look at him! You saw him. Look at the way he is. How can it make her happy? Seeing him like that? How can she bear to live with herself? She's prepared to tear us all apart to keep him. She says it's for the family. She calls it happiness.' Delilah sank back into the bench and sighed bitterly. 'Happiness!' she exclaimed.

'And what do you call it?' asked Hildamay.

'Don't you see?' cried Delilah. 'That's why I let him go. Because I love him. That's why I won't see him any more, to stop him destroying himself. And me,' she whispered. 'It went on and on, to and fro until I thought I was going mad. That's not love, it's bloody war.' She groaned and covered her face with her hands. 'A bloody, bloody war. How can she be happy, living like that?'

'Can you be happy now?'

'Oh, what's happy?' said Delilah irritably. 'I sometimes wake up in the morning and look around me and think, "Is this it?" Just me and the kids stumbling our way through the days, waiting for something to happen.'

'What are you waiting for?' asked Hildamay curiously.

'Someone to save me from myself,' said Delilah with a hard laugh. 'Even though I know that they won't and that, even if they wanted to, they couldn't,' she added in a low voice. 'Oh, at first I thought that Ned could do it. Dan, well, Dan was just an addiction. Not a good one, either. Like smoking, I suppose. I had to give him up before he made me ill. Or killed me. Ben, too. You start even though you know it's bad for you and at first you enjoy it. You don't see the damage it's doing. You don't even feel it. Then gradually you begin to feel the very cells of your body rotting and stinking and you know that you must give it up. And you try and try and every fibre of your body screams out to have it back. You think, for a long time –' she sighed, a long, anguished sigh – 'for such a long time you think you can't live without it but gradually the need begins to diminish. But it never goes away. After it, you always feel that life is somehow empty, that something is missing. Even years after, you long for it, to feel that way again. And then sometimes you long never to have felt it, you long never to have had that knowledge so that life could be as simple as it was before it. Oh, innocence!' Delilah laughed suddenly. 'Sweet innocence. At first, that's what I thought I'd found with Ned. Innocence. He seemed so content, so in tune with his world that at first I thought that he could give me that, too. Make me content.' She sighed again. 'To begin with he did. His world was so new to me, so sweet and gentle and uncomplicated, that I was mesmerised. Then the kids came along and a whole new world opened up. But suddenly they were grown and had their own world and I looked back at Ned and saw that nothing had changed, that he was just the same as he had always been. The children and I hadn't expanded his world,' she said with sudden bitterness. 'He'd simply absorbed us into his. We made no difference to him. We just added on to the population a bit. It was then that I realised that he had no imagination, that he saw only his own world and nothing outside it. And always will. Of course he's content,' she exclaimed scornfully. 'He lives in a world of his own making. I seem to live in somebody else's or at least in one which is not my own invention. The only time I feel happy in it is when I'm in love and the excitement of that obliterates everything else in one great, consuming, destructive surge. So I sit and wait,' she sighed, 'for someone to save me from myself.'

'It is bad to depend so heavily on other people for happiness,' cried Hildamay passionately. 'It is better not to.'

'It's safer, certainly,' said Delilah, with a slight shrug. 'But I'm not sure it's ultimately as satisfying.'

'Satisfying' cried Hildamay in disbelief. 'How can pain satisfy? Most of the time I think I would rather be as I was. Safe and alone.'

'But you weren't alone before,' Delilah pointed out. 'You didn't

know what it was to be alone until you'd let someone in. It is only when they leave us that we realise that we are alone. Once we have found love.'
'So unkind,' murmured Hildamay.
'What?'
'Love.'

CHAPTER
TWENTY FIVE

'HERE he is,' whispered Liz. 'Here's your godson.' They tiptoed over to the cot and peered down at the bundle of blankets. Through the gloom Hildamay could just make out the rounded curve of a cheek and a head, slightly dented, mottled pink and white, covered in patches of red scabrous skin and a fuzz of dark hair. She glanced briefly at him and turned to go but Liz still hung adoringly over the side of the cot and, by the stillness of her posture, made it clear to Hildamay that she had not paid full or proper attention. She bent down again and occupied herself by studying the honeycomb weave on the handkerchief of a blanket while Liz smiled and talked some unintelligible nonsense at the baby's sleeping head. 'Here's your godmother, Harry,' she crooned. 'Her name is Hildamay Smith but you can call her just plain Hilda.'
  'He cannot,' said Hildamay loudly.
  'Shhhh!' hissed Liz. 'You'll wake him up.'
  She bent over and readjusted the blanket then, putting her hand out to him, rubbed his back, rocking him gently for some time.

Hildamay had a crick in her neck so she straightened up and stood with patient attention over the two of them. Liz looked up at her, her lips parted in an eager, expectant smile.

'Very nice,' whispered Hildamay eventually.

'Very nice?' hissed Liz. 'Is that all you can say? The miracle of birth, this small, beautiful and perfectly formed creature, this triumph of genetic engineering who is my son, is very nice!'

What else do you say, thought Hildamay, about a dented, scabrous scalp? 'Handsome,' she whispered doubtfully.

'Better,' said Liz.

'Handsome and clever?' suggested Hildamay.

'I'll divest you of godmothering rights,' Liz grumbled.

'Oh, fuck off, mother,' whispered Hildamay, but even as she smiled Liz's eyes widened in horror and she clapped a hand across Hildamay's mouth. 'Harry,' she hissed, 'is very sensitive about sexual matters.'

'He'll be even more sensitive,' murmured Hildamay, 'when he grows up and finds out how he was conceived.'

'Wash out your mouth,' whispered Liz as they crept out of the room. She pulled the door until it was open a crack then opened it another inch, closed it half an inch, then opened it another two inches.

'Shall I get a tape measure?' said Hildamay, after a while.

Liz looked at her, puzzled.

'For the door,' said Hildamay, nodding her head at it.

'There might be a draught,' muttered Liz. 'And I need to hear him if he cries,' she added crossly.

'I thought babies made a lot of noise.'

'They do,' said Liz grimly. 'They do.'

She walked into the sitting room and flopped on to the sofa. Hildamay sat in a deep armchair facing her and stared at the sofa, thinking of the night when Harry was conceived. What a game it had seemed then, to play with life! How careless it seemed to her now, to treat love with such carefree, abandon. She wondered suddenly if Thomas knew that his son had been born.

'Have you spoken to Thomas?' she asked, her manner diffident.

'He sent me flowers.' Liz closed her eyes. 'And a love letter,' she added, with contemptuous indifference. 'I'd love a cup of tea.' She groaned and turned over and pressed her face into a cushion. 'I'm so tired,' she wailed, her voice muffled. 'You can't believe how tired I am.' She looked up at Hildamay. 'Be an angel?' she pleaded, smiling wanly.

As Hildamay made the tea she wondered at the irresponsibility of human beings, treating love as if it were a brightly coloured toy, which when first received is played with, examined, toted around in fumbling, adoring hands; then later discarded, left out in the rain to spoil or dumped in some forgotten cupboard to be retrieved years later and exclaimed over, in wonder. Did this bring me so much pleasure? Ah, yes, I remember! And there were those who, growing angry with their toy, smashed it and then, repentant, went back to gather up the pieces, holding them in clumsy hands as they tried to stick them back together. If they were lucky, and the fragments were large enough, they mended it to form some image of its former self but one still cracked, spoiled. And then there were still others who, seeing the toy, turned their heads away and said coldly, like petulant children, 'I don't want it, take it away.' She thought of Sky, holding out her love like a brightly wrapped parcel, her face eager with hope, and how she, shaking her head, had said, 'I don't need this. What do I need this for?' She sighed, watching the teabags float in their mugs, the surface of the water broken like crazy paving; and then she fished the teabags out and poured in the milk which glued all the mineral deposits in the water together as soap does with oil. She stared at the tea and thought of George, of his kind, shining face and the sudden, impenetrable shadow which sometimes clouded his pale eyes. Was that pain, she wondered, or terrible loneliness? 'Alone,' he had said. 'For some people it is the only way.' She understood what terrible thing had happened to George, for she understood now that it was terrible. A child had disappeared. Gone, perhaps for ever. She thought of him watching the children in the park, trapped by some solitary agony. That George had some mystery in his past she did not doubt, what it was she dared not ask. Some things are better left untold, she thought, picking up the mugs of tea and carrying them through to the sitting room.

Liz lay on the sofa, sobbing.

'What is it?' said Hildamay, alarmed. She put the mugs on the floor, spilling tea on the carpet in her haste, and went and knelt by Liz. 'What is it?' she asked again, putting her arms around Liz, rocking her as she wept, so that their bodies swayed and danced in the grey morning light.

'I don't know!' wailed Liz, burying her head in Hildamay's neck so that tears warmed her flesh and ran, in little streams, down into the collar of her sweatshirt. 'I feel so lonely,' she cried, her voice muffled. 'I look at Harry and I feel so lonely.'

'Why lonely?' asked Hildamay, curiously, sitting back to look at Liz's face.

'I sat on the loo this morning with him clasped to my tit. He was bawling, I was bawling,' said Liz, rubbing at her face with the cushion. 'I can't even have a crap by myself!' She started to cry again. 'He's there, all the time. He never goes away,' she sobbed, 'and every day and every night I run around, feeding him, washing him, changing him, winding him, worrying about him, and he just lies there, staring at me with those eyes of his. How they seem to judge, those eyes! And sometimes when he cries and cries, I don't know what to do, or when he doesn't put on weight, I worry and stare at the ceiling all night and think that I have failed him and I have no one to ask for help. No one to help me. I want someone to look after me,' she screamed, battering her fists on her knees like a child in a temper. 'I'm so tired and nobody says when I cry, "There, there, go back to sleep and I will look after you. It will be all right." And what shall I do when he's four? Which school will he go to?' She turned over and flung herself, head first, into the cushions of the sofa.

Hildamay laughed. 'School?' she said. 'Why are you talking about schools?' She ruffled Liz's hair.

'Oh, you don't understand!' shouted Liz, sitting up. 'I have to make that decision for him. I have to make it on my own. He can't make it. Nobody else can make it. I have to do it. I have to bear it all.'

'But I thought this was what you wanted,' protested Hildamay.

'Of course it's what I wanted,' exclaimed Liz. 'That doesn't mean to say it's not hard. I love him but then I sometimes resent him so much that I hate him. But that doesn't mean I don't want him.'

'Good grief,' said Hildamay.

'You're not to do it,' said Liz suddenly.

'Do what?'

'Have a child.'

'Did I ever say I would?' protested Hildamay, staring at her curiously.

'That child you're so obsessed with,' said Liz. 'Give her up. Forget the whole idea.'

'But she's nine years old!' exclaimed Hildamay. 'It's hardly the same as having a baby.'

'I don't care,' muttered Liz. 'You must let her go. You're not a person who should have children.'

'Why not?' said Hildamay, her voice cold.

'Because they're so demanding,' said Liz, too caught up in her own frustration to notice how Hildamay shrank back from her and folded herself away, her face closing as some flowers do when the light of day has gone. 'You have to give all of yourself to them. Once you have a child, you are never free again.'

'Do you think me so selfish?' murmured Hildamay.

'Oh, no,' said Liz abstractedly, reaching out to pat her hand. 'It's just that you don't understand what you would be giving up by having a child. You can't possibly know, until you have one.'

Hildamay wondered for a while what hormone it was that turned women with children into patronising bullies. 'I am not two years old!' she protested after a time. 'My rational mind is fully formed. Of course I've thought about the consequences of taking Sky in.'

Liz looked at her and on her face was the same look of surprised astonishment that a parent shows to a child when it questions a conventional wisdom. 'Well, your imagination is obviously not,' she grumbled, hurt. 'Anyway,' she protested, 'it's not even as if she were your own flesh and blood! And it's not as if you were adopting because you desperately want children. You've never wanted to have children and suddenly you're picking up some waif, literally off the street. Why do you want her?' she demanded, her voice accusing.

'Because I love her!' shouted Hildamay. 'Is that so difficult to understand?'

'Oh, love!' said Liz in exasperation. 'We're talking about a child.'

'Can you not love a child?'

'Yes, of course you can,' said Liz impatiently. 'But if it's love you're after, why don't you go out and get yourself a man?'

Why, she is not listening to me at all, thought Hildamay. Or perhaps she simply cannot understand. 'I don't want a man and I'm not after love,' she said quietly. 'It's that I've found love. She sees love in me, I see love in her, I want to be with her. Is that so difficult to understand.'

Liz was silent.

'If I'd come to you,' said Hildamay slowly, watching Liz's face, 'and said that I'd met a man whom I loved, would you still presume to tell me that I don't know what I'm doing, that I'm too selfish to love, that I don't understand what I'm taking on?'

'Men aren't children,' said Liz petulantly.

'Say you,' flashed Hildamay. 'And what if it had been a woman? What then?'

'I would have told you to be careful.'

'Why?' Are women more dangerous to love than men?'

'No,' said Liz, her voice sharpening with irritation. 'Stop being so obtuse. Loving a woman is more difficult because you face constant disapproval. It's hard to fly in the face of convention.'

'Oh, Lizzie,' said Hildamay, her voice suddenly tired. 'Love is love and why should it matter where you find it? I found it and now I've gone and thrown it away. I thought my life was full and now I see that it was empty.'

Liz stared at her in silence for some minutes and then, flushing, looked away. 'Do you think I should let Thomas come and see Harry?' she asked, her voice low.

'I don't see that it could do much harm,' said Hildamay slowly.

'He says in his letter that he loves me. He says he wants to look after me. And Harry,' said Liz, pulling herself up on the sofa, dragging a cushion on to her lap, and hugging it protectively against her breasts.

'And what do you want?'

'Oh, I don't know,' grumbled Liz in irritation. 'One minute I think, "Yes, why can't he come and see us? Why shouldn't I let him love me?" And the next I think that I don't want anyone at all. Just me and Harry. What if he was simply pretending to love me so he could come and steal Harry away?' she demanded, looking up at Hildamay, two patches of red burning in her pale face.

'He's hardly the type to snatch a baby,' protested Hildamay.

'He's mine,' said Liz, clutching the pillow to her belly. 'I won't give him up.'

'I don't think Thomas is asking you to give him up,' said Hildamay, looking at her curiously. 'I think he is only asking you for permission to love Harry. And, perhaps, you.'

'It sounds so rational when you put it like that,' complained Liz. 'What if Harry loved him more than he loves me?' she added, her voice dropping to a whisper.

Hildamay looked at her in silence and then said, her tone careful, 'Why should he do that? He will love you if you give him love. He may love Thomas, too, if you let him.'

'He's my child!' said Liz, flaring up suddenly.

'And what about Thomas? Technically, he is his too.'

'Technically!' shouted Liz in frustration. 'One sperm. One lousy sperm. If the plan hadn't gone wrong, he would never have known.

He would have looked at Harry and perhaps thought, What a nice baby, and then he would have turned his head away and thought no more of the matter. Does knowledge suddenly give him rights?'

'Yes.'

'No!' screamed Liz. 'No, it doesn't.' She threw herself down on the sofa and began to sob. Hildamay did not move but sat and waited until the storm of tears had abated.

'I'm sorry,' said Liz eventually, sniffing weakly. 'I seem to be in such a jumble at the moment.' She smiled pathetically. 'I don't even know what I'm frightened of, except that it was such a big decision and I did it by myself and went through the pregnancy and the bad, as well as the good, times. And now I have this baby, have Harry, and I love him more than I can bear sometimes and yet he makes me feel so isolated. But still, he's mine, and suddenly –' She whimpered like a child. 'Suddenly there's this man, this stranger, who says that Harry is his and I feel like he wants to take him away from me!' She sobbed, open mouthed, and the tears ran down her face and joined the saliva which dripped down her chin.

'He doesn't want to take him away,' said Hildamay, going over to the sofa and sitting down to put her arms around Liz. 'He just wants to share him. Not even to share,' she added hurriedly, 'just to see him. When you're feeling stronger, why don't you invite him over for tea and let him meet Harry and you can sit and talk to him, get to know him? You liked him well enough before and, who knows, you two might grow to be friends. Which,' she said, stroking Liz's hair soothingly, 'might be very good for Harry.'

'Good for Harry,' murmured Liz in a defeated voice.

'Hildamay, it's Thomas.'

'Oh,' she said, her voice slow with surprise. 'Hello, Thomas.' She stared out of her bedroom window at the winter trees, their branches bare and mournful, bereft of life and leaf, and as she looked at them she thought about loneliness.

'Are you lonely?' she asked.

'Lonely?' he exclaimed and then was silent. 'Sometimes,' he said softly. 'What is it, Hildamay? Are you lonely?'

'Lonely,' she echoed and then sighed. 'No, I'm not lonely but I am alone. Alone,' she repeated mournfully.

'Are you all right?' His voice was loud and the sudden urgency of his tone shook her, as if out of a dream, so that she started and turned her head to stare at the telephone receiver in her hand.

'I'm sorry,' she said, her voice quickening, 'just a bad case of the blues. I used to take them to the bathroom, wash them away,' she explained. 'But now the bathroom is all closed up. The magic, you see, has gone.'

'I see,' he said which she thought kind as he could not possibly have seen.

'Did you want something, Thomas?' she asked.

'I wondered if we could meet?'

'Well –' she said, dubious. 'I'm not sure that's a good idea.' There was silence. 'I don't, you see, want to get –'

'Involved,' he said, finishing the sentence for her.

'No,' she said quickly, 'that's not what I was going to say at all. I am involved. What I don't want is to have to take sides. I don't want to hear both sides of the story,' she added, her voice apologetic. 'Because if I did then I would have to be disloyal.'

'I see,' he said slowly. 'So you do, at least, see that I have a right to love him?'

Hildamay was silent. 'Hildamay,' he pleaded, 'see me. I need someone to talk to. I have no one, you see, and I need to talk. I can't tell anybody else about this and it –' he stumbled, 'it hurts very badly,' he finished, his voice breaking.

'Yes,' she said gravely, thinking of Sky, 'I can see that it would.'

'So you will see me?' he said, his voice brightening with hope.

'I didn't –' she began, but was interrupted by Thomas almost shouting, 'Thank you, thank you. At The Globe, then. At six.'

'At six,' she echoed.

The Globe was empty except for a small group of people who sat in the coveted comfortable armchairs and sofa which stood in a plump group over by the window, chatting in a desultory fashion and drinking coffee. As Hildamay walked in they looked up, examining her curiously. Failing to recognise her they lost interest and turned back to each other.

'It's a fabulous synopsis and, if the sample chapters are anything to go by, we're on to a winner. Sort of *Money* meets *Ambition*,' mused a woman with a sleek, brilliant red bob of hair and pronounced freckles.

'No, no!' exclaimed a small, intense woman with very pale skin and dark, blinking eyes. 'It's more of a contemporary *Vanity Fair* with naughty bits.'

'Cynthia, don't be so pompous!'

'I am not being pompous!' she protested. 'It's a romping great saga and although the central character's a he, not a she, you have to admit that he's utterly compulsive; charming, immoral and quite, quite delectable,' she added, with a longing sigh.

'Oh, who cares?' drawled a man with wild, curly grey hair and round red glasses. 'It'll sell thousands. Millions, even.'

'Ah, the pecunious delights of clit lit,' said another and was greeted by shouts of laughter.

'What was her name again?' drawled red glasses.

'Cassandra Montrose,' said the redhead. 'Rather good, I thought.'

'It's a fiction,' declared red glasses again. 'Nobody has a name like that.'

So Cassie's really gone and done it, thought Hildamay wonderingly. How extraordinary that Cassie, whom we all thought would tumble through life in that giddy, colourful, irresponsible way of hers, trying always to force herself like a square peg into round holes, should suddenly find a form that fits. She heard Cassie's voice, the pink-painted mouth drawn into a pout of reproach: 'But darling, I told you I would. I told you I'd be good.'

Hildamay laughed out loud, ignoring the group who turned at the sound of her laughter and, seeing her standing alone, shook their heads at each other in amused concern. She flashed a brilliant smile at them and walked over to sit on a stool at the bar.

'Champagne, please,' she murmured to the barman who smiled at her with a look of such interested speculation that she began to feel not only cheerful, but intensely optimistic. She'll be there, she thought. She'll be sitting on the bench in the middle of the station, her cap pulled down low over her eyes and her cheeks flushed with the pleasure of seeing me and she'll say in that high little voice of hers, 'I've been here, waiting, for half an hour!' She'll be slightly aggrieved and I'll laugh and tell her that if she must be early then it's entirely her fault if I am late.

'Hildamay?' said the barman as he put down her glass of champagne, its base dressed in a little paper mat with a neat, scalloped edge. She looked up from her dream.

'Yes?'

'Thomas is waiting for you,' he said, 'in the back room.'

'Too crowded in here for him?' she asked, getting to her feet and picking up the champagne which she sipped at as she walked through the bright, comfortable room, down a long corridor, emerging into a cavernous, dimly lit bar. It was a cold, gloomy room; the walls painted dark, concrete grey and the uncarpeted floor dotted here and there with tables and chairs of sharp black steel. Thomas was sitting at a table right in the far corner of the room.

'Hildamay!' he called, as she emerged through the gloom.

'What kind of hell is this?' she said, groping her way over to him.

'Designer,' he said with a bleak smile. He looked tired, his hair no longer flopped boyishly over his forehead but fell in a sort of exhausted sprawl into his eyes. He blinked at it and stared up at her.

'The mourners like it. The ones who will wear black,' he explained.

'I suppose it has a certain morbid elegance,' said Hildamay, staring around her, 'if you think discomfort elegant. I didn't even know it existed.'

Thomas shrugged. 'We only open it late in the evening,' he said, 'for the pre-club crowd. Makes them feel at home. Most of them feel so at home, they don't even bother to go on to the clubs. Good for the profits,' he added with a shrug.

'You look tired.'

'I was here, with this lot,' he said, jerking his head at the room, 'until four in the morning.'

They looked at each other and, not knowing what else to say, smiled vaguely and gazed with elaborate concentration around the room. Hildamay sipped at her champagne and waited.

'Well,' said Thomas, at last.

'Well,' echoed Hildamay and turned to look at him.

'Now that you're here,' he said, his face creased in an anxious, apologetic smile, 'I'm afraid I don't know what to say to you.'

'Perhaps there is nothing to say,' she said gently but he shook his head in protest, shaking the hair out of his eyes, and a torrent of words, like water which has been stopped too long, came pouring out of his mouth.

'I have no one to talk to,' he exclaimed, staring at Hildamay in mute appeal. 'I really liked her,' he added mournfully. 'I really, really liked her. I thought, that night, that it was the beginning of something.' He sighed and looked away. 'She seemed so pleased, happy even, to be with me. And I thought then that here was a woman who I would like to bear my child.' He laughed bitterly. 'But I had thought that it might be a decision that we would share.' He shook his head. 'When I found out that she had just used me, like some sort of siring bull, I was so angry. Furious with her. And then the anger started to fade and I thought instead of the child and realised that, however it happened, my child was growing inside her. Then I didn't know what to think,' he went on, his voice so low that Hildamay had to strain to hear him. 'I felt love and anger and hate and pride.' He looked up at her. 'It was all blended into one, into this lump that sat in my belly and gnawed away at me. I remembered thinking that night that we were making love to make a child, that it was not just fucking.' He spat out the word in disgust and rubbed at his eyes with his knuckles. 'When I discovered that she was pregnant I felt so abused that at first I just wanted to hurt her. Make her understand that she couldn't just come and take something from me and grow it into my own flesh and blood, cheating me of even my consent. Women,' he said bitterly, 'claim that they have no power, when they have in their bodies the ultimate power, the veto of life or death.' He stared at Hildamay and in his eyes she saw something close to hate.

'Can you imagine?' he asked, his voice strained, 'how it feels to be so impotent over something as fundamental as life?' Hildamay shook her head dumbly. 'It is terrible to be deprived of choice, of the freedom to say whether your child is born or not. The child may not grow inside me, but it is part of me that is growing and I don't know if she is taking care of it, I don't know if she loves it as much as I need her to love it, to love me.' He groaned. 'I saw him,' he added, his eyes bright. 'I went to the hospital. I didn't touch him!' he protested. 'Just stood and looked at him through that glass wall and thought, this is my son. How will you be, my son? What sort of man will you become? And as I was looking at him I understood suddenly that I was allowed no part of it, of his life, and the pain was so terrible that I thought suddenly that I was ill.' He shook his head and smiled at her, a pale smile which hovered dimly in the gloom. 'I'd been counting the weeks. I ticked them off, week by week and when the time was near I went to the hospital and made friends with one of the nurses, took her out a couple of times and spun her this line about Liz being my estranged sister and the family not allowing me to see her, but that I wanted to keep an eye on her. Shame about Sue,' he sighed. 'The nurse,' he added, seeing her puzzled look. 'She was a sweet little thing. Pretty, too. Blonde, like you. I think she liked me. She's still waiting for me to call. I think I may have hurt her. So much pain,' he exclaimed suddenly, 'for one small life. I don't want to hurt Liz,' he said again, patting Hildamay's hand as if to reassure her. 'It's just – it's just that he is my son.' Taking her hand he pressed it to his face, covering it with his hands so she felt his mouth move against the palm of her hand, and tears wet against her skin. 'I didn't even have a chance to say what he might be called,' he protested, his voice muffled, 'although I quite like Harry. My brother's a Harry,' he said bleakly. She gently removed her hand which he still clasped between his own.

'Can you love when you feel so much pain?' she asked, as much to herself as him.

He shrugged. 'Why does one love anyway?' he said harshly and then grimaced. 'Why do I care so much about this one, tiny sperm when I have spilled millions? When I may, for all I know, have made a child before? I don't know. Perhaps it's some primal instinct deep in us which forces us to protect our own. I wish, often,' he mused, 'that it didn't exist. How much nicer to say to Liz, "Oh, that's our son then? How terribly interesting," and then to be able to walk away and not feel this unbearable wrenching of the soul every time I think of him.' He looked up at her and shrugged again. 'It's stronger than reason.'

'What will you do?'

His mouth twitched. 'Hope?' he said and looked away. 'It's all I can do,' he murmured. He looked back at her. 'Will you ask her,' he said hesitantly, 'just ask if I could at least go and see him? And her? Just to talk. Please,' he begged, the hair spilling into his eyes so that he blinked owlishly and looked for a moment like a small boy begging his mother to buy him a toy.

'I will ask,' said Hildamay gravely. 'But I can't promise that she will listen.' She looked at her watch. It was half past seven. 'I must go now.'

'A lovers' tryst?' said Thomas, smiling suddenly, and she looked at his face and thought that she liked him very much.

'No,' she said, laughing and shaking her head ruefully. 'I've lost a child, not found a lover.'

'A child?' He frowned in question.

'It's too complicated to explain,' she said, with a half smile, and put out her hand to push herself up from the table.

'Please,' said Thomas, putting out his hand and taking her by the wrist. 'I'd like to understand.'

She shook her head. 'Even I don't do that.'

'Do what?' he asked, confused.

'Understand.'

CHAPTER TWENTY SIX

HILDAMAY sat in her office and stared bleakly at the pile of papers on her desk. She sighed and then her sigh turned to a hiss of irritation as Jack Rome put his head around the door.

'A little matter,' he said with a triumphant smile, 'which I think needs urgent consideration.'

'Yes?' said Hildamay, her voice bored.

'Seems good old Bonham has closed the account,' he said, his smile thinning to one of pure malice. 'Young Mr Stone's just been on the phone to me. Seemed to think that you were losing your grip. I told him that you had seemed,' he paused, 'rather preoccupied recently and that I would handle the matter personally myself.'

'I'll call Bonham,' said Hildamay in a tired voice. 'I'm sure –'

'No need. No need' exclaimed Jack. 'Consider it done. Seems he wants me to handle the account personally. So,' he added, grinning, 'does Young Mr Stone. Seems the profits were down a bit this quarter. Can't have that now, can we?' he said wagging an admonishing finger at Hildamay. 'You've been a naughty girl.'

Bugger Bonham, thought Hildamay. Sod Si Stone and fuck Jack Rome. But she smiled. One of her better smiles.

'How good are your ankles, Jack?'

'What?'

'Never mind,' she said pleasantly. 'Now, if you'll excuse me.'

George shot into the office at a half run. 'That woman,' he panted, 'who rang yesterday.' He whirled his arms in agitation at Hildamay's puzzled frown. 'Sky's mother!' he shouted. 'On the phone.'

'Put her through,' said Hildamay, patting at her face and hair in agitation, trying to make herself look presentable. Good grief, she thought, as her extension buzzed. What am I doing? Cautiously, she picked up the receiver.

'Hildamay?' said a voice. 'Is that Hildamay?'

Hildamay froze, the telephone receiver hard against her ear.

'Sky?' she said, forgetting in the sudden panic of her excitement that it was not Sky. 'Sky? Is that you?'

'No,' said the voice apologetically. 'I'm sorry. It's not Sky. It's Blanche.' The voice was small and soft, like Sky's, but infinitely sad.

'Where are you?'

'I'm at my mother's house in Woodside Park. I want to meet you. Would that be all right?' She sounded hesitant and woven through her sad, small voice ran a thread of guilt.

'Yes, yes,' said Hildamay impatiently. 'When?'

'At one o'clock. But I don't know where . . . ?' Her voice trailed off hopelessly.

'At St Pancras station,' said Hildamay firmly. 'By the ticket office.'

'St Pancras?' Blanche's voice echoed doubtfully down the line.

'You can get the tube,' urged Hildamay. 'It's a direct line.'

'Yes,' said Blanche faintly. Her voice seemed so insubstantial that Hildamay wondered fleetingly if she even existed.

'At one o'clock,' she repeated urgently. 'At the ticket office. Is that all right?'

'Yes,' sighed Blanche.

'You will be there?'

'Yes. Yes, I'll be there.' Her voice seemed to be getting fainter.

'Do you know what I look like?' shouted Hildamay, to rouse her. The voice strengthened slightly.

'Sky told me.'
'Good. One o'clock, then.'
'One o'clock,' echoed Blanche, and the line went dead.

Hildamay was not prepared for Blanche Matthews. The only thing she recognised about her was her hair. 'Stiff,' Sky had said. Stiff and lustrous as old straw, it stuck out in a peroxide halo around her pinched, white face.

'Hildamay?' she said and Hildamay nodded mutely, staring at her to find any traces of Sky in her face. They existed only in her eyes which were a deep blue, almost navy, and so lustrous they were shocking, shining out from the anaemic paleness of her skin which was further accentuated by the brittle deadness of her straw blonde hair. She was so thin she looked as if she might topple over or snap in two, folding up on herself like a flimsy garden chair. Alarmed, Hildamay put out a hand to steady her and Blanche accepted it with a gesture so habitual that it seemed she was used to steadying hands fluttering around her as she moved. Her stick-like legs were encased in jeans so tight that light shone through the sharp triangle between her thighs, and her little feet were forced into shiny black boots with high, thin heels; the toes scuffed and the heels so worn that her ankles bent outwards, emphasising the triangle of light. She wore a pink sweater, the pink of strawberry ice cream, tight and ribbed, with a high polo neck. Over this was a scuffed black leather jacket and in each ear dangled several gold earrings. She looked at Hildamay then down at her hands and picked at the remains of the bright pink polish which clung steadfastly to her nails. Both index fingers were stained a deep yellow. She scrabbled suddenly in the capacious black shiny bag she carried and extracted a packet of cigarettes and a book of matches, the cover ripped off.

'Shall we sit down?' she said in a high, hesitant voice.

'Yes,' said Hildamay and led her to a bench, wondering how this could be Sky's mother. This thin, pale creature with her hesitant air and cheap, shabby clothes. She heard Sky's voice. 'She likes people to think that she's my sister. I have to call her Blanche.'

They sat on the bench and Blanche lit a cigarette and began to suck at it furiously; the end glowed brilliant red and ash began to flutter down on to her jeans. She stared down at the ground in silence for some minutes then scrabbled again in her shiny bag. Out of it she drew a stained, creased piece of paper which she handed to Hildamay.

'Dear Blanche,' it said in Sky's round, childish hand. 'I am writing to tell you that I am all right. I could not live with grandmother any more because she does not like me and since you left, she is always cross. So I thought it was better if I went and lived somewhere else. I wanted to go and live with my friend Hildamay, but she said that I can't. She likes to live on her own. Please do not worry about me, I have found a friend and she looks after me. I hope grandmother is not cross and that you are having a nice time in Spain. I hope I've got the address right. I remembered it from all those letters I posted. Love from Sky.'

Hildamay read it three times and then sat in silence, staring at the crumpled piece of paper.

'When did this arrive?' she asked eventually.

'Three days ago,' said Blanche. 'So I got on a plane and came home.'

'I thought Mary had telephoned you to tell you that Sky had disappeared?' said Hildamay curiously.

The soft voice hardened. 'Of course not. She wants Sky for herself.' She glanced sharply at Hildamay, eyes narrowed. 'Hates you, of course.' Hildamay frowned. 'Well, it stands to reason, doesn't it? You tried to take Sky away from her. "Ruined her," is what she says. Wouldn't even give me your telephone number until I threatened her with the police.'

'The police?' said Hildamay in confusion.

'The police,' said Blanche, her thin face sharp with satisfaction. 'Well, she hadn't told them about your and Sky's little friendship, now, had she? About her seeing you all the time. Withholding evidence I think they call it.' She smiled, remembering. 'So she had to give me your number,' she added, obviously pleased by the small victory.

'Sky told you about me?'

'Told me most things. Like kids together, we were. Secrets they were, mind.' She shrugged. 'Well, had to be really on account of *her*,' she said with a sharp jerk of her head. 'I'd try and get her all the stuff that *she* wouldn't let her have. Not that the poor kid got much,' she added bitterly, 'and even then we'd have to keep it a secret. Even books. It wasn't as if she wanted much.'

'No,' said Hildamay, thinking of the dictionary. She looked curiously at Blanche. 'What did you mean when you said she wants Sky for herself?'

Blanche shrugged. 'What I said. She's never been my daughter. Or I've never been her mother. I've never been much,' she added, with a sudden flash of bitterness. 'My mother,' she explained, looking at Hildamay warily, 'is not an easy woman.'

'There are better ways of describing her,' said Hildamay drily.

Blanche laughed suddenly, a high squeaky giggle. 'Like bitch, you mean?' she cried with childish glee. Hildamay said nothing. 'Oh, it's all right,' said Blanche, shrugging irritably, 'you don't have to go all proper on me. I'm sure you hate her, too. Seeing as you love Sky so much.'

Love? thought Hildamay. How does she know I love Sky? She gazed at Blanche speculatively, refusing to be drawn in on the complicity of hate. You can never tell with families, she thought.

Blanche watched her expectantly for a few minutes and then shrugged. 'Oh, she means well enough. It's just she's got this thing about what she calls "values". She'd love us if we were good. That's always been her threat. "Such a disappointment,"' said Blanche suddenly, mimicking Mary Matthews' harsh voice. '"You've always been such a disappointment to me." Trouble is, she never had time, after attending to all "the values", for living. No time for emotion or affection or all the soft bits. I think she believes that if she showed an ounce of softness then the world would crumble around her. Don't know what happened to her when she was a kid. Something nasty. The sins of the mothers,' she muttered under her breath. 'And my sins,' she added with a sudden, bitter smile, 'got dumped on Sky. Thinks she was too soft on me,' she explained, seeing Hildamay's questioning frown. 'So she's even harder on her. I never had a childhood,' she whined, her voice shrill with self-pity. 'Never even had a life, if it came to it. Not until now, anyway.'

'And what about Sky?' exclaimed Hildamay, contemptuously. 'What kind of life have you given her? What have you done to protect her?'

Blanche snatched the cigarette which was stuck between pale, bloodless lips and stared at Hildamay in astonishment. 'Me!' she cried. 'Me? Protect her?'

'Well, you are her bloody mother,' muttered Hildamay.

'And you don't bloody listen, do you?' cried Blanche. 'I've just told you how it is.'

'No, you bloody haven't,' exclaimed Hildamay in a passion of fury. 'All you've told me is how you neglected your own daughter – no, abandoned her! Abandoned her and then let your mother mistreat her. Worse than mistreat her. Be actively cruel to her. And you just sat there and did nothing. Nothing!' she cried furiously. 'Except buy her a bloody baseball cap.'

'And you're so wonderful, are you?' shouted Blanche, so loudly that passers-by stopped to stare at the two women who faced each other on the bench, their faces white, stricken with guilt and anger. 'You're so fucking wonderful that when she came to you for help, you turned her away! You made her go away. It was you,' she screamed, tears spurting out of her eyes.

Hildamay stared at her in horror and then, with a slow sigh of despair, sank back against the hard back of the bench, her head bowed to her chest. She raised her hands to her face and slowly, carefully, dug her knuckles into the sockets of her eyes until the lights exploded and the pain crashed in her head. 'I'm sorry,' she whispered brokenly. 'I'm really very sorry.' She felt a hand fumble clumsily at her head and then it began to stroke her hair, awkwardly, in an embarrassed, jerky movement.

'I was only fifteen,' Blanche whined, pleading for understanding. 'I wanted attention. Love, really. Was desperate for it. My dad died when I was twelve. A good man, he was, a nice man. He softened her up a bit but she hated him for it. I think she was pleased when he popped off.' She sighed and then laughed bitterly. 'After he'd gone, she dried up, all the warmth left her. She has these stupid rituals she does. Like cleaning the stairs every other day, even though they're clean enough already. At nine o'clock. If she starts them a minute late she's in a temper all day.' She sighed. 'She has hundreds of little routines like that. Polishing the brass on the front door, cleaning the kitchen floor. And those are just the domestic rituals, or the "values" as she calls them. We must have values, without values we are just animals. The values mean speaking right, dressing right, standing right, sitting right.' She shook her head. 'That house's no place for a young girl. I wasn't allowed any friends home, in case they messed up the place. Did something criminal like rumple a cushion. After a while, none of them came home, anyway. After a while I didn't have any friends. Well, you can't really, can you? It's too difficult, living like that.'

There was silence for a while. 'I don't think,' she said musingly, 'she's ever kissed me. Not in my memory, at least. Not even when dad died. So I went out to find love somewhere else. I thought you could fuck your way to love. I fucked and I fucked and all I got was a baby. By the time I realised what had happened to me I was four months gone.' She sighed heavily. 'I thought about running away but I didn't have Sky's courage. Don't know where she gets it from,' she added reflectively. 'Her dad, I expect. He always had an appetite for living. Too much for me. She made us get married, of course. Made him come and live with us.' She shrugged her thin shoulders. 'What else could we do? We were young, had no jobs, no money. He was only seventeen. Said he wanted to be a writer. A writer! That went down well with her. He lasted two months in that house after the baby was born. I was so knocked out, I didn't know if he was there or not half the time. It was him called her Sky. Said she might have something to reach for. He hated my mother. Ended up hating me, too.'

She glared defensively at Hildamay. 'It wasn't my fault! I didn't know what to do with a baby. She said I was to have nothing to do with her. Said if I did, she'd grow up just like me. Wouldn't even let me breastfeed her. Took her away and put her in a cot in her room. Got up and did all the night feeds. Changed her nappies. Bought her clothes. Everything. Wouldn't even let me pick her up. When I tried she'd just stand and stare at me. I was so nervous that I'd start to fumble. Let her head go back or pick her up awkwardly, so the baby'd start to cry. Then she'd say in that icy voice she has, "She doesn't like you." Then there was the time I dropped her. That was it. After that, every time I went near her she'd say, "Trying to kill her, are we?" I was too nervous after that even to touch her. Thought I might really kill her. I was too young in those days to understand that babies bounce.' She laughed harshly. 'Anyway, by that time, the damage was done. Sky cried whenever I went near her. I suppose I was pleased, in a way. The birth and pregnancy were such a nightmare, I couldn't find any joy in the child. So I let her get on with it. I just sort of shrivelled up. Lay around the house and did nothing. She ignored me. She'd shout sometimes and when I'd had a drink, I'd shout back. I had a drink every night after a while. We were always shouting. Then I met Steve.' Her voice softened. 'Ever so nice, he is. Said I was a valuable human being.' She repeated the words slowly. 'A valuable human being. The kindest man I've ever met. Nobody's ever been kind like that, not since Dad. We saw each other for a year. Then he got this job in Spain. He's a builder. The best!' Her voice strengthened and she flushed with pride. 'He wanted me to go with him but I said I wouldn't because of the kid. I wrote to him every day and then I couldn't stand it any more. So I left. Like I said, I thought she could handle it. Spunky little kid. Like her dad.'

Blanche sighed heavily and sank back against the bench as if exhausted by her story. Hildamay stared at her in silence for some time, remembering the cold, bright stream of Sky's loneliness, her eager, terrible need for love. 'But you left her in that house,' she said coldly, 'you left her in that house with that woman. With no love and no joy. You, who understands how terrible it is. Why didn't you take her with you?' Anger and distress made her voice harsh but Blanche just shrugged.

'You won't listen, will you?' she said wearily. 'Like I said, she's not my child. Not really. You don't take your kid sister away with you when you run off to a lover, now, do you?' She looked at Hildamay curiously. 'So why didn't you take her, then? Let her come and live with you? She said in her letter that she'd asked you. Something about you having to live on your own.'

'I am used to being alone,' murmured Hildamay, looking away.

'Not married then?' said Blanche. 'No fella?'

'No fella.'

'But you're looking, right?'

'Wrong.'

'Like girls, then, do you?' said Blanche sharply, squinting at her through the smoke which curled out of the cigarette stuck in her mouth. It had burnt down almost to the filter but she did not appear to notice.

'No,' said Hildamay patiently. 'I just like being on my own. You'll burn your mouth.'

Blanche took the smouldering butt out of her mouth and lit a fresh cigarette with it. 'Someone leave you, then? Mess you around?'

'No.'

'Oh, well,' sighed Blanche, stretching her legs as she leaned back against the bench and made herself comfortable, 'takes all sorts, I suppose.' She stared at Hildamay with Sky's eyes. 'Why're you so interested in the kid?' she demanded suddenly.

'She's unhappy,' said Hildamay shortly.

'Do you want her, then? Want to take her in?' asked Blanche, squinting at her.

Hildamay said nothing at first, feeling a sudden hatred for this woman with her absurd stiff hair and her thin legs and her soft, high voice, saying in that matter of fact way that she didn't want her daughter. 'So you're not coming back, then?' she said flatly.

'I've just told you how it is,' protested Blanche. 'Of course I'm not coming back.' Her voice was defensive, edgy with guilt. 'Oh, look,' she pleaded, bending forward to take Hildamay's hand, 'she's not my kid. Not any more. I can't go back and live there. I'd kill the woman, or myself.' Hildamay stared at her. Guilt at not having listened to Sky – oh, not to her words, to her silence – that guilt gave her gaze the steely brightness of contempt. Blanche dropped her hand and looked away. 'Oh, why should I expect you to understand?' she murmured and then sighed. 'Not that it makes much difference now. She's gone.'

'What are you going to do?' said Hildamay, more gently.

Blanche sighed again, a great gulp of despair. 'Wait,' she said bleakly. 'Sit in that house and wait. See what more damage we can do each other. She's suffering, too, mind,' she muttered suddenly. 'She loves her. In her own way. Not that it amounts to much.'

'No,' said Hildamay quietly. 'Not much.'

Blanche glanced at her sharply and seemed about to make some remark but then her face grew sullen and closed in on itself, her mouth slackening in defeat. 'What about you?' she mumbled.

'I'm going to find her,' exclaimed Hildamay and smiled; a hard, brilliant smile to give herself, and Blanche, the courage she did not feel.

Blanche looked at her curiously. 'I'd like to be a person like you.' She sighed and, picking up her bag, stood up, tottering in her down trodden heels. She looked down at Hildamay and smiled, a shy, sad smile. 'Sky would have liked that. I know I don't amount to much either, but I love her, too.' She walked away, swaying slightly on her thin, frail legs.

George was hovering by the door of Hildamay's office when she walked in. He looked at her, his eyebrows peaks of expectation above round, excited eyes. She smiled slightly but said nothing. He watched her take off her jacket in silence and then disappeared, returning a few minutes later carrying a mug of tea.

'A nice hot drink,' he said, blinking sympathetically.

'She was nothing like I imagined,' she murmured, sipping at the tea. 'Although I'm not sure what I was expecting,' she added wearily.

'Was she any help?' he said, his voice gentle.

'She's scarcely more than a child herself,' said Hildamay with a sigh. 'She can hardly look after herself, let alone Sky. She certainly couldn't protect her from that woman,' she exclaimed bitterly. 'Although she maintains she loves her. Mary Matthews, I mean. Not Blanche. She loves her, too. But not enough.' She sighed.

'Everyone has different ways of loving,' he said quietly.

'It was you who said she suffered from a lack of kindness, George,' Hildamay pointed out. He watched her steadily, in silence. 'Oh, why didn't I listen to you? Why did I tell her I didn't love her!' she cried in a sudden passion of self loathing. 'She only wanted someone to love her!' George blinked at the pain and horror in her face, but still he said nothing.

'What happened to your daughter?' said Hildamay, too caught up in the urgency of her own pain to worry what effect her words might have on him.

'She went away,' he said, so quietly that she almost did not catch his words.

'Away?' she cried. 'Where did she go?'

But he shook his head at her and his face crumpled in despair. 'Not yet,' he said. 'Not yet.' He left her, closing the door quietly behind him.

'I'm sorry, George,' whispered Hildamay. 'I'm really very sorry.'

CHAPTER TWENTY SEVEN

ST Pancras station was crowded with people. Time hung heavy on some faces; faces vacant as empty moons suspended above limbs heavy with resignation, blindly waiting until the clock struck 12.21 or 12.32 or some such minute when they would suddenly clatter with life, clambering on to trains bound for Leicester or Derby, where seats would be argued over and newspapers read, Walkmans listened to and babies fed. On other faces time, or the lack of it, registered in a sort of surprised astonishment as they ran or stumbled, hampered by heavy suitcases, around groups of people huddled here and there in little knots, warming themselves on each other as if seeking protection from the loneliness of the great, grey hall. Others stood motionless, their heads tilted back to watch the huge board on which the times of trains were marked. As each train arrived or left, the printed boards clicked and whirred, making the noise of a hundred electronic birds coming home to roost. The people looked as if they were waiting for a message from the heavens, so attentive and still were their poses. Or perhaps they feared that if they turned their heads away from the board, their train would disappear and they would never find their way home.

Hildamay sighed and looked around her, watching the people as they queued to buy tickets. Most fidgeted and exclaimed in exasperation, glancing around them impatiently, their gazes always returning to the watches they wore on their wrists which they examined every other second, as if by looking at them they could hurry time along.

There was one who stood perfectly still in the queue, so still that he seemed scarcely to be breathing and on his face was an expression of sublime resignation as if he were not standing in a railway station at all, but in some distant and pleasant place. Hildamay supposed that he must be practising some form of meditation and did the same, concentrating hard. She thought for a minute that if she could see through Sky's eyes, she might be able to make her real. She concentrated so hard that she was not surprised to see a small figure over in a crowd by platform three. She pushed hurriedly through the crowd, knocking against people, causing those who were carrying heavy suitcases to stop and call after her in exasperation, but she did not stop to apologise or even to look behind her at the long trail of disconsolate faces. Her eyes were fixed firmly on the khaki nylon jacket and the thin wrists which protruded from the lumpy bracelets of the rolled-up sleeves. And on the baseball cap, black and a little too big, jammed down hard to hide the face. Hildamay's heart quickened, as did her step, until she was about five yards away when she slowed down and assumed a cautious walk, a parody of stealth, tiptoeing up to the small figure; anxious not to alarm it lest it should disappear. She was not conscious of her exaggerated movements until the child in the khaki jacket and baseball cap turned round and fixed her with a suspicious gaze.

'Don't think I didn't see you!' he said, for it was a little boy. 'I knew you were behind me. Why are you walking like that? Are you playing a game and can I play? I want to play!'

'No,' said Hildamay, her voice curt with disappointment. His mouth pursed into an obstinate little rose.

'Why not?'

'Because I'm looking for somebody and you would just get in the way.'

'I would not!' He stamped his small foot and put his hands on his hips, perhaps as he had seen his mother do. 'Who are you looking for, anyway?' he said sulkily.

Hildamay did not want to tell him. His mouth had settled in

an obstinate, hard little line; strange against the rounded, childish contours of his cheeks. She did not trust that mouth, but then she thought that he might have noticed Sky because she wore a cap so like his own. Children seemed proprietorial about such things.

'A little girl. She has a cap almost exactly like yours.'

'Like mine?' He put his hand to the peak of his cap and tugged sharply at it then stared up at Hildamay with disbelief. 'Exactly like mine?' he said, frowning.

'Yes,' she said. 'Exactly.'

'It can't be exactly like mine. This is mine.'

'I said exactly like, not exactly,' said Hildamay irritably.

'But you said –' he began.

'Oh, do be quiet,' she said sharply, glancing around her. 'I'm trying to think.' She looked down at him. His face was beginning to crumple. 'There's a nice little boy,' she said cajolingly and stretched out her hand to pat him on the head. His face turned bright red and seemed to disintegrate altogether. Tears ran down his cheeks and out of his mouth came a piercing wail.

'Mummy, Mummy, that mad lady tried to hit me,' he bawled, running to clutch at the hem of the coat of a woman who had been standing with her back to them, deep in conversation with a young, blond-haired man. She turned round. She had thick, glossy red hair swept back off her face and held in place with a broad ribbon of emerald silk. She was immaculately, if a little heavily, made-up and wore an olive covert coat of unimpeachable cut, fastened at the waist with a broad belt of crocodile leather dyed a glossy chestnut brown and clasped with a golden buckle. On her fingers were many rings, all of them diamond.

'What did you say, darling?' she said, her low voice stretched in a fashionable drawl.

'That lady,' cried the boy, tugging at his mother's coat and pointing at Hildamay. Hildamay noticed that his tears had miraculously vanished but that his face was still red and creased with petulance. 'She's mad. She tried to talk to me and then she tried to hit me.'

Sweeping her coat out of his grasp, the woman walked over to Hildamay. She did not stop until their noses were almost touching. Hildamay smiled at her.

'Fuck off,' said the woman in a precise, cultured voice. 'Filth.' And then she spat full in Hildamay's face and, turning on her high spiked heel, walked back to her companion. 'Bloody loonies,' she said, her voice loud. 'I don't know where they all come from. I blame the government myself. They should lock them up, where they belong.'

Hildamay stood, speechless, the woman's saliva dripping down her face and hanging off her chin in a shining string. Mutely she wiped it off her face with the sleeve of her sweater and walked slowly back to the ticket office. She looked down at herself. Her sweater had holes in it and her sweatpants were badly stained at the knees from the rubbish she had crawled through that morning in the burrows and holes behind King's Cross station, where she had patiently lifted every cardboard box, turning up each one in case Sky should be asleep underneath. She pushed her fingers hurriedly through her hair, remembering that she had not combed it that morning, and then scrubbed at her face with the ends of her sleeves which she wore pulled down over her hands, like mittens. She looked up to see a young man staring at her. He had pale brown hair backcombed to form a Cochran quiff, and the skin of his face was roughened but shiny with grease. From the line of his jaw, down his neck, crawled red snakes of acne, which disappeared into the collar of his cheap black leather jacket. 'I should worry!' she called, jamming two fingers stiffly in the air in a gesture of contempt. He reddened and turned away and she went back to her position by the ticket office, her arms crossed aggressively and her gaze fixed and staring. The people in the queue shuffled away from her, leaving a berth of some yards around her, as if she were contagious.

She had never felt so close to despair.

'Hildamay?' The voice came from behind her head and a hand took her elbow. She jumped.

'It's OK,' said George, steadying her with his other hand. 'It's only me.'

'How did you know I'd . . . ?'

'It's Saturday. Three o'clock,' he said gently, his voice so full of affection and his eyes so bright with sympathy that Hildamay felt a great sob start somewhere in the pit of her chest and barrel up out of her throat. Contempt she could bear; kindness, she knew, would break her.

'Nooo!' she screamed, pushing him away and throwing her head back, baying like a dog. She could not stop the strange sound coming out of her mouth, so she fell to the ground and sat there, pulling her knees up and throwing her arms over her head to hide her howling. The people in the queue shuffled further away until it snaked in a huge semicircle around them. Even as she howled, she worried about George. George, so neat, so tidy, so proper – so embarrassed. Suddenly she felt him sit on the ground behind her and, straddling her with his legs, pull her backwards until she rested against his chest. He cradled his arms around her and rocked her, making low, soothing noises, like growls from a baby bear. Hildamay cried even harder and the people stared, watching open-mouthed as the odd couple rocked and crooned upon the ground.

Finally, Hildamay stopped crying. 'George,' she squeaked, scrubbing at her face with a dirty sleeve. 'George,' she said again, and began to mumble his name like an incantation, as if it calmed her. He sat and listened attentively then pushed a clean white handkerchief into her hand.

'Better now?' he said.

'Ummm,' she said, for her lips were so swollen from crying that it was difficult to form words properly.

'Want a cup of tea?' he asked.

She nodded that she did, so he got up and hoisted her to her feet. She was three inches taller than he but he still managed to put his arm around her shoulders and led her to the cafe.

'Not there,' she said, finding her voice. His grip tightened.

'Yes,' he said.

'No, I don't want to go there!' she exclaimed. 'That's where Sky and I sometimes used to eat.'

'All the more reason for going there,' he said firmly. 'She might come in search of you.'

Protesting weakly, Hildamay walked into the cafe and sat at a table while George went to get the tea. She blew her nose strenuously, wiped her eyes, lit a cigarette and was almost composed by the time he got back with it.

They drank their tea in silence. 'Want some cake?' he said.

She shook her head and, although she did not speak, he could see that she seemed calmer and this made him relax. Leaning back in his chair, he watched her steadily.

'What happened to your daughter?' she asked suddenly, looking up at him.

He said nothing, for a full five minutes. Hildamay thought he had forgotten the question, or chose not to answer, so she began to think again of Sky, worrying through all the places they had been together. Portobello! She hadn't asked the Rastafarians. Perhaps they had seen her? Her mind raced with possibilities and she was just about to say to George that they must go immediately and at once to Portobello, when he spoke.

'She died.'

Hildamay's mind was by then so far away from the original question that she had forgotten she had asked it.

'Who did?' she said stupidly.

'My daughter.'

'She died? How did she die?' said Hildamay, her face still stupid, but this time with shock.

George looked steadily at her. 'My wife killed her,' he said. 'And then she killed herself.'

Hildamay closed her eyes. 'She killed her?' she whispered unsteadily.

George was silent for a minute. Then he began to speak, his voice flat and emotionless, as if he were talking about a stranger. 'We lived in the country. We wanted Louise – that was her name – to grow up surrounded by fields and animals. London's such a dreadful place for a child. So we bought a house in Suffolk, on the coast. We kept our flat in London because of my work. I lived there all week and went to Suffolk every weekend. I used to arrive at seven o'clock, every Friday evening. My wife, Ann, said she could set her watch by me. She would keep Louise up especially late, so I could see her when I arrived. We would put her to bed together and later open a bottle of wine and sit by the fire, discussing the week's events. Anyway, I arrived as usual one Friday evening and walked into the sitting room. I could see the back of Ann's head. She was sitting in the armchair by the fire, so I tiptoed up behind her and bent over to kiss her. Louise was lying in her lap. Her throat had been cut. At first I thought that Ann was simply suffering from shock; her eyes were closed and she was deathly pale. I picked Louise up. There was blood all over Ann's cream sweater. I thought it was Lousie's but then I realised, as I touched her, that Ann was dead. The blood was from a deep chest wound. There was a knife; the carving knife from the kitchen. It lay by her side, the handle sticking up and the blade buried down the side of the chair. I thought, of course, that they had been murdered and picked up the knife and ran through the house, searching it. Then I called the police. They examined the bodies, then took them away. Then they took me to the police station. I was there all night. In the morning they told me what they thought had happened. The only fingerprints on the knife, other than my own, were Ann's. And Louise's,' he said bitterly. 'She must have tried to stop her mother.' His voice tailed off and he took a deep breath. 'They think, the police, that Ann cut Louise's throat and then stabbed herself in the heart. But they were puzzled because there was no note.'

Hildamay moaned and bent her head down to the cold formica table, where she rested it, feeling the hard metal edge digging into her forehead. George went on talking.

'There was a full investigation, of course. They still thought I might have done it, or at least, set it up. Many of the village people did think that. My wife was very popular, you see. Such a cheerful, happy woman. So sane. The only thing she seemed to really worry about were environmental issues, which she talked about constantly. More and more each week, and her fears became more and more extreme. I didn't really notice at the time, but in retrospect I suppose her fear had become obsessive. She talked incessantly about the planet being doomed and fretted about dying, leaving Louise to grow up in it alone. She adored my daughter. Particularly because we had been told we could never have another child.'

He stopped speaking. Eventually Hildamay lifted her head to look at him. He seemed to have slipped into a trance.

'How old was she?' she asked, very quietly.

'Three. It was nearly six years ago. She would have been exactly Sky's age.' He smiled. 'She even looks a bit like her. I mean,' he said, hesitating, 'looked. She had that same red gold hair, strawberry blonde I think they call it. My wife had red hair and I'm blond. Was blond,' he said with a shrug, running his hand through the few limp pale brown hairs which still clung to his head. 'It all disappeared after – after they left,' he said carefully. 'I seemed to fade. All the colour gradually leached out of me and my whole body seemed to shrink.' He laughed harshly. 'A shadow of the man he used to be. I sold the house, of course,' he said, frowning at her, as if he was wondering why she was there, sitting in front of him. He looked away and sat motionless for a while, gazing at the bustle of people over by the hot food counter.

'Memories?' said Hildamay gently, after a time.

His eyes came back into focus and he looked over at her and shrugged. 'Hate mail. Even though my name was cleared in the eventual inquest, the letters kept on coming. I suppose they still believed that I had done it. I'd find dog excrement put through the letter box and dead birds or rats on the doorstep.' He shrugged. 'It wasn't that so much. I couldn't bear to go on living there. I wanted to die or at least to be somebody else. Which is when I had the idea.'

'The idea?'

'To become somebody else. I gave up all my possessions. Everything that had once had anything to do with the man I used to be, I sold. My house, my flat, my cars, my business.'

'You had a business?' said Hildamay, incredulous.

He looked at her and an edge of pride sharpened his voice. 'Oh, yes,' he said, and smiled. 'I wasn't always a maker of tea.' She shook her head but he ignored her. 'I had a very successful graphic design business. But after the –' he paused – 'after the accident, I sold it and changed my name.'

'Your name's not George Brown?'

'Who,' he said with a wry smile, 'who really has a name like George Brown?'

'There are two hundred Browns without an e and with the initial G in the telephone directory,' said Hildamay automatically.

He looked at her questioningly but she just shook her head and motioned at him to go on with his story.

'My real name is Arthur Dogwood. You probably read it in the papers. The investigation went on for months and the press –' he shrugged – 'well, the press love a good murder mystery. So when it was all over, I became somebody else. Somebody who has nothing, because if you have nothing,' he said softly, 'nobody can ever take it away.'

He fell into a deep silence while Hildamay sat and thought about Harry Dogwood. Of course, the waiter at Langan's. No wonder the name had seemed familiar. It had been all over the newspapers, for weeks. She remembered the case well. She had wondered at the time, about that and other similar cases, what happened to those people after something so terrible had devastated their lives. She had always wondered how they survived. How, even, they went on living. This, at least for one of them, was how. She looked at George.

'So you reinvented yourself?'

'Yes. I learned to type, to file, to do simple bookkeeping. I wanted a nice, safe, secure nine to five job where I could give little and ask nothing in return. No questions,' he said, with a brief smile. She smiled weakly, remembering their lunch. 'I bought a tiny two-room flat in Streatham. It has a bed, a table, two armchairs and a cooker. When I moved in my whole personality seemed to change. I became this,' he said indicating himself, 'this person. This George Brown. The only thing I couldn't give up were the coloured ties. I've always loved colour and pattern.' He laughed suddenly. 'The only uncharacteristic thing that George Brown ever does is buy his ties from Paul Smith.' He shrugged. 'I suppose he has to have one little vice. One vanity. I eat lamb chops every evening and pickled herring and cucumber sandwiches every lunchtime because it means that I never have to make a decision, never have to have an appetite or go out and join in the real business of living. The only indulgence I ever allow George Brown is to go to the park on Saturday afternoons to look at the children. Between three and five o'clock each Saturday afternoon, I sit there and remember Louise. I've been going for years now. I watch the children grow, much as I would have watched Louise. Amazing,' he murmured, 'how much they change.'

'Which is why you know so much about children?' said Hildamay softly.

He looked at her, his eyes seeming to come back into focus. 'Yes,' he said slowly, 'I suppose it is. I talk to their mothers often. At first they were suspicious.' He shrugged. 'There are some odd men around and I suppose I must have looked very odd. But after a while they began to accept me and then they began to greet me. One of them,' he laughed softly, 'her name is Ann. She has a daughter who is almost exactly the same age as Louise would have been. She asked me if I had any children and I told her that I had one but that she had died. She sort of took me under her wing after that; sits and talks to me every Saturday. She talks about her child, Emily she's called, and how she changes over the months. Emily comes and talks to me, too. She calls me Uncle George. At least, she used to. They moved away. About two months ago. Went to live in the country. Ann said she thought the city was bad for Emily. I miss her,' he said softly. 'I miss her very much.'

Hildamay bent her head and rested it once more on the cold edge of the table. Her head felt swollen and heavy; too great a weight for her neck to support. 'I'm so sorry,' she murmured and then, to her fury and embarrassment, began to cry again.

'Oh George,' she sobbed. 'I'm so sorry,' but whether she was crying for George or Sky or even for herself, she did not know.

She felt his hand on her hand and then he began to gently stroke her hair.

'You mustn't be sorry,' he said quietly. 'Don't ever be sorry.' He sighed, suddenly. 'You can waste a whole life in regret.' He put his hand under her chin and lifted it so she was staring directly into his face. 'You must find her,' he said, his voice urgent. 'You must find her and then you must bring her home.'

'But how will I ever find her?' she cried. 'And if I do, will she want to come home? Will she ever believe me again?'

'Yes,' said George, cradling her face in his hands and wiping the tears from her eyes. She closed them, feeling the cool, soothing pressure of his fingers. 'She'll believe you. You understand about love now.'

'Yes,' whispered Hildamay bleakly. 'I understand about love now.'

George was silent for a moment. 'Smile, Hildamay,' he said. She opened her eyes and looked at him, astonished. She did not feel like smiling. 'Smile, Hildamay,' he said again, dropping his hands from her face.

She smiled.

'Well,' he said, looking at her thoughtfully, 'I suppose it's a start.'

CHAPTER TWENTY EIGHT

HILDAMAY stood in the doorway of Luigi's and blinked at the unaccustomed noise and colour. She had spent so many weeks sitting alone, waiting, that she had forgotten that life still went on. Everyone was laughing and talking and she stood for a moment, bemused, wondering what it was that they were so pleased about. Luigi saw her and came bustling over to enfold her in a bear like hug. His starched white apron crackled and she was suddenly enveloped in the scent of basil and garlic laced with the heady, sweet perfume of the lavender hair oil with which he tried, without apparent effect, to sleek down his dark, unruly curls.

'Luigi,' she murmured, blinking at him.

'Hildamay!' he exclaimed, kissing her loudly on both cheeks.

'*Bella, belissima*, how we have missed you!' He held her out at arm's length. 'But you look so pale! So thin! We haven't seen you for over a month. You have been away?' He frowned at her sternly. 'You have been working too hard. No! No, let me guess. You have been on one of those reducing diets which you young girls insist on doing.' Hildamay smiled at this but he shook his great head sadly and wagged an admonishing finger at her. 'You women will never understand. Never!' he said emphatically. 'We men, we don't like thin, pale women. We like something to get our hands on.' He curved his hands in the air, fingers twitching as if testing imaginary melons for ripeness. 'All those beautiful curves,' he said, squinting at her with a lugubrious eye, 'where have they gone?' He smiled then and looked at her enquiringly, his little black eyes twinkling under the dark hedges of his eyebrows. She shook her head mutely and smiled back at him. 'Even your smile has been on a diet!' he exclaimed. 'So! We feed you! Your friend is here. Go and sit down, eat. Enjoy!' So saying he took her by the shoulders and pushed her gently in front of him as though she were a child. She stepped forward a few paces then stopped to look for Kate. Not seeing her, she stood irresolute in the middle of the room. One of Luigi's sons, Leonardo, swooped past her, his arms laden with steaming platters of food.

'*Bella!* She's over there,' he said, jerking his head at a table in the far corner. 'We have very good linguine today,' he called back over his shoulder. 'Your favourite. We knew you were coming. Luigi, he felt it in his waters.'

Hildamay laughed and walked over to the corner. 'Kate, Kate, is that you?' she called, threading her way between the tightly packed tables.

Kate turned around at the sound of her name and began to pat nervously at her hair. Her round face was considerably less rounded than it had been the last time Hildamay saw her and her deep set eyes were bright and piercingly blue. They looked so startling that at first Hildamay blinked, but as she stepped closer she realised that they were framed in an artful blend of shadows, and Kate's once fair and unobtrusive eyelashes were coated with thick black mascara. Her usually flushed pink skin was hidden under an even film of freshly painted beige and her lips were glossed in deep coral. Hildamay stopped a few feet away and examined her. Even the hair did not belong to Kate. The fine, fair wisps which had once straggled around her face were coloured a rich honey and swept into an elegant chignon, and in her ear lobes diamonds glittered.

'Good grief,' said Hildamay. 'Is it you?'

'You don't like it!' Kate's voice was shrill, accusing.

'I'm not sure about *it*,' said Hildamay, laughing. 'Are you under there?'

Kate's eyes were bright with embarrassment and she fiddled nervously with her napkin. 'I've been made over,' she said querulously.

'You've been what?' Hildamay kissed her carefully.

'Made over,' explained Kate, looking down and pleating her napkin into a rigid concertina. 'Oh, you know.' She shrugged defensively. 'Like they do in the magazines. I went to this place and they did my make-up and gave me a chart to follow so I could do it myself at home. The man there said I have very good skin,' she said proudly. 'But that my features could do with a little help,' she added slowly. Hildamay frowned, perplexed. 'To bring them out,' explained Kate earnestly. 'Anyway, when he'd finished he said that now my hair wouldn't do at all, that the colour was all wrong for me, so he sent me off to this other place where they dyed it. This colour, Sunny Honey, is warmer for my face,' she explained, patting nervously at her hair. 'And they put it up like this but then they said that the new hair and the new face didn't suit my old image at all and that I needed some new clothes, so I went to see this woman who's called an image consultant and she showed me what to wear. She said I was much better tailored than layered and I'd got all my proportions wrong and what with my new colouring all those old pastels I used to wear were killing my face. So she put me in these blues, which she said were good for my eyes, and recommended red for confident days, well, a coral red really, a blue red's too harsh against my skin, and navy, never black, for elegant evenings. Navy's the new black, she said. And better for a spring person, which I am; much more than an autumn type. Although she said I had a bit of summer in me, too,' she added thoughtfully.

'Good grief,' said Hildamay, sinking back in her chair, exhausted. 'Which bit of you is left?' she asked curiously.

'Oh, it's all *me*,' said Kate earnestly. 'It's making the best of me, don't you see?'

Hildamay did not see, but did not say so.

'It cost me a fortune,' Kate added reflectively, 'and I get such a shock every time I see myself in a mirror or a shop window. But Ben likes it,' she said triumphantly.

'Well that's all right, then,' said Hildamay, peering at her closely. She thought Kate looked as if she had been dipped in a thin layer of gloss, although the fresh paint did not quite disguise the old cracks which still showed through. Even her gestures were artificial and brittle, as if she were contained in a mould which might suddenly crack and tumble in pieces all around her. She frowned at the thought of little bits of Kate scattered over the floor while in her place sat her core, gleaming palely; an exposed, monstrous pupa.

Kate noticed the look and bridled. 'The image consultant said it would be my women friends who'd find the New Me difficult,' she said, and a shiny pink flush crept through the matt beige of her foundation. 'She said women were always jealous if they saw an old friend transformed. She said women are always undermining other women and that I was to expect it.' A challenging note crept into her voice.

'I didn't say I didn't like it!' protested Hildamay. 'I'm just slightly unnerved. I'd arrived expecting to see an old friend, and in her place is this glorious stranger.'

Kate relaxed. 'It is a bit strange, isn't it?' she giggled, and in an habitual gesture ran her fingers through her hair. They stuck in the first inch of hair they encountered. 'Oh, shit!' she said, disentangling them gently. 'I keep forgetting. Does it look all right?' She peered anxiously at Hildamay.

'I think so,' said Hildamay doubtfully, bending forward to get a closer look. 'It's rucked up a bit to the left. There, just there,' she urged as Kate patted at the offending lump. 'That's it. Does it take you hours in the morning?'

'Don't be horrid, Hildamay. It's only a chignon. A child could do it.' Kate wriggled self-consciously in her chair. 'Well, what do you think?' Her expression was a mixture of doubt and triumph.

'Nice,' said Hildamay smiling. 'Very nice.'

'I suppose I really did look awful before,' sighed Kate, her face crumpling anxiously.

'I rather liked the old you.'

'So you don't like the New Me!' she flounced. 'No, you don't. I can tell. You're just being kind. I looked awful before.'

'I'm glad you got some of that weight off, anyway,' said Hildamay comfortingly.

'I wasn't that fat!' said Kate furiously. 'And what do you mean, *some*? Some! As if I've only lost a couple of pounds. I've lost two stone. I've been dieting for weeks and weeks!' she said triumphantly. 'The way you're going on, you'd think I was some sort of monster.'

'Champagne?' asked Hildamay brightly, thinking it better to get off the subject of Kate's appearance as quickly as possible.

'My diet,' Kate murmured piously.

'Nonsense,' said Hildamay firmly. 'It's a diuretic. You pee all the sugar away.'

'Well, if you're sure –' Kate looked doubtful.

'Perfectly.'

'What are we celebrating?'

'What?' Hildamay frowned at her.

'Why the champagne?' asked Kate. 'What are we celebrating?'

'Champagne's not a celebration!' exclaimed Hildamay. 'It's a medicine. It cures everything, but particularly boredom. The French have a glass when they're doing the Hoovering.'

'Oh,' said Kate thoughtfully. 'They must have very clean houses, then.'

'Well,' said Kate, snapping the menu shut after only five seconds. 'Now, what's all this about a child? Ben came home with some extraordinary story about finding you sitting on your own in the middle of St Pancras station at ten o'clock at night looking for a lost child.' Hildamay regretfully abandoned the menu to listen to Kate. 'He said you seemed unhappy. He was terribly distressed for days afterwards. He's so fond of you, Hildamay.' She leaned across the table and patted Hildamay's hand.

Hildamay smiled wanly but was saved from answering by Luigi who came to take their order. Hildamay looked up at him.

'Kate will toy with a little green salad, no dressing, just lemon juice, and then she'll chase a bit of grilled sole around her plate. Not butter, Luigi. Promise,' she added sternly.

Luigi looked aggrieved but shook his head sadly in assent. Hildamay ordered pasta to start followed by fish baked in olive oil with extra mashed potato. The ordering of each dish was punctuated by horrified exclamations from Kate. 'And some red cabbage,' finished Hildamay, ignoring her.

'But it's full of sugar,' hissed Kate. Luigi raised a reproachful eyebrow so she shut up until he had left the table. 'You're not going to eat all that!' she exclaimed in a loud whisper once he was out of earshot.

'You get on with your diet, and I'll get on with mine,' said Hildamay mildly.

'That's a diet?' said Kate, incredulous.

'For the soul,' said Hildamay and smiled briefly at her.

Kate shrugged. 'Well, it's your body,' she murmured, her mouth pursed into a prim little bud of coral gloss.

'Is Puritanism the credo of New Meism?' asked Hildamay sharply.

Kate looked hurt. 'I was only trying to help,' she protested.

Hildamay relented. 'I have never needed help with food,' she said and smiled. Kate simply shrugged, folded her mouth back into its prim bud and retreated into silence. But silence was not for Kate a natural state.

'One does eat a great deal when one's unhappy,' she exclaimed, after a minute. 'And Ben said you were very, very unhappy.' Her face had taken on such an eager, excited look that Hildamay wondered if her unhappiness had somehow pleased her. 'Now, I want to hear about this child,' said Kate in a voice that brooked no argument. 'I want to hear all about it,' she added, her eyes bright with curiosity.

'She's a child.'

'Yes, yes. I know she's a child. But who is she? And why are you looking for her? And what has she done to upset you so badly?' she demanded. 'Ben said you were very upset,' she added, her tone insistent.

'Her name is Sky,' began Hildamay.

'Sky!' interjected Kate scornfully. 'What kind of name is that for a child? Honestly, the names that people give children,' she grumbled. 'It's all wrong, really it is.'

'Her name is Sky,' continued Hildamay, ignoring her, 'and I've got to know her over the past six months. Her mother ran off to Spain and she hates her grandmother, whom she lives with. She asked me if she could come and live with me and –'

'*Live* with you!' interrupted Kate incredulously.

'If she could live with me,' continued Hildamay patiently. 'And I told her that she couldn't, so she ran away. So now I'm trying to find her.'

'*Why?*' demanded Kate imperiously.

'Because I love her,' said Hildamay gently. 'Because I realise that I do want her to come and live with me.'

'Yes,' said Kate impatiently, 'but *why?*'

'Why what?' Hildamay frowned at her.

'You can't just have a child come and live with you!' spluttered Kate. 'Children need people to look after them. What do you know about bringing up children?'

'What do you know?' said Hildamay sharply. 'Do you need qualifications to love children?'

'Well, yes, as a matter of fact you do!' said Kate indignantly. 'I've brought up three children and I can tell you, it's a full-time job. You've already got a full-time job. What are you going to do about that? I suppose you could get a nanny, although I can't see you dealing with her terribly well,' she added dismissively. 'And what about that flat of yours? It's hardly suitable for a child, is it? All those pale colours and fragile old bits and pieces. Anyway, you can't just decide that you're going to have a child and pick one up off the street. You don't even know where she's been!' she exclaimed.

Hildamay frowned. 'I do know where she's been. I just don't know where she is now.'

'But you can't decide you want a child and have one just like that,' said Kate, shaking her head crossly.

Hildamay put down her fork and looked at her. On her face was an expression of deep interest. 'Why not?' she asked innocently.

'Because you can't!' exploded Kate.

There was silence. Hildamay picked up her fork and began to twirl linguine loaded with cream and cheese into her mouth. Kate looked at her with disgust and poked at a lettuce leaf.

'Anyway,' she said primly, 'I think it better, if you want a child so much, to have your own and not go around picking up other people's as if they were toys.'

'Do you?' said Hildamay indifferently, tearing her roll in half and mopping up the sauce on her plate. She looked up and, smiling, shoved it, whole, into her mouth.

'Oh, really, Hildamay,' said Kate in exasperation. 'You're like a child yourself, just playing at life. It's what I always say to Ben. You've got this grand title and you swan around the place as if you know what life is all about when you don't even know the half of it. And now you're talking about taking some child in, just as if you were getting a cat! You have to devote yourself entirely to children.' She jabbed at her salad for emphasis. 'You can't mother part time. You don't even have a minute to yourself and certainly not an ounce of privacy. And you, of all people, have to have your privacy!' she exclaimed. 'No, no. You're really not the sort of person who should have children. One sacrifices everything to be a mother.' She smiled complacently. 'You never have time to think about yourself, let alone read a newspaper.'

'And you think that's a passport to adulthood?' said Hildamay, her voice dangerously quiet.

'No,' snapped Kate defensively, 'but I do think it's a passport to life. It's women who do the real business of living. And that's not smart jobs and flats and drinking champagne whenever you feel like it. When I had those three under my feet I was much too busy being involved with life to pay attention to any of the fancy details like nice clothes or self important job titles.'

'So I noticed,' said Hildamay, provoked.

Kate looked surprised, then wounded. 'What?' she exclaimed, but Hildamay shrugged irritably. Luigi appeared with their food and they ate in silence for a while.

'How are the kids?' said Hildamay eventually, her voice carefully neutral.

'The boys have gone off to school,' said Kate, eyeing her cautiously. 'I thought I'd hate them being away but really, I don't mind that much. In a way it's rather a relief.'

'I can imagine,' said Hildamay pleasantly.

'No you can't!' snapped Kate.

Hildamay looked up from her mashed potatoes in surprise.

'Well, really,' grumbled Kate, 'a childless woman can't possibly understand the exhaustion of having children and I do wish they'd stop pretending they could. There aren't two sexes, but three. Men, women, and women with children. Women who pretend to understand what it's like to be a woman with children are as bad as men who pretend to understand what it's like to be a woman. A woman without children can't possibly understand how a woman with children feels.'

'I think they can,' said Hildamay innocently. 'It's smug, isn't it?'

Kate looked at her in astonishment.

'Smug!' she said furiously. 'Smug? There's nothing smug about cleaning up shit and vomit.'

'Oh, I don't know.' Hildamay's voice was airy. 'There's nothing like a bit of mortification for encouraging complacency. It's always seemed to me that cleaning up shit gives women licence to call themselves women. The shit free are a sub species of women.'

'You don't know what you're talking about,' said Kate angrily.

Hildamay shrugged. 'Maybe not.'

But Kate was by this time shrill with indignation. 'If anybody's being complacent around here, I think it's you,' she exclaimed.

Odd, thought Hildamay, how children, the thing that supposedly binds women together, always seems to set them apart. 'Fine,' she said calmly and spooned the last mouthful of potato into her mouth.

'Well, really, Hildamay!' exclaimed Kate. 'I sometimes think you couldn't give a damn about anybody else. You sit there in your perfect flat and live your perfect life and if you can't be bothered to see anybody, or even talk to them, you don't.' Her cool beige face had turned a hot and brilliant pink.

'Why does that upset you?' asked Hildamay with interest.

'I am not upset! It's just I don't think – it's just not right.'

'Not right?' echoed Hildamay, her smile mocking.

'It's – it's so cold!' said Kate triumphantly. There was silence. 'It's not that you're cold,' she added quickly. 'Well, not really. It's just that you don't seem to need other people. And you don't like children.' The words came tumbling out, falling over each other.

'Don't I?' How odd, thought Hildamay, when I have just told her that I want a child to come and live with me.

'Well, you don't seem to,' said Kate peering at her, worried suddenly that she had upset her. 'You look at my children as if they irritate you,' she blurted out, colouring.

'Well, they do.'

'Really, Hildamay!' exclaimed Kate. 'That's not a very nice thing to say.'

'It's not their fault,' protested Hildamay. 'Some children interest me just as some people interest me. Others don't.'

'And I don't?' Kate's eyes were bright.

'How did you get to that?' asked Hildamay, puzzled.

'Well, if my children irritate you they obviously don't interest you and as they are my children then I don't either,' explained Kate breathlessly.

'Good grief,' said Hildamay. 'That's not what I said at all.'

'Oh, why are we arguing?' asked Kate, crossly.

'Because you think I'm cold and incapable of love and don't answer my telephone and find your children irritating.' Hildamay shrugged and smiled suddenly. 'Because we're the shit full and the shit free.'

Kate giggled and returned the smile, her face suffused with an affectionate, almost maternal glow. 'Sometimes,' she said soothingly, 'I don't understand you, Hildamay. I really don't understand you at all. Anyway,' she added more briskly, 'I'm glad we've had this chat. Sometimes little disagreements aren't such a bad thing, now are they?' She smiled, a faintly benign smile. 'But don't you ever feel left out?' she asked.

'Left out of what?'

'Having children, of course. Unless, of course, you go ahead with this mad idea of picking up a stray child,' she added doubtfully. 'Don't you ever feel excluded from life?'

The unconscious cruelty with which women treated their own sex never ceased to astonish Hildamay. She thought that perhaps breeding limited the brain, narrowed the vision until the only social order that was recognised as happy, acceptable even, was that of the family, while everything outside it became undesirable, abnormal.

'Life?' she said, her voice dangerous. 'Don't you mean rules? Oh, don't frown so, Kate. You'll spoil your new face. What's normal? Are rules normal? Normal, according to the rules, is a man and a woman and two and a half children. That's happy. A man and a woman and no children; that's happy but for an unfortunate accident of nature or an unfortunate nature of selfishness. A man alone. That's happy, possibly the happiest state of all given the popular portrayal of women. Then there's a man with a man. Unhappy. Two cocks can't make happiness, they can only make AIDS. A woman alone? Bitter, unhappy, frustrated, cold. A woman with a woman? Now there's the killer! Cockless, unhappy and plain misguided. To be welcomed back into the flock at all costs. There's nothing like society's approval of a converted lesbian. She's seen the light and the light is the cock that shall lead her back to all understanding.'

'It's unnatural,' said Kate, flushing.

'Oh, sod unnatural!' shouted Hildamay.

'There's no need to shout,' said Kate reprovingly.

'Well, you're the one who's always preaching about love,' said Hildamay, her voice suddenly tired. 'And then you condemn that which you praise.'

'It's just not a proper sort of love,' said Kate, flushing.

'And what's proper?'

'You know,' Kate shifted uncomfortably in her chair. 'Married love!' she exclaimed after a while.

'Must love be officially registered in order for us to know it exists?' asked Hildamay.

'There is no love so absolute as married love,' said Kate firmly. 'Marriage changes everything, it gives you sort of a warm glow inside.' She leaned forward eagerly in her chair. 'Oh, it does, Hildamay. Really! When you get married, you'll understand.' Hildamay did not respond but stared at her, a curious smile on her face.

'Oh, why should you understand?' complained Kate. 'But once you are married and have children, you will understand how important it is. How sacred!' she exclaimed. 'That's why nothing – nothing,' she repeated, her voice rising in excitement, 'must be allowed to break it up.'

'How is Ben?' said Hildamay, still with a smile.

'Oh, he's wonderful. Perfectly, blissfully, gloriously, wonderful!' exclaimed Kate.

'He fucked you last month then, did he?' drawled Hildamay.

'Hildamay!'

'Well, did he? What's he done to deserve that many adjectives? He must have made the universe shake.'

'Sometimes,' said Kate primly, 'I really think you're rather a bitch, Hildamay.'

'Joke, Kate, joke,' said Hildamay, her smile tight. She leaned across the table. 'Remember? When we used to laugh?'

'Sex is no laughing matter,' said Kate primly.

'Oh, come on. There's nothing so comic as a penis,' said Hildamay, grinning. Kate's face darkened.

Good grief, thought Hildamay, what has happened here? Perhaps Ben's constant infidelity has turned the penis into a tragedy? Perhaps Ben's penis is a tragedy? She held up her hands in a gesture of surrender. 'Sorry, Kate,' she said, her smile contrite. 'Why's he so particularly wonderful at the moment?'

'He's changed,' said Kate thoughtfully. 'He was in such a state for a while.' Her face darkened. 'After that business with Delilah. But the day he really changed was the day I tried to kill him.'

'I could see that might have an impact on a person,' said Hildamay gravely, but she could not help smiling.

'It wasn't funny!' protested Kate but Hildamay burst out laughing.

'Oh, I'm sorry, Kate,' she said, wiping at her eyes. 'It must be the way you tell it.'

'Well, he did change,' said Kate crossly. 'Afterwards he seemed relieved, pleased almost.' She shook her head. 'I don't know why.'

'How did you try to kill him?'

'Oh, you remember,' said Kate, fiddling with a diamond earring. 'The ginger biscuits. The rat poison. I told you about the time I made them. Anyway, he got back late, after a business dinner, and was starving. God knows why he was starving after dinner.' She frowned. 'Anyway he was, and went into the larder and found the biscuits. He woke me up in the night and looked so ill I called an ambulance. It was only when we were in casualty that he explained to the doctor what he'd eaten that day and I had to confess.' She blushed. 'I was so humiliated, but Ben started to laugh. At first we all thought it had gone to his head. Poisoned his brain,' she explained, 'which apparently can happen but he said that, no, he was laughing because he thought it funny.' Kate giggled suddenly. 'The doctor didn't think it was very funny at all. Anyway, then Ben started crying and held on to me and thanked me over and over again and said that he was so glad I'd made the decision for him.' Kate shrugged. 'I thought he must be delirious but he kept on repeating it. They kept him in overnight and since then he's been a lamb.'

'When was this?' asked Hildamay, curious.

'Oh, about a week ago,' said Kate. 'I know the accident happened after he saw you at the station. Before that, when he had just seen you, he became quite strange again and kept on going on and on about you losing the thing that you loved and how you must find it again. He's so fond of you, Hildamay,' added Kate, smiling brightly.

'So you said,' said Hildamay abruptly.

'Well, I told him not to be so silly. You're not going to go ahead with this silly idea, are you, Hildamay?' she said, frowning at her. Hildamay said nothing so after a minute Kate leaned back in her chair with a satisfied smile. 'Good,' she said brightly. 'What you need is a decent man, not some stray child. Now, where was I? Oh, yes. Ben kept on saying, "We must go after the thing that we love and not lose it." Those were his words. I told him that I had no intention of going away or ever letting him go.'

'And what did he say?'

'He gave me all this money so I could go and become a New Me,' said Kate eagerly. 'I've never known him be so generous before. He said he wanted to be sure that I was ready for a new life. That things were going to be quite different from now on and that in a few years' time I'd understand how wonderful life could be. When I teased him about it taking a few years he said that that was how long it took to completely change your life.' She hugged herself excitedly. 'He wants me to go and get a job, too. Said I was far too clever to sit at home now that the boys have gone off to school. He's been so helpful about it all, arranging for interviews for me for secretarial jobs in the City. He's even paying for me to do a refresher course in typing and shorthand. He won't say what they are, but I know that he's got some amazing plans.'

'Oh, God,' said Hildamay. Poor, slow Kate. Ben was setting her up, sending her off to be turned into someone new so he could leave her with a clean, or a less dirtied, conscience. 'Find the thing that you love.' Of course. Delilah. And then Hildamay looked at Kate's face and saw in it the stupid cruelty of blind convention. She'll do anything to keep him, she reflected. Anything at all. He doesn't stand a chance. Poor Ben. Poor, foolish Ben.

'What?' Kate was peering at her, a puzzled smile illuminating the excitement which still shone in her face.

'Good,' said Hildamay, smiling bleakly. 'Oh good.'

CHAPTER TWENTY NINE

'DARLING!' Cassie stood in the entrance to the bar at The Globe, her arms spread in a gesture of benediction. Across her shoulders and arms were draped scarves; scarves of chiffon, silk and cut work velvet, each in a different shade of violet and all embroidered with beads, birds and flowers. Her auburn hair was dyed a shining blue-black and on her heavy lidded eyes, powdered violet shimmered.

'Good grief,' said Hildamay.

Cassie swooped on her and smothered her in a scented embrace.

'Violets,' breathed Hildamay. 'Nice.'

'It's my new trademark, darling,' said Cassie, wrinkling her nose and giggling. 'You look a trifle wan, sweet,' she added, frowning and patting Hildamay's cheeks. 'Try a bit of rouge – or sex. Sex first, then if you're not getting any of that try Bourgois Number 5. It's the closest thing there is to that contented sexual glow.'

Hildamay looked at Cassie's cheeks, which were very pink. 'You look like you've been getting quantities of both,' she said drily.

Cassie laughed and collapsed into a chair. 'That would be telling, darling.' She smiled coyly and draped a languid arm across the back of the chair. She looked at Hildamay expectantly. 'Anyway, the scent is my trademark,' she said after a brief silence and, sighing dramatically, closed her eyes. 'We novelists must have a trademark, darling,' she murmured, 'and mine is bruised violet; violet scent, violent sex, purple prose.' She half opened one eye and squinted at Hildamay to gauge her reaction. 'You know, for the interviews,' she explained and, opening her eyes, sat bolt upright. 'You can just see it, can't you? The opening paragraph – "Cassandra Montrose opened the door of her enchanting little cottage. She was dressed entirely in purple (those journalists can never tell the difference between the two) and as I followed her into her country hideaway, the scent of violets flooded the air with their sharp, sweet perfume. It was a fitting setting etcetera, etcetera . . ." All the women's magazines will adore it, darling. I've got all the interview outfits worked out, too. Quantities of scarves, darling. Metres of them. Violet, of course, although I might add flashes of pink occasionally,' she added musingly. 'My publicity girl says she doesn't know why I bother to employ her. But then, darling, I've been selling people things they don't want all my life. Not that they won't want the book, of course, but they must be told that they want it. Do you think they'll take any notice of me, darling?' she asked, wrinkling her nose anxiously.

'Not a chance,' said Hildamay, laughing. 'Is the book finished?'

'Very nearly.' Cassie stretched both arms above her head and heaved a satisfied sigh. 'It just writes itself. Good old Jack comes walking off that page, large as life.' She laughed mischievously. 'And twice as nasty. Although he does,' she said wistfully, 'have a certain charm. Why is it that women love cads, darling?' she demanded suddenly. 'Cads and bounders. I tried to make him nice, or at least, redeemable, but my editor said that no, that wouldn't sell at all. Must be their higher pain threshold,' she murmured thoughtfully. Her face darkened momentarily and then a smile glittered on her painted face. 'How is darling Jack?'

'Just darling,' said Hildamay with a shrug.

'Not beaten? Not destroyed? He's still walking!' Cassie's voice was high with outrage.

'Men like Jack,' said Hildamay contemptuously, 'don't have the imagination for defeat.'

'Or the grace,' muttered Cassie crossly. She made a sharp gesture, somewhere between a shrug and a flounce of petulance. 'You'd think he'd mind about his wife, Beth, if not about me.'

'Of course he does,' lied Hildamay. 'I'm sure it's all an act.' She paused. 'You look happy anyway. Better.'

Cassie appeared not to hear. 'And I suppose he's fucking some little secretary,' she said furiously.

'No,' said Hildamay slowly. As far as she knew he was living with one of the girls from marketing; a defeated blonde with a tired mouth and surprising, blinking, bright blue eyes. Hildamay suspected that contact lenses might be a shared interest. 'He's changed the colour of his eyes,' she added. 'They're violet.'

'So he did not go unscathed,' said Cassie, cheering up. 'And you look worse, darling,' she said suddenly.

'Thanks.'

'Oh, darling, I'm sorry. I didn't mean that you look awful or anything like that. It's just that you seem –' She frowned and peered closely at Hildamay. 'Some of that annoyingly bright shine you used to have seems to have rubbed off. You look a bit tarnished, somehow.'

'I wondered where those black marks on my clothes came from,' said Hildamay drily.

'Well?' Cassie's eyes were bright with curiosity.

'Well what?'

'Well, what's the matter? You look,' she added slowly, 'like a woman who's been left. Yes, that's what it is. Have you been left, darling?' she asked, her voice gentle.

'I suppose,' sighed Hildamay.

'Did you love him very much?' said Cassie wistfully.

'Her,' said Hildamay shortly. Cassie flushed. 'It's not –' began Hildamay but Cassie held up her hand in protest.

'You don't have to explain,' she said quickly. 'I understand. As a matter of fact,' she added, her voice dropping to a low, excited whisper, 'the same thing's happened to me!'

'You've adopted a child?' said Hildamay, puzzled.

'A child?' Cassie frowned. 'Darling, what on earth are you talking about? I'm having an affair,' she hissed. 'With a her!'

'Good grief,' said Hildamay.

Cassie pouted and tossed her head, causing the flock of silver butterflies hanging from her ears to tinkle gently. 'You're not going to go all disapproving on me, are you?' she asked, frowning. 'You said you'd done it with girls yourself!' Her voice was high with outrage.

'Surprise,' corrected Hildamay. 'Not disapproval.'

'Don't be silly, darling!' exclaimed Cassie. 'You know I've always been desperate to try it. But it's not,' she added, her mouth puckering in a pout of disappointment, 'quite as fabulous as I thought it might be. Oh, it's nice, darling! It's just that after the novelty wore off it seemed like boring old sex again. But sex with locks on. All that forbidden stuff was thrilling at first and tits are quite as nice as I thought they were going to be. Still, it's not. . . .' Her voice tailed off.

'Beth, I suppose?'

'Of course, darling. The countryside's not exactly littered with lesbians, you know. Well, only very old ones who are as good as heterosexual, they've been together so long. You don't mind, do you, darling? You, of all people. I thought you'd be pleased for me.'

Hildamay smiled. 'Yes.'

'It's perfect!' Cassie exclaimed, clapping her hands. 'You can't believe how perfect it is. Even the children don't mind, although I think that really they're a bit small to understand. But they say they like having two mummies, so that's all right. I thought at least Jack might mind,' she added petulantly and Hildamay wondered, with a pang of regret, whether this was simply the final act in Cassie's revenge. No, not that; it was only that Cassie couldn't bear to be ignored. She hoped that Beth understood Cassie; realised that her desperate need for love did not necessarily equip her to return it. She hoped that Beth did not love her. Women, she thought, can be just as cruel as men. Often crueller because they are, for the most part and certainly past a certain age, coolly practical about love. Pragmatism is unkind to the heart.

'And Beth of course is utterly divine,' said Cassie, cutting into her thoughts. 'She was a bit surprised at first, like me, but I said to her, what can you expect when you have two such gorgeous women locked away in the country together?' She giggled then frowned suddenly. 'Of course it'll all have to stop when the book comes out. Can't have the sexy new author being a dyke now, can we? The public simply won't understand.'

'Good publicity,' murmured Hildamay, her tone dry.

Cassie's head snapped back and her eyes grew narrow with possibility. 'Do you think so?' she asked in a high, excited voice.

'Guaranteed tabloid coverage.'

'Maybe,' said Cassie thoughtfully, 'if I wrote in some rude bits about girls –'

'What about love?'

'Oh, love!' Cassie blinked her eyes in amusement. 'Love's for the fairies, darling. Only children believe in magic.'

'Do they?' Hildamay looked thoughtful.

'Yes, yes, darling. All those years I spent searching for love when what I was really after was attention. Fulfilment, perhaps.' She stretched and yawned complacently. 'And now, of course, I've found it.'

'With Beth?'

'Don't be silly!' Cassie exclaimed. 'With the book.'

'Of course,' murmured Hildamay. 'Silly old *moi*.'

Cassie glanced sharply at her. 'Are you quite sure you're all right? You seem a little odd. Not like you at all.' She did not wait for an answer. 'Although, of course, if the right sort of thing came along, one might be tempted.'

'The right thing?'

'Oh, you know, darling,' said Cassie flapping a hand at her dismissively. 'Men, children, that sort of thing.'

'Oh,' said Hildamay. 'And what about Beth?'

'Oh, Beth,' said Cassie regretfully. 'Beth might turn out to be a tiny little problem. Well, quite a big one, really. She's so convinced that this is it, darling. Although I tell her that really it's cloud cuckoo land. I mean, you can't even hold hands in public. Certainly not where we live. There'd be a local scandal. We'd be tarred and feathered and drummed out of the village with everyone chanting "shame!" or they'd hang bells around our necks and we'd have to go around calling "unclean, unclean!" Girls together are all very nice, darling, but it does get a tiny bit claustrophobic after a while. All those messy female feelings flying around the place. It's like living in an emotional sauna.'

'Don't you worry about her?' asked Hildamay curiously.

'Like I said, darling,' sighed Cassie with an apologetic pout. 'I'm so insecure that if someone tells me they love me, I find them completely irresistible. I can't help it,' she exclaimed, glaring at Hildamay quite crossly. 'We must take what we can, darling. When we find it,' she added loftily.

'Until the real thing comes along,' said Hildamay drily.

'We all have a dream.' Cassie smiled at her in agreement.

'That's a pretty cynical view of love,' murmured Hildamay.

'Cynical!' Cassie stared at her in astonishment. 'Me, cynical! I believe in love. I believe in the happy ever after. I'm quite the most romantic person I know. There's nothing cynical about believing that one day the right person will come along,' she protested.

'The right what?' asked Hildamay. 'The right height, the right eyes or the right sex?'

'The right cock,' said Cassie, giggling. 'Now what's this about you being left?'

'That child I told you about,' began Hildamay.

'Child?' said Cassie, looking puzzled. 'Oh, that child. Has she reappeared? Oh, don't look like that, darling. She'll come back. Funny,' she added thoughtfully. 'I never knew you had any maternal feelings. I suppose they strike us all, in the end. I can feel that clock just ticking away, the alarm buzzes every so often and jolts me into this state of heightened awareness, a sort of nervous anticipation when I'm filled with this awful sense of destiny. Trouble is,' she added, laughing, 'I'm never quite sure if it's the muse or mother earth calling. I suppose,' she mused, 'I could slot them in, between the books, couldn't I? Well, I hope you find her, darling, but what's all this about being left?' She glanced abstractedly at Hildamay but kept peering over her shoulder. 'It's Liz!' she exclaimed. 'Look, over there. Sitting at the table in the corner. And I do believe she's with Thomas. Are they having an affair?' She frowned crossly. 'Why didn't you tell me?'

'As far as I know,' said Hildamay, glancing over her shoulder, 'an affair's the last thing on Liz's mind.'

'Don't be silly,' said Cassie, 'she's female. And there's my agent. See? That fat man over there in the corner. Cooeee!' she shouted, fluttering her fingers at him. 'He adores me, darling. Simply adores me. So he should, after that ten per cent he took. Oh lord, look, I'd better go over and talk to him. I want to make sure he hasn't forgotten about trying to tie up film rights. I thought Kevin Costner would do nicely.' She slapped her cheeks hard until they glowed pink then took a small gold perfume bottle out of her handbag and shook a few drops on to her wrists. 'The trademark,' she said, winking. 'You go and talk to Liz and Thomas,' she added, patting Hildamay on the shoulder. 'And I'll come and join you when I've finished. Sorry, darling.' She smiled brightly. 'But this is business and you know how we career girls must take care of that.' She fluttered off, scarves and essence of violet trailing behind her.

Hildamay walked over to the table where Liz and Thomas sat, their heads bent close together; Thomas's shiny gold hair looked, against Liz's dark curls, as bright as if it had been newly minted. Liz was laughing.

'Parents' evening?' said Hildamay. Liz blushed and looked at Thomas who nodded his head gently. They both smiled up at her.

'We're clucking,' said Liz with satisfaction, 'about the strength of Harry's grip. He's trying to hold his bottle all by himself.'

'That's nice,' said Hildamay brightly and sat down.

'She's articulate about babies,' said Liz affectionately and leaned over to kiss Hildamay.

'They are those things you pick up by the loose skin at the back of the neck, aren't they?' said Hildamay, making a face.

'Only at three o'clock in the morning.'

'Where's Harry?' asked Hildamay, looking from one to the other.

'Evening classes in the interpretation of dreams,' said Thomas laconically, 'with a gorgeous eighteen-year-old blonde. Trouble is, he has a worrying tendency to sleep on the job but we think it's something he'll grow out of.' He looked at her curiously. 'Did you find the child?' he asked, his voice hesitant. Hildamay was silent.

Liz stared at him. 'Have you two been meeting behind my back?' she said sharply.

Thomas shrugged. 'Yes.'

'Why?'

'Your back was so fully turned away,' he said gently, 'that it didn't leave us much option.' He smiled bitterly. 'We weren't planning a baby snatch, if that's what you mean,' he added quietly.

'What did he say to you?' Liz's voice was loud. She glared at Hildamay who frowned.

'He told me he loved you,' she murmured.

'What?' asked Liz, bending her head to hear.

'We talked about love,' said Hildamay, more loudly.

'Oh, love!' exclaimed Liz, flushing, and jerked her head in irritation.

'It's a dirty word around here,' said Thomas bitterly and, getting up from the table, smiled briefly and walked away.

Liz stared after him regretfully. 'Now look what you've gone and done. We'd just managed to get off the subject,' she said. 'He's got this ridiculous, sentimental notion that we're going to get married and live happily ever after. He thinks, just because he wants it enough, that it will happen. As if love could spring from me fully formed, like a baby. He confuses the two,' she added. 'Love is Harry, Harry is us, therefore we are love.' She shook her head. 'I told him I couldn't love –' she snapped her fingers – 'just like that! These things take time.'

'Do they?'

'Sure.' Liz shrugged and laughed. 'They definitely take time if you're doing them backwards; starting with a baby and ending up with an affair.'

'Could you love him at all?'

Liz shrugged again. 'Maybe.' She stared down at the table. 'Maybe not,' she added softly and then shook her head impatiently. 'I don't know if I know him enough to love him yet. And then there's Harry. I've got over the jealousy bit. At least I think I have. And he is very good with him.' Her face softened. She was silent for a moment and then exclaimed, 'Oh, I don't know! Why must he be so impatient? Men have this infuriating logic. It's almost childlike. I love you therefore you must love me. Men think they deserve love, women think they have to earn love.' She laughed suddenly. 'It's all connected to their dicks, of course. The penis expects instant gratification whereas the clitoris has to be teased and cajoled and persuaded and is doubtful, right up to the last minute, whether it'll ever get there in the end.'

'Speak for yourself.'

'Don't boast.'

Hildamay laughed. 'I'm not!' she protested. 'It's been so long I think mine would need more than gentle persuasion. I can't even remember the last man I slept with.'

Liz looked at her curiously. 'Do you think you'll ever end up with one?'

'You mean it shows already?'

'A man, idiot. Not a penis.'

'I thought they were somehow connected.'

Liz frowned at her. 'I'm serious.'

'They're not really my type,' she began but Liz's frown deepened. 'Stranger things have happened,' she said, shrugging.

'Lord,' said Liz smiling. 'You must be getting old.'

'Senile.'

'But you've never minded,' Liz's voice was hesitant. 'You've never minded about being on your own, have you?'

'Never used to,' murmured Hildamay. 'I used to think it was the only sensible way to be. I never understood it before,' she added thoughtfully.

'Understood what?'

'The fear.'

'What changed?'

'My heart,' said Hildamay bleakly and wondered suddenly if hearts, like minds, could be changed back again. She doubted it.

'Oh, that,' said Liz with a slight smile. 'I've always thought that falling in love is like washing your hair.'

'Stings the eyes?'

'No, idiot. If you wash your hair once, just once, you have to go on washing it for the rest of your life. If you never wash it, it never needs washing.'

'Now she tells me.'

Liz was silent. 'Are you still determined to take that child in?' she said after a while.

'Yes.'

'It'll change your life.'

'It's already changed,' said Hildamay with a slight smile.

'No lovers staying over.'

'Good grief, woman. Don't you ever stop thinking about cocks?'

'Only when I've got my hands on one.'

'Don't be vulgar. Talking of which, what are you going to do about Thomas?'

Liz shrugged. 'I've told him he can come and see Harry once a week. And as for me – well, we can be friends. I do like him!' she exclaimed. 'I like him very much. He's good and he's kind and he is very cute,' she added, leering slightly. 'And he fucks like a dream.'

'You mean you can't remember anything about it in the morning,' said Hildamay, laughing.

'Up your bum.'

Thomas walked over and stood hesitantly by the table.

'What are you two giggling about?' he asked, his voice nervous. 'And can I join in?'

'No,' said Liz but she smiled up at him and took his hand. 'It's girls' talk.'

'Babies?' said Thomas brightly.

'Don't be silly,' said Hildamay. 'Dick dialogue.'

CHAPTER THIRTY

'KNEW you'd be here.'

Hildamay looked up to see Blanche Matthews squinting at her through a curl of smoke which snaked out of the cigarette attached to her freshly painted mouth. Her lips glowed orange, startling against the dead pallor of her skin.

'You'll burn your mouth,' said Hildamay automatically.

'Knew you'd be here,' repeated Blanche, nodding at her with satisfaction. 'Love her, don't you?' she said sharply, tugging the cigarette from her mouth and grinding it into the ground.

Hildamay stared at the crushed end of it. 'Yes,' she said, adding in a bleak whisper, 'much good it'll do her.'

'She'll turn up,' said Blanche reassuringly. She patted Hildamay's shoulder with a soft, hesitant hand. 'She will,' she soothed and then suddenly, in a fierce undertone, 'she must.'

'Must?' Hildamay looked up at her, startled.

'Must,' exclaimed Blanche, glowering at her. She dropped her eyes and looked away. 'She must be happy,' she insisted. 'She must.'

She looked back at Hildamay and shrugged thin shoulders. 'She is my daughter, isn't she?' she demanded.

'She is your daughter,' agreed Hildamay slowly, watching her.

'My mother,' said Blanche heavily. She sank back into the bench and stared bleakly over at the crowds hurrying through the platform gates. 'My mother,' she began again, with a tired sigh. 'She's been locking her in her room. Tied her to her bed.'

Hildamay closed her eyes.

'I got it out of her. Why Sky'd been so miserable. It started after I'd gone. Poor little bugger had a rough enough time of it when I was around but after I'd gone –' Her small, sad voice trailed off into the air, as insubstantial as her cigarette smoke. She sat in brooding silence for a few minutes and then took a few deep reviving breaths. 'Said she wanted to knock some sense into her head. Said she had to learn discipline. Said she didn't want her turning out wild, like me.' She sighed again, heavily. 'She doesn't mean to be wicked. She thought it was for Sky's good. Loves her, you see.'

Hildamay kept her eyes closed and thought about love. Love and possession. The love that binds, that ties people up in other people's egos, that strangles faith and trust, that locks, she thought bleakly, small children in rooms. She sighed. What was it George had said? 'Love is kindness.' She felt her shoulder being shaken sharply and opened her eyes. Blanche was leaning over her.

'She doesn't mean it, you see!' She looked at Hildamay with Sky's eyes, pleading. 'She's not a bad woman, really she's not. It's just –' Blanche looked away. 'It's just,' she whispered, her voice trembling, 'it's just that she doesn't understand about loving.' She ducked her head and scrabbled in her black, shiny bag for a packet of cigarettes. When she eventually managed to extract one from the flattened, torn pack her hands were shaking so badly that she could not light it. Hildamay sighed and took the matches from her, took a cigarette from the pack for herself and lit them both. 'Didn't know you smoked,' said Blanche, sucking furiously. 'Shouldn't, you know. Bad for you.' Hildamay smiled slightly.

'Better,' said Blanche and smiled back and there, suddenly, was Sky's face. 'What are you going to do?' she asked.

'I told you. I'm going to find her.'

'Yes, yes,' said Blanche impatiently. 'But when you've found her? Then what?'

Hildamay shrugged and looked away from the woman's sharp face. She hadn't thought about after. Just about when. 'I don't know,' she said slowly. 'Show her kindness,' she murmured.

Blanche looked at her curiously for a moment, a frown tracing the fine white skin between her fiercely plucked eyebrows. Then the frown cleared. 'So you want to keep her?' she exclaimed eagerly.

'Keep her?' echoed Hildamay.

'Keep her!' Blanche's voice was triumphant, happy even. 'You know,' she added encouragingly. 'Have her come and live with you, full time like. Be your little girl.' Her voice was shrill with excitement.

Hildamay turned to stare at her. Blanche flushed, her thin, pale face mottling with confusion. 'Don't look at me like that!' she cried, irritable with embarrassment. 'I only said it because you said you loved her, because I thought it would make you happy, the idea of keeping her.'

'She's not a dog,' said Hildamay shortly, looking over at platform three.

'I know she's not a dog!' cried Blanche, hurt. 'You know I didn't mean it like that,' she wheedled but Hildamay remained silent, her head slightly averted. 'Oh, I don't know why I bother,' she muttered, growing petulant. 'I came all the way here to see you and all I get is you being snotty, behaving as if I'm doing something criminal. I thought you'd be pleased, really I did.'

'I'm sorry,' said Hildamay and patted the thin hand which picked restlessly at some flaking paint on the bench. 'I know you're not doing anything criminal. It was just when you said that she'd kept her locked in her room –' They stared at each other in a sort of horror.

'I told her,' said Blanche fiercely. 'I told her she wasn't fit. Told her that when we got her back that I'd –' Her eyes slid away from Hildamay's and she lapsed into silence.

'That you'd what?' prompted Hildamay.

'Told her that I'd give her to you,' she muttered, defiant.

'Give her?' echoed Hildamay.

'You could adopt her! Make her your little girl.' She clutched suddenly at Hildamay's hand. 'She'd like that.'

'So you could go back to Spain,' said Hildamay slowly.

Blanche's face darkened. 'It's for her own good,' she said sullenly. 'It's not for me. I'm thinking of her.'

'And what if I said no?' cried Hildamay.

Blanche sighed heavily. 'Then I'd stay, of course and look after her. Keep her safe from – I'm not wicked,' she exclaimed. 'I know I'm not a very good mother but I'm not wicked,' she added in a low, fierce voice.

'No,' said Hildamay, looking at her white, defeated face. 'I know you're not wicked.' She watched Blanche carefully. 'What about your mother?'

Blanche shrugged and looked away. 'She'll have to put up with it. Sky's my daughter and legally, it's my decision.' She glanced back at Hildamay. 'I took proper advice,' she added proudly.

'Well,' said Hildamay, her voice breathless as excitement caught at her throat. 'If you're sure.'

'So you will?' said Blanche, her face suddenly alive with hope. 'Adopt her? Be her mum?'

'Well, I couldn't be worse at it than you, now could I?'

'There's no need for that,' grumbled Blanche, but she smiled.

The next morning George walked into her office carrying two cups. 'Tea,' he said, putting them down on her desk and sitting neatly in the chair facing her.

'Nice and hot, George?' said Hildamay, teasing. He smiled faintly but not enough to disturb the gravity of his expression. 'We have to talk,' he said slowly.

Hildamay looked at him in alarm. 'You're going to leave me,' she exclaimed, reaching across the desk and clutching at his hand in a sudden panic. He blinked rapidly, his pale eyes suddenly reddening, then took her hand in his, stroking it firmly with his thumbs. Such firm, reassuring hands, thought Hildamay in surprise. 'Please don't leave me, George,' she whispered.

He blinked again, nodding in sympathy, and went on stroking her hand. 'It's not that I'm leaving you. Not really.' A pale smile hovered uncertainly at his lips. 'It's just that it's time to start again,' he said gently. 'I have mourned for long enough.' He sighed suddenly. 'Six years is a long time, Hildamay.'

'Yes,' she whispered and closed her eyes. Six weeks is a long time when you have lost a child, she thought. How much more terrible is six years? 'Is the pain better now?' she asked, thinking of the time she had caught him, unawares, crying on the street. She opened her eyes and gazed at him solemnly. He smiled slightly at the childlike quality of the question. 'It is healing,' he said, and a look of faint astonishment crossed his face. 'Drink your tea,' he added, nodding at her cup and gently disentangling his hands.

She leaned back in her chair and picked up her cup. She sipped at the hot tea in silence for a few moments then looked at him thoughtfully over the rim of the cup. 'What will you do?'

'Go back to my original profession,' he said, shrugging. 'It may take a while to get a job and I shall probably have to accept a fairly junior position but at least it will be a start.'

'A start,' echoed Hildamay.

'Of a new life,' said George.

'A new life,' said Hildamay slowly and they raised their cups and clinked them in celebration. 'Toasting your new life with tea,' she said gravely, 'doesn't seem quite right. We should be drinking champagne.'

'George Brown,' said George, 'has never seemed to me a champagne sort of a person. I think it only fitting that he should be laid to rest with tea.'

'You will always be George Brown to me,' said Hildamay firmly. 'George Brown, champagne or not, is a person of whom I am inordinately fond.'

George blinked again and turned his head away. Pulling a starched white handkerchief out of his pocket, he dabbed at his face. Hildamay looked at the familiar handkerchief and blinked in sympathy. George looked back at her and they gazed at each other in silence for a moment, blinking in unison, and then suddenly ducked their heads to their cups to cover their embarrassment. Eventually, George looked up. 'I won't be leaving immediately,' he said briskly. 'It will take me a while to find a job.'

'Yes, yes, of course,' said Hildamay, equally briskly, and then she gazed at him sadly. 'And for me to find a replacement for you.' She shrugged suddenly and sighed. 'Or maybe not bother. Maybe it's time for me to start a new life, too. All this,' she gazed around her, 'suddenly doesn't seem so important any more. Maybe I'll go, too,' she added slowly, 'and make Jack Rome a happy man.'

'That man will never be anything but a fool,' said George heatedly. 'And I'm sorry to say it, but you're a fool, too, if you think Jack Rome an equal to the job. And all this,' he gestured sharply with his hand, 'has not changed. You, perhaps, have changed and if you have decided that work is no longer the ruling force in your life, then all well and good. Everything in its proper place. But that is no reason to leave. On the contrary, it's a reason to stay.' He was silent for a while. 'Running away will not bring her back,' he added, more gently.

'Maybe you're right,' sighed Hildamay in a defeated voice.

He looked at her, his eyes sharp. 'I think it's time you bought a new pair of silk stockings and took Young Mr Stone out for lunch. You have neglected him of late.'

'How did you know about the stockings?' exclaimed Hildamay.

George shrugged. 'He's not the only man around here who appreciates a fine pair of ankles,' he said quietly, smiling.

Hildamay gazed at him in astonishment.

'And you'd better polish up those smiles,' said George sternly. 'Now smile,' he said. She smiled. 'No, no,' he exclaimed fretfully. 'The way you used to do.' Hildamay smiled again. 'I think you need to put in some mirror work before next week,' said George, gazing at her thoughtfully. Hildamay looked at him questioningly. 'You have a lunch booked in with Young Mr Stone on Wednesday next.'

'I do?'

'You do,' said George firmly. 'And I have organised a lunch with Mr Bonham for Monday. Which should give you time to sort out that little problem before you see Mr Stone on Wednesday. The lunch was originally scheduled by Jack Rome, who has decided to take the matter into his own hands and thus try to usurp you. I took the liberty of calling Mr Bonham to explain that you would be taking the lunch and I told Jack Rome that Mr Bonham has been forced to cancel but that he will be calling him to rearrange it at some later date.'

'You did?' said Hildamay staring at him in amazement.

'I did,' said George, picking up the two empty cups and walking to the door of her office.

'So we need to get all the figures out and analyse them before your lunch on Wednesday. Personally, I think Jack Rome is exaggerating about the drop in profits. A bit of creative accounting, to his own advantage. And one other thing. He has been cheating on his expenses. A case of fraud more than petty theft,' he added mildly. 'I have collected all the necessary information. Do with it as you wish. The details are on your desk.'

'Thank you, George,' said Hildamay meekly.

George hovered in the doorway, a slight frown of reproof twitching at his hairless eyebrows. 'There is much to be done,' he said.

Hildamay raised her hands in a gesture of surrender. 'I'm doing, George, I'm doing.'

'Good,' he said, not moving from his position by the door.

Hildamay looked over at him and raised an eyebrow. 'Sod off, George,' she said.

'That's more like it,' he murmured and left.

*

Hildamay sat, bent over the sheets of paper on her desk, analysing the last quarter's figures. 'Shit,' she exclaimed in exasperation, 'what a mess,' and wondered how she could have let them get in such a state. Then she thought of Sky and felt a familiar dull ache in her stomach. 'It's all your bloody fault,' she muttered crossly and thought of the pale, heartshaped face and lustrous navy eyes and dropped her head to her hands in despair. Someone tapped on the door of her office. She rubbed angrily at her eyes, composed her face into an expression of bored irritation and looked up, expecting to see Jack Rome.

'My God,' exclaimed Delilah in admiration, 'no wonder they're all so bloody terrified of you here.'

'Someone's got to be,' said Hildamay, smiling. 'My friends most certainly aren't.'

'Do try to act more surprised,' complained Delilah, prowling around Hildamay's office. She arrived at Hildamay's desk and dropped a kiss on the top of her head. 'Are you feeling faint with pleasure? Is that why you haven't jumped to your feet for a fond embrace.'

'Kiss me, you fool,' said Hildamay, hugging her.

'You all right?' whispered Delilah, her thin arms holding Hildamay in a fierce embrace. Hildamay nodded. 'Good,' said Delilah releasing her, 'because I've got a surprise for you.'

'A surprise?'

'Yes, it's called going out to lunch. Remember that? I telephoned George to see if you were free and he said, rather despairingly I thought, that you'd been free for weeks.' She looked at Hildamay and raised a sleek eyebrow. 'You hadn't forgotten that it was your birthday, had you?'

'My birthday?' said Hildamay in astonishment.

'Well, that makes us all feel better. We thought you'd just forgotten your friends,' said Delilah with a cool smile. 'But if you've managed to forget your own birthday as well then I suppose we could forgive you.' She paused and picked a sheet of figures up off Hildamay's desk. 'She hasn't appeared, I take it?' she said, not looking up from the piece of paper.

'Not yet,' said Hildamay.

'Well,' said Delilah, tossing the paper casually back on to the desk, 'if wanting is getting, she will.'

'Is it?'

'Not in my experience,' said Delilah, shrugging. 'But what do I know?'

'What I love about you,' said Hildamay, picking up her bag and taking Delilah by the arm, 'is your sunny, optimistic nature.'

'Endearing, isn't it?' said Delilah, hugging Hildamay's arm close to her body. 'We must hurry. We're late.'

'Late for what?'

'For the others, Cassie and Liz. Oh, and Harry. Liz seemed convinced that Luigi, or rather Mrs Luigi, would be thrilled to have a baby to play with while they're busy trying to run a restaurant.'

'She will be.'

'Yes,' said Delilah thoughtfully. 'Some people are just plain weird.'

'No Kate,' said Hildamay, forgetting.

'We were trying to avoid an international incident. Cassie was all for it, said it would be fabulous material for her book, but Liz, who had the casting vote, said that fresh blood gave her indigestion. So we decided not to invite her. Not that it matters, any more,' added Delilah, her voice neutral.

'It's over then?'

'Clever, aren't you,' said Delilah flatly, her smile mocking.

Hildamay patted her hand consolingly and Delilah's mouth quivered suddenly. 'He told her he was leaving her so she took an overdose. So, of course, he stayed.'

'Kate! An overdose?' cried Hildamay in alarm.

'Enough to frighten him,' said Delilah roughly. 'Not enough to do herself any real damage. She's not as foolish as she pretends.'

'No,' said Hildamay slowly, thinking of Kate in the restaurant, picking bits of bloody meat out of her teeth. 'No bitch is ever going to take my husband away from me.'

'She understands him,' said Delilah thoughtfully. 'Men like Ben, they need to be made to feel that life can't go on without them. Emotional dependency gives Ben a hard-on. Kate knows that and she's good at it. Very good. If it's not her, it's the kids. They play it in turns.' She sighed suddenly. 'I've never learned that particular skill. I've never made him feel that I can't survive without him.'

'And can you?'

Delilah's smile glittered. 'Yes,' she said slowly. 'I can survive. There's the pity of it.' They walked in silence for a while. 'Oh, fuck men!' Delilah exclaimed in sudden exasperation.

'Regularly,' murmured Hildamay.

'Wednesdays and Sundays,' amended Delilah. Hildamay raised an eyebrow. 'Ned's days with the children,' she explained.

'Who is he?'

'Height, six feet two. Hair, dirty blonde. Age, three erections a night. Profession, medical. Car, beaten-up Spitfire. Marital status, damaged goods. Hobbies, oral sex. Bedside manner, good to excellent.'

'Sounds perfect.'

'Well, he doesn't make the earth move,' said Delilah, shrugging, and then smiled. 'But he sure as hell makes the bed shake.'

'What more could you want?' asked Hildamay, laughing.

'Blind adoration. Selfless devotion.' Delilah's smile sharpened. 'Someone to save me from myself?' Hildamay shrugged in sympathy and Delilah hugged her suddenly. 'Oh well, thirty-five-year-old divorcees can't be choosers, the available population's too limited.'

'Nor can thirty-six year-old spinsters,' said Hildamay, 'but that never stopped us asking. Come on, we really are going to be late.'

'But you don't want saving, do you?' asked Delilah breathlessly, as they hurried along. 'Must we go so fast?'

'Yes and no,' said Hildamay, increasing her pace.

'No what?' cried Delilah in exasperation at Hildamay's retreating back.

'No, I don't want saving,' called Hildamay with some of her old spirit. 'It sounds so dull. Grey and worthy, trapped forever in a spiritual bank account.'

'You know the trouble with you, Hildamay?' shouted Delilah across the stream of traffic which now separated them.

'Yes,' called Hildamay, feeling suddenly, absurdly, optimistic. 'I know the trouble with me.'

CHAPTER
THIRTY ONE

HILDAMAY was asleep on a bench. It was a few minutes past midnight on the Northern line platform. The last tubes of the night still slid through the station, but between the hiss and squeal of the doors opening and the drunken shouts of the men who had fallen out of their offices and into the pubs at half past six, intent on having just a few halves before they went home for supper, but who were even now still staggering resentfully home to their angry wives, Hildamay slept.

'Hildamay,' said a voice. 'Hildamay!'

She opened her eyes. Sky was staring at her, her nose inches away from Hildamay's face. Out of the dirty, pinched white triangle of her face shone eyes blue and round with astonishment. Her teeth chattered between bloodless lips cracked and rough with cold but her baseball cap, now scuffed and splitting at the seams, was nonetheless still pulled down low over her forehead.

'There you are,' said Hildamay, her voice deep with sleep. She thought she dreamed still.

'What are you doing here?' said Sky, frowning. 'You shouldn't be asleep here, on a bench. It's dangerous.'

'Is it?' said Hildamay, sitting up and blinking at her in confusion.

'Well, of course it is,' said Sky, shivering and looking around nervously. 'There are some very nasty men around, you know. Anything could have happened to you. It was Patty who said I should come and wake you up. She said it was no wonder that women got themselves into trouble, going to sleep on a bench at this time of night. I didn't know it would be you.'

'Who's Patty?'

'She's my friend. She looks after me. She's over there. Oh! She's gone. She's probably hiding somewhere. She's very shy,' whispered Sky confidingly. 'She doesn't like people much, says she finds them a bit of a trial, really. She has a house behind King's Cross station. It's all made of cardboard but it's really quite comfortable. When you get used to it,' she added thoughtfully. 'You can't have baths, though.'

'No,' said Hildamay. 'I can see that.' She examined Sky minutely. Her face was thinner, almost gaunt, with hollowed cheeks and purple circles, like bruises, smudged beneath her eyes. A matted wool scarf was knotted around her neck and on her shoulders lay a triangle of brown, crocheted wool trimmed with improbable orange tassles. Beneath this peeked out her old khaki nylon jacket, now blackened and stiff with dirt. She wore thick wool socks, far too big for her, and held up with pieces of knotted elastic.

'Are you all right?' said Hildamay gently.

Sky ignored the question. 'What are you doing here?' she demanded again.

'Looking for you,' said Hildamay, watching her warily. It struck her again, as it had many times in the past few weeks, that perhaps Sky did not want to be found. She seemed so distant and composed and, although she had always shown a composure remarkable for her age, there was a new gravity about her which Hildamay found disturbing. 'I've been looking for you for six weeks.'

Sky frowned and looked down at her hands. Her fingers poked out of dirty navy blue gloves, the fingers of which had been cut off at the tips. 'So I can feel properly to pick things up,' she explained, seeing Hildamay looking at them. 'For six weeks?' she added, her eyes round with surprise. 'You've been looking for all that time?'

'You should have said something before you went,' said Hildamay sternly. Sky looked down at her hands again, inspecting them minutely. She did not say anything. 'I thought we were friends,' added Hildamay more gently.

'I thought you didn't want to be my friend any more,' whispered Sky, her eyes still cast down.

'Why? Because I said you couldn't come and live with me?'

'Yes.' The word was almost inaudible. 'I told you I couldn't stay and live with grandmother. Not with Blanche gone. I told you I'd go away.'

'Yes,' said Hildamay, watching her carefully. Sky still would not look at her. 'But I didn't believe you.' Sky's head snapped back and she looked at Hildamay in astonishment. 'I know,' said Hildamay with a sigh. 'It was foolish of me.'

'I'm not going back,' said Sky, her mouth a thin pink line. 'I won't go back there.'

'Blanche is here.'

'Blanche?' said Sky. 'She's in Spain.'

'No,' said Hildamay. 'She's here, waiting for you.'

Sky shrugged and looked away but her mouth quivered. 'Why?' she demanded.

'She's worried about you. She got your letter.'

Sky shrugged again. 'I said I was all right,' she repeated, obstinate.

'I met Blanche,' said Hildamay carefully.

'You did?' cried Sky in astonishment.

'We had a long talk. She's very worried about you. She wants you to be happy.' Sky was silent.

'Why did you run away?' asked Hildamay, after a time.

Sky's face darkened and she looked away again, kicking the ground with her old, tattered trainers which were no longer white but blackened with dirt.

'What did your grandmother do to you?' asked Hildamay, her tone urgent. 'Look at me,' she demanded.

Sky looked up, her mouth set in a mutinous line. 'Nothing,' she said, indifferent, but her eyes darkened with pain.

'Blanche and I had a long talk,' said Hildamay slowly. 'She said that if it was all right with you, then it would be all right with her if you came to live with me. She said, if you'd like it, that I could adopt you and make you my daughter. I could be your mother.'

'I know what adoption means,' said Sky coldly, but her eyes glittered with sudden hope. Then the light in them died. 'Grandmother,' she said, with a small, defeated sigh.

'Blanche can fix that,' said Hildamay, watching her. 'Legally you belong to her.'

'Belong,' muttered Sky, kicking a foot viciously at the leg of the bench. 'I belong to them. Like a broken toy,' she exclaimed, her voice bleak.

Hildamay looked at her in astonishment. 'You mustn't talk like that, Sky,' she cried in despair. 'You're only nine years old.'

'I'm ten now,' said Sky. 'And that's what you said before,' she added contemptuously.

'Before what?'

'Before when. When you said I couldn't go and live with somebody else. When you said I couldn't come and live with you,' she cried, her eyes glittering with tears.

'I was wrong,' whispered Hildamay brokenly.

Sky shrugged and kicked at the ground but as she looked away, Hildamay saw the shine of tears on her cheeks.

'Will you come and live with me now?' whispered Hildamay.

Sky looked up, wiping the tears angrily from her eyes with the corner of the dirty, crocheted shawl. The tears had left clear white streaks on her skin. 'And that's not all you said,' she exclaimed, thrusting out a bright, perfectly pink lower lip and turning her back, suddenly a child again.

What does she mean? thought Hildamay in despair. What is she talking about? 'Sky? What do you mean?' she whispered, the tears thick in her throat, but Sky just shrugged and stood, staring at the advertisements on the wall of the tube. Her back was rigid and she made no sound. Hildamay knew that having once had her trust destroyed, Sky would not willingly allow it to happen again. She followed her gaze. 'Don't let love and life pass you by,' said the poster. Hildamay squeezed her eyes shut, but a tear still forced its way out of the crack of her eyes. Mother was right, she thought in a haze of despair, I did not learn to love. Or maybe I learned too late. She remembered looking at that same poster and wondering what love really had to do with life. Now she thought she knew. 'Without love,' she mumbled, 'I am alive but not engaged. Not connected.' And then she thought, and now I am engaged but the connection is broken. How can I live alone now? For she thought, suddenly, that now she understood what her mother had meant by the love that says you are not alone. What her mother had not told her was that, having once found that love and let it go, then, and only then, will you understand what it is to be alone. Of course she did not tell me, she reflected, she thought I learned by example.

And she remembered her mother, standing over the kitchen sink. 'Today is a new day,' she said every morning, in a voice bright with optimism. And every night, even as she dragged her thin body to bed, and even though the defeated slope of her shoulders said otherwise, she would call to her daughter in a voice charged with hope, 'Goodnight, Hilda. Tomorrow is another day.' And on it would go, day after day, the eternal circle; the bright, shining ring of hope. 'I was unkind,' murmured Hildamay. 'I thought she was foolish, without imagination. Now I see that she had too much. I never understood her. I never understood what it was to be alone.'

And then she knew that she had never been alone before now and felt a pain so sharp that she gasped and opened her eyes. She saw Sky's ungiving, unforgiving back and her despair became a fury, leaving her restless and agitated. 'Sky,' she pleaded, 'will you come home with me?' The back stiffened but Sky still did not move. Hildamay put out her hand to touch her on the shoulder and she ducked sharply and then ran up the length of the platform. Hildamay stared after her and called despairingly, 'Sky. Please?' But Sky stood, motionless, her back still turned.

Then Hildamay knew that she must do something, anything, to escape the pain, so she pulled herself wearily up from the bench and began to walk towards the stairs. She reached the stairs and climbed them, then fumbled her way down the long, curving corridor which led suddenly into a great square room where the shiny escalators still rumbled. As she put her foot on the first stair, they stopped, for the last train had just drawn into the station and disgorged its final load. She let out a sudden cry but then began to climb up the unmoving steps. When she was halfway to the top, she heard her name being called and turned to see Sky below, at the foot of the escalator. A tiny figure standing alone in the enormous room.

'Hildamay!' she called.

'Yes?'

'Are you going home?'

'Yes,' she called and stood there waiting. Sky stood and watched her, but she did not move, nor did she call out. Hildamay waited for what seemed like hours but the tiny figure still did not move and so, with a sigh, she turned and began to walk on up the unmoving stairs. She heard her name again, echo through the vast room.

'Hildamay!'

'Yes?'

'Do you love me?'

That's what she meant, thought Hildamay, she does not know that I love her. 'Yes,' she said with a wrenching sob. 'Oh, yes.' Still the small figure did not move but seemed poised instead for flight and Hildamay watched her, far below, and thought that the future would always be like this. A great, grey hall peopled with tiny figures she could not reach. Why does she not answer? she cried to herself until she realised that she had spoken only to herself. 'Yes!' she called, as loudly as she could. 'I love you. Sky, I love you,' and sat, her legs giving way in the suddenness of relief, as Sky ran up the shining stairs.

In the morning Sky sat at the kitchen table and swung her legs, scratching with her still gloved hands at the scarred wooden table top.

'Good grief,' said Hildamay as she walked into the kitchen. 'You're even dirtier than I remember.'

'It was dark last night,' said Sky. 'What shall we do today?'

'I thought perhaps we might ask George to come and have tea.'

'Does he like shop bought cake?' said Sky.

'I think he might acquire the taste.'

'And can I have an egg for breakfast?' said Sky hopefully. 'It's Saturday. I promise to eat it,' she added quickly.

'I think it might be a good idea to have a bath before breakfast, don't you?' said Hildamay briskly, and led her through to the bathroom.

'Why are we in this bathroom?' said Sky, glaring around her. 'We never have baths in this bathroom. What's happened to the magic bathroom?' she demanded.

'It's all closed up.'

'Why?'

Hildamay shrugged. 'It seemed to lose all its magic when you left.'

'How?' said Sky, looking at her curiously.

'It looked so empty,' whispered Hildamay and Sky, sensing her distress, asked no more questions but took her hand.

'Never mind,' she said kindly. 'Let's go and see what we can do.'

They walked into the bedroom and Sky stood patiently by the door while Hildamay picked up the old, violet painted vase, and shook it on to the bed. The key was stuck but, after some shaking, she managed to dislodge it and it tumbled out into her hand. She unlocked the door and they stood in the doorway.

'Good grief,' said Sky, looking at the fragments of mirror and shards of glass which littered the floor. 'Did you have a fight?' she asked, looking up at Hildamay.

'In a manner of speaking,' said Hildamay and smiled at her.

'Will the magic come back?' asked Sky doubtfully.

'Yes, if we make it.'

'How?'

'We'll make a wish,' said Hildamay, taking her by the hand and leading her into the room. It seemed to Hildamay that the time passed in hours, although she knew it to be only minutes, and finally she whispered, 'Sky?'

'What?' said Sky, opening her eyes.

'Have you wished?'

'Yes,' she whispered loudly. 'For love.'

'Is that magic?'

'Yes,' said Sky impatiently. 'Of course it is. Shall we go and get ready for George now?'

The doorbell rang and Hildamay peered out of the window to see George waiting patiently on the doorstep, his arms filled with brightly wrapped parcels. She ran to fling open the door and they stood for a moment gazing at each other solemnly. Then Hildamay smiled, a smile radiant with happiness, tremulous with joy, brilliant with hope.

'That's more like it,' he said, blinking.